✦ MAGIC ✦
TREE HOUSE®

THE KNIGHT AT DAWN

MARY POPE OSBORNE'S

MAGIC TREE HOUSE®

THE KNIGHT AT DAWN

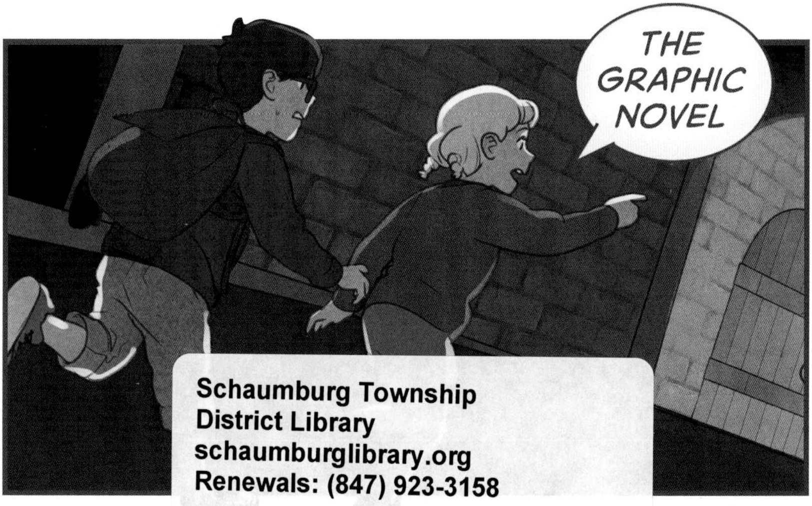
THE GRAPHIC NOVEL

ADAPTED BY
JENNY LAIRD
WITH ART BY
KELLY & NICHOLE MATTHEWS

A STEPPING STONE BOOK™
RANDOM HOUSE NEW YORK

Text copyright © 2021 by Mary Pope Osborne
Art copyright © 2021 by Kelly Matthews & Nichole Matthews
Text adapted by Jenny Laird

All rights reserved. Published in the United States by Random House Children's Books, a division
of Penguin Random House LLC, New York. Adapted from *The Knight at Dawn,* published by
Random House Children's Books, a division of Penguin Random House LLC, New York, in 1992.

Random House and the colophon are registered trademarks and A Stepping Stone Book
and the colophon are trademarks of Penguin Random House LLC. RH Graphic with
the book design is a trademark of Penguin Random House LLC. Magic Tree House
is a registered trademark of Mary Pope Osborne; used under license.

Visit us on the Web!
rhcbooks.com
MagicTreeHouse.com

Educators and librarians, for a variety of teaching tools, visit us at RHTeachersLibrarians.com

Library of Congress Cataloging-in-Publication Data
Names: Laird, Jenny, adapter. I Matthews, Kelly (Comic book artist), artist. I
Matthews, Nichole, artist. I Osborne, Mary Pope, author.
Title: The knight at dawn, the graphic novel / adapted by Jenny Laird; with art by Kelly & Nichole Matthews.
Description: First graphic novel edition. I New York: Random House Children's Books, [2021] I Series: Mary Pope Osborne's
Magic tree house I Summary: "Retells, in graphic novel form, the tale of eight-year-old Jack and his younger sister,
Annie, who are whisked back in the magic tree house to the time of knights and castles" —Provided by publisher.
Identifiers: LCCN 2021009066 (print) I LCCN 2021009067 (ebook) I
ISBN 978-0-593-17472-2 (hardcover) I ISBN 978-0-593-17475-3 (trade paperback) I
ISBN 978-0-593-17473-9 (library binding) I ISBN 978-0-593-17474-6 (ebook)
Subjects: LCSH: Graphic novels. I CYAC: Graphic novels. I Time travel—Fiction. I
Knights and knighthood—Fiction. I Middle Ages—Fiction. I Tree houses—Fiction. I Magic—Fiction.
Classification: LCC PZ7.7.L28 Kn 2021 (print) I LCC PZ7.7.L28 (ebook) I DDC 741.5/973—dc23

The artists used Clip Studio Paint to create the illustrations for this book.
The text of this book is set in 13-point Cartoonist Hand Regular.

MANUFACTURED IN CANADA
10 9 8 7 6 5 4 3 2
First Graphic Novel Edition

This book has been officially leveled by using the F&P Text Level Gradient™ Leveling System.

For Gail Hochman
—M.P.O.

For Randy, a royal, steady keeper of the light
—J.L.

For Jan Morgan
—K.M. & N.M.

CHAPTER ONE
The Dark Woods

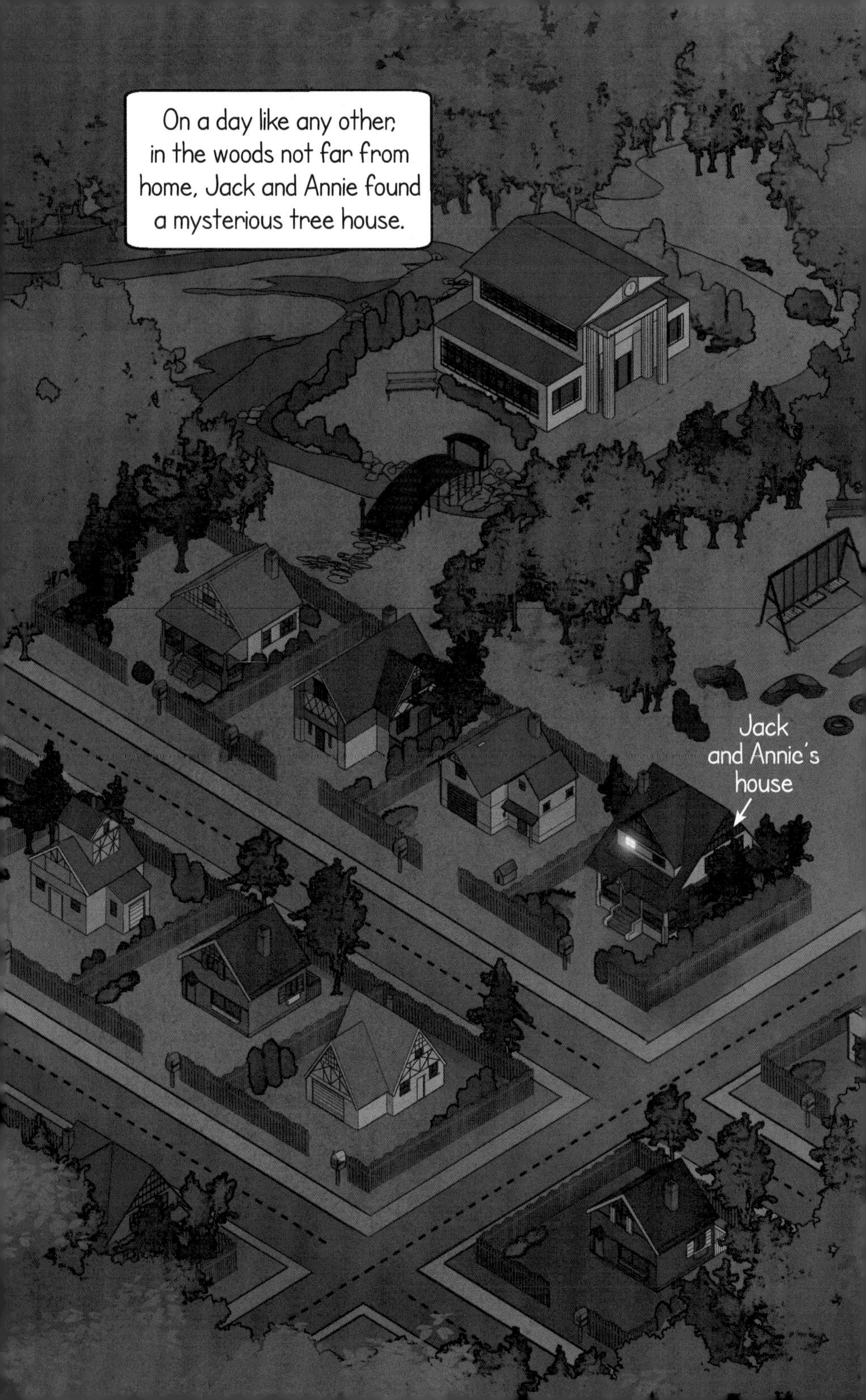
On a day like any other, in the woods not far from home, Jack and Annie found a mysterious tree house.
Jack and Annie's house

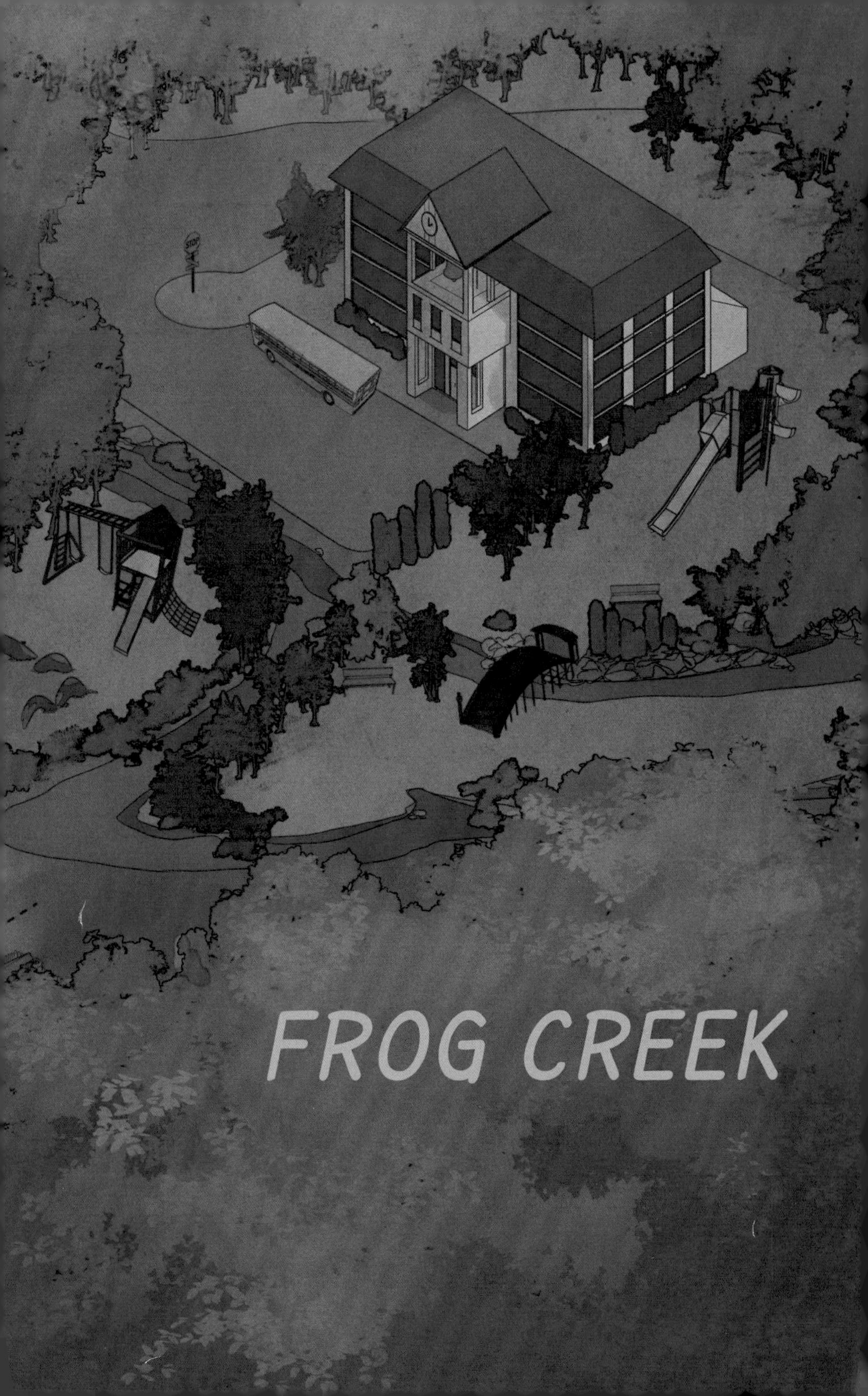
FROG CREEK

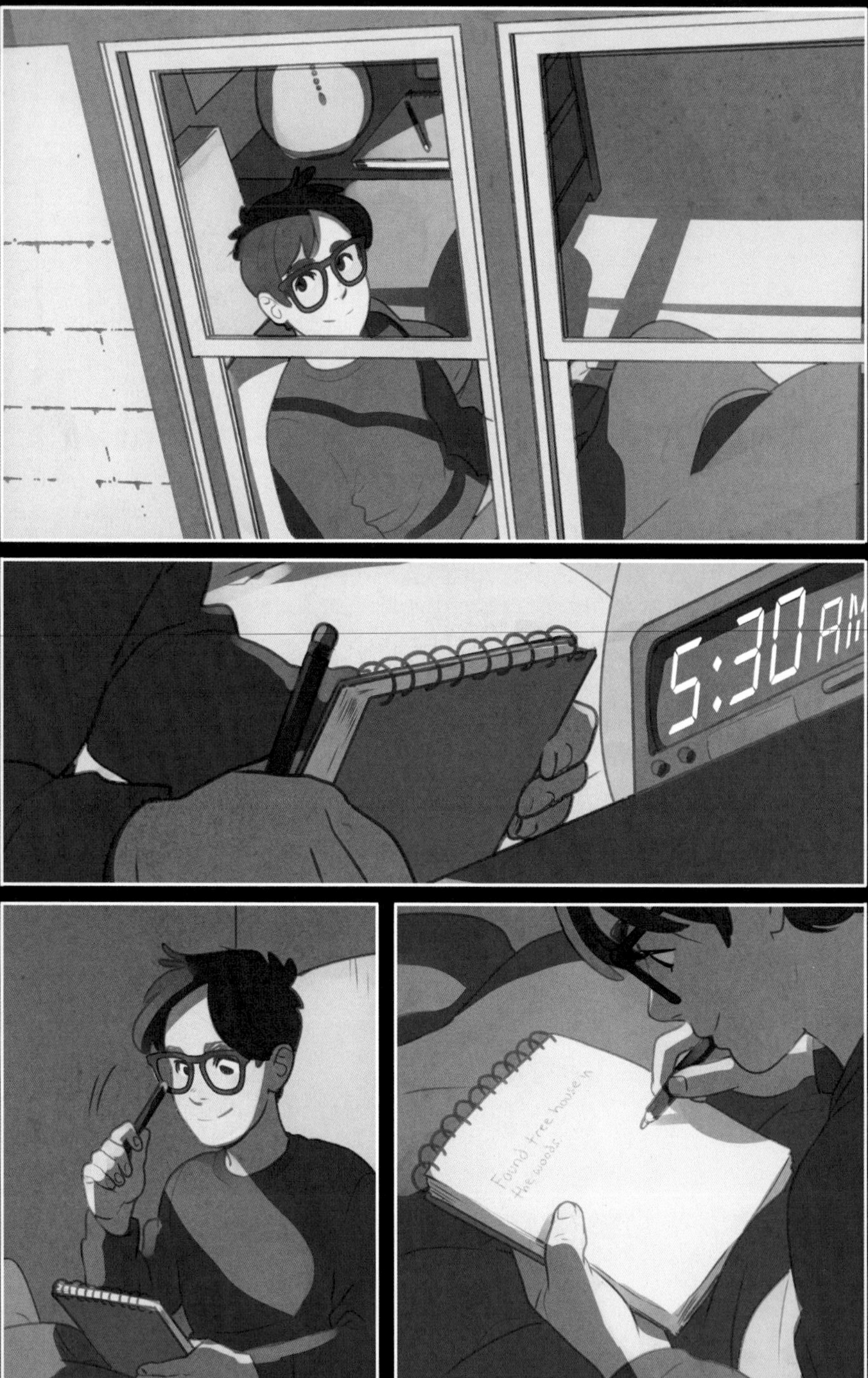
5:30 AM
Found tree house in the woods.

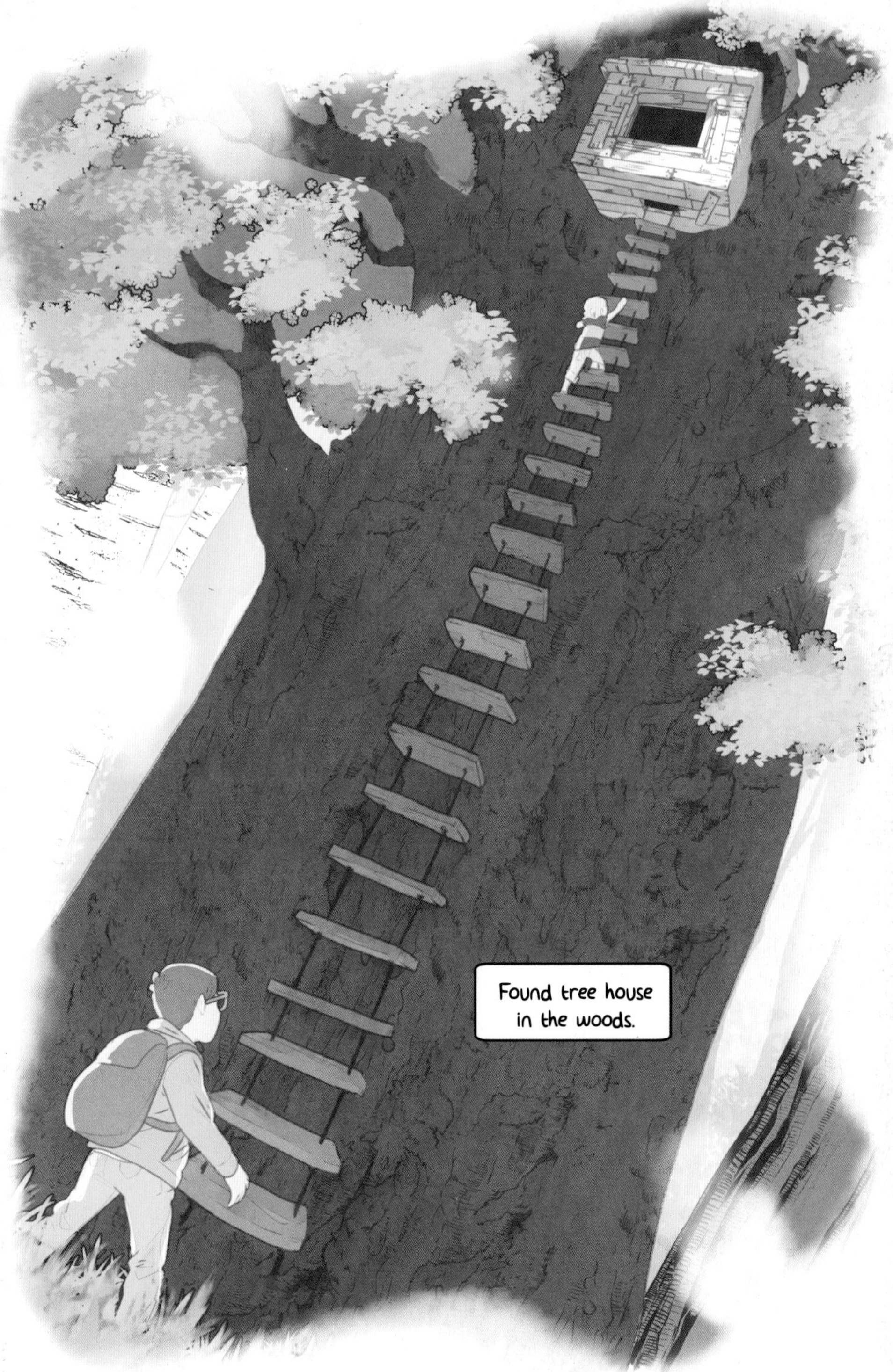
Found tree house
in the woods.

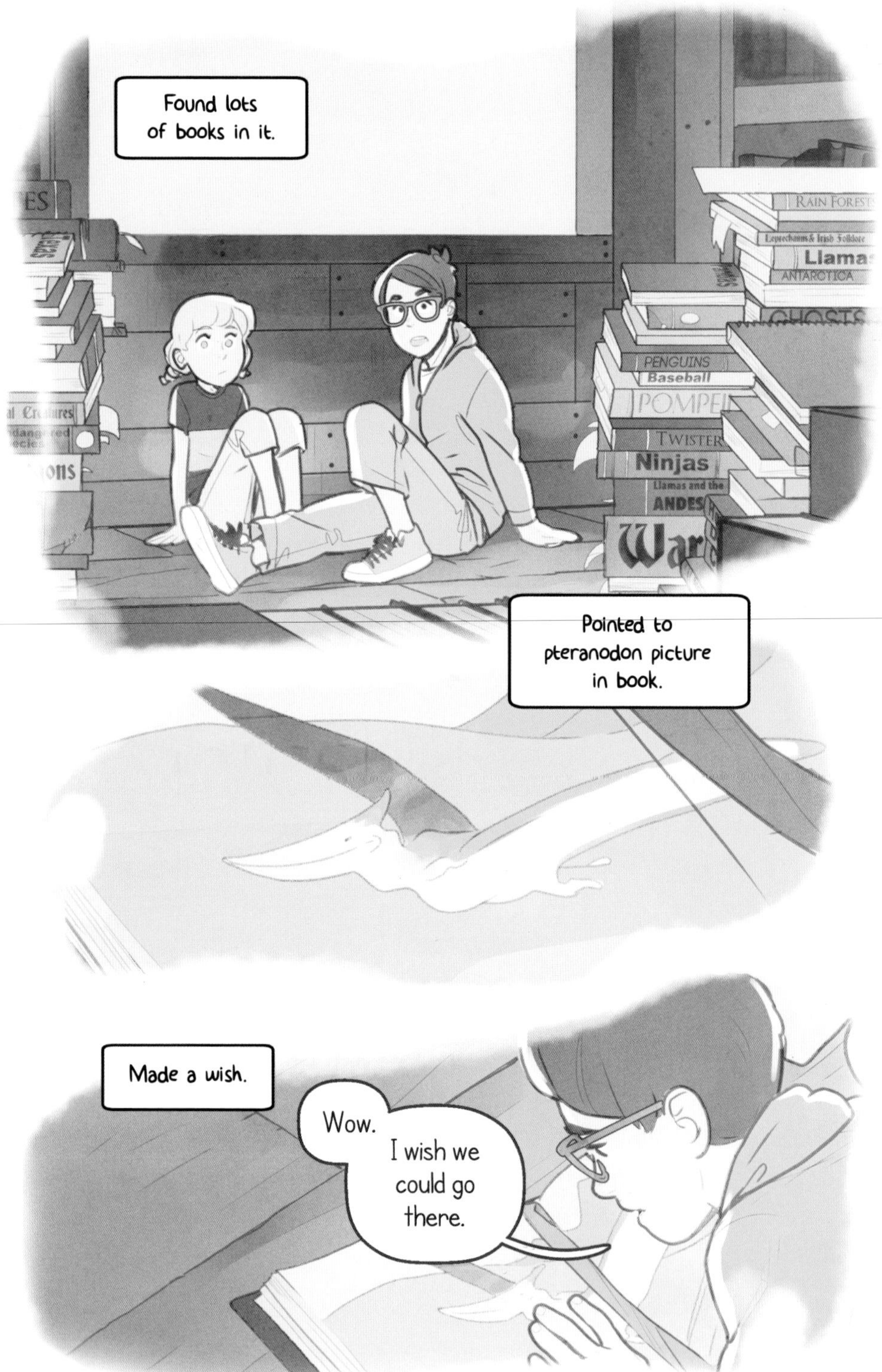

Found lots of books in it.
Rain Forests
Leprechauns & Irish Folklore
Llamas
Antarctica
Penguins
Baseball
Twister
Ninjas
Llamas and the Andes
Pointed to pteranodon picture in book.
Made a wish.
Wow.
I wish we could go there.

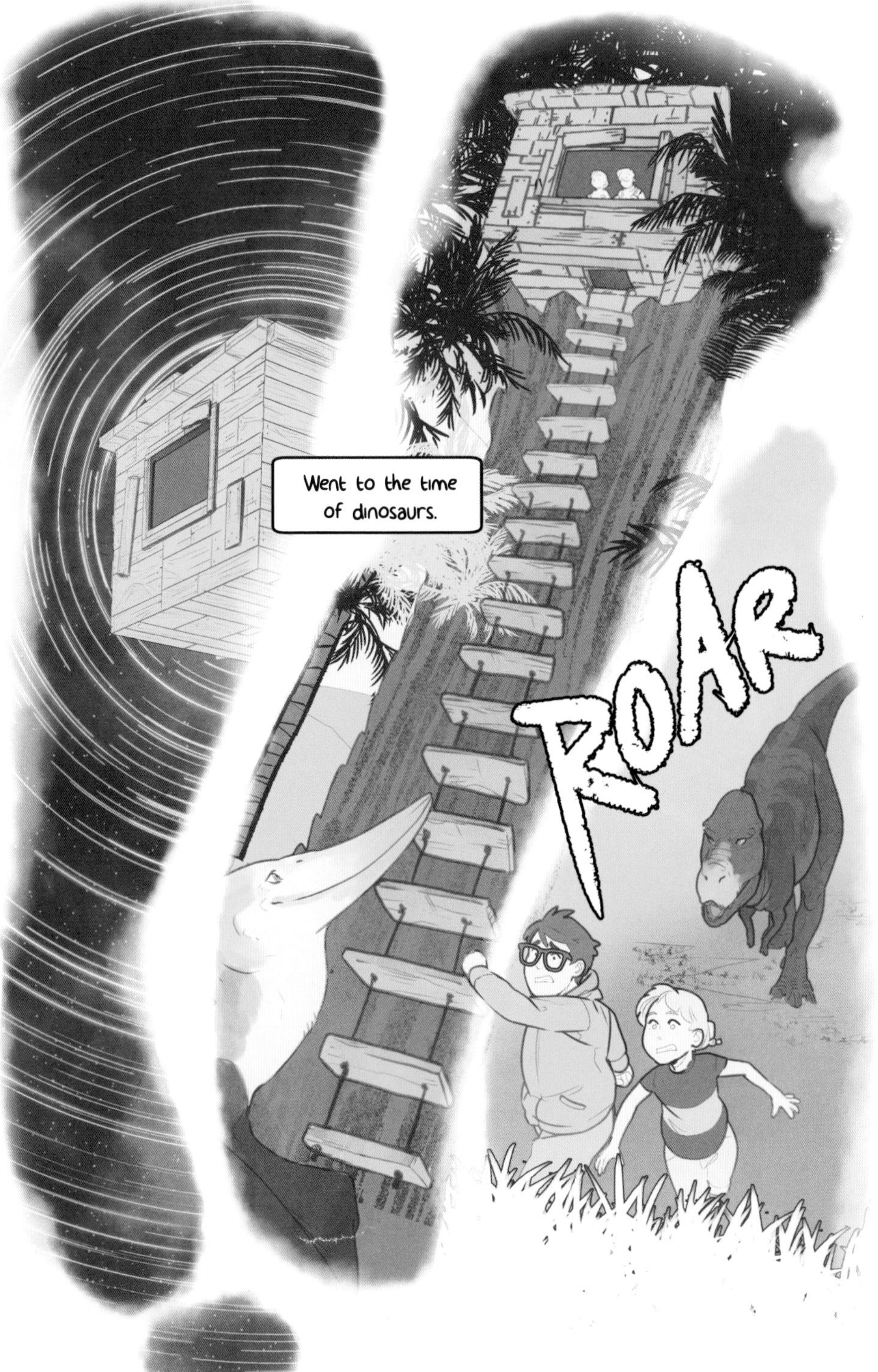
Went to the time of dinosaurs.
ROAR

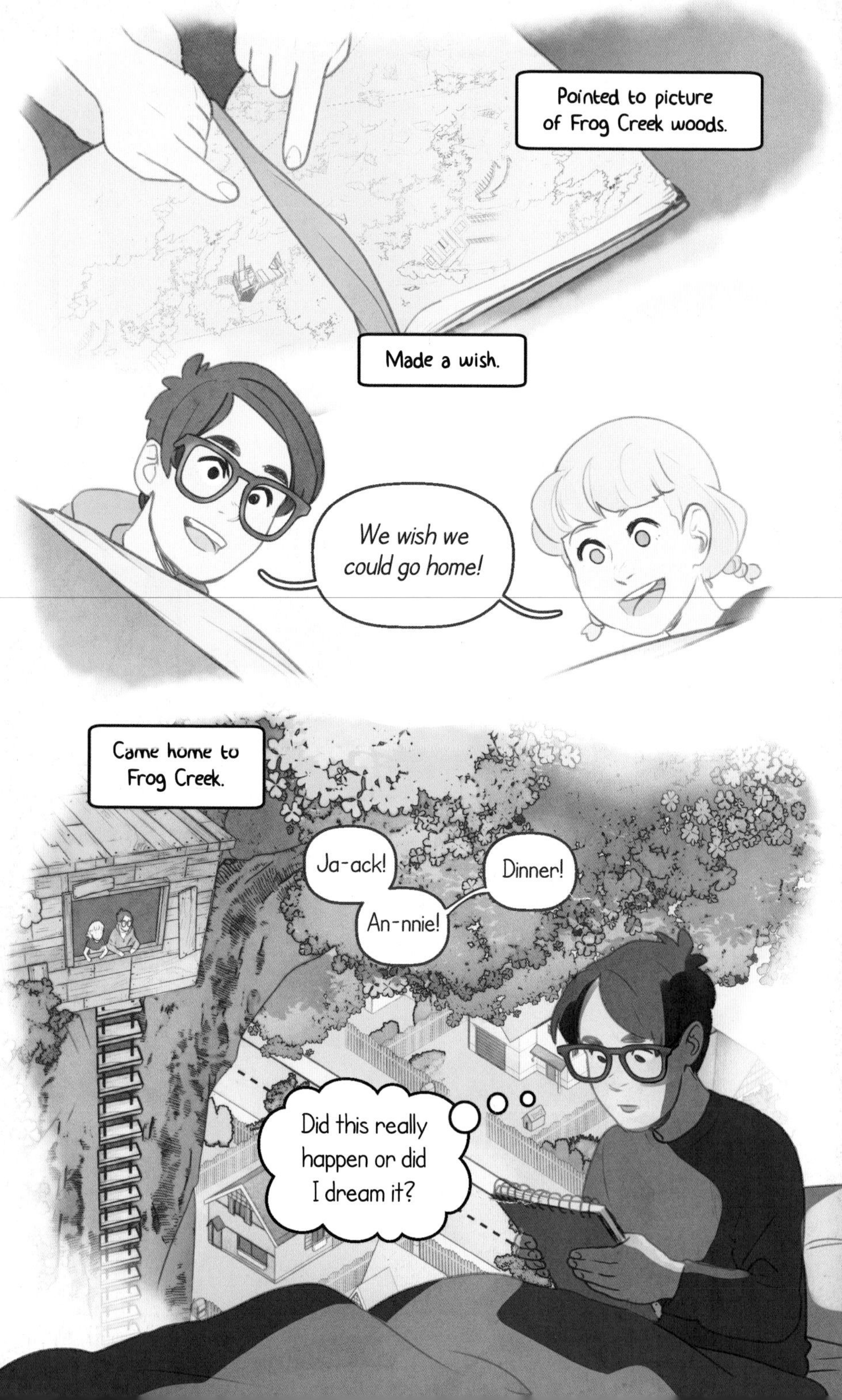
Pointed to picture of Frog Creek woods.
Made a wish.
We wish we could go home!
Came home to Frog Creek.
Ja-ack!
An-nnie!
Dinner!
Did this really happen or did I dream it?

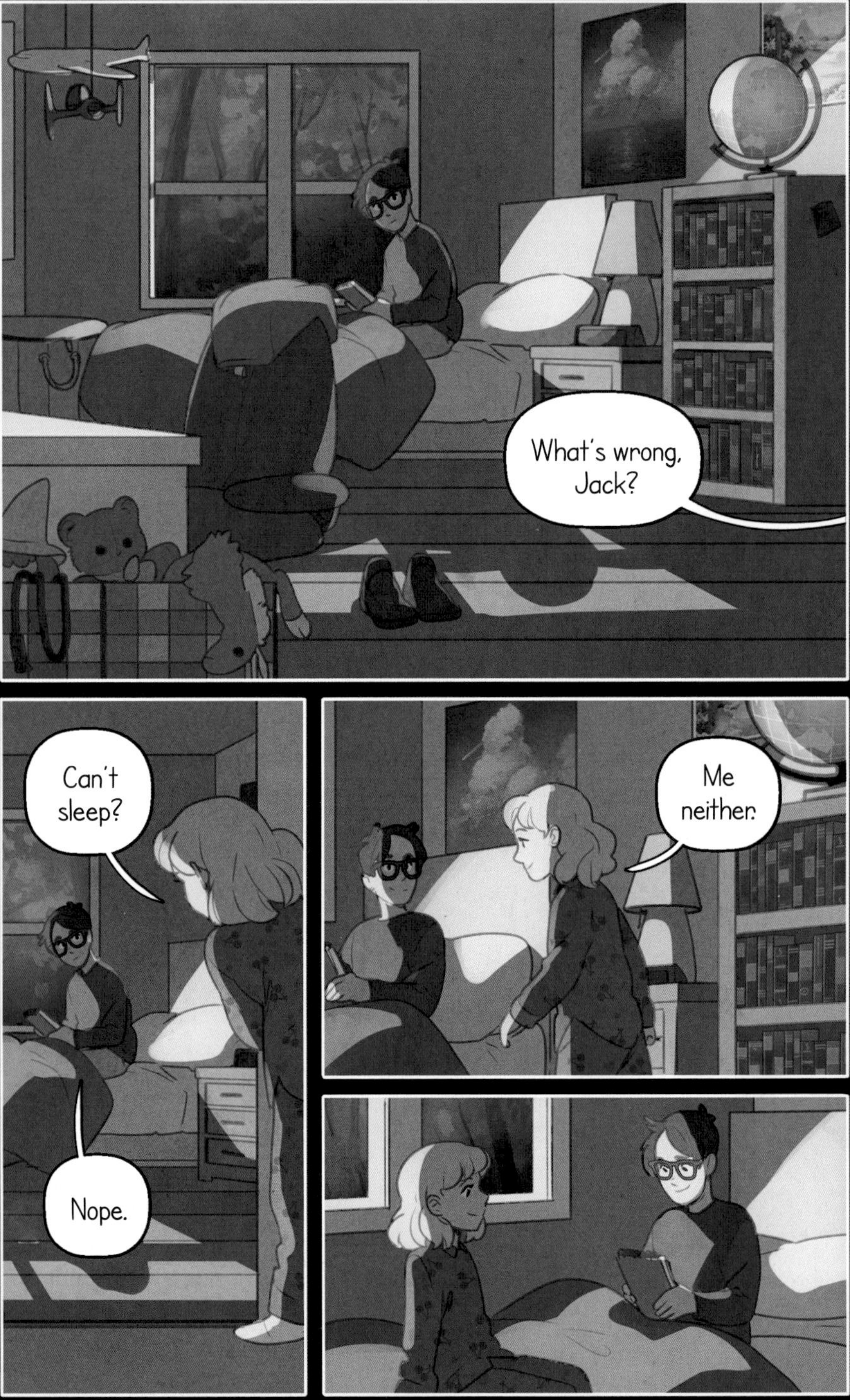
What's wrong, Jack?
Can't sleep?
Nope.
Me neither.

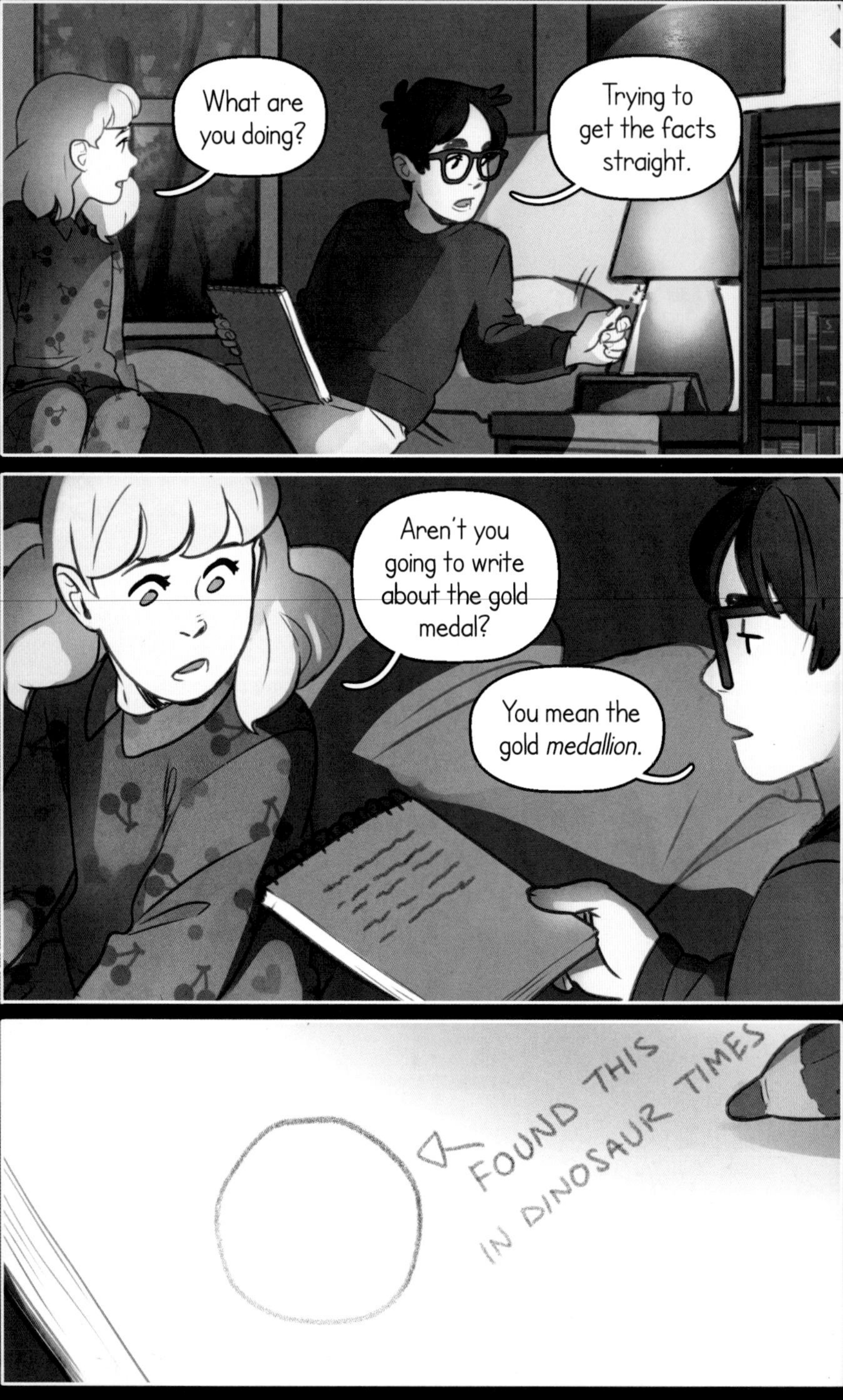
What are you doing?
Trying to get the facts straight.
Aren't you going to write about the gold medal?
You mean the gold *medallion*.
FOUND THIS IN DINOSAUR TIMES

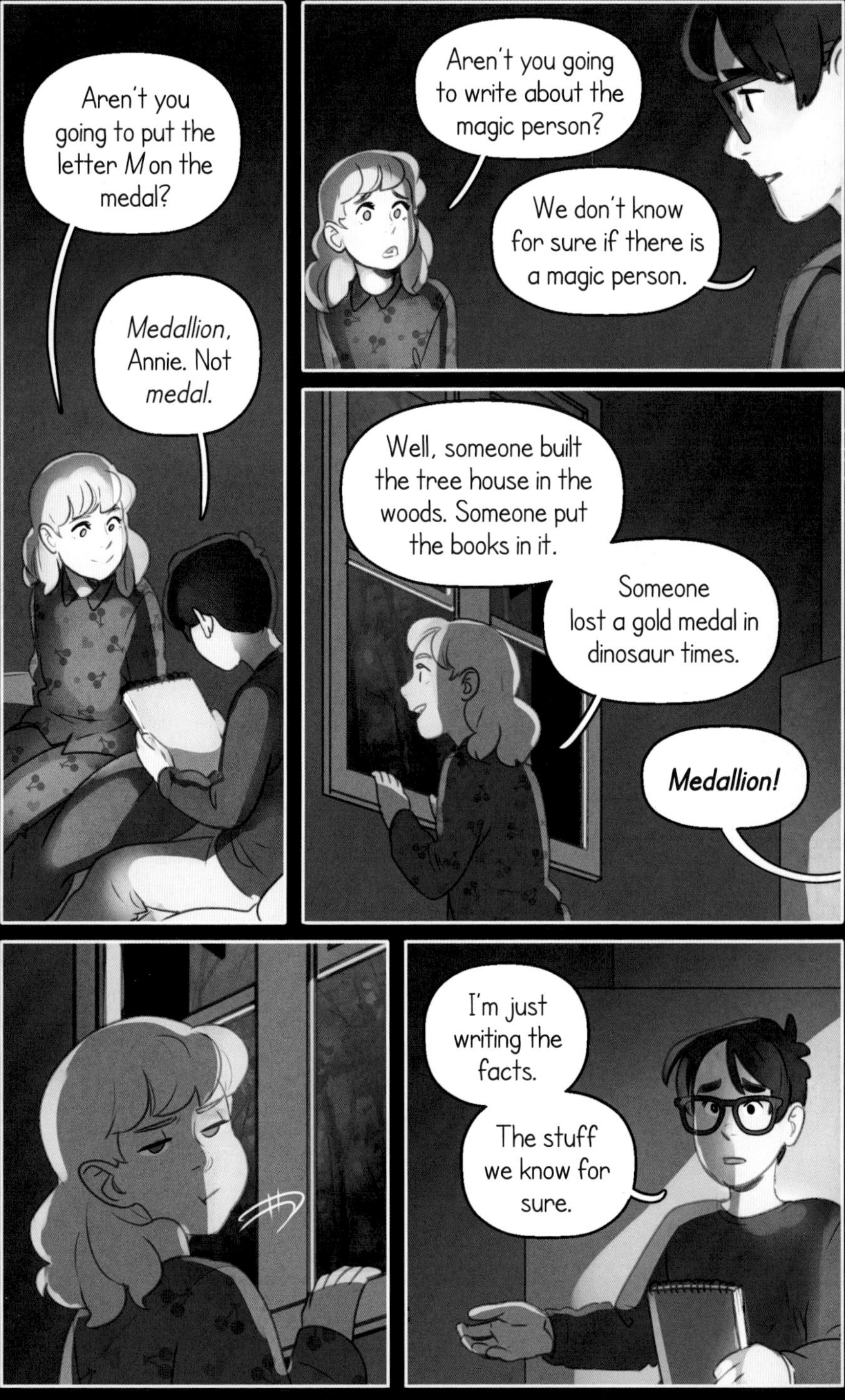

Aren't you going to put the letter *M* on the medal?
Medallion, Annie. Not *medal*.
Aren't you going to write about the magic person?
We don't know for sure if there is a magic person.
Well, someone built the tree house in the woods. Someone put the books in it.
Someone lost a gold medal in dinosaur times.
Medallion!
I'm just writing the facts.
The stuff we know for sure.

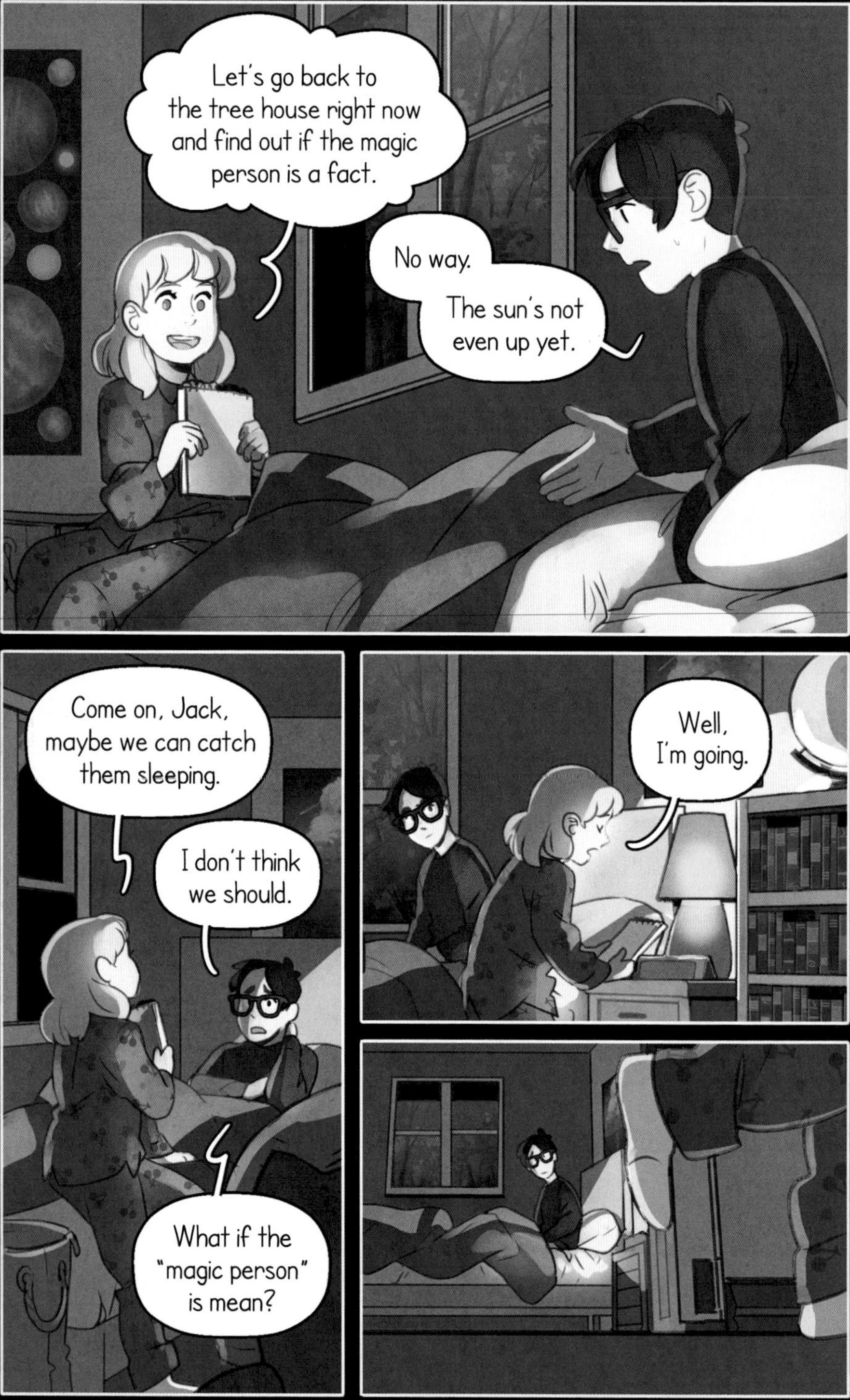
Let's go back to the tree house right now and find out if the magic person is a fact.
No way.
The sun's not even up yet.
Come on, Jack, maybe we can catch them sleeping.
I don't think we should.
What if the "magic person" is mean?
Well, I'm going.

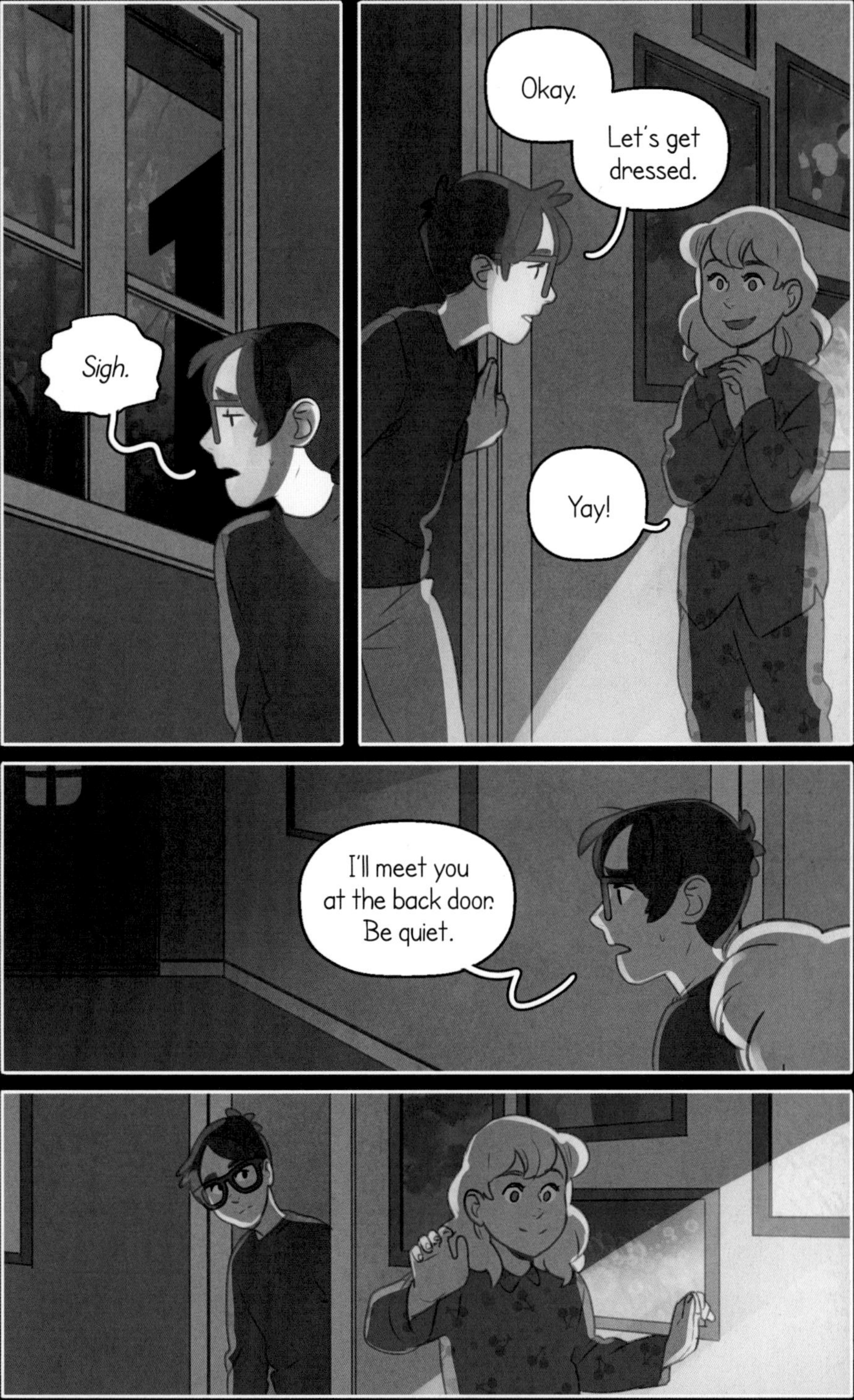
Sigh.
Okay.
Let's get dressed.
Yay!
I'll meet you at the back door. Be quiet.

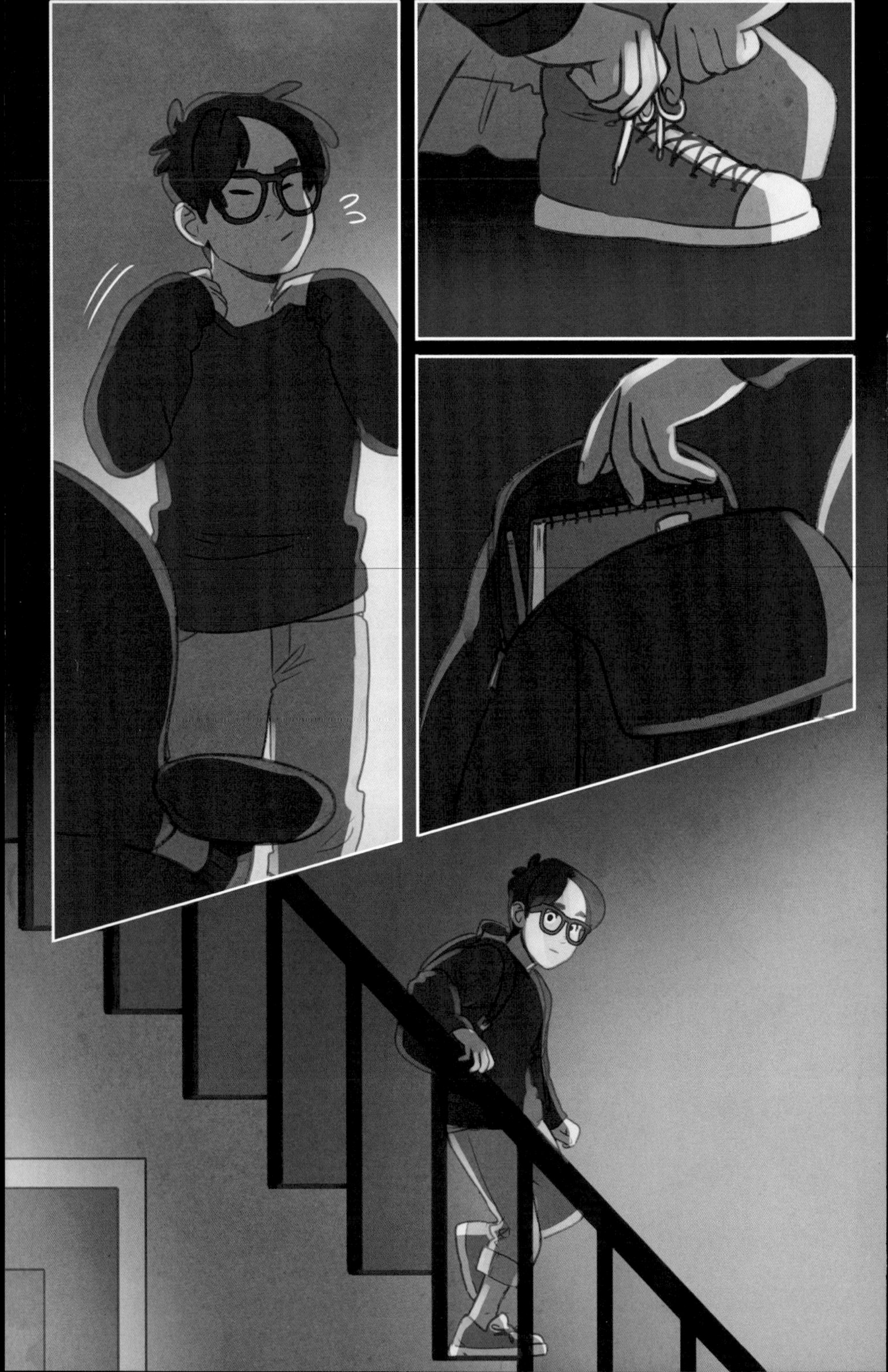

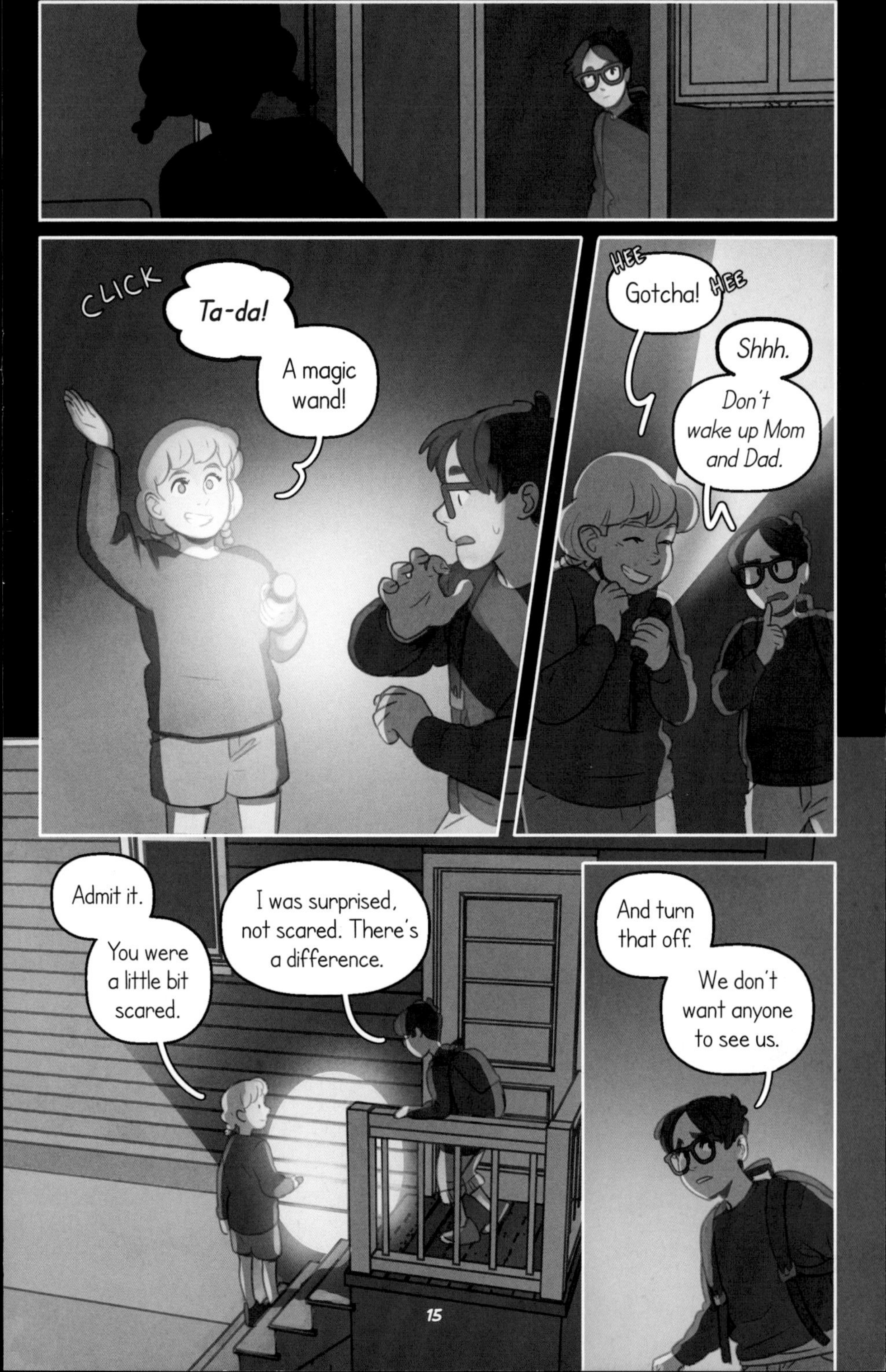
CLICK
Ta-da!
A magic wand!
HEE
Gotcha!
HEE
Shhh.
Don't wake up Mom and Dad.
Admit it.
You were a little bit scared.
I was surprised, not scared. There's a difference.
And turn that off.
We don't want anyone to see us.

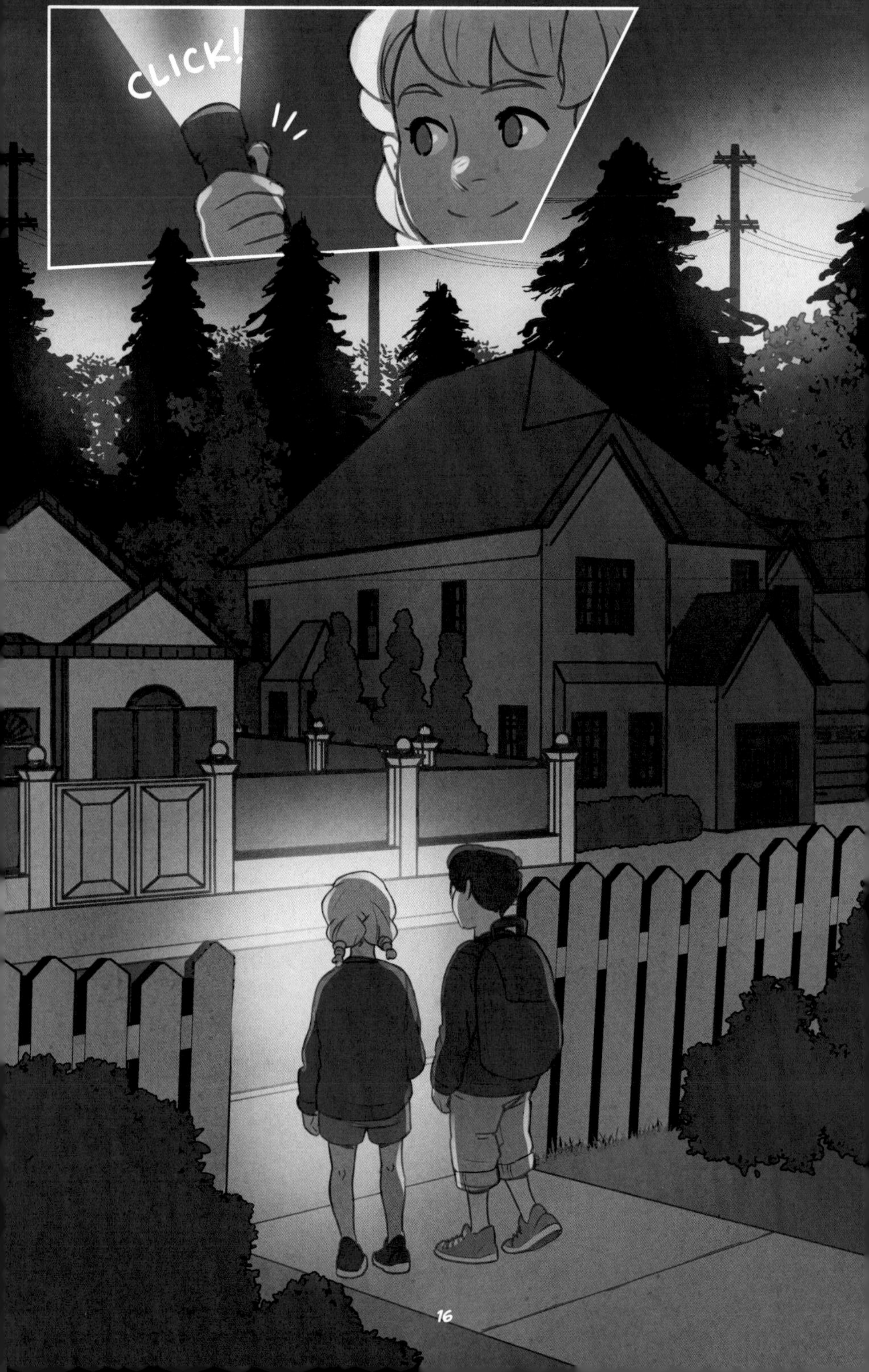
CLICK!

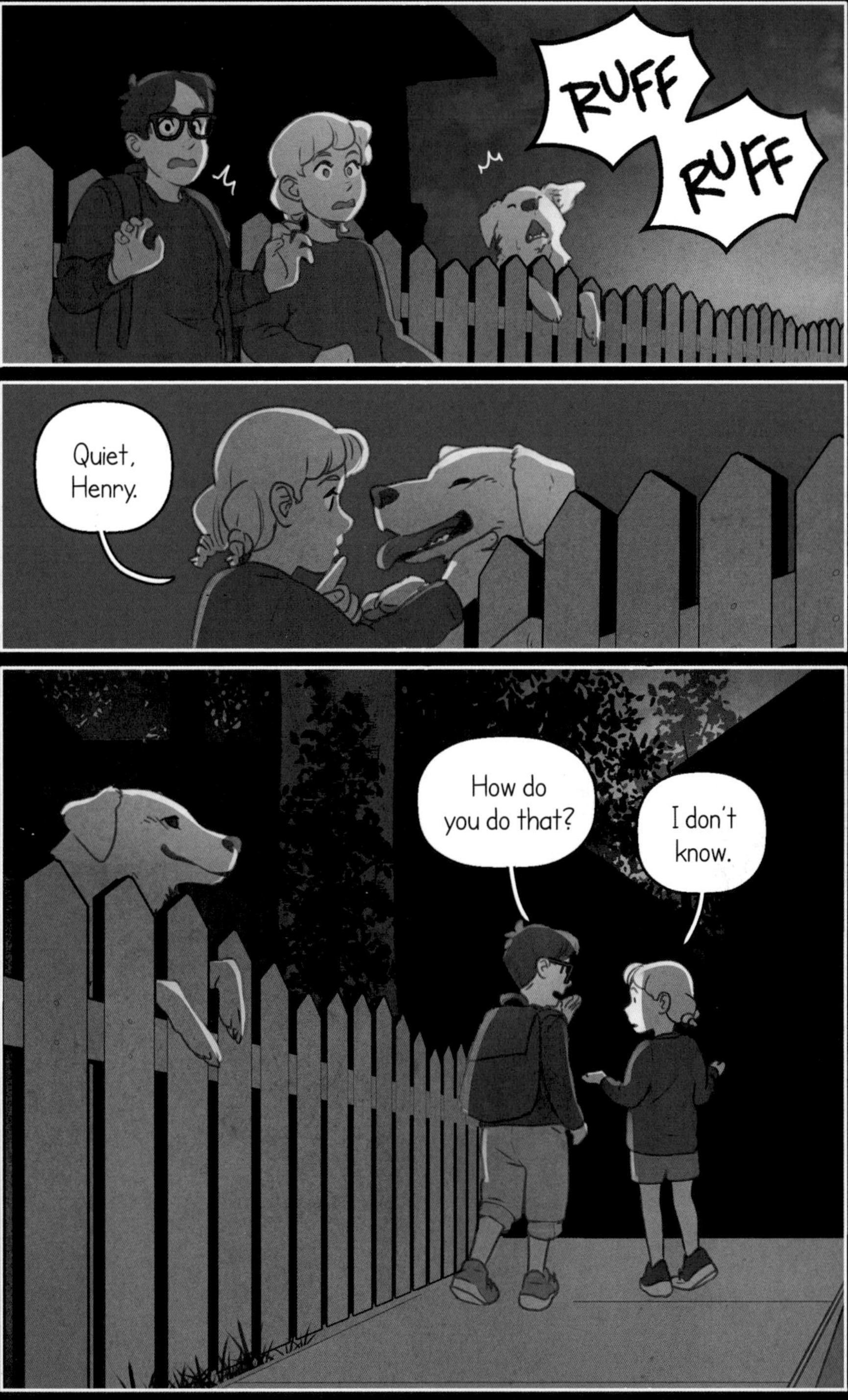
RUFF
RUFF
Quiet, Henry.
How do you do that?
I don't know.

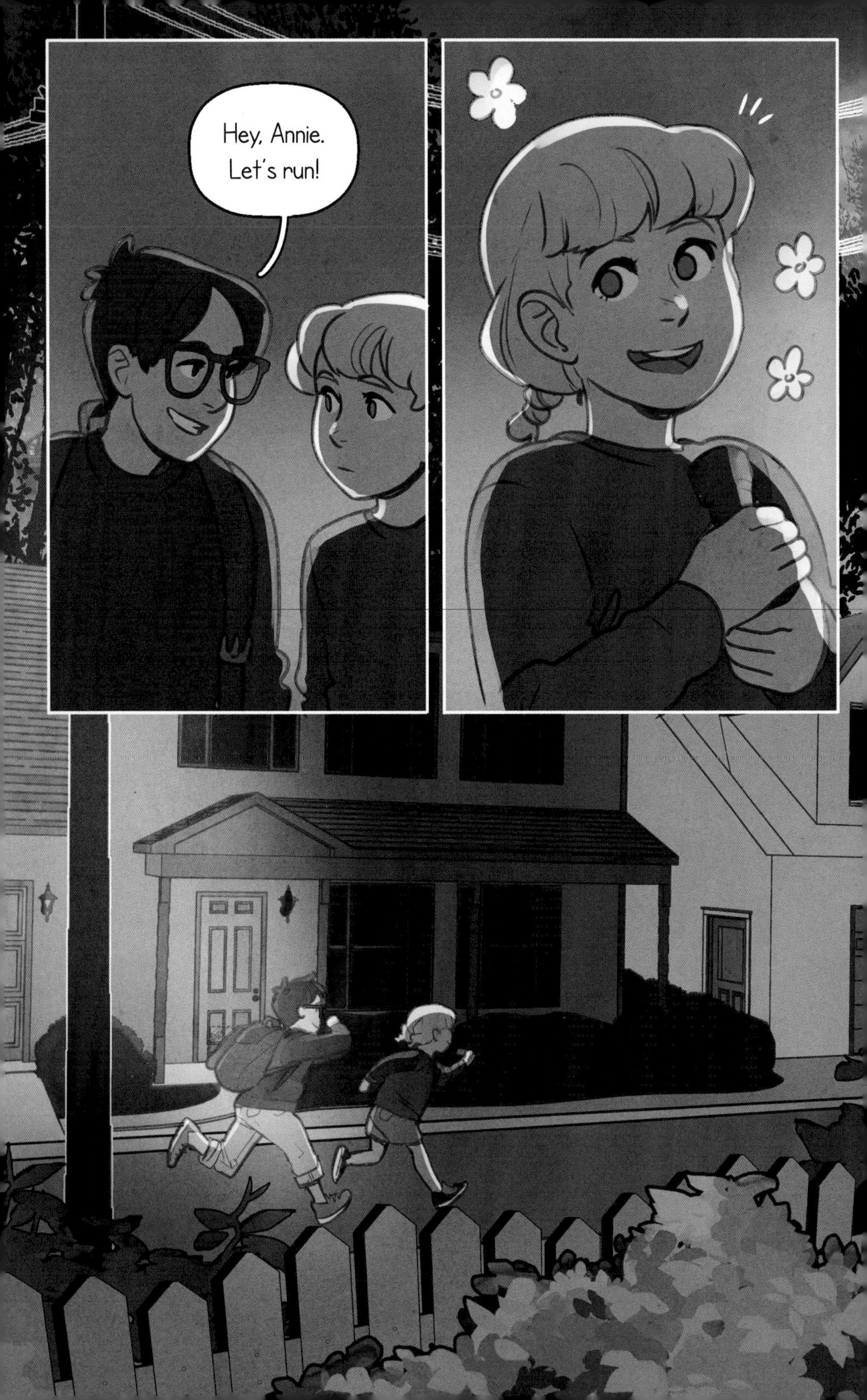
Hey, Annie. Let's run!

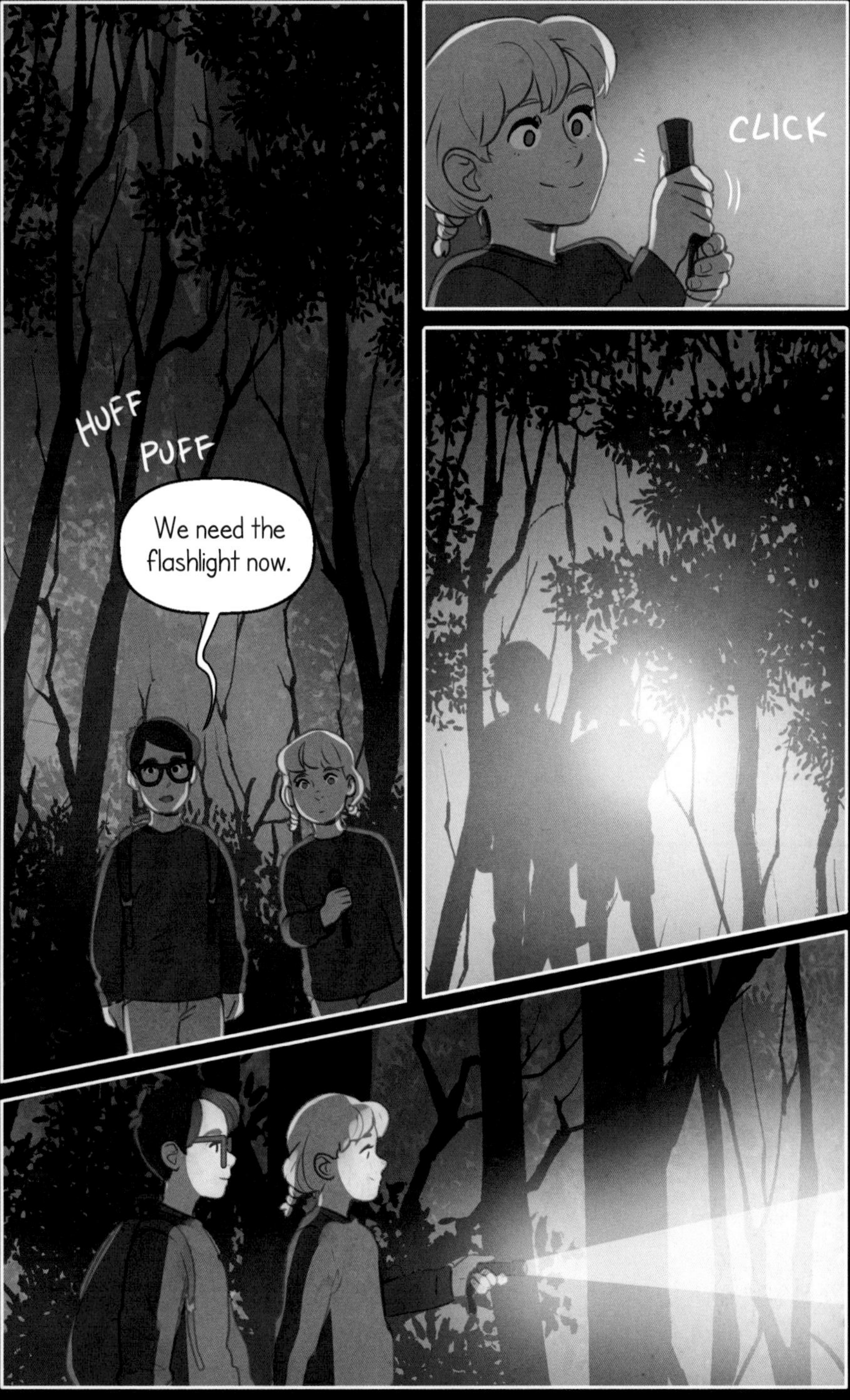
HUFF
PUFF
We need the flashlight now.
CLICK

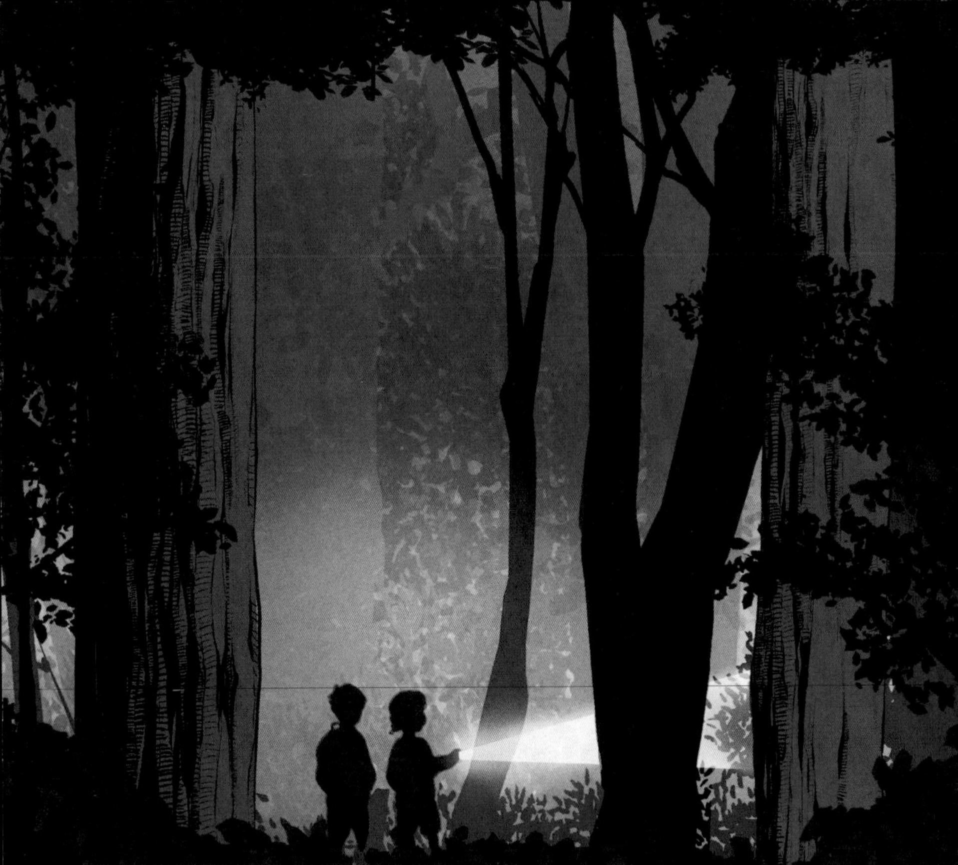

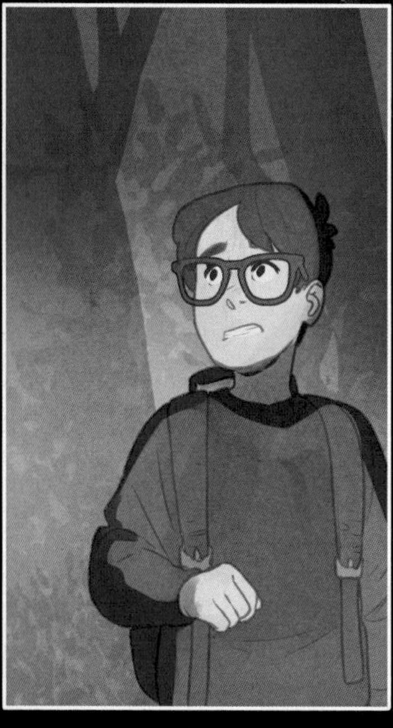

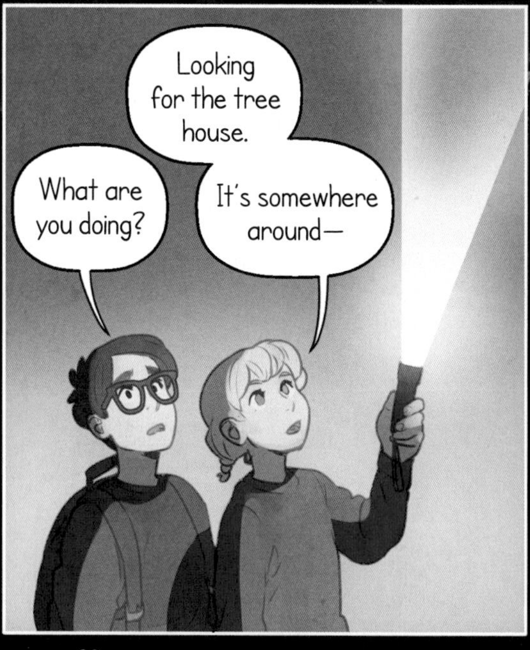
Looking for the tree house.
What are you doing?
It's somewhere around—

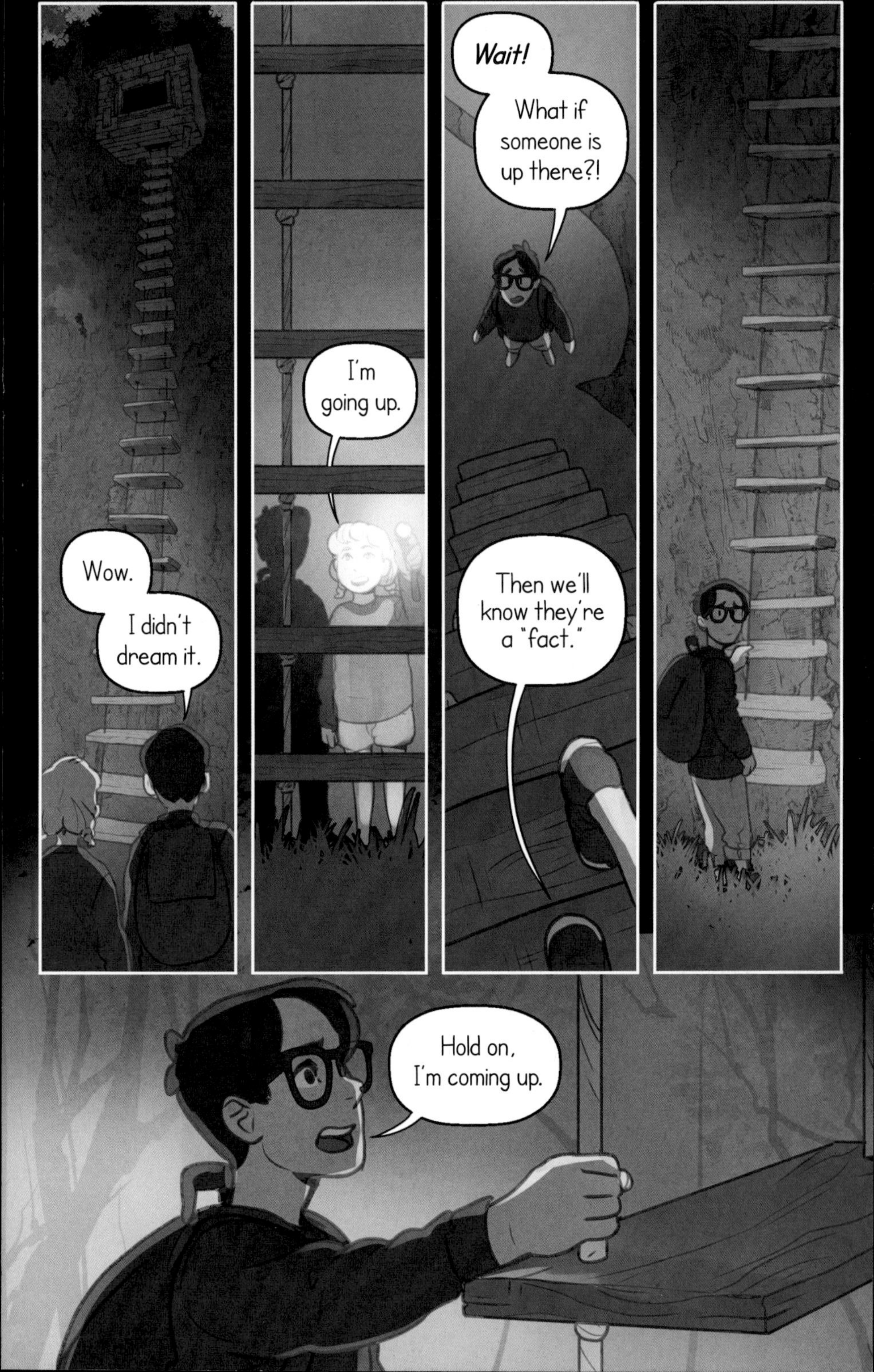
Wow.
I didn't dream it.
I'm going up.
Wait!
What if someone is up there?!
Then we'll know they're a "fact."
Hold on, I'm coming up.

CHAPTER TWO
Leaving Again

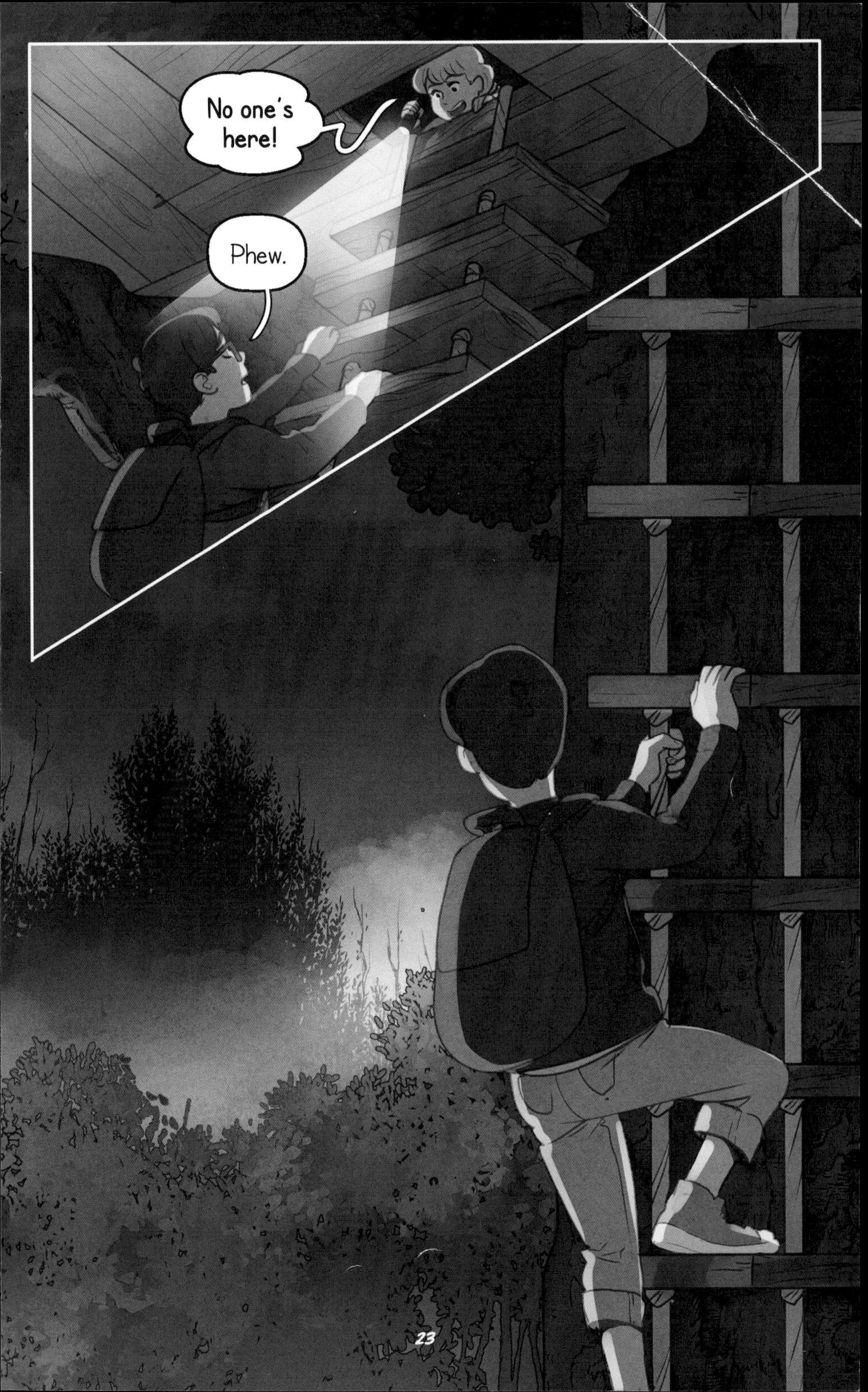
No one's here!
Phew.

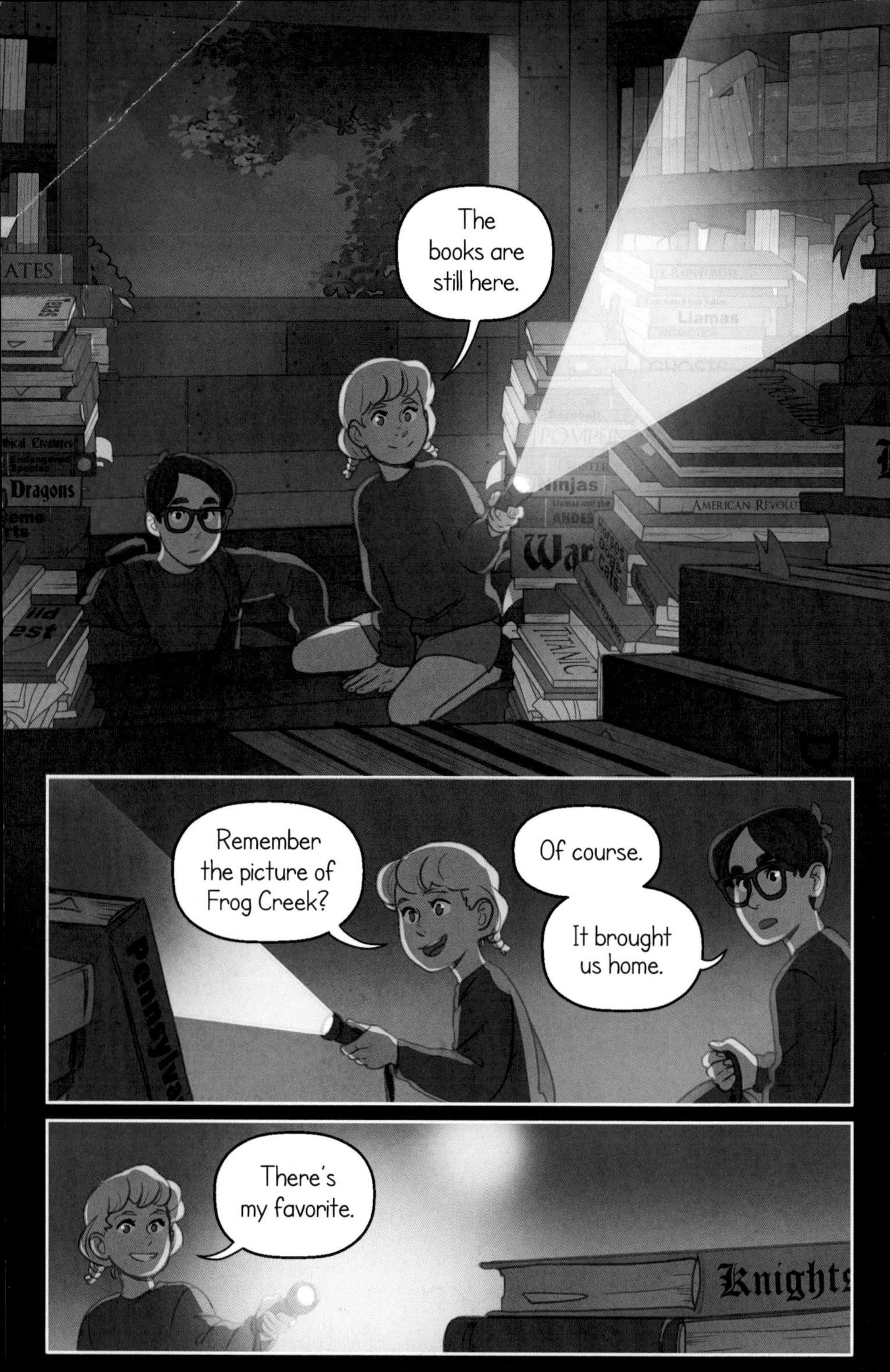
The books are still here.
Dragons
Llamas
POMPEII
Ninjas
TITANIC
AMERICAN REVOLUT
Remember the picture of Frog Creek?
Of course.
It brought us home.
There's my favorite.
Knights

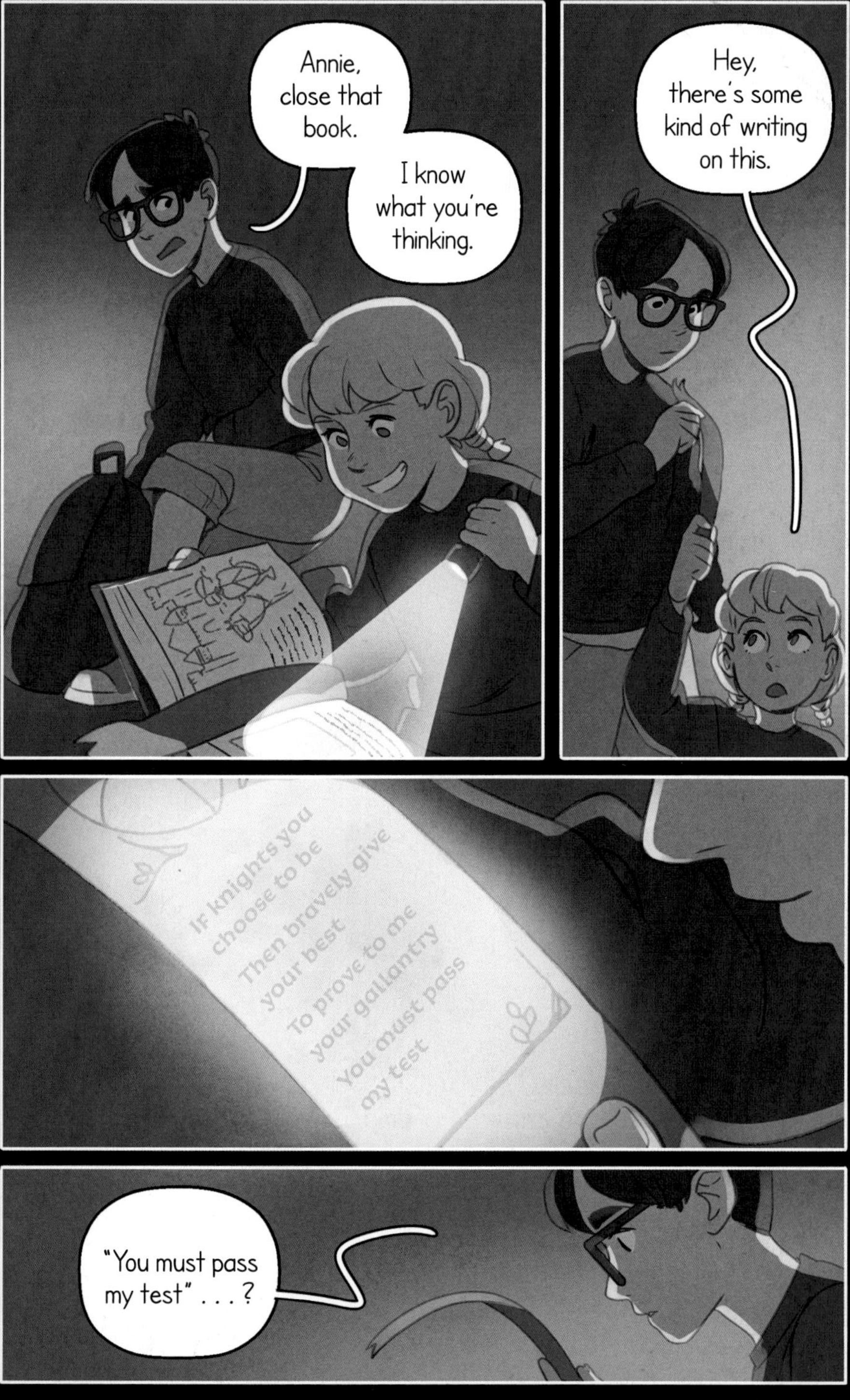
Annie, close that book.
I know what you're thinking.
Hey, there's some kind of writing on this.
If knights you choose to be
Then bravely give your best
To prove to me your gallantry
You must pass my test
"You must pass my test" . . . ?

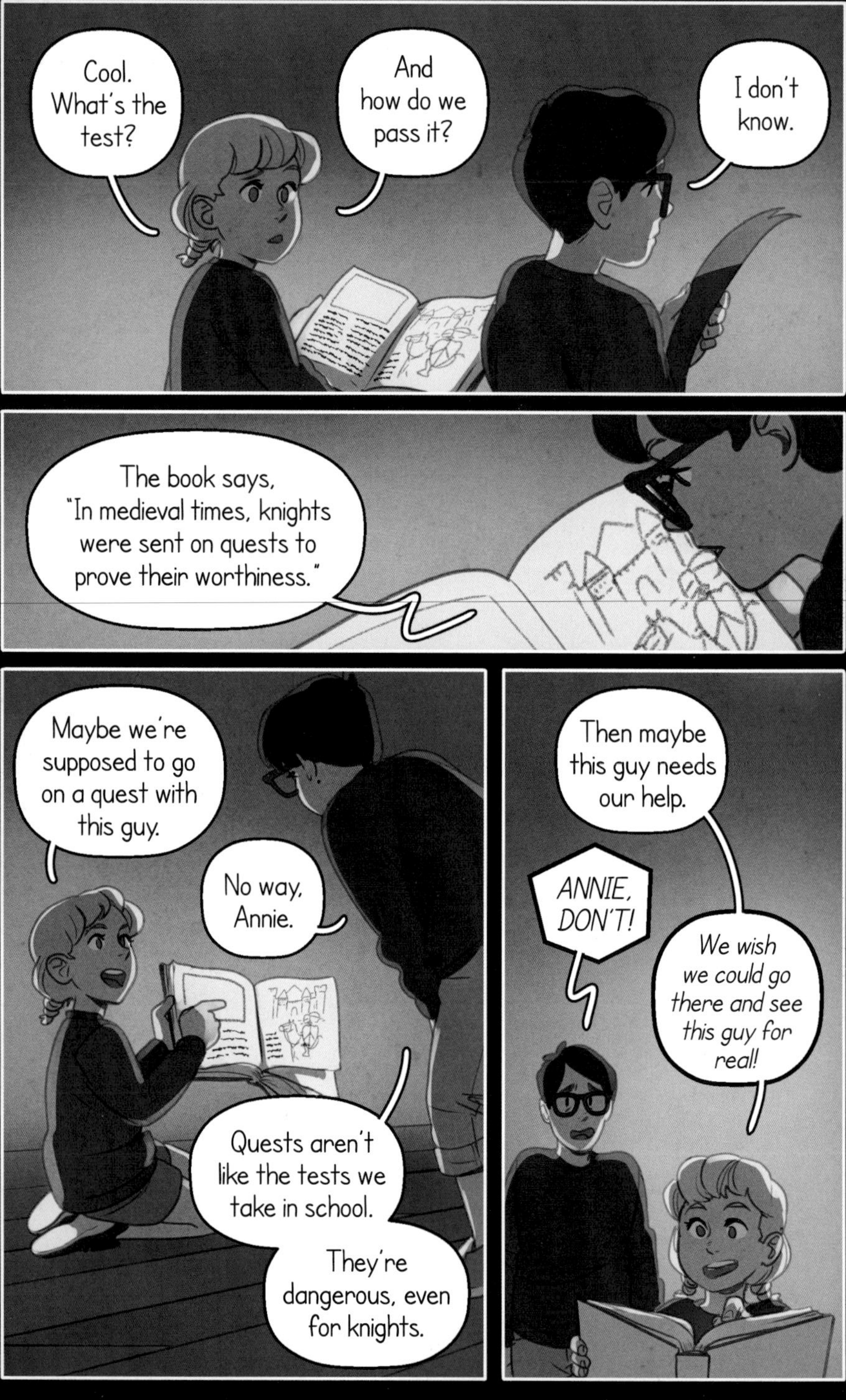
Cool. What's the test?
And how do we pass it?
I don't know.
The book says, "In medieval times, knights were sent on quests to prove their worthiness."
Maybe we're supposed to go on a quest with this guy.
No way, Annie.
Quests aren't like the tests we take in school.
They're dangerous, even for knights.
Then maybe this guy needs our help.
ANNIE, DON'T!
We wish we could go there and see this guy for real!

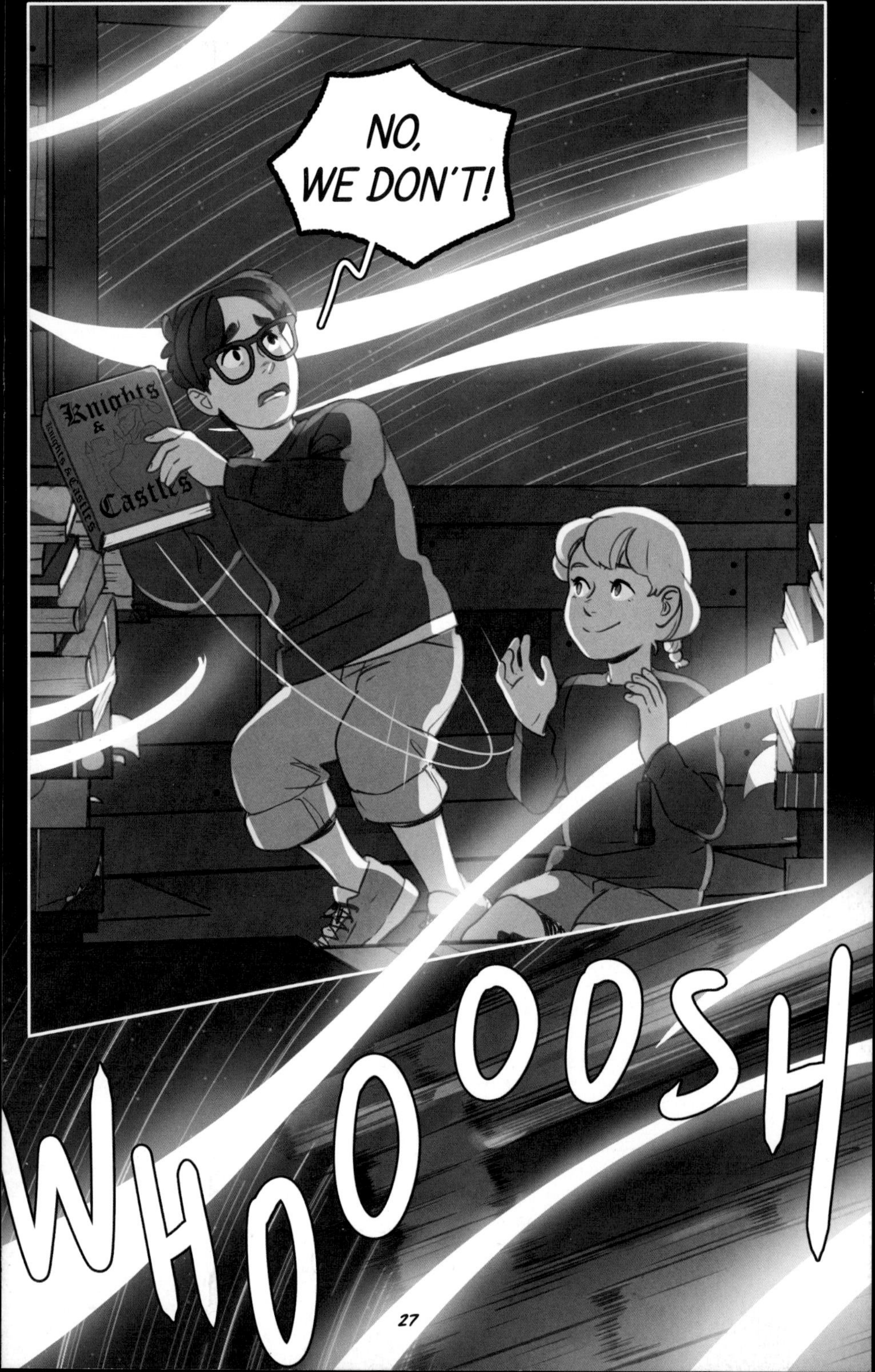
NO, WE DON'T!
Knights & Castles
WHOOOOSH

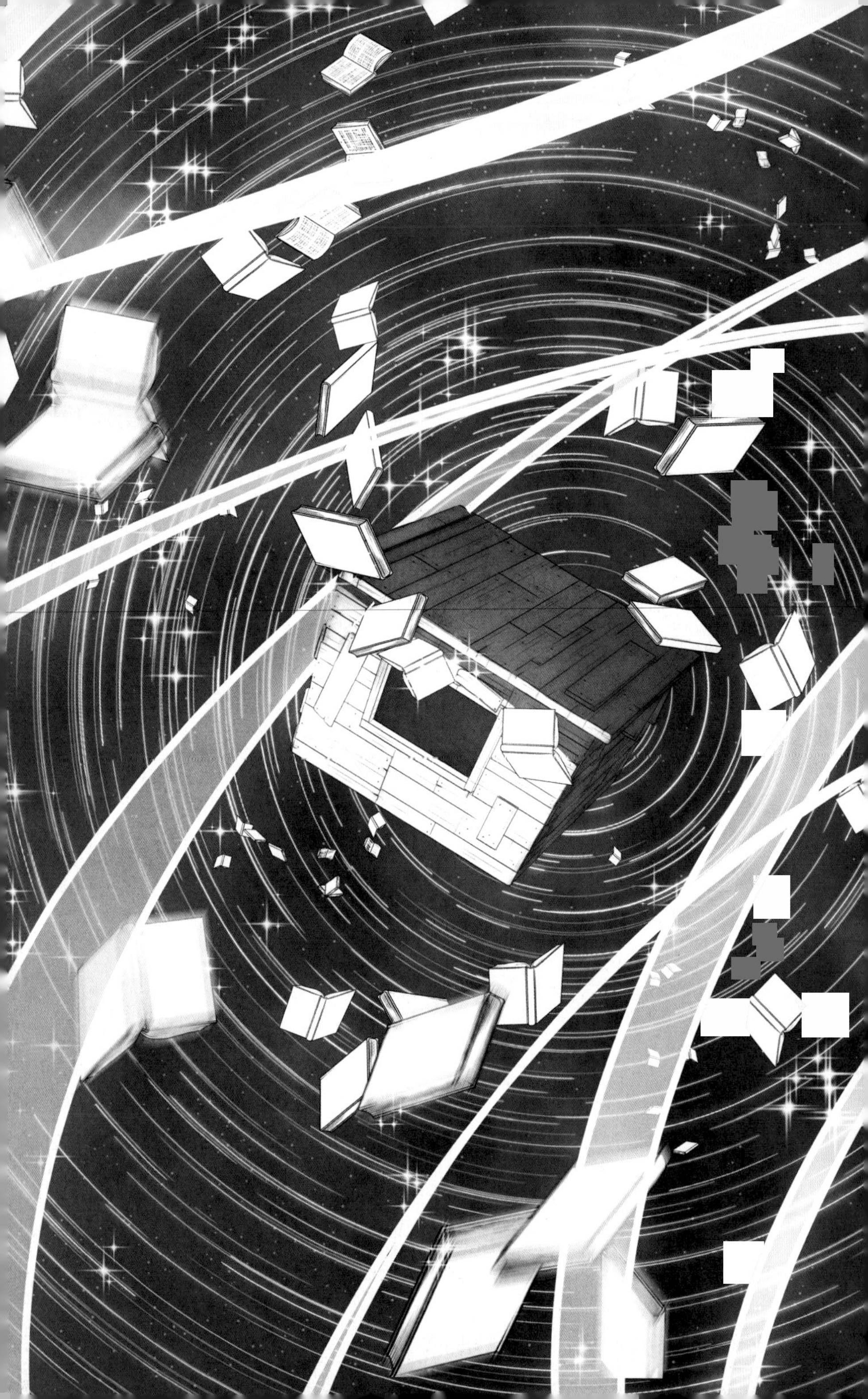

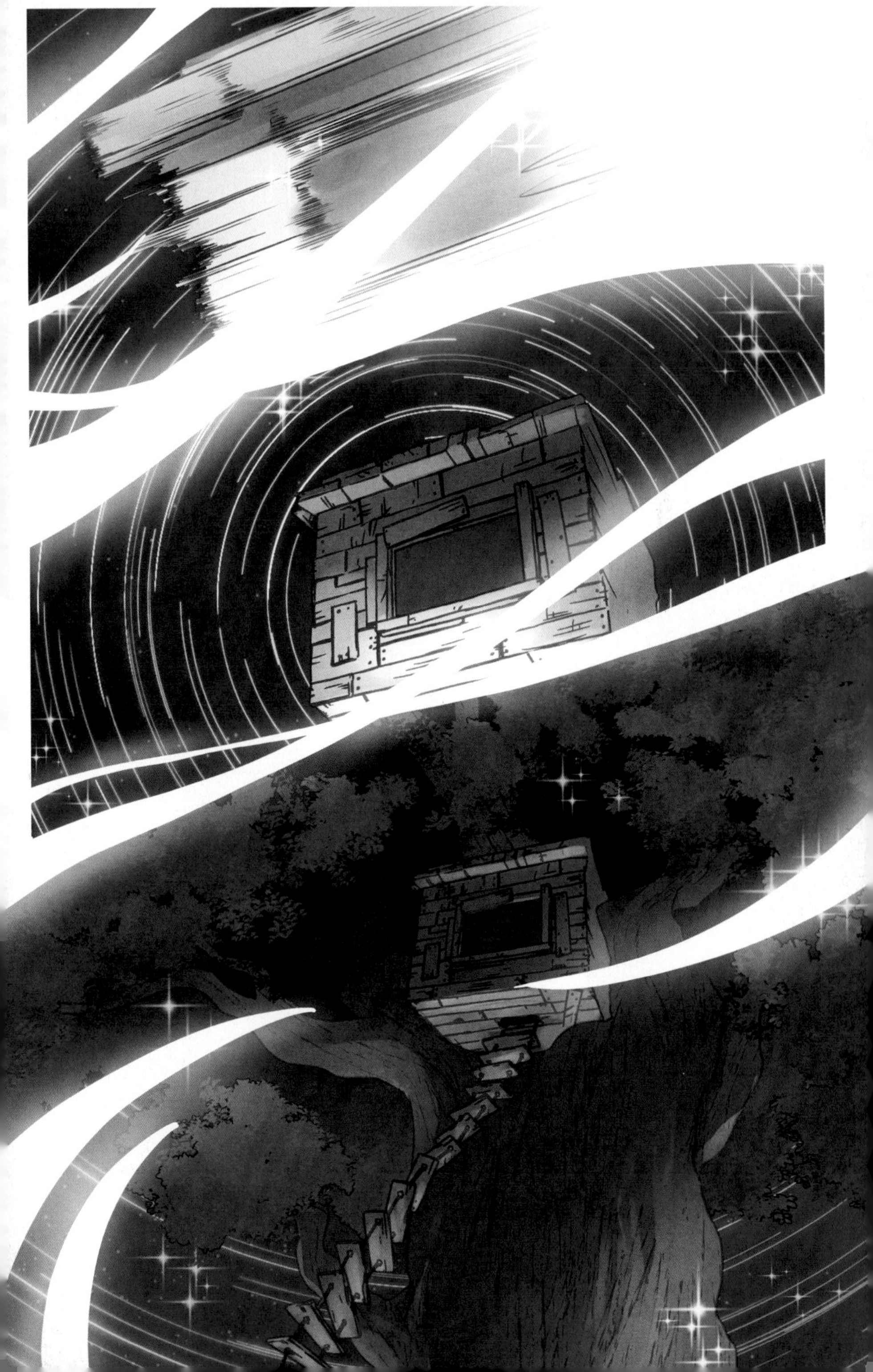

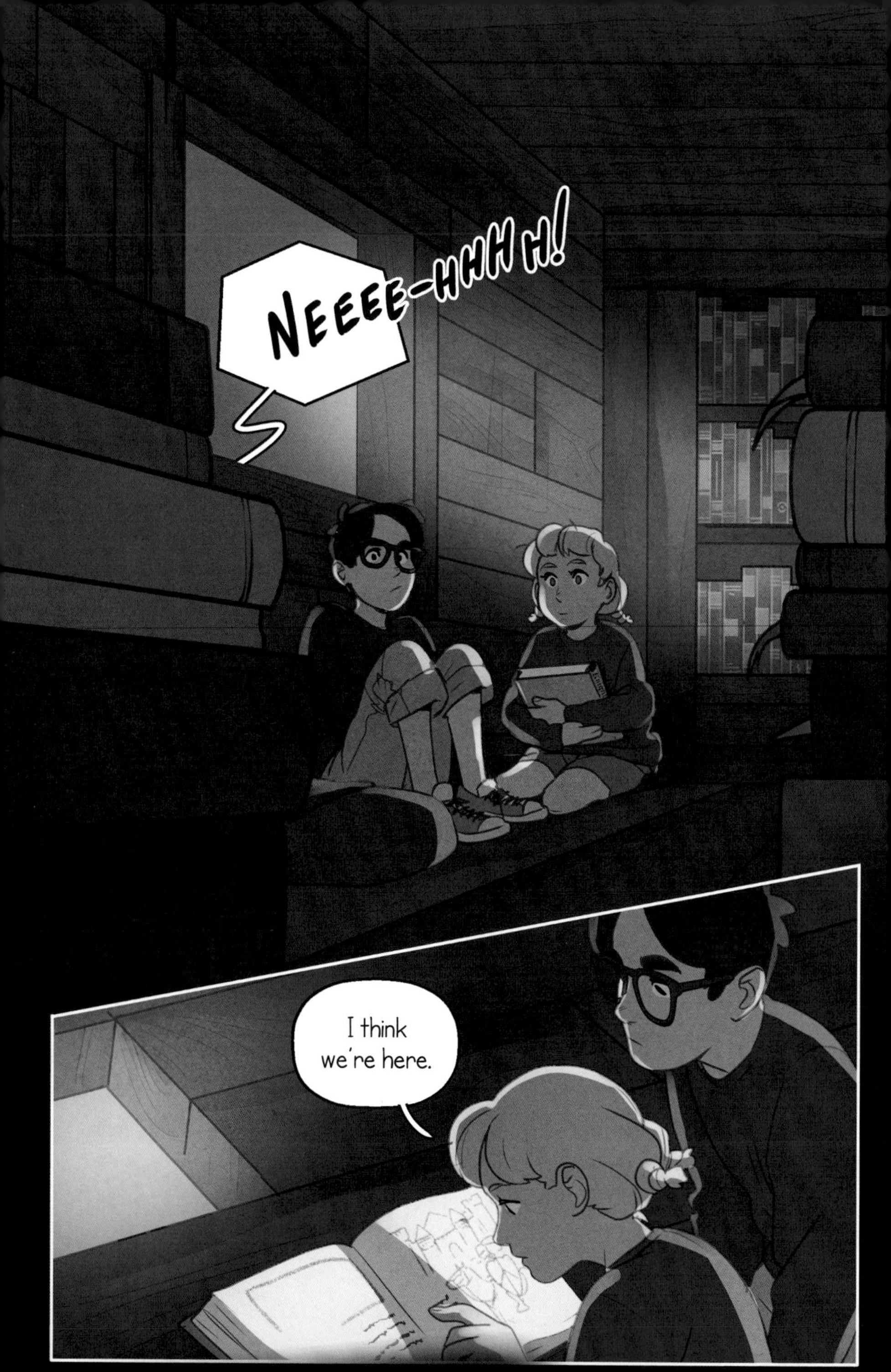
NEEEE-HHHH H!
I think we're here.

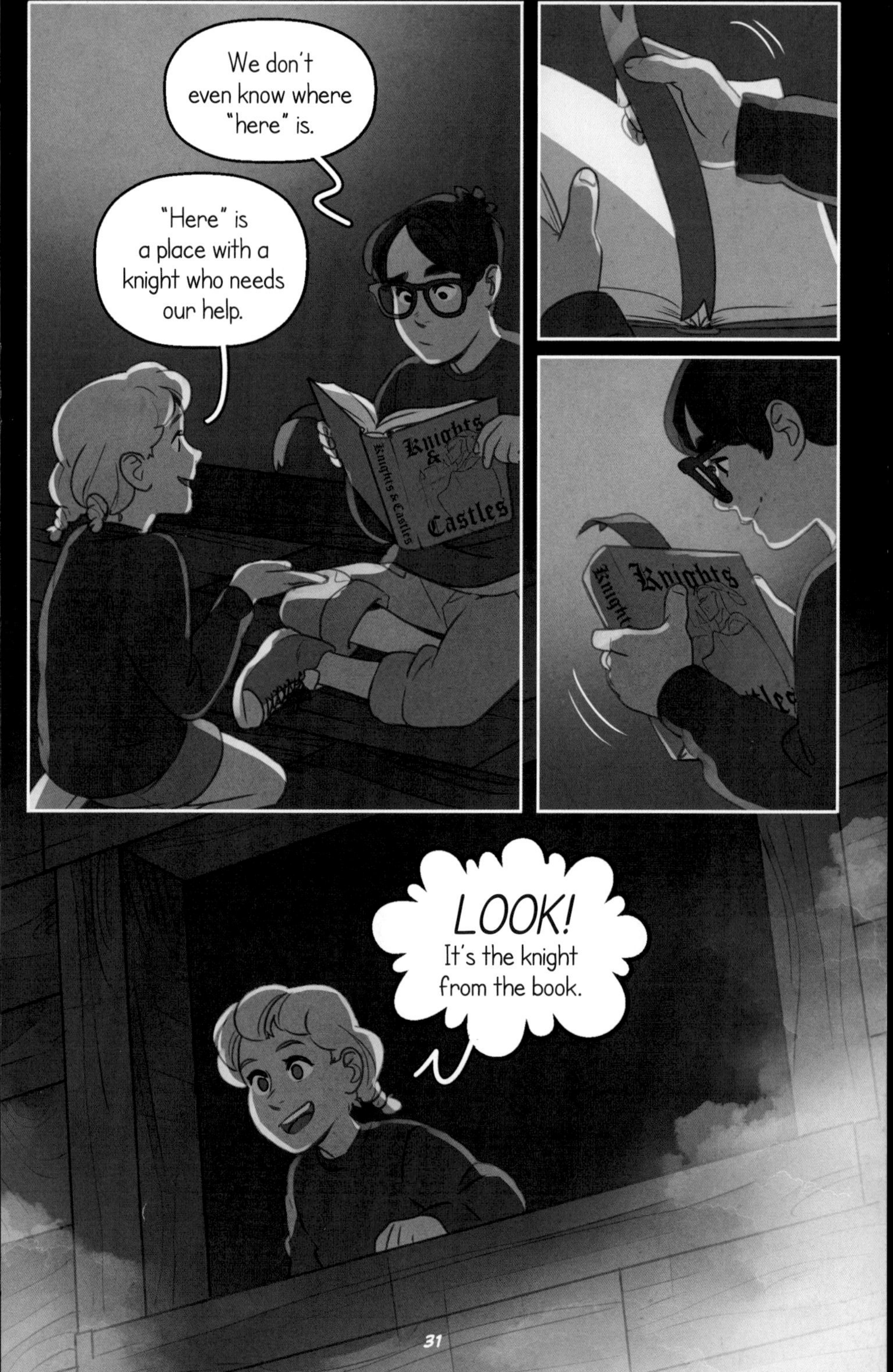
We don't even know where "here" is.
"Here" is a place with a knight who needs our help.
Knights & Castles
Knights & Castles
Knights
Knights
LOOK! It's the knight from the book.

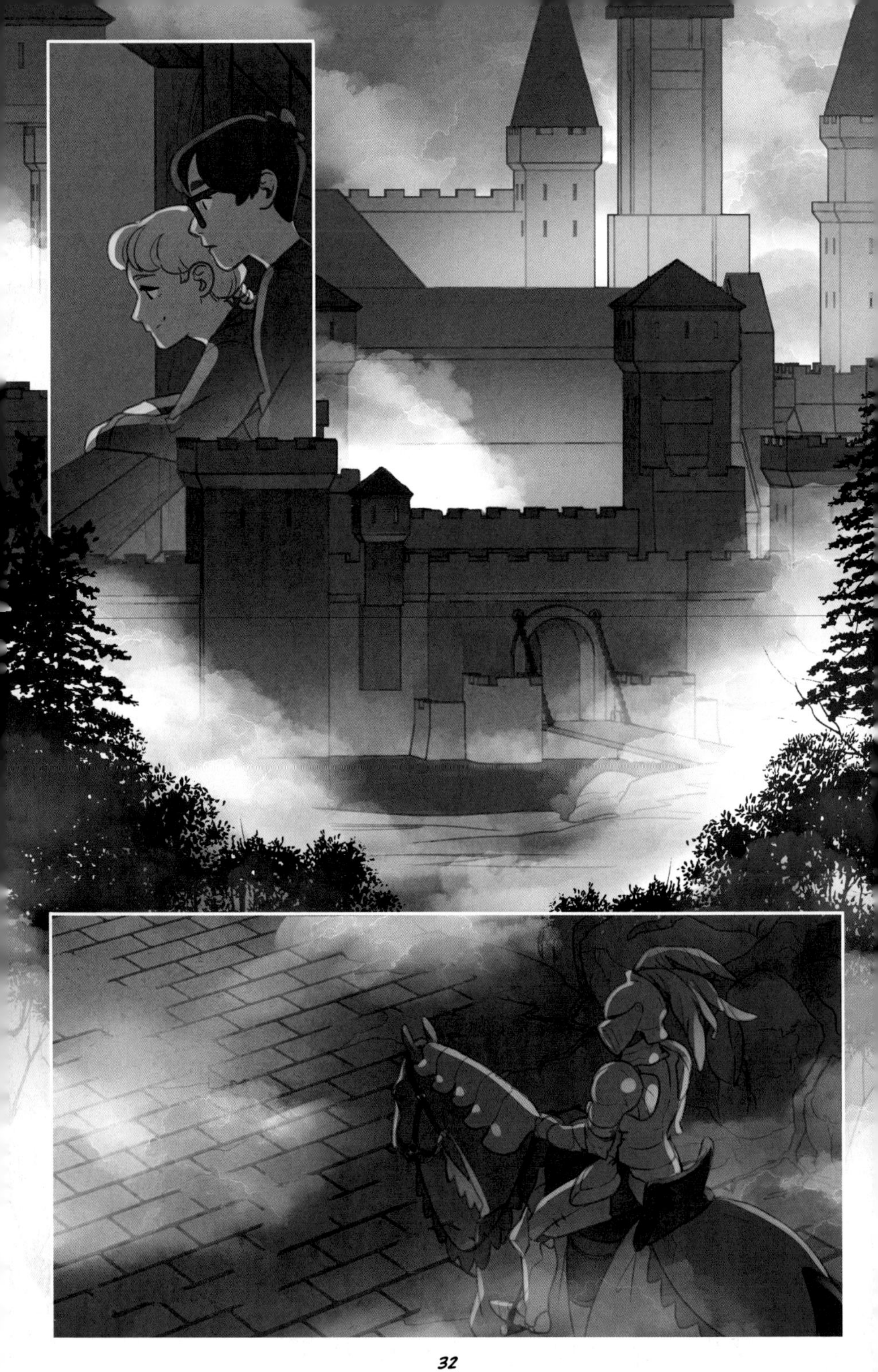

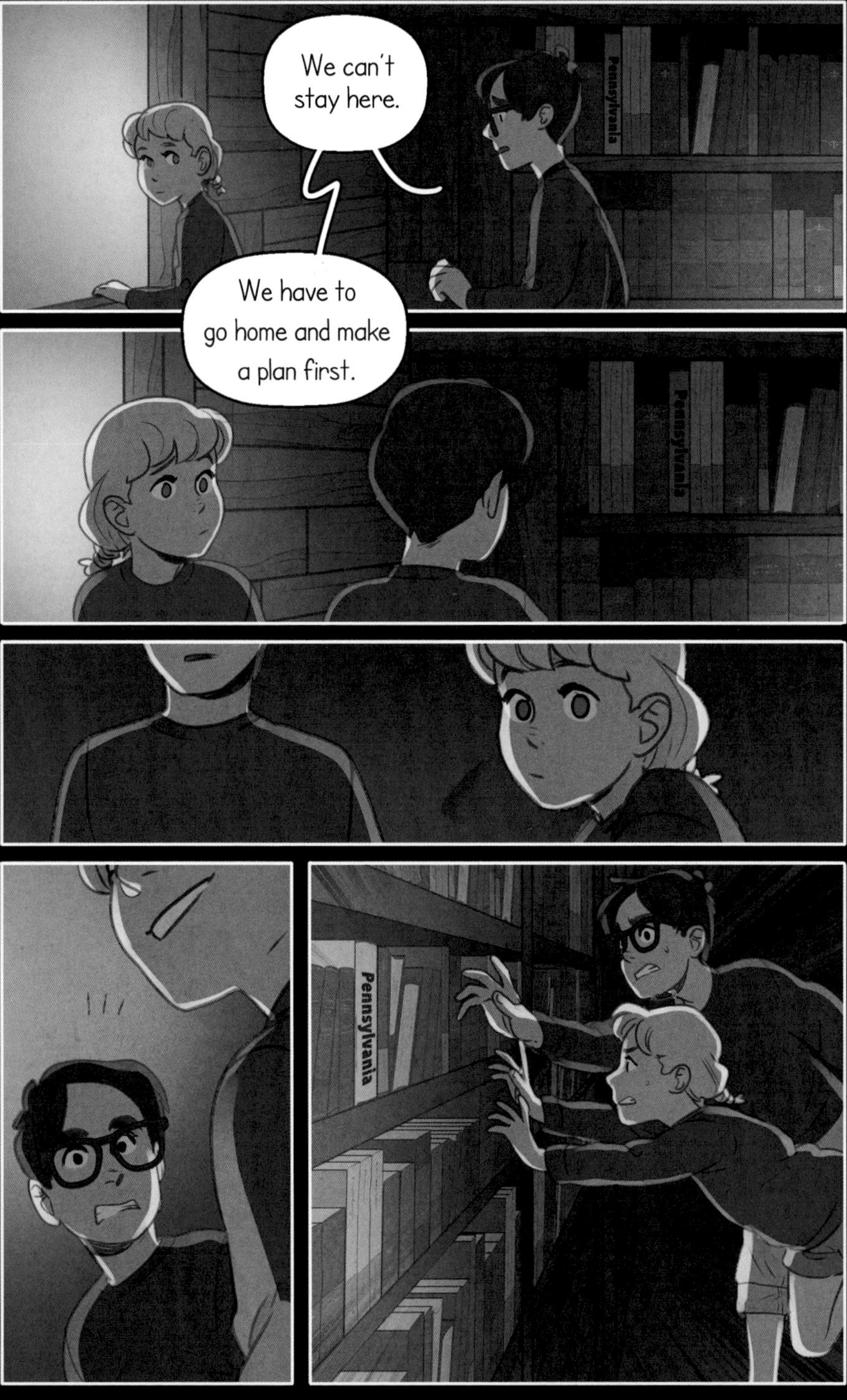
We can't stay here.
We have to go home and make a plan first.
Pennsylvania

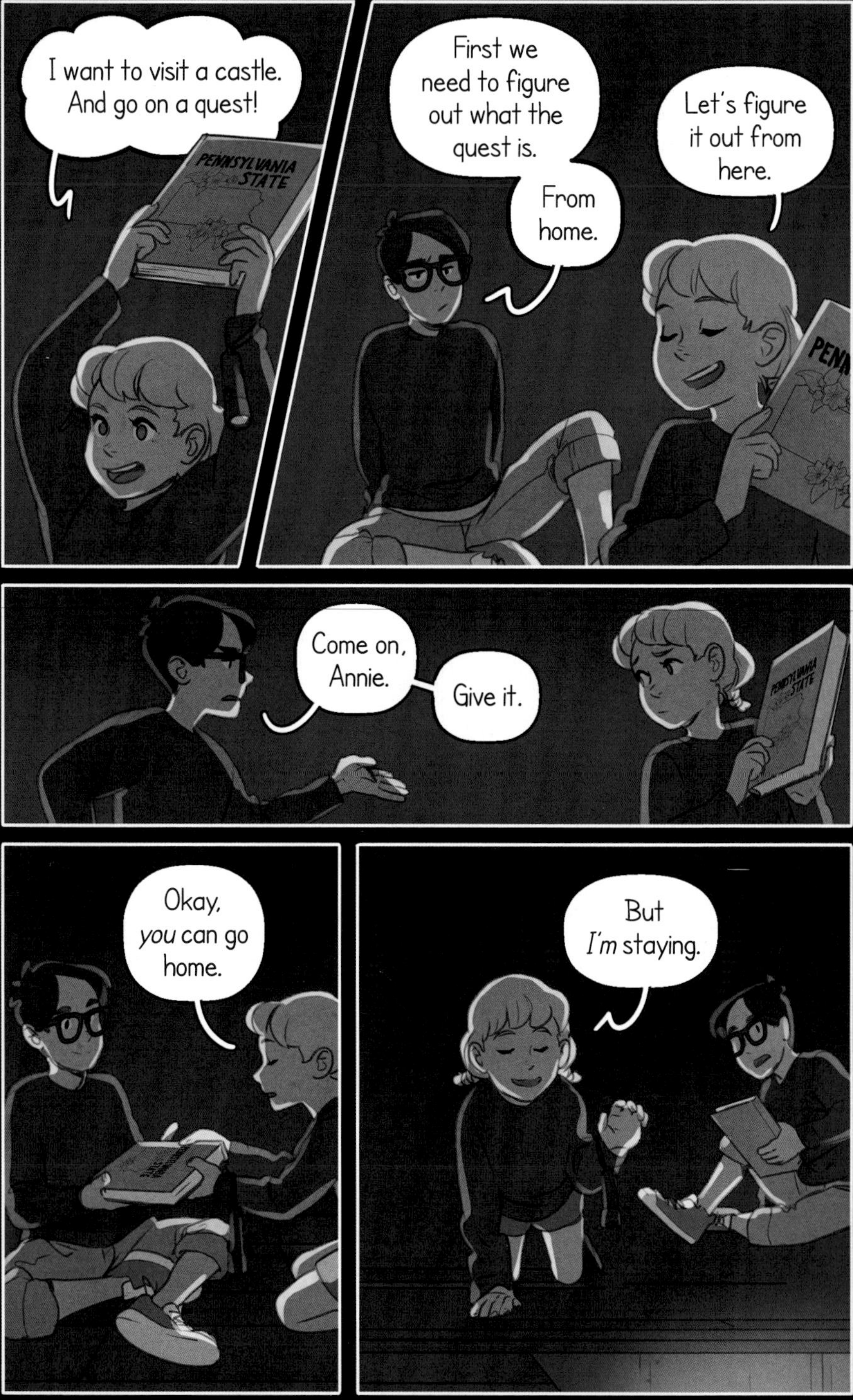
I want to visit a castle. And go on a quest!
PENNSYLVANIA STATE
First we need to figure out what the quest is.
From home.
Let's figure it out from here.
Come on, Annie.
Give it.
Okay, *you* can go home.
But *I'm* staying.

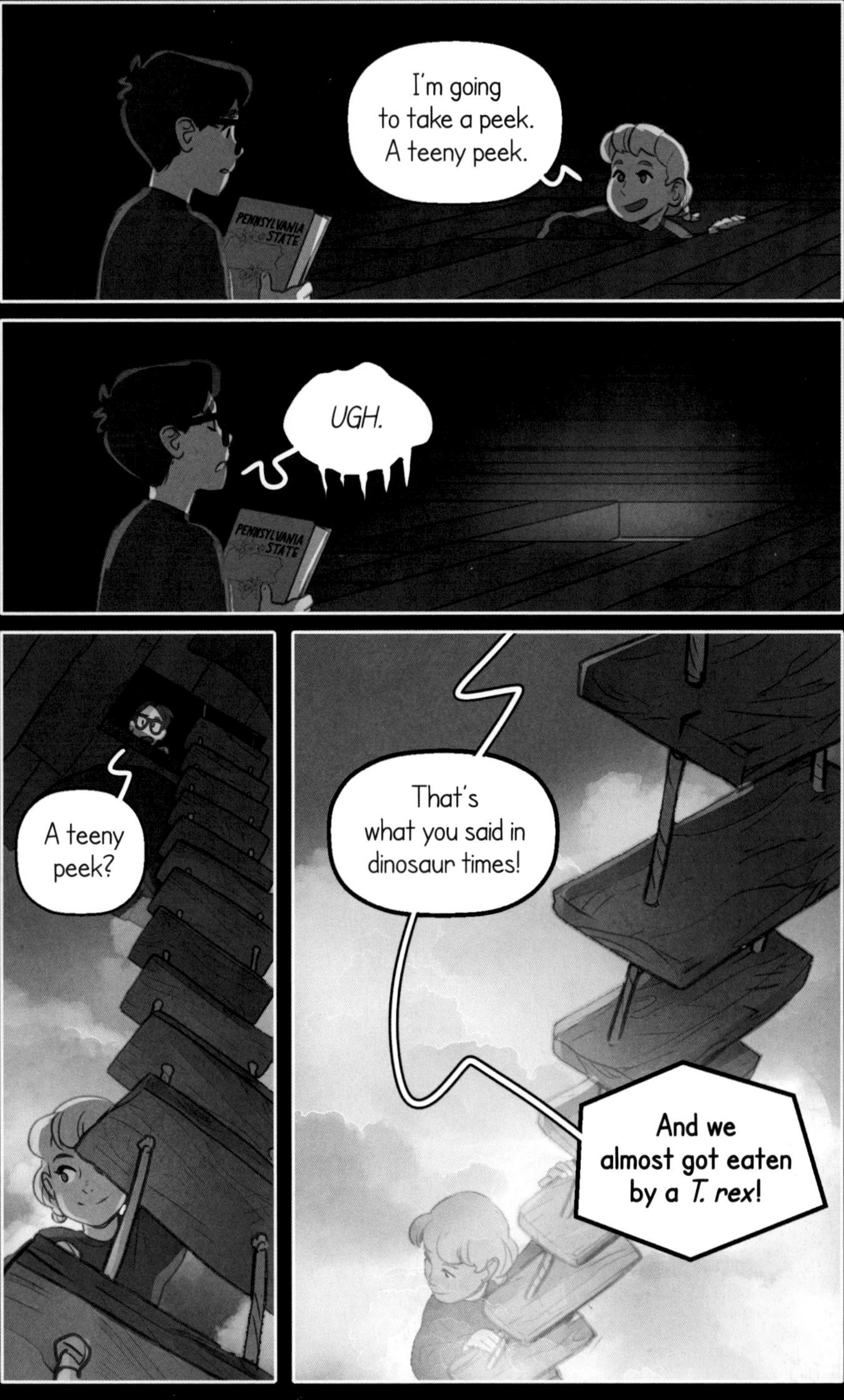
I'm going to take a peek. A teeny peek.
PENNSYLVANIA STATE
UGH.
PENNSYLVANIA STATE
A teeny peek?
That's what you said in dinosaur times!
And we almost got eaten by a *T. rex*!

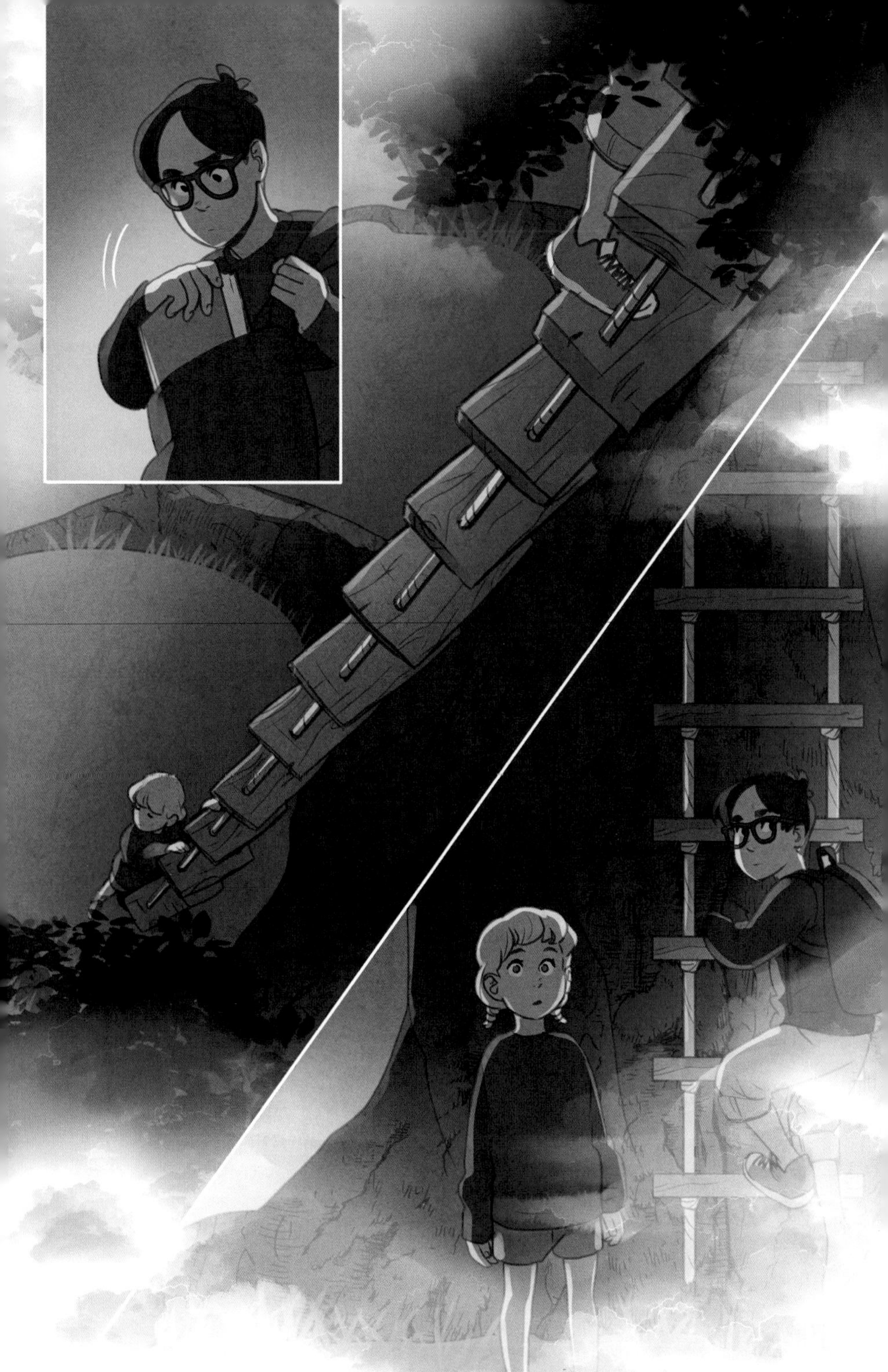

CHAPTER THREE
Across the Bridge

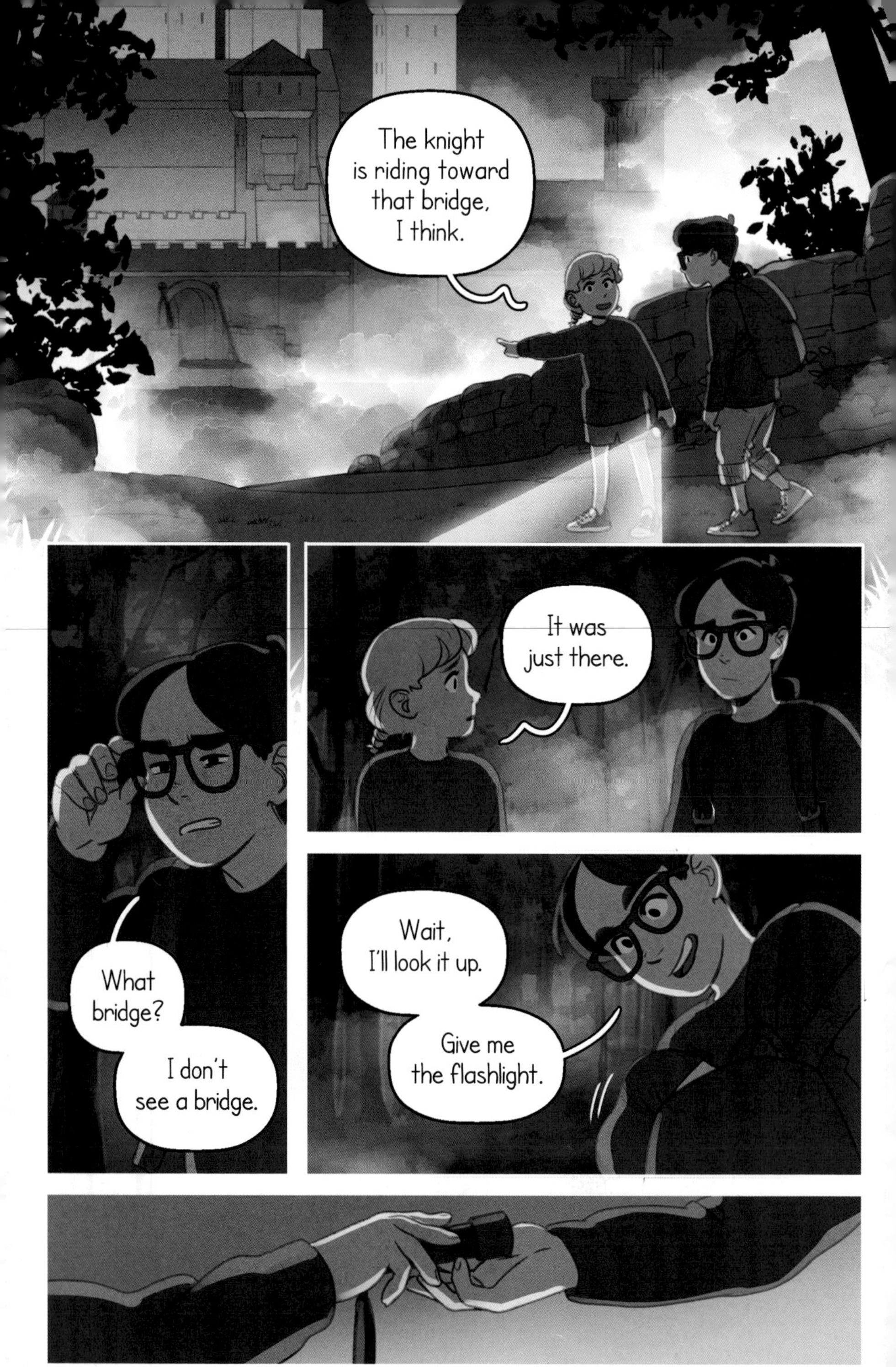
The knight is riding toward that bridge, I think.
What bridge?
I don't see a bridge.
It was just there.
Wait, I'll look it up.
Give me the flashlight.

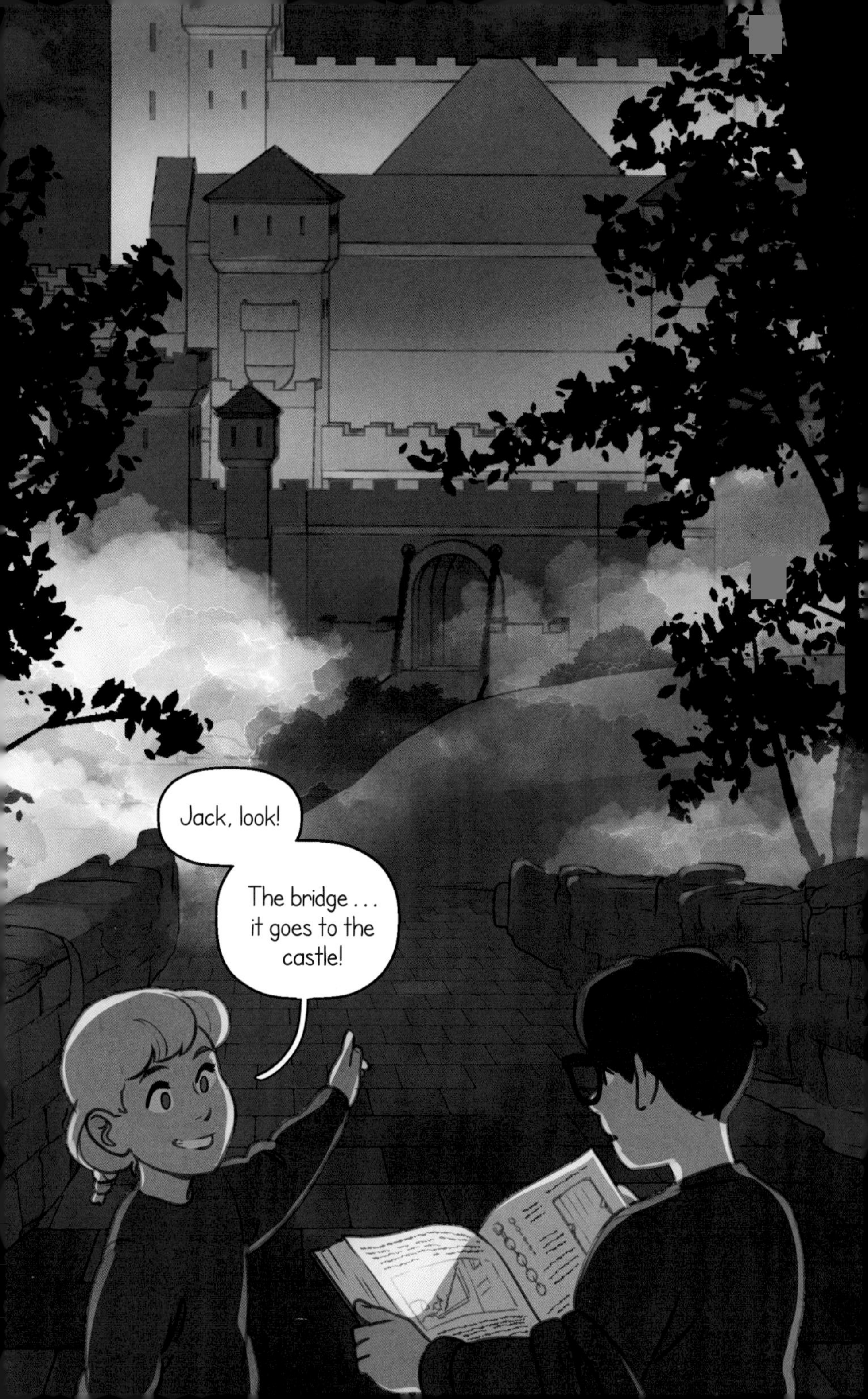
Jack, look!
The bridge . . . it goes to the castle!

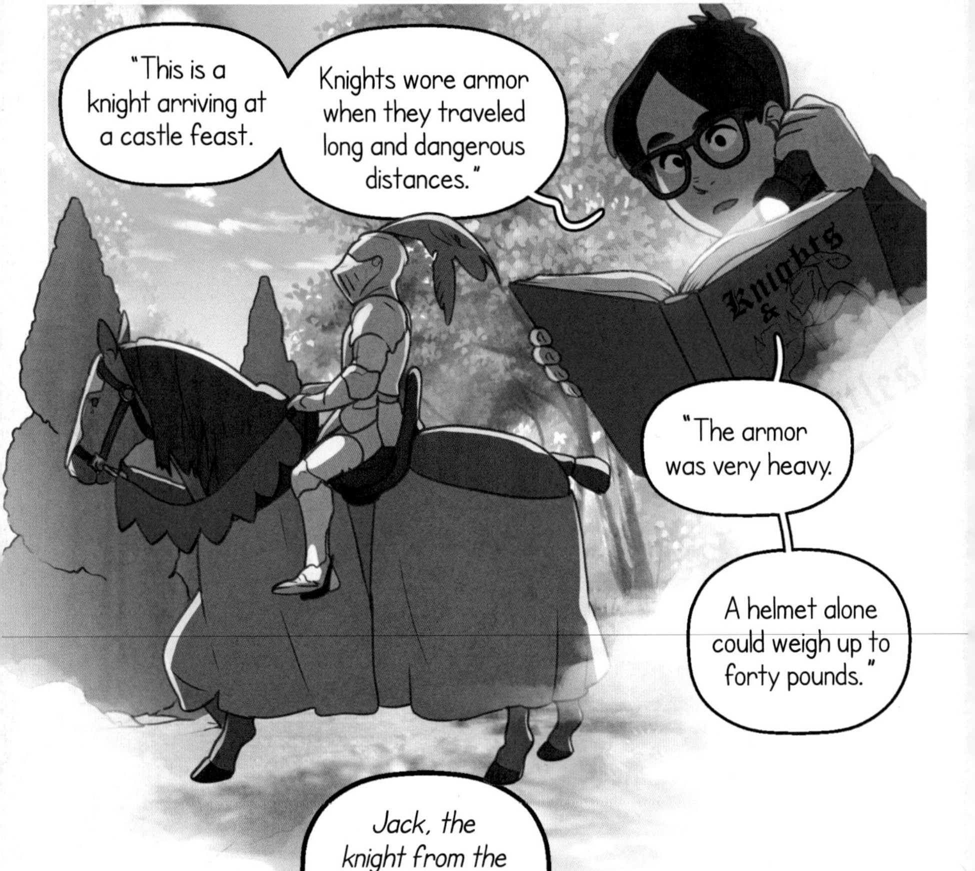
"This is a knight arriving at a castle feast.
Knights wore armor when they traveled long and dangerous distances."
"The armor was very heavy.
A helmet alone could weigh up to forty pounds."
Knights &

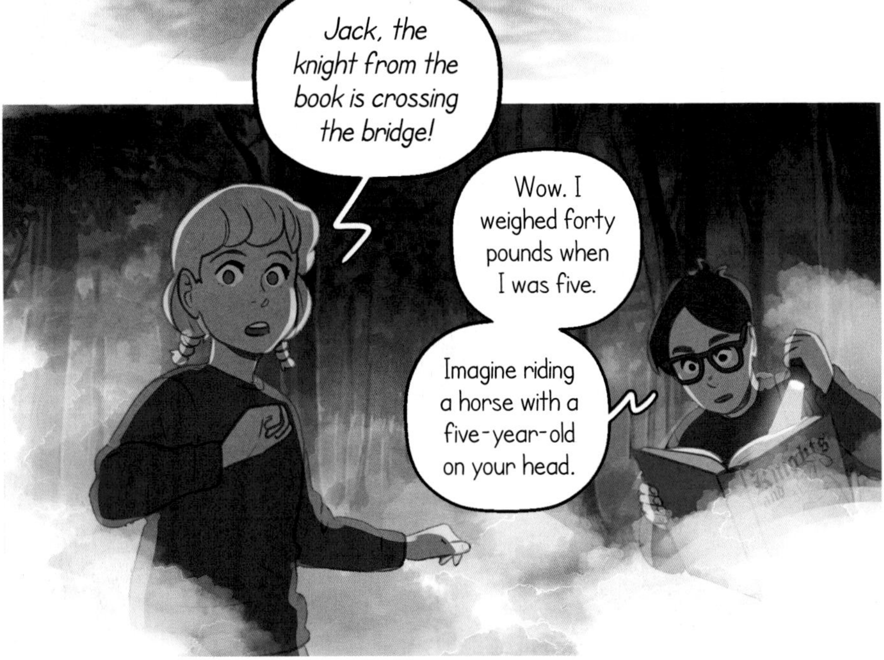
Jack, the knight from the book is crossing the bridge!
Wow. I weighed forty pounds when I was five.
Imagine riding a horse with a five-year-old on your head.

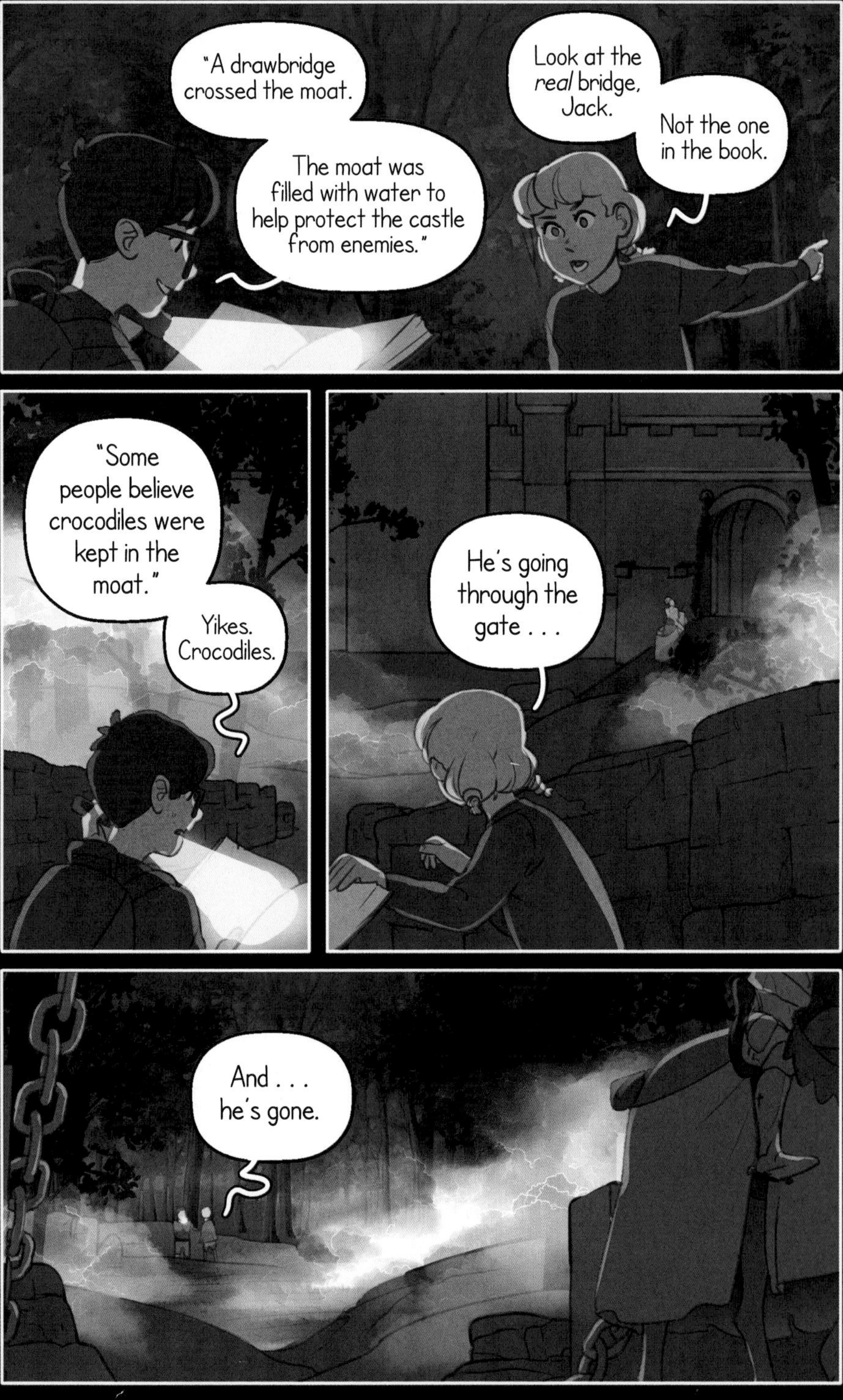
"A drawbridge crossed the moat.
The moat was filled with water to help protect the castle from enemies."
Look at the *real* bridge, Jack.
Not the one in the book.
"Some people believe crocodiles were kept in the moat."
Yikes. Crocodiles.
He's going through the gate . . .
And . . . he's gone.

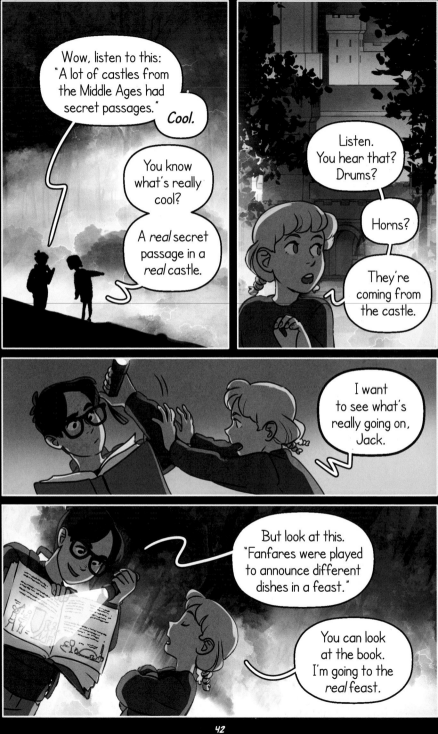

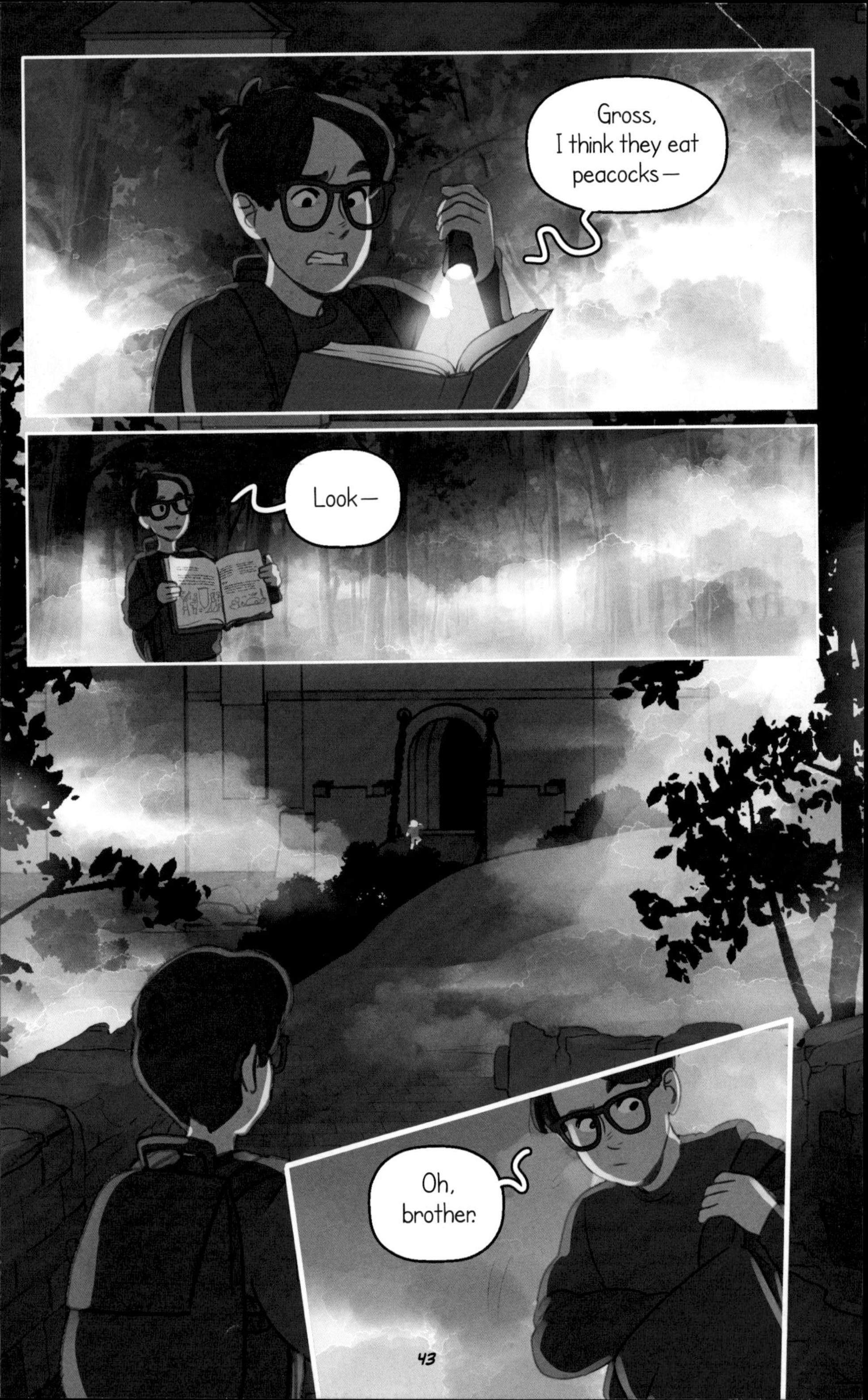
Gross,
I think they eat
peacocks—
Look—
Oh,
brother.

CHAPTER FOUR
Into the Castle

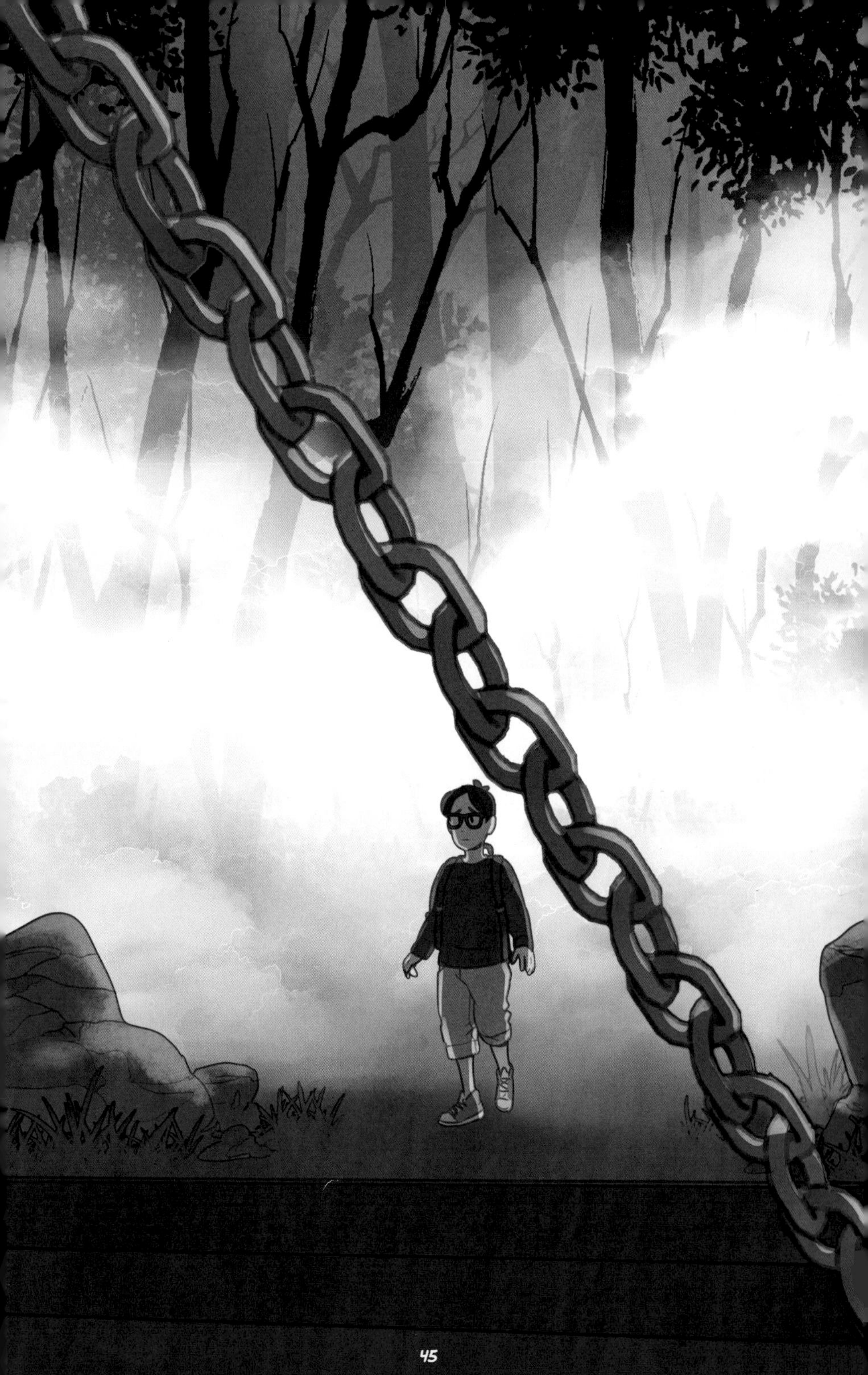

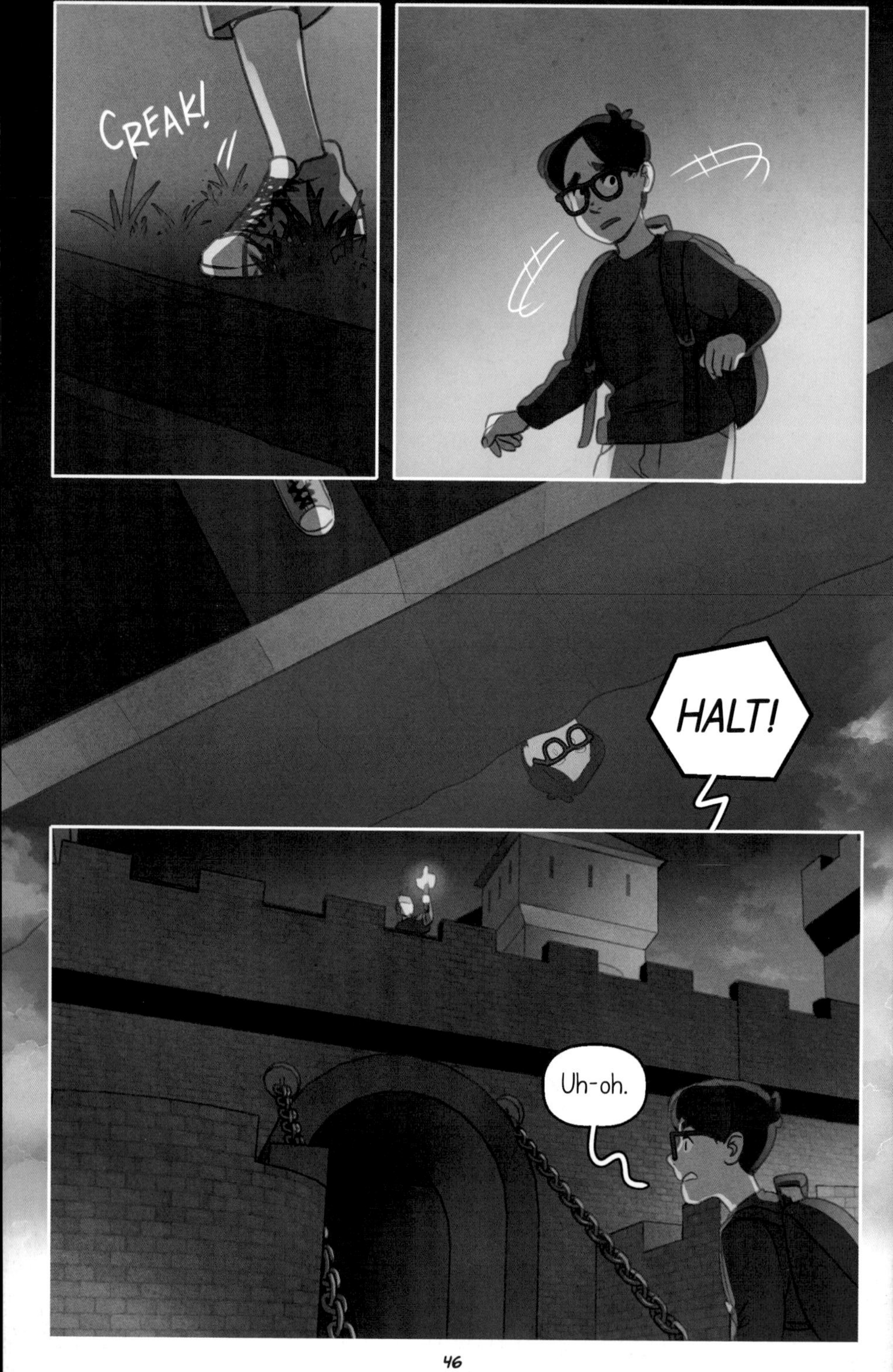
CREAK!
HALT!
Uh-oh.

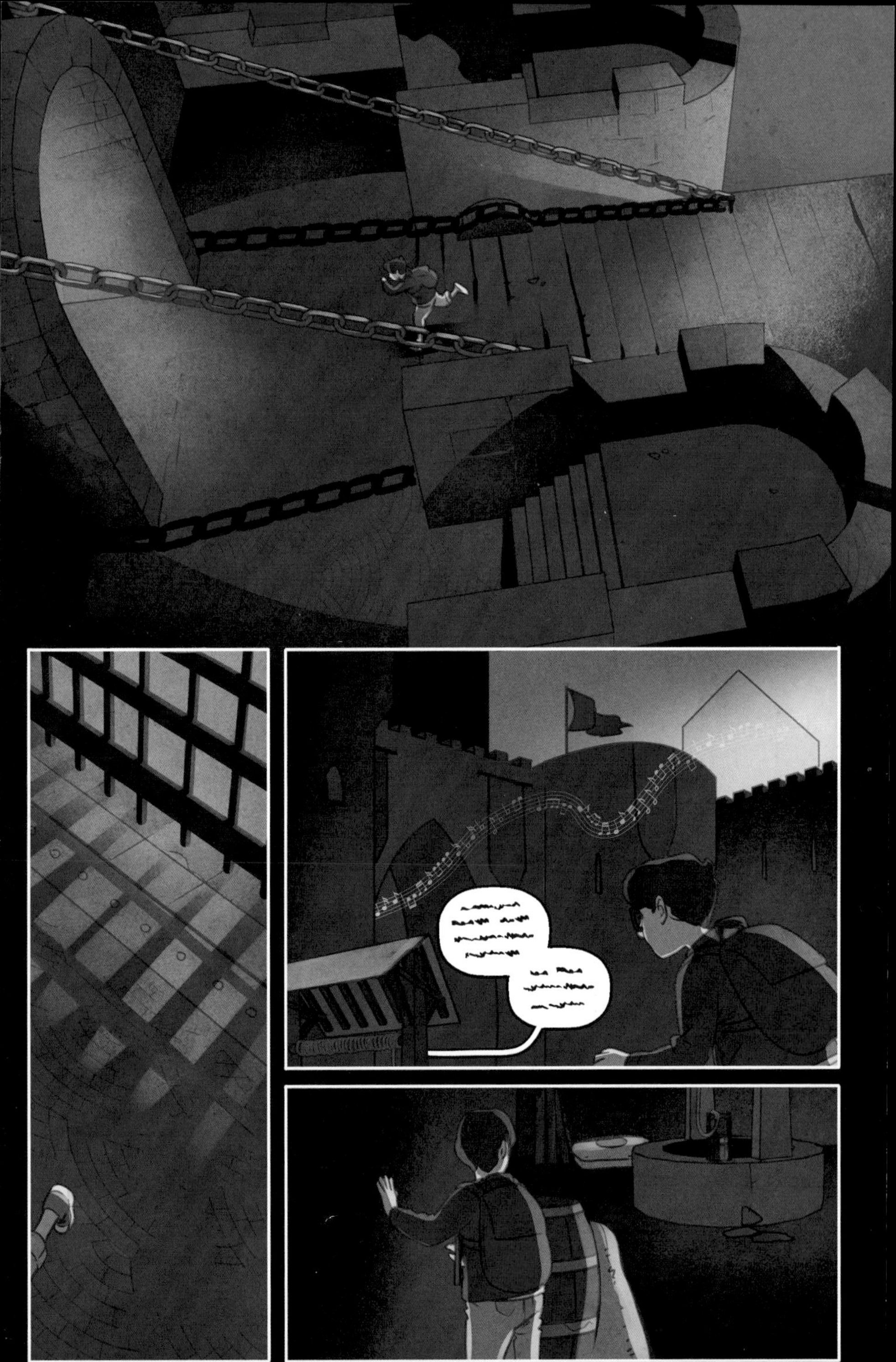

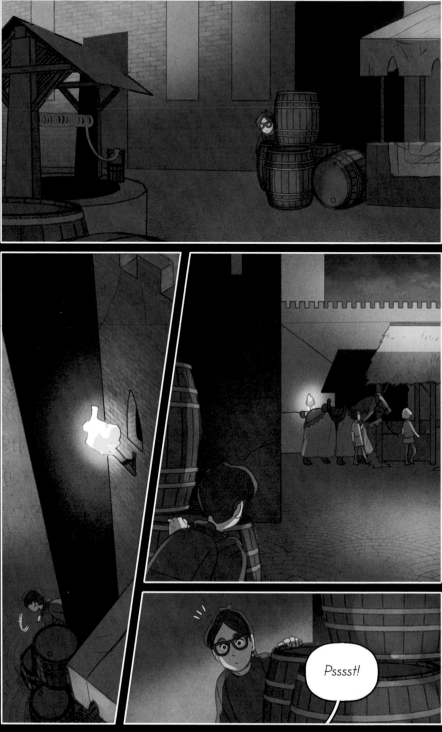

Pssssst!

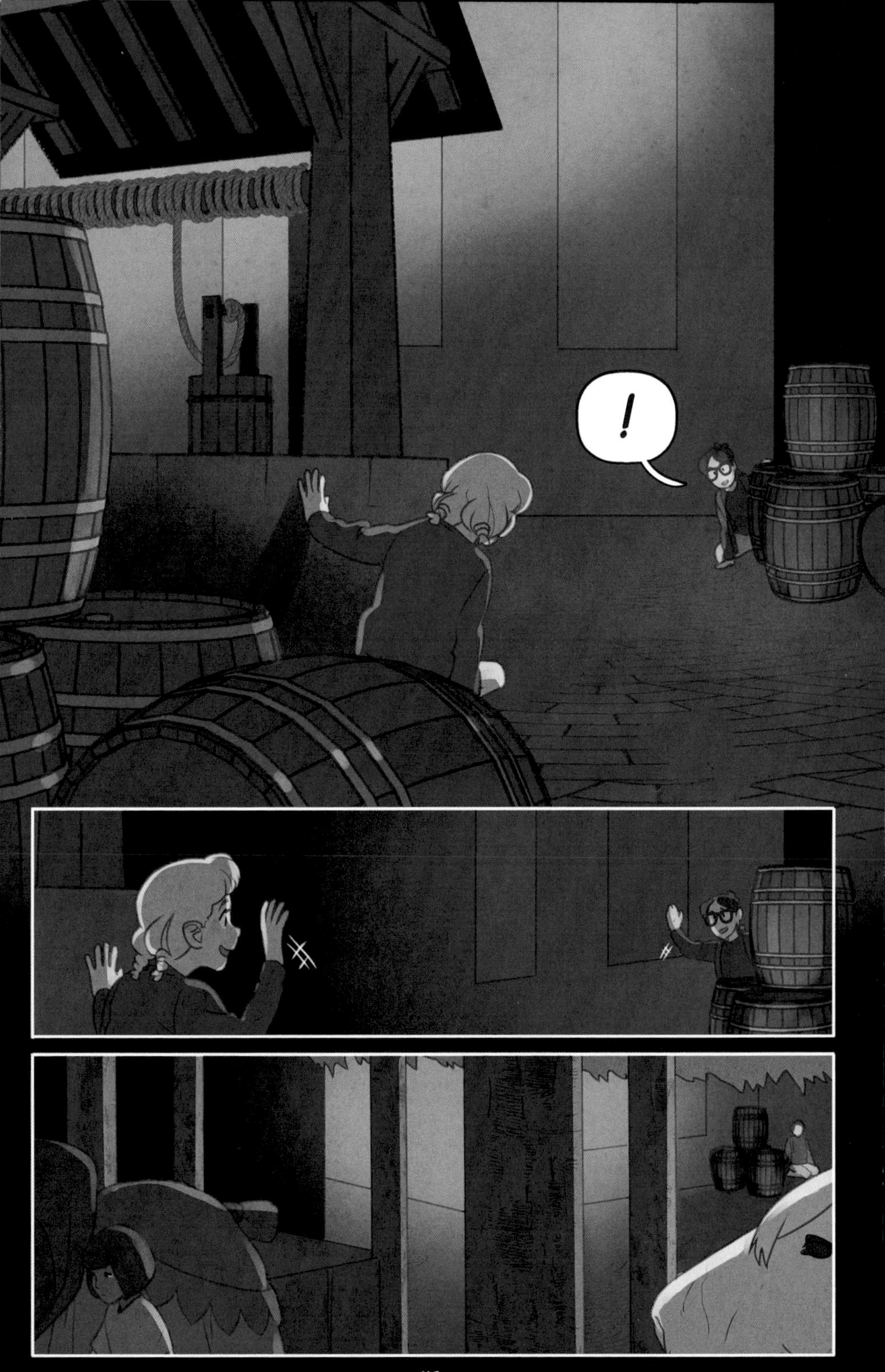
!

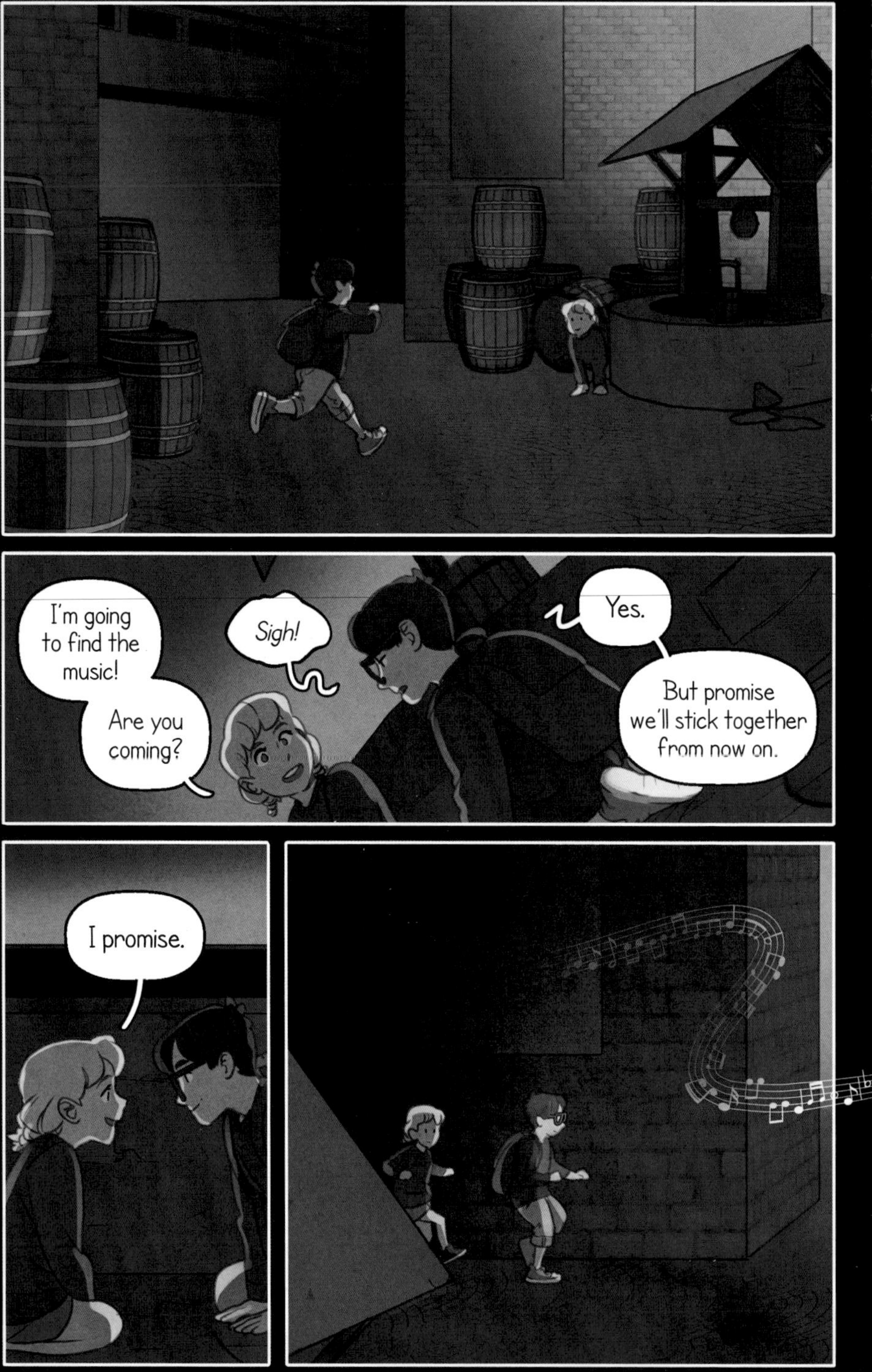
I'm going to find the music!
Are you coming?
Sigh!
Yes.
But promise we'll stick together from now on.
I promise.

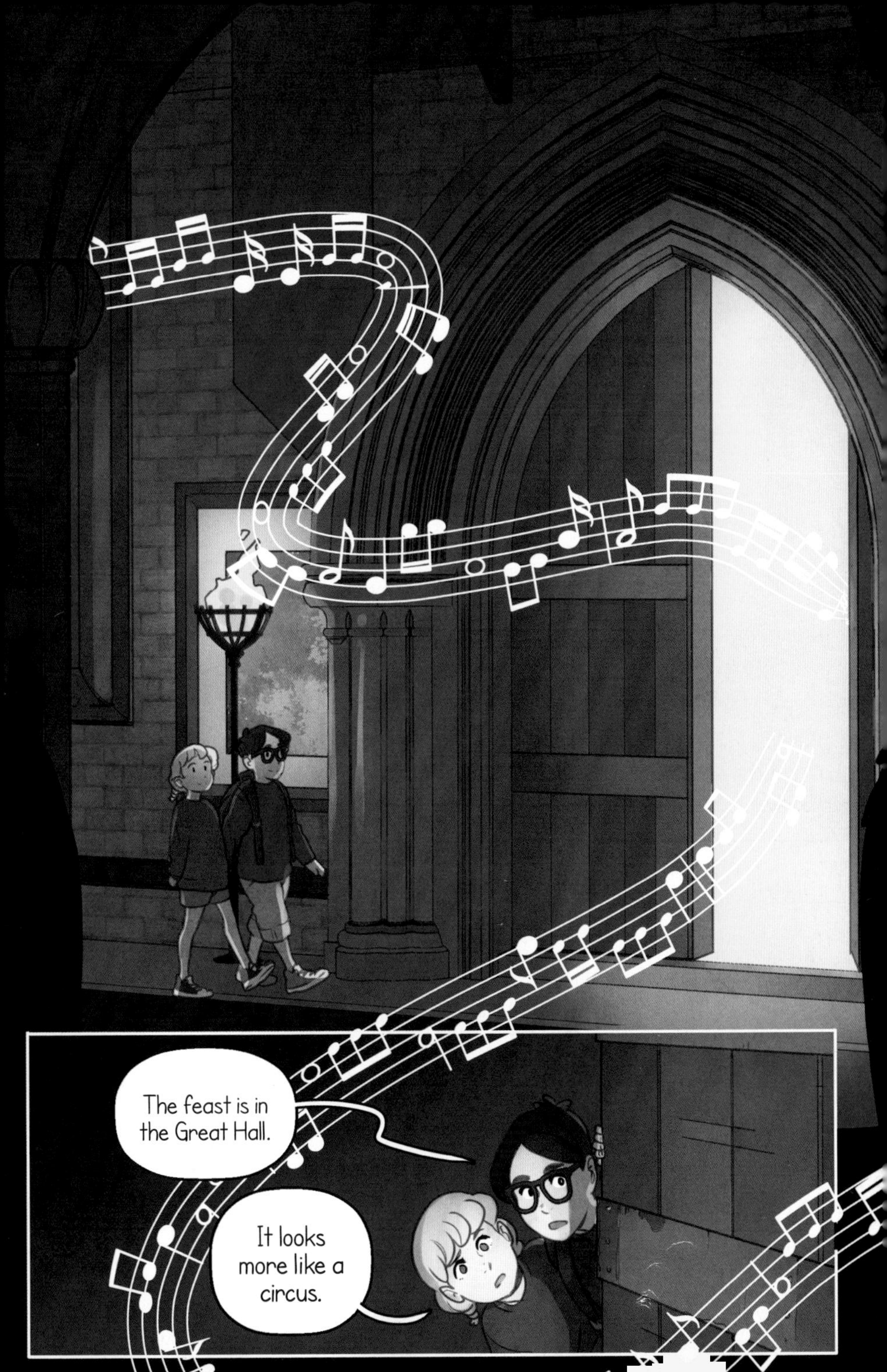
The feast is in the Great Hall.
It looks more like a circus.

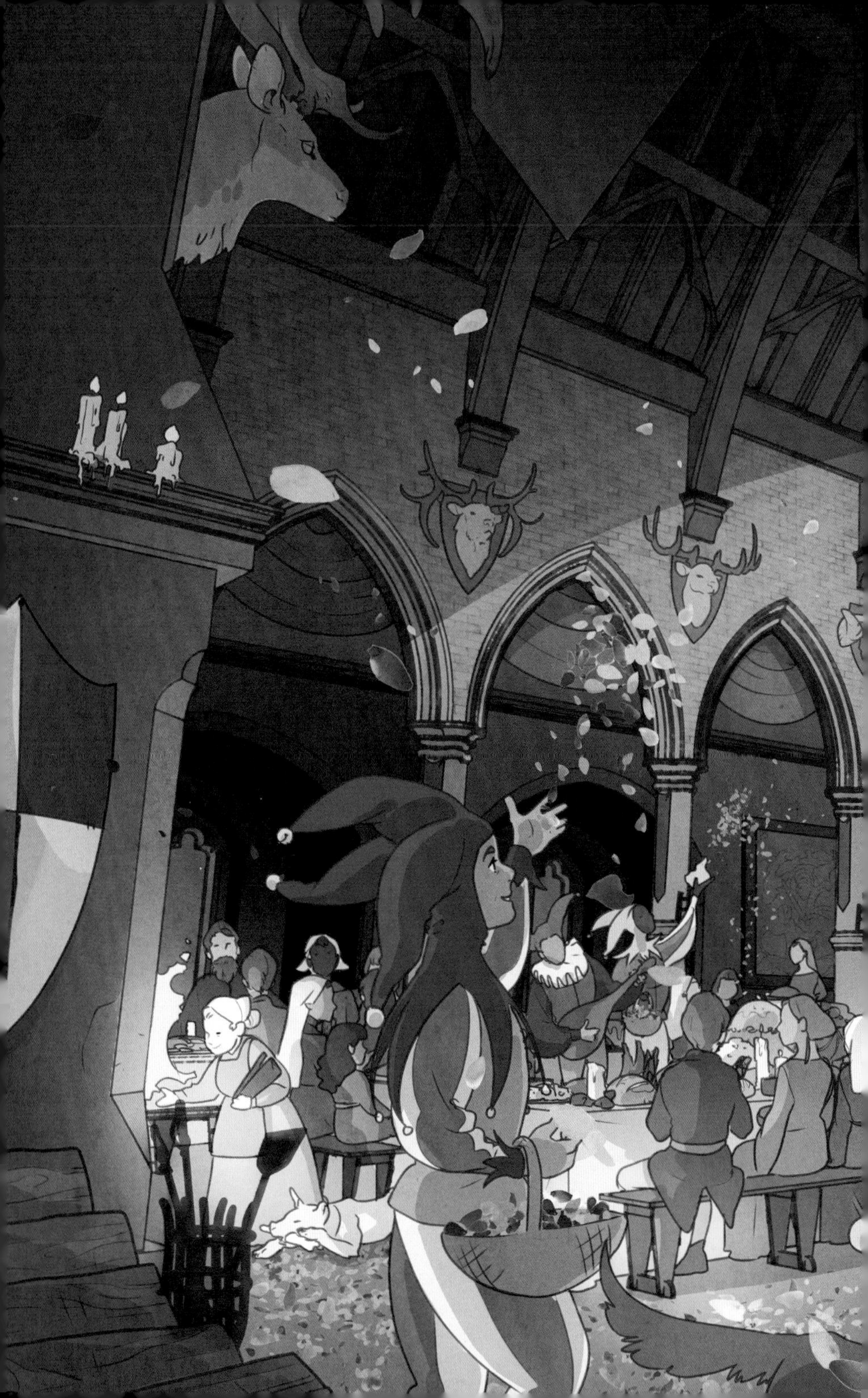

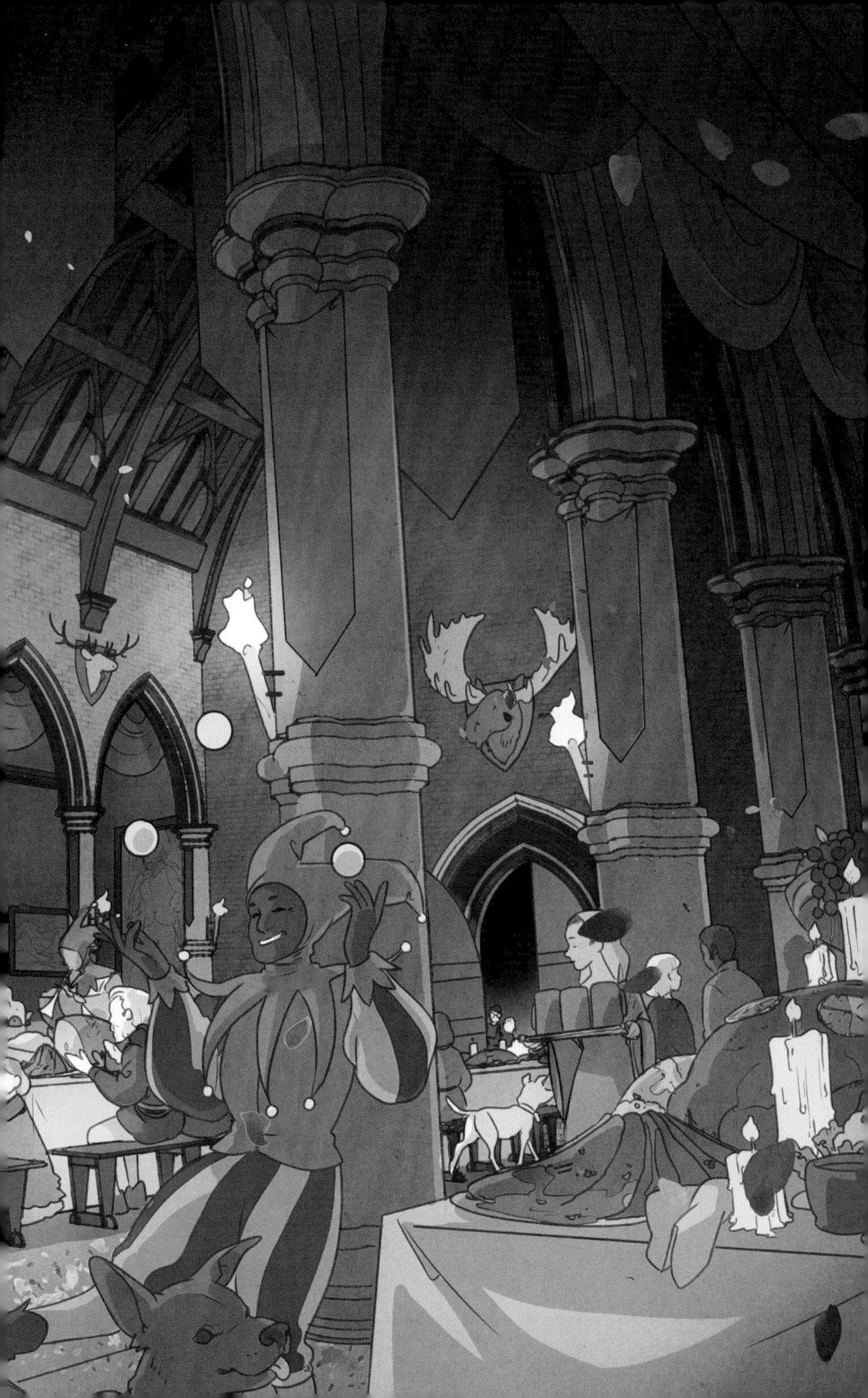

55

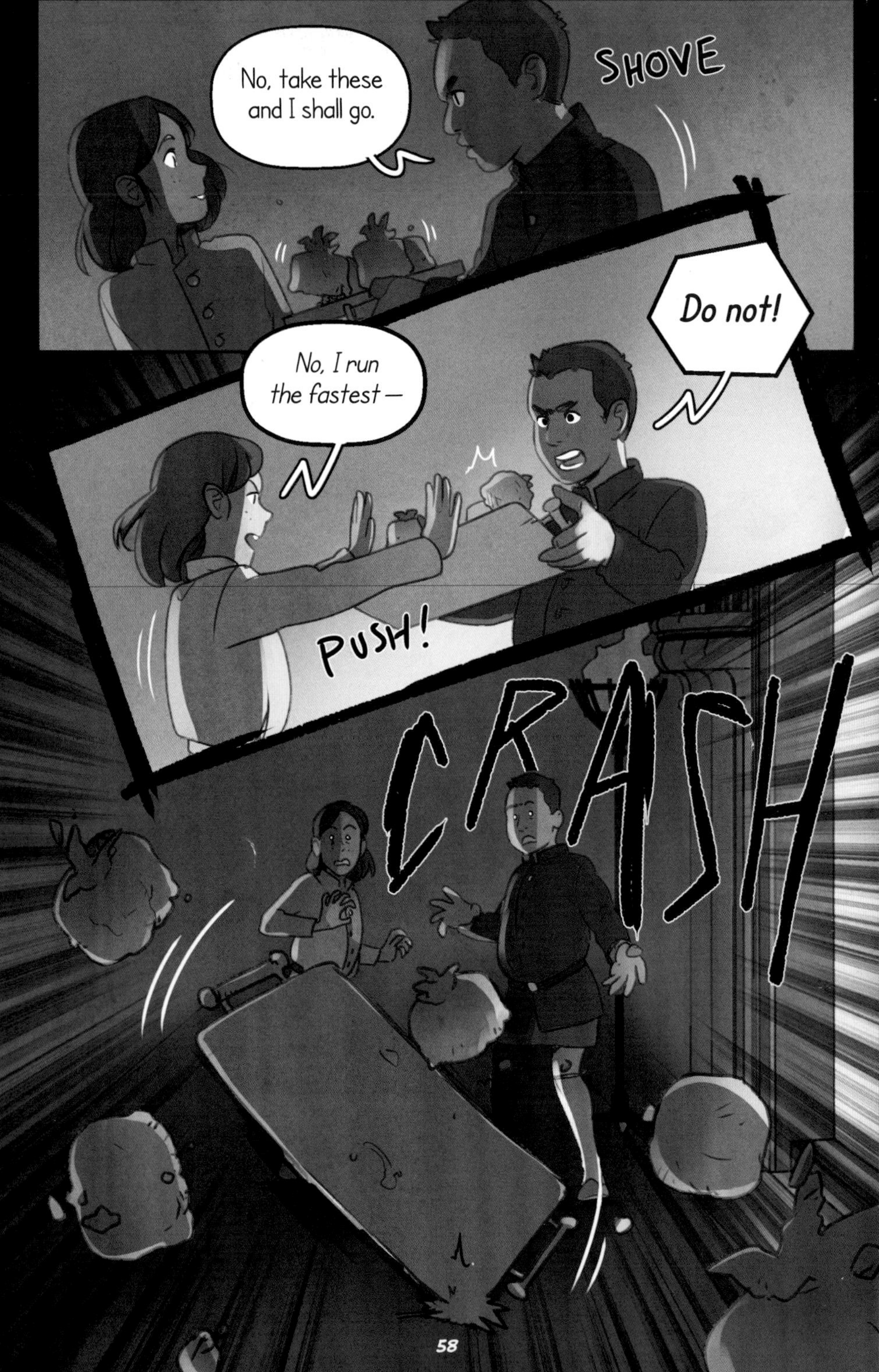
No, take these and I shall go.
SHOVE
Do not!
No, I run the fastest —
PUSH!
CRASH

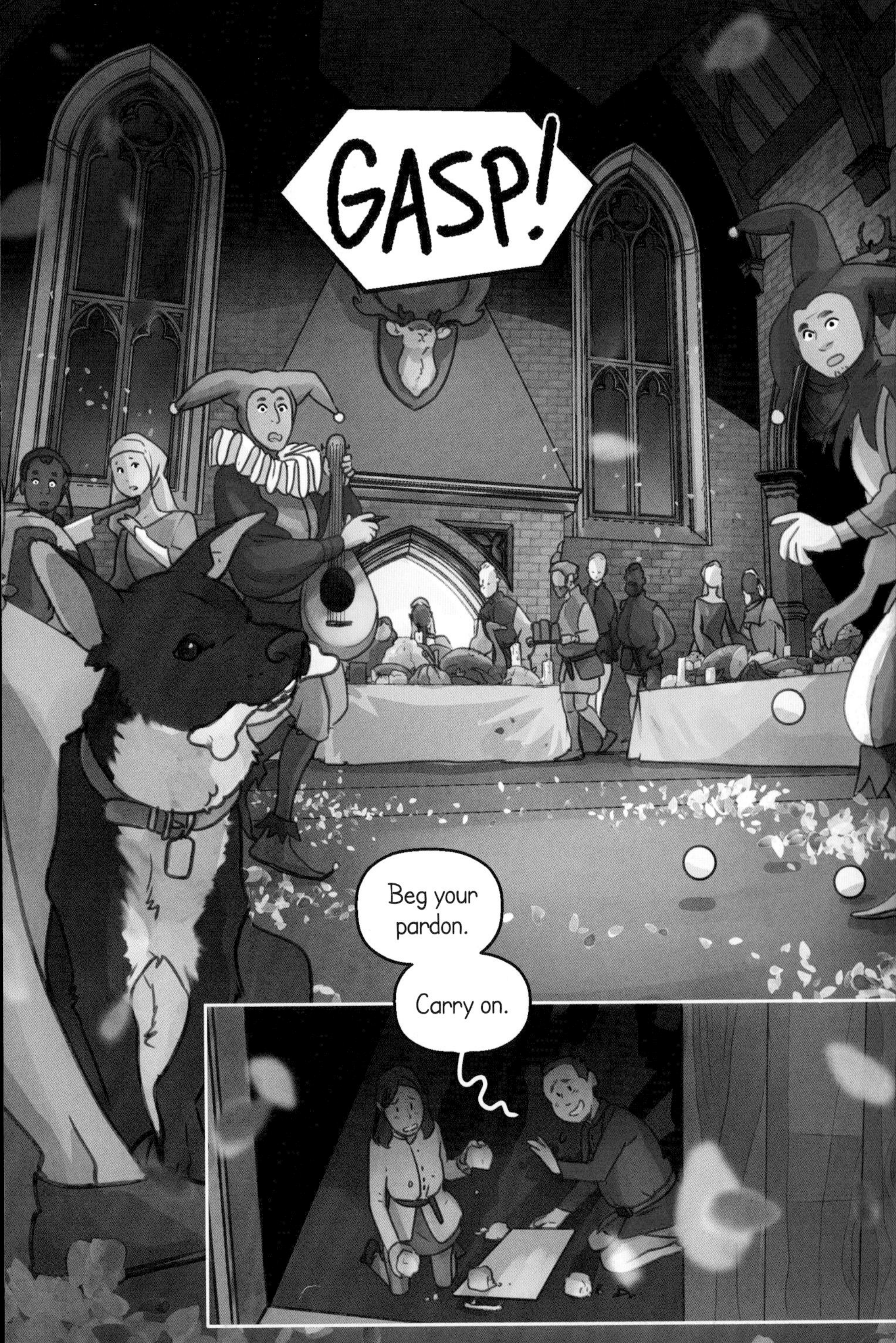
GASP!
Beg your pardon.
Carry on.

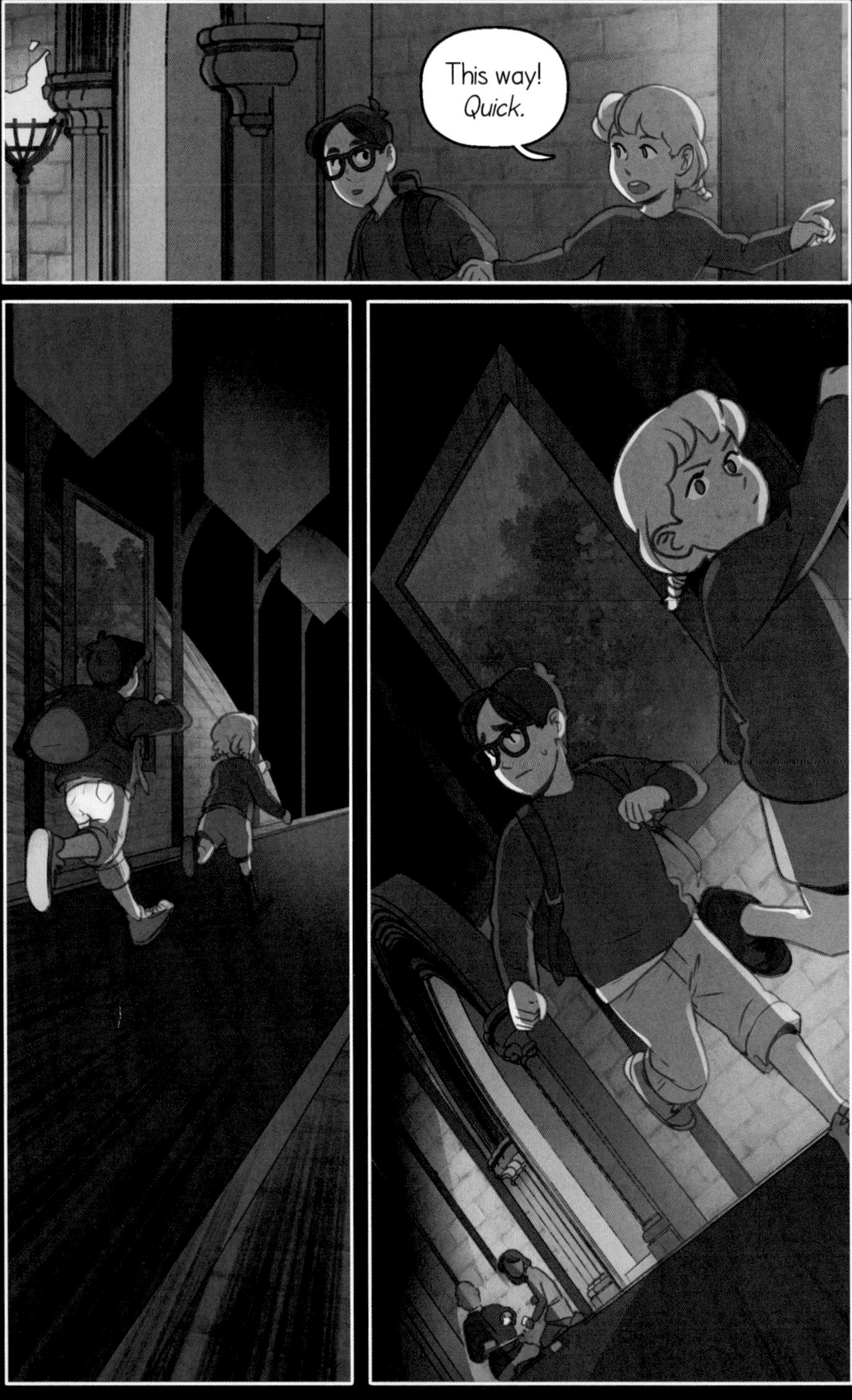
This way! Quick.

CHAPTER FIVE
Trapped

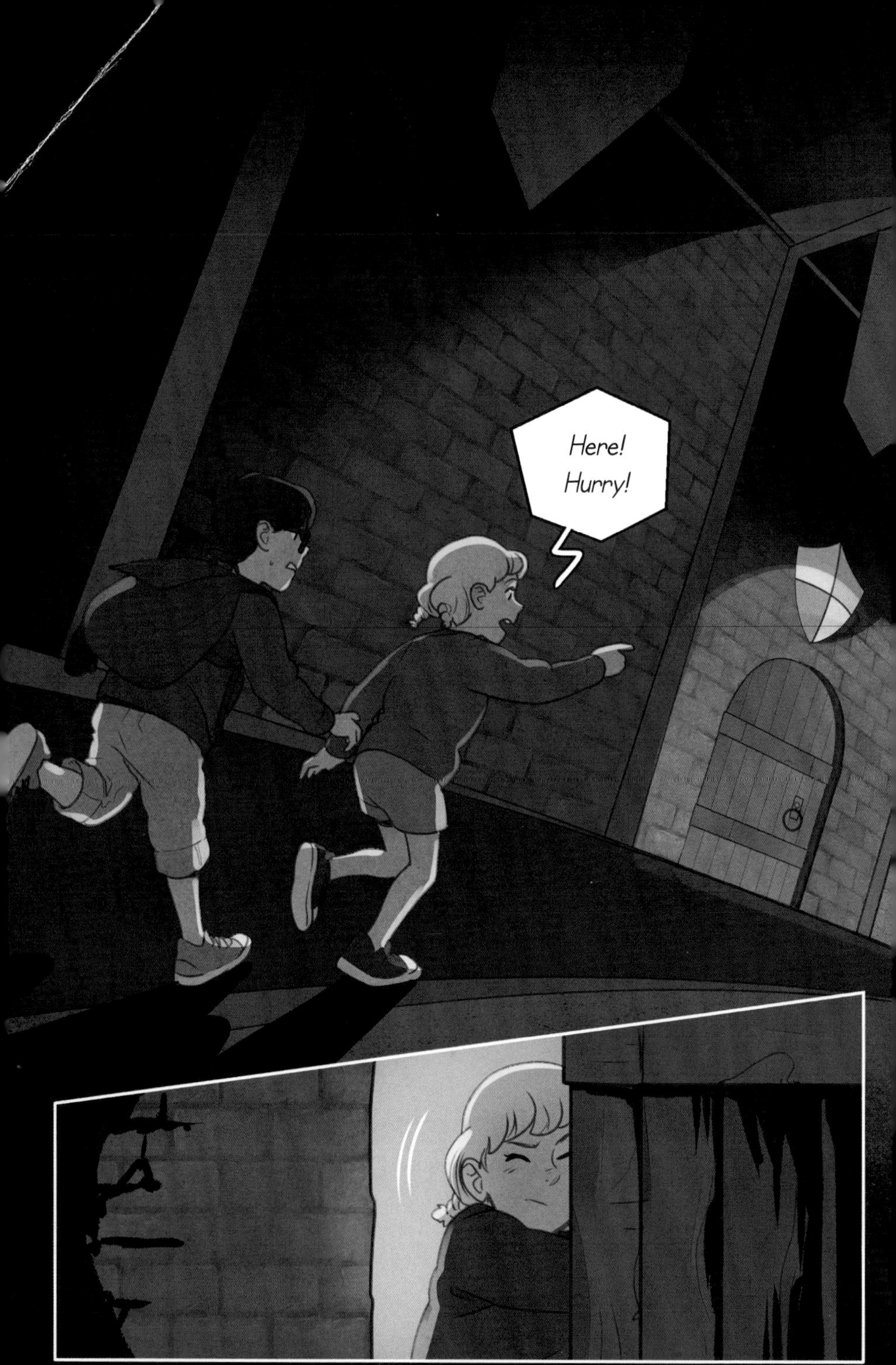
Here! Hurry!

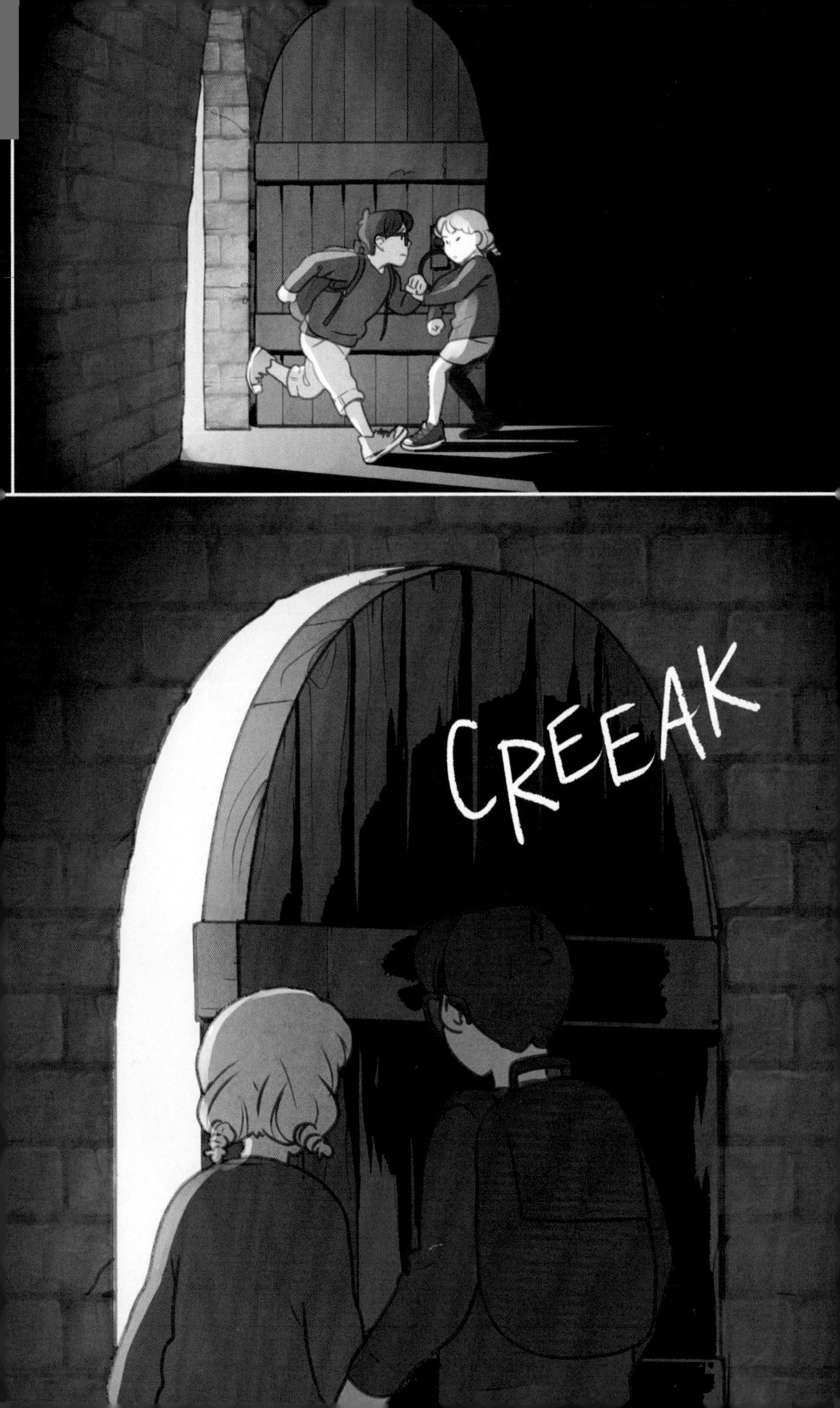
CREEAK

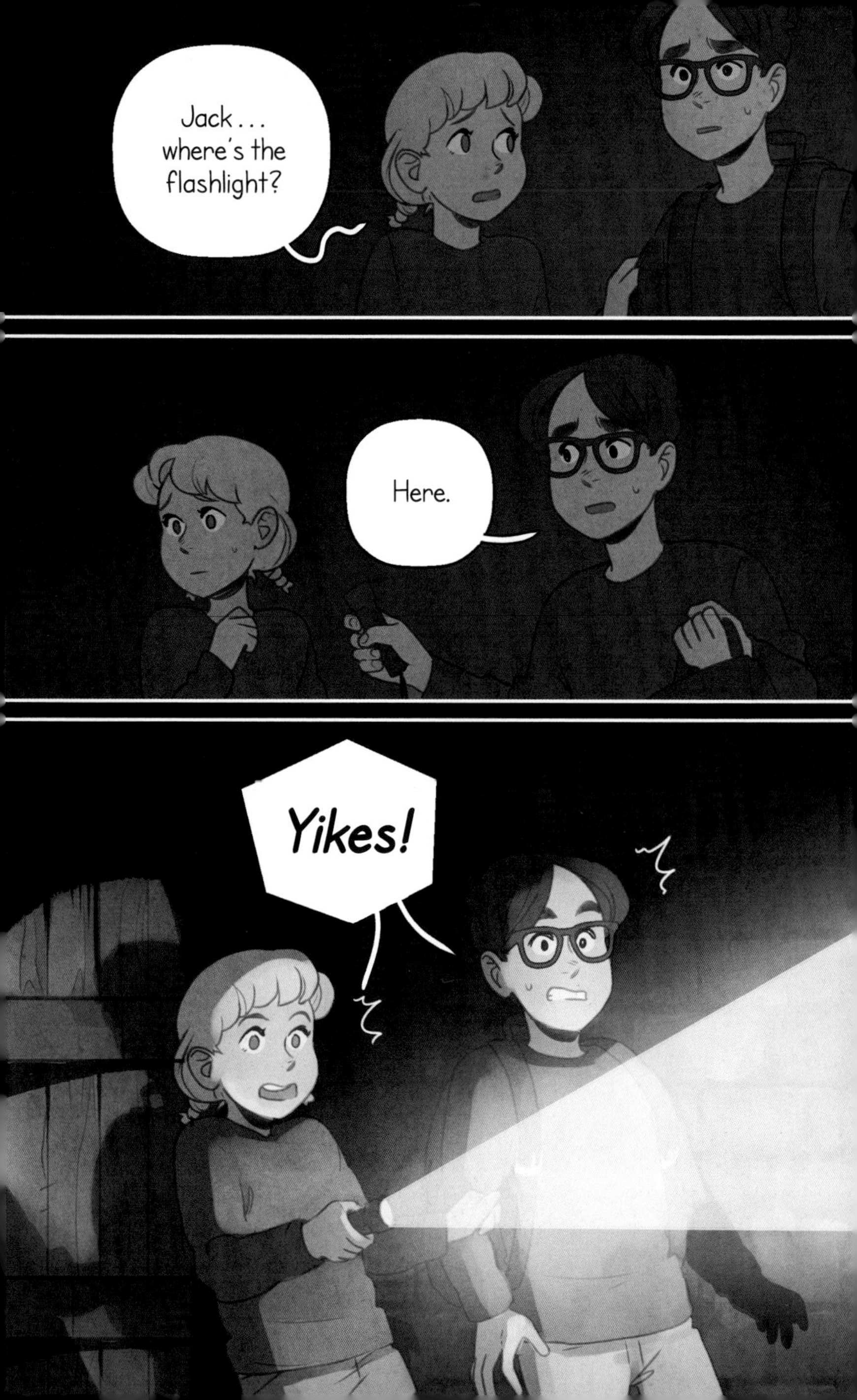
Jack . . . where's the flashlight?
Here.
Yikes!

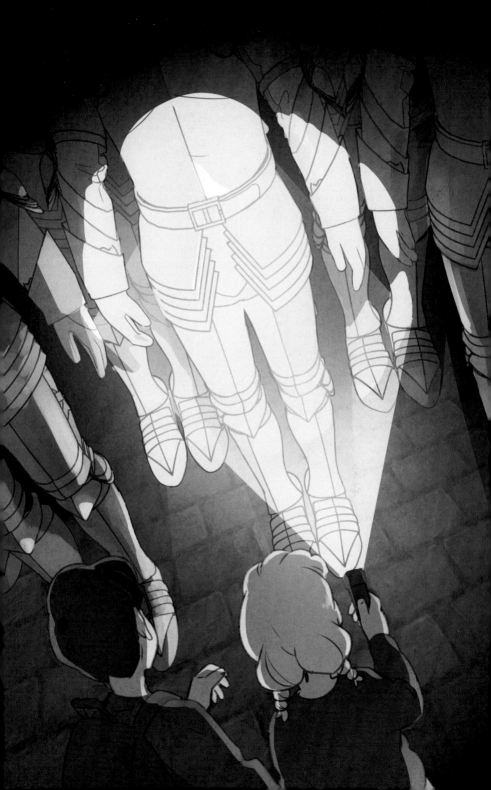

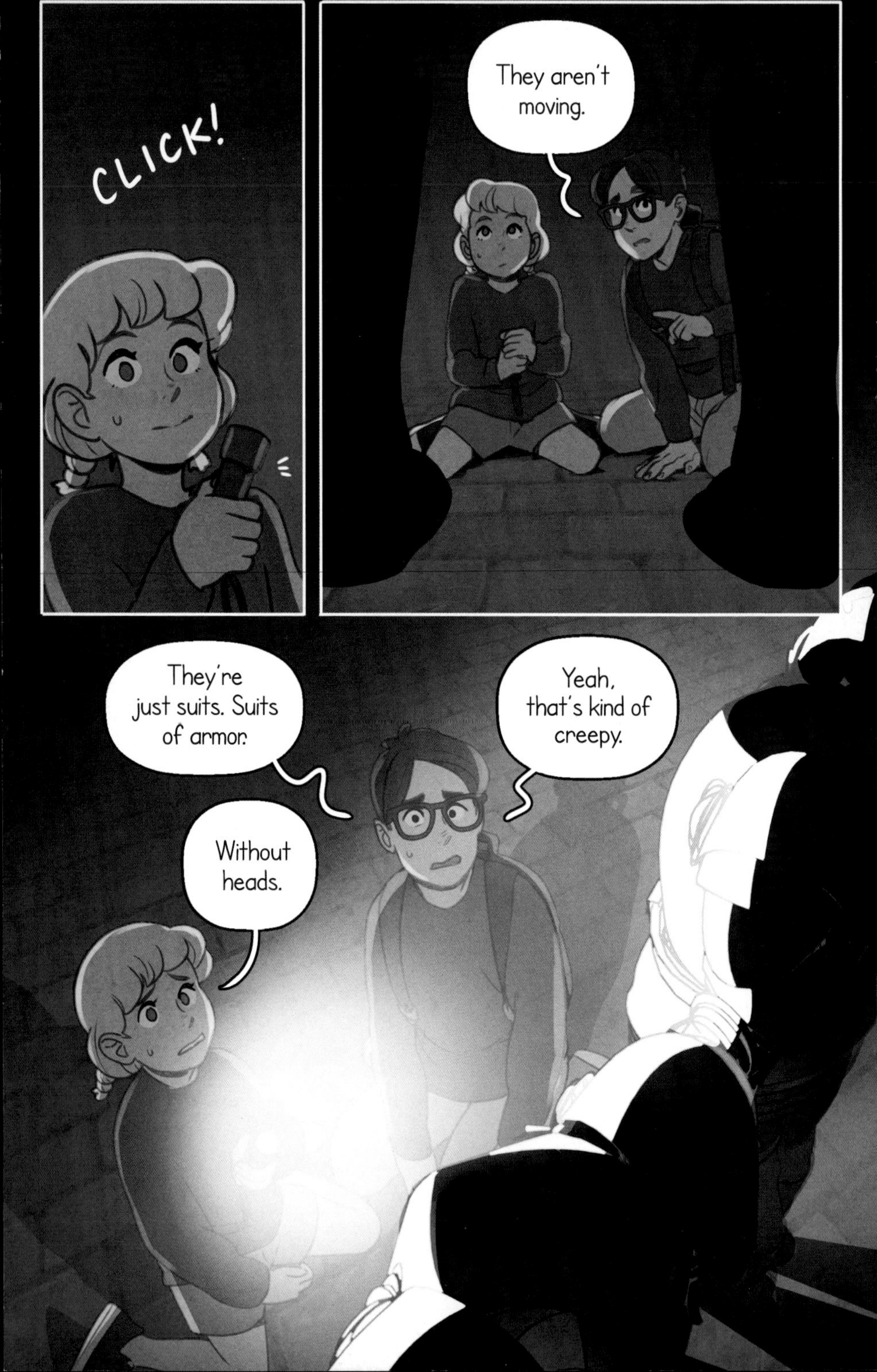
CLICK!
They aren't moving.
They're just suits. Suits of armor.
Yeah, that's kind of creepy.
Without heads.

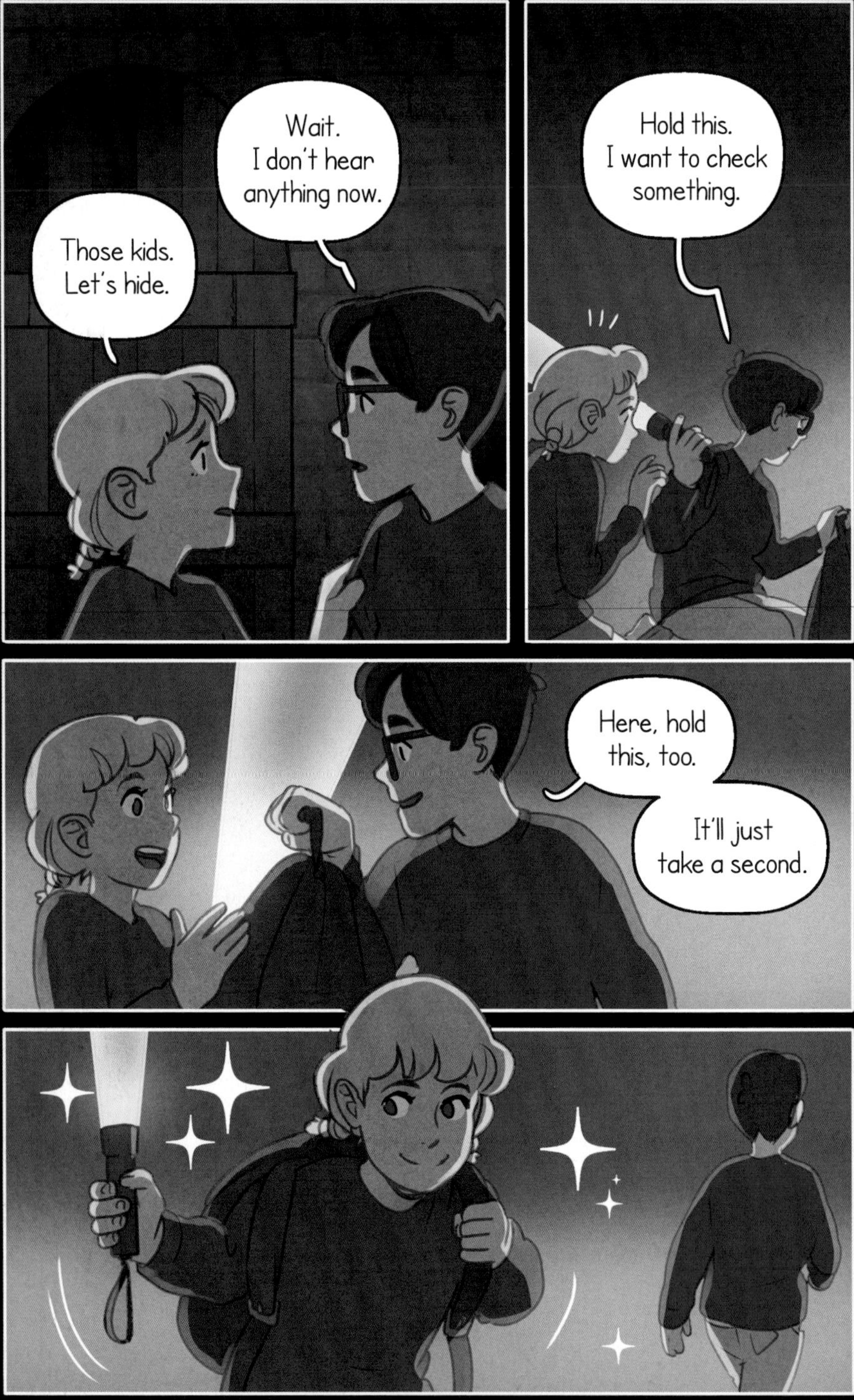
Those kids.
Let's hide.
Wait.
I don't hear
anything now.
Hold this.
I want to check
something.
Here, hold
this, too.
It'll just
take a second.

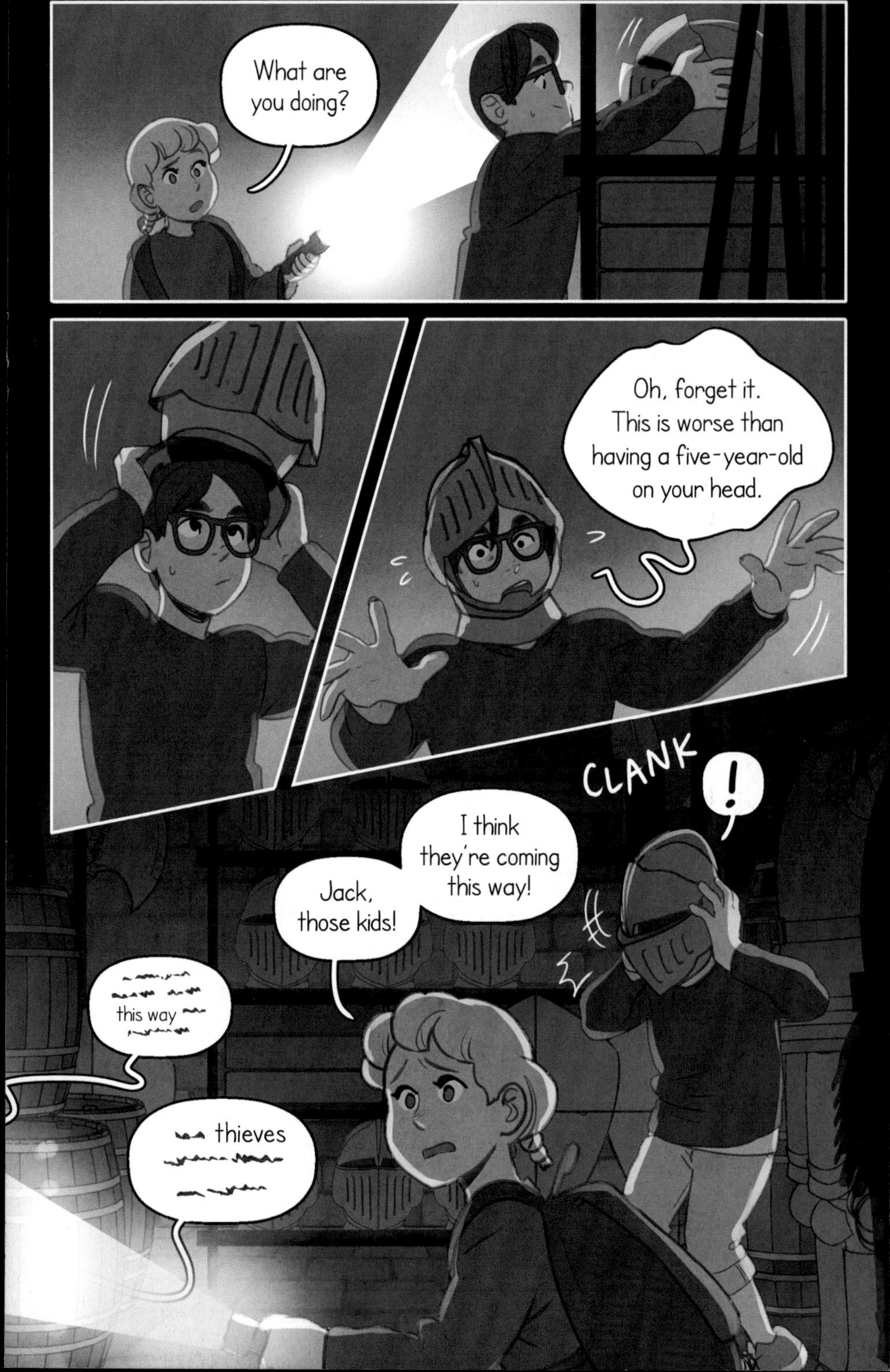
What are you doing?
Oh, forget it. This is worse than having a five-year-old on your head.
CLANK
!
I think they're coming this way!
Jack, those kids!
this way
thieves

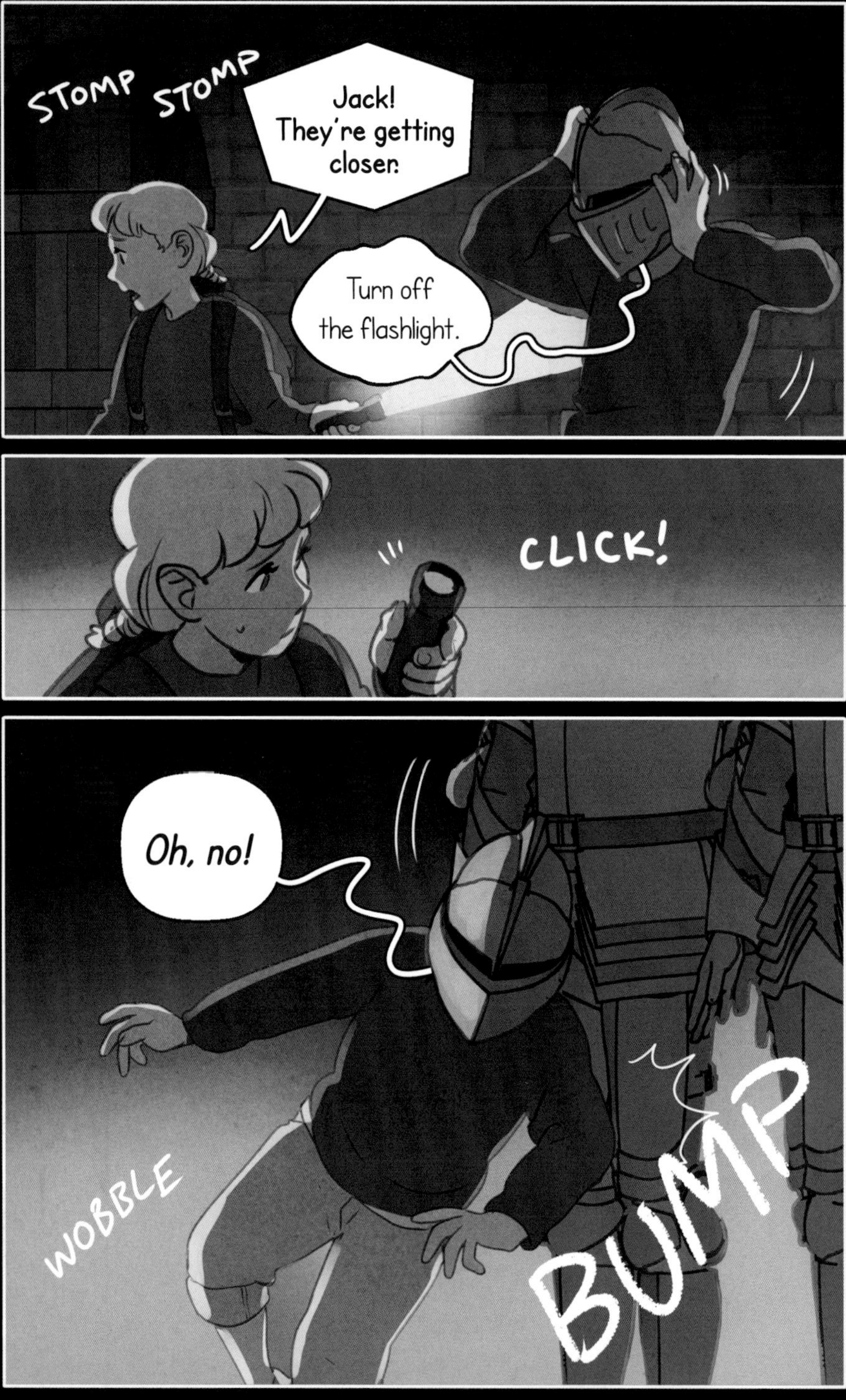
STOMP STOMP
Jack! They're getting closer.
Turn off the flashlight.
CLICK!
Oh, no!
WOBBLE
BUMP

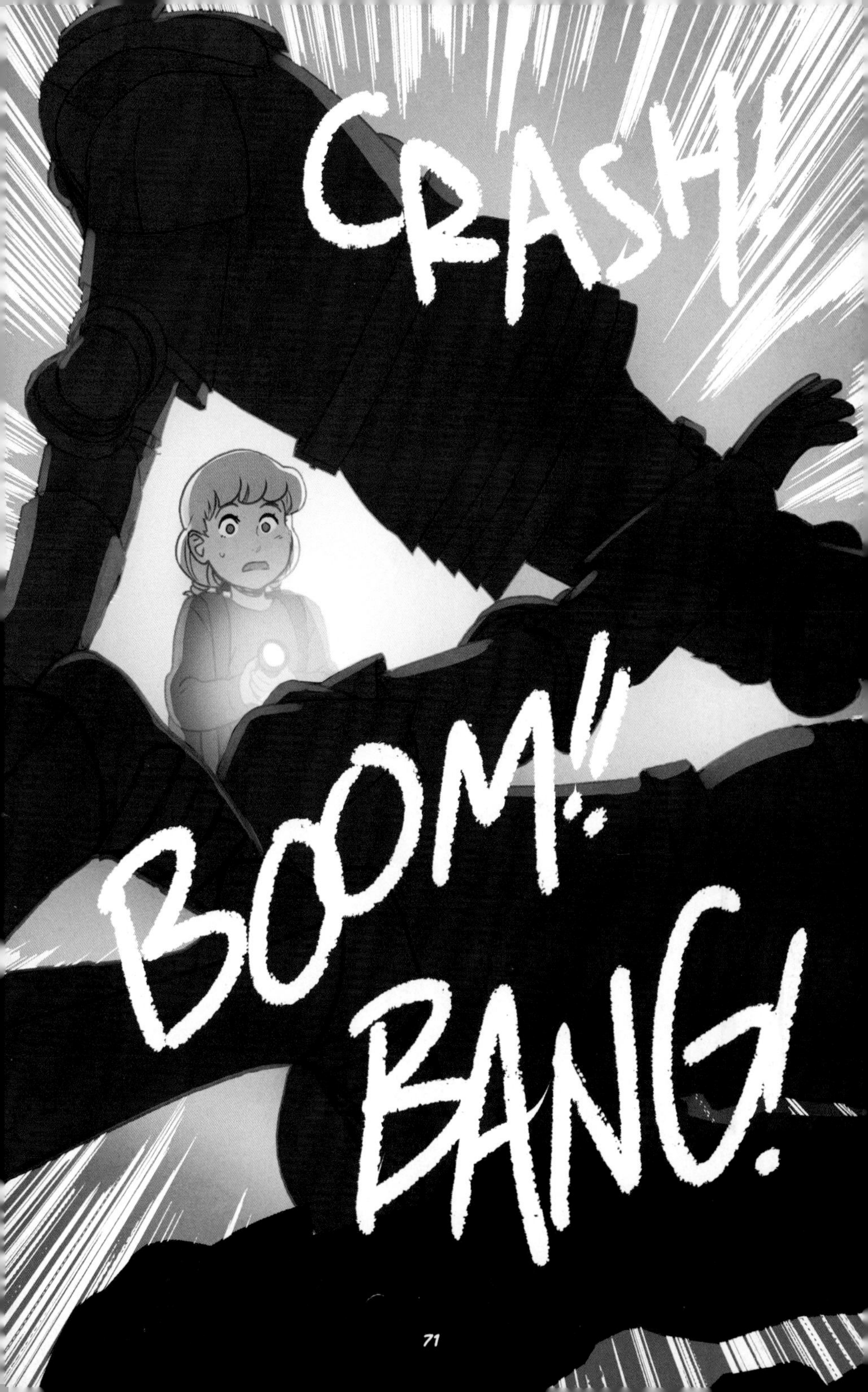
CRASH!
BOOM!!
BANG!

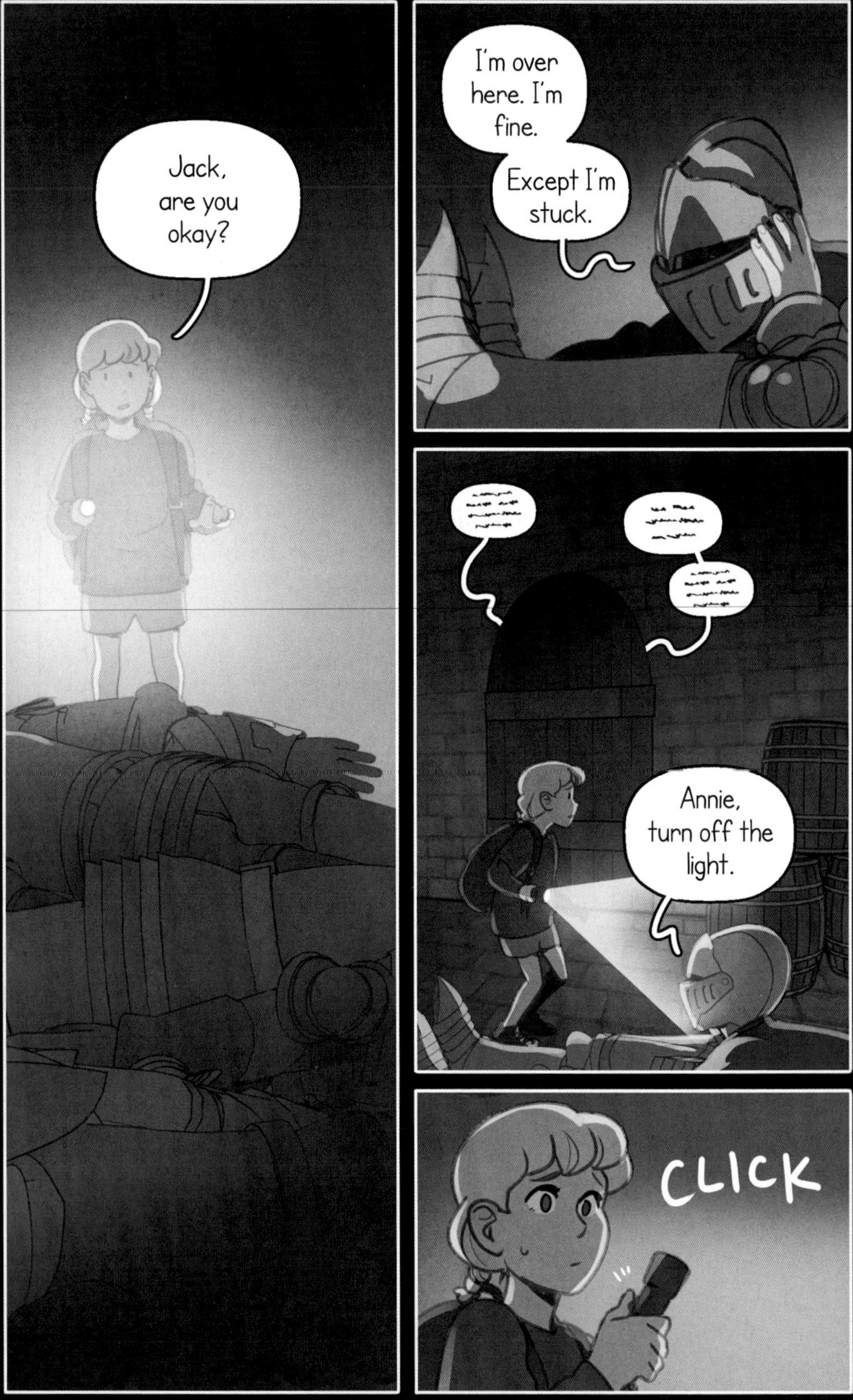

Jack, are you okay?
I'm over here. I'm fine.
Except I'm stuck.
Annie, turn off the light.
CLICK

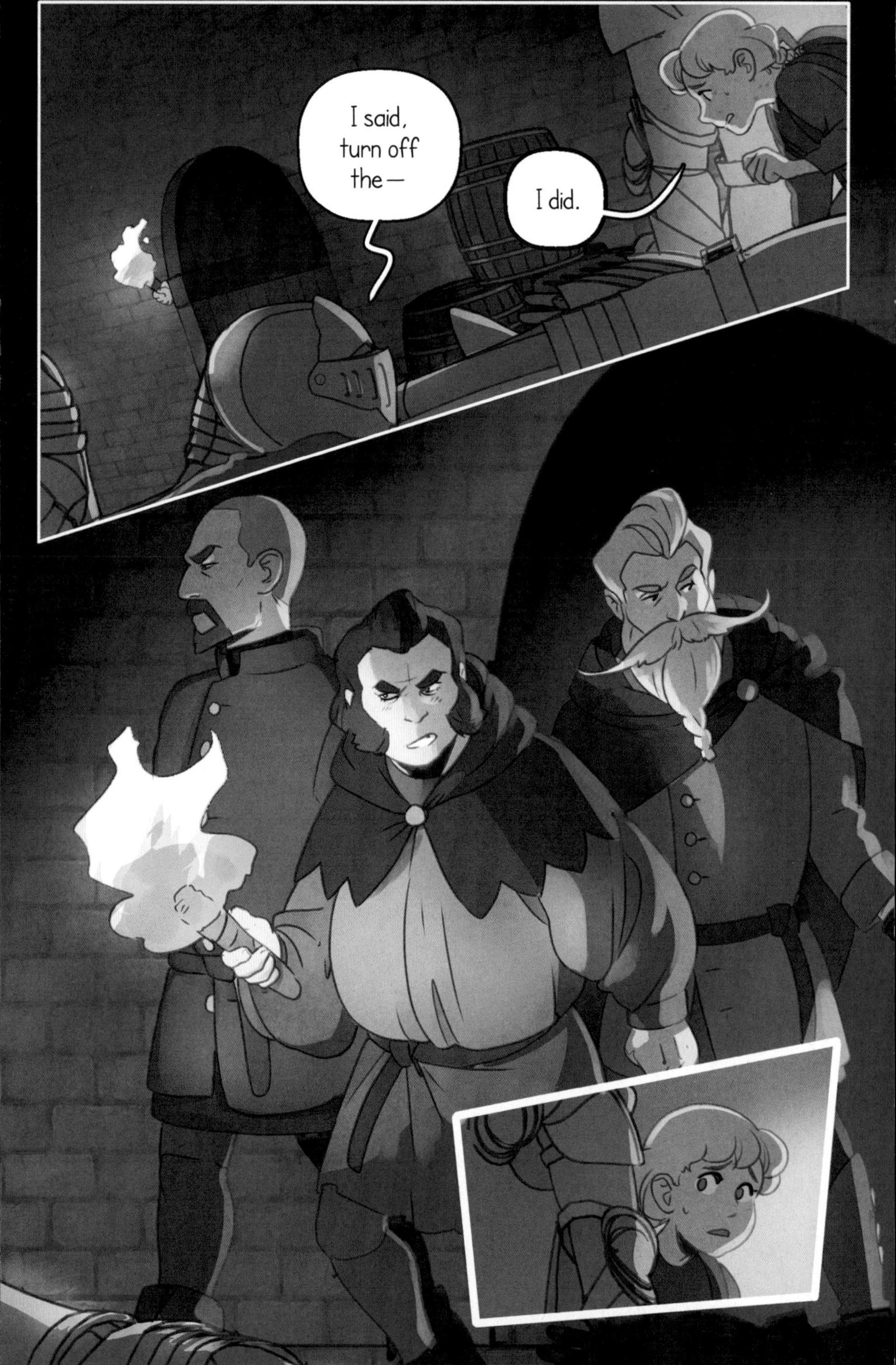
I said, turn off the—
I did.

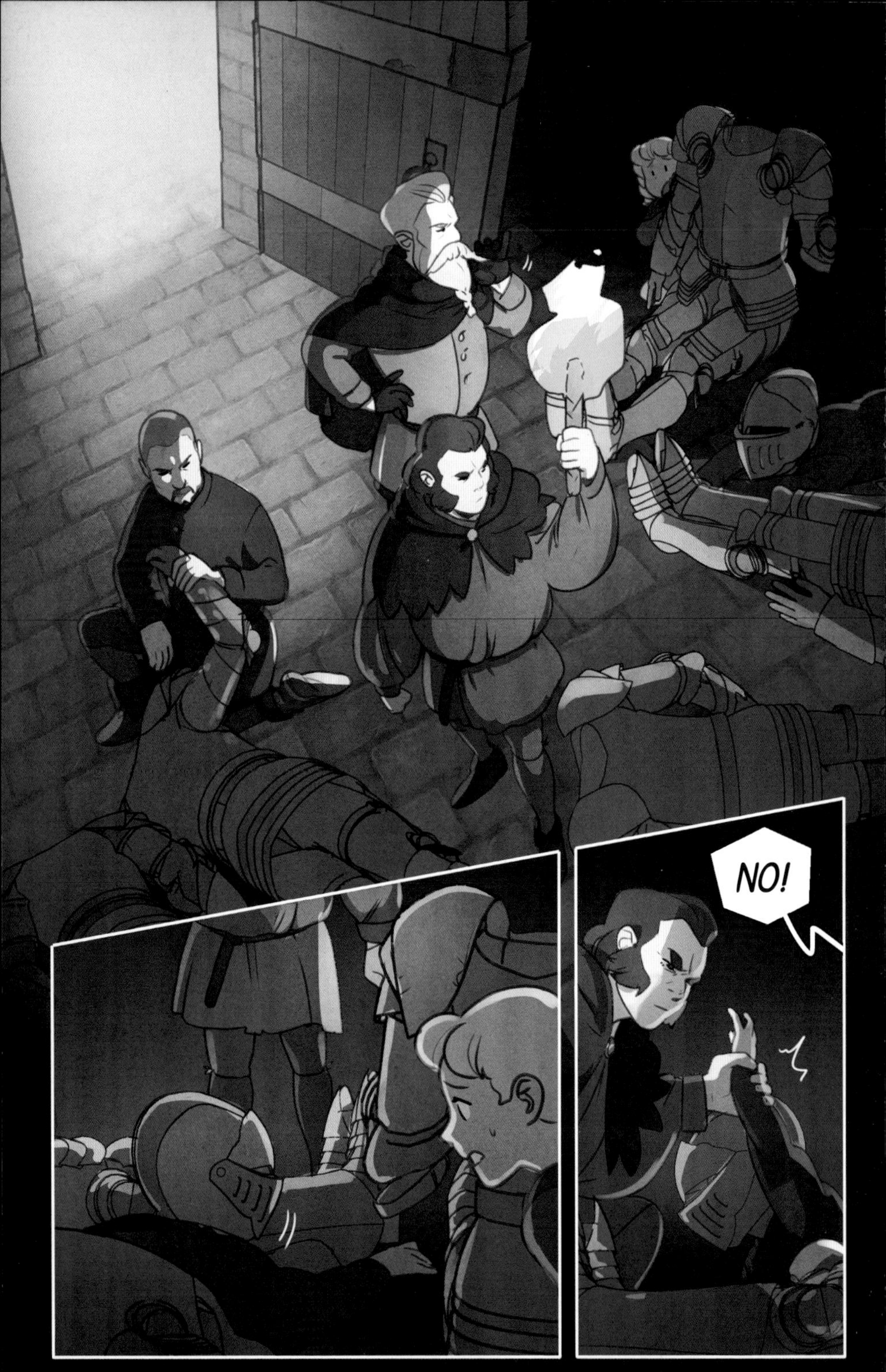
NO!

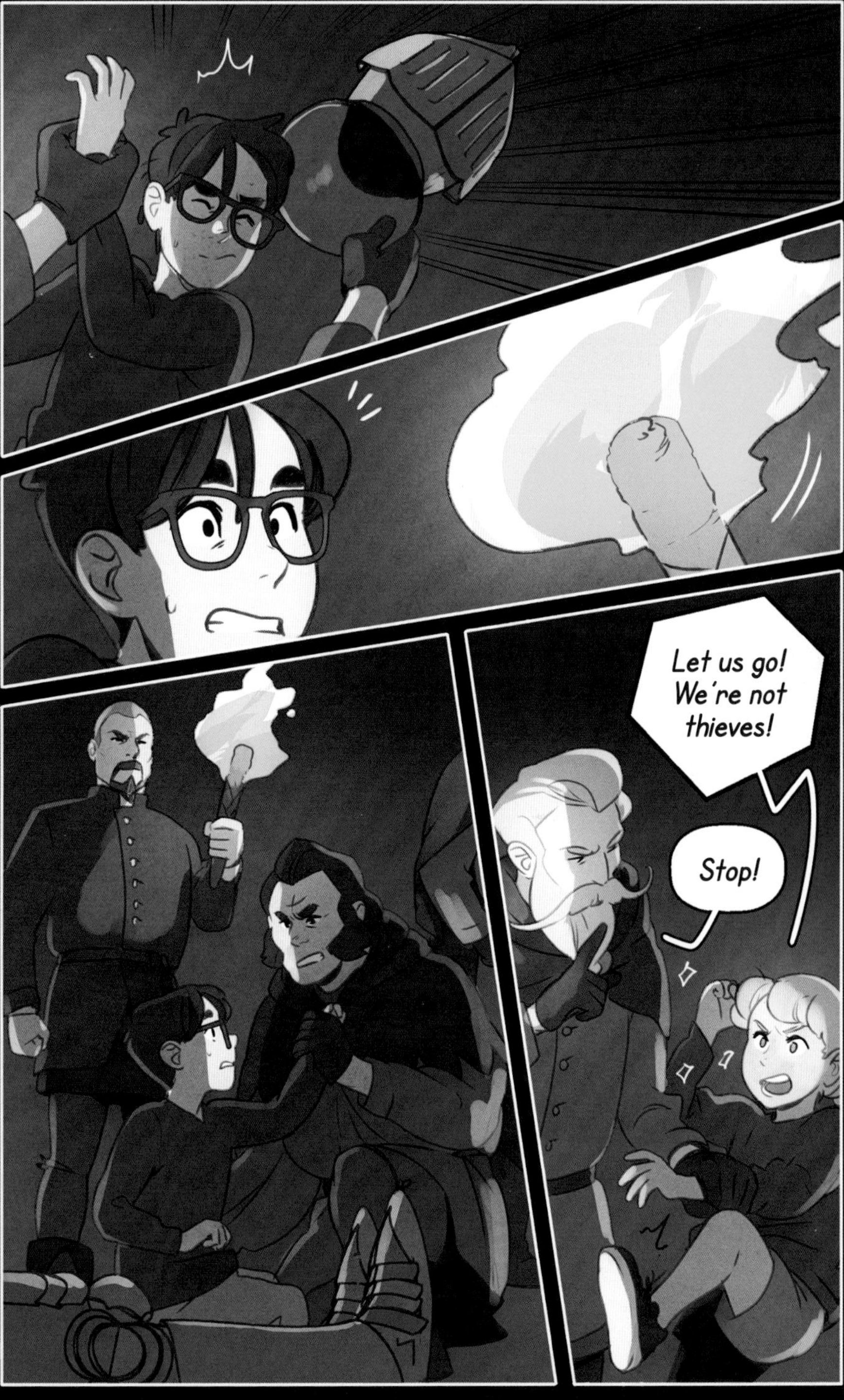
Let us go! We're not thieves!
Stop!

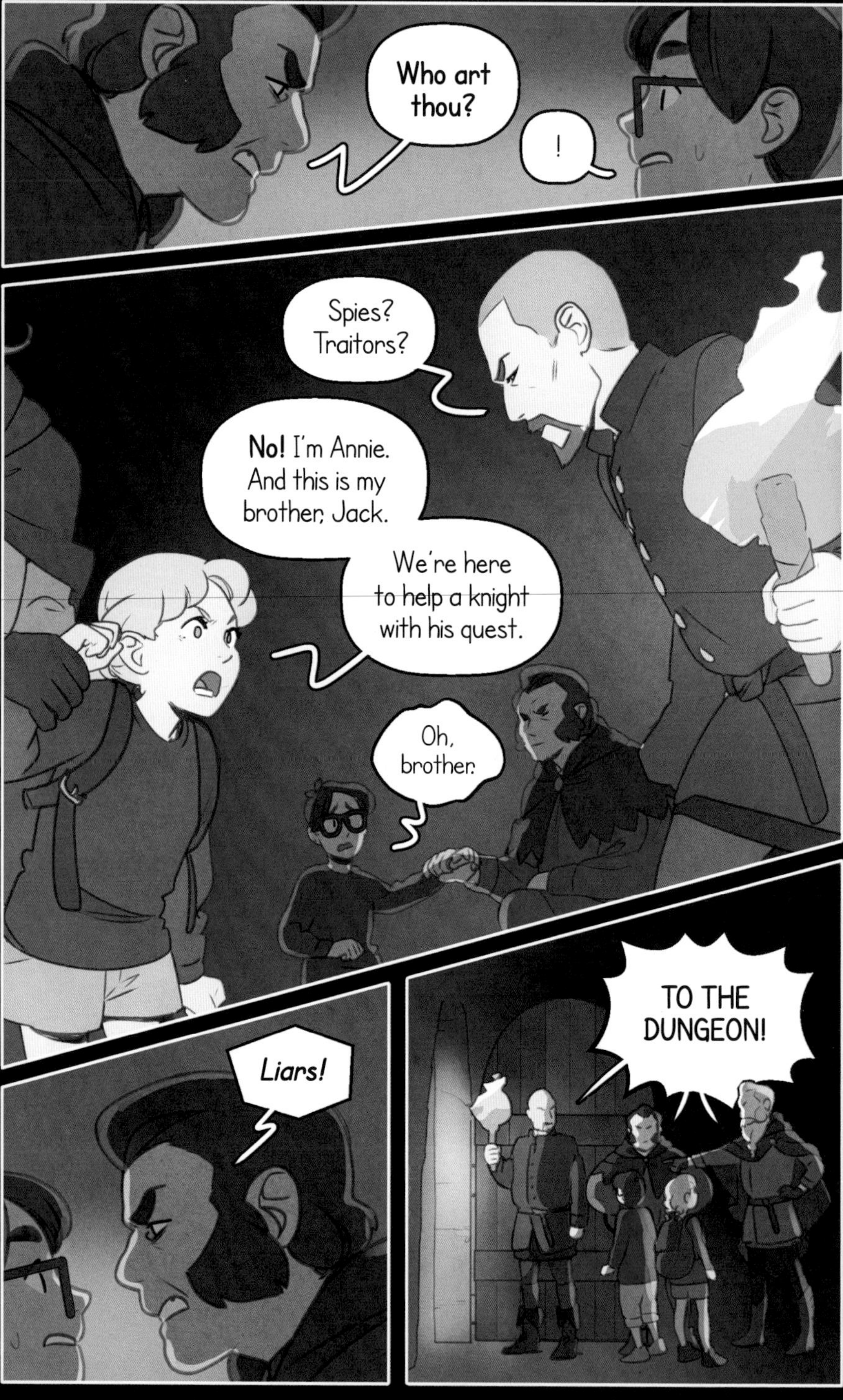

Who art thou?
!
Spies? Traitors?
No! I'm Annie. And this is my brother, Jack.
We're here to help a knight with his quest.
Oh, brother.
Liars!
TO THE DUNGEON!

CHAPTER SIX
The Dungeon

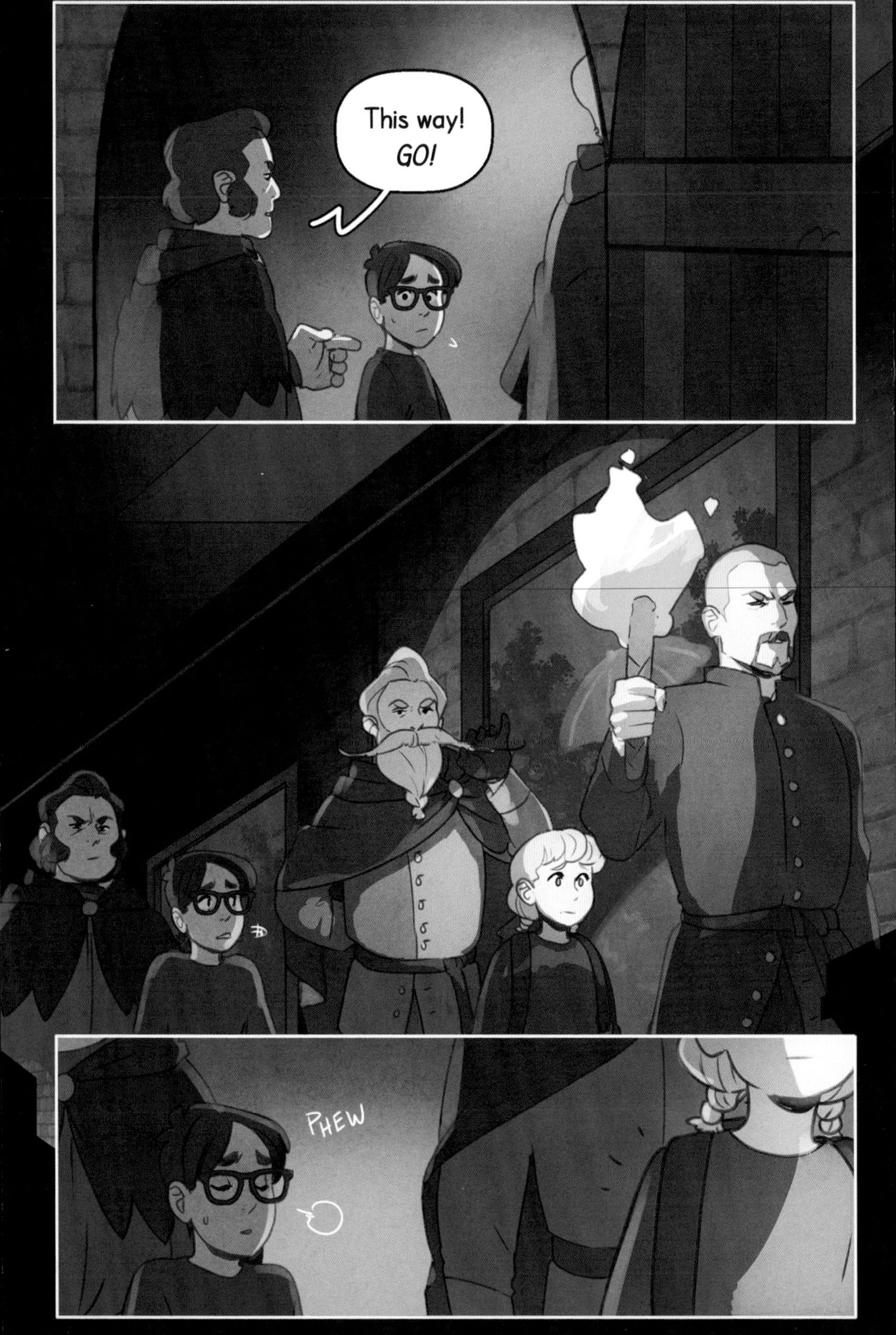
This way!
GO!
PHEW

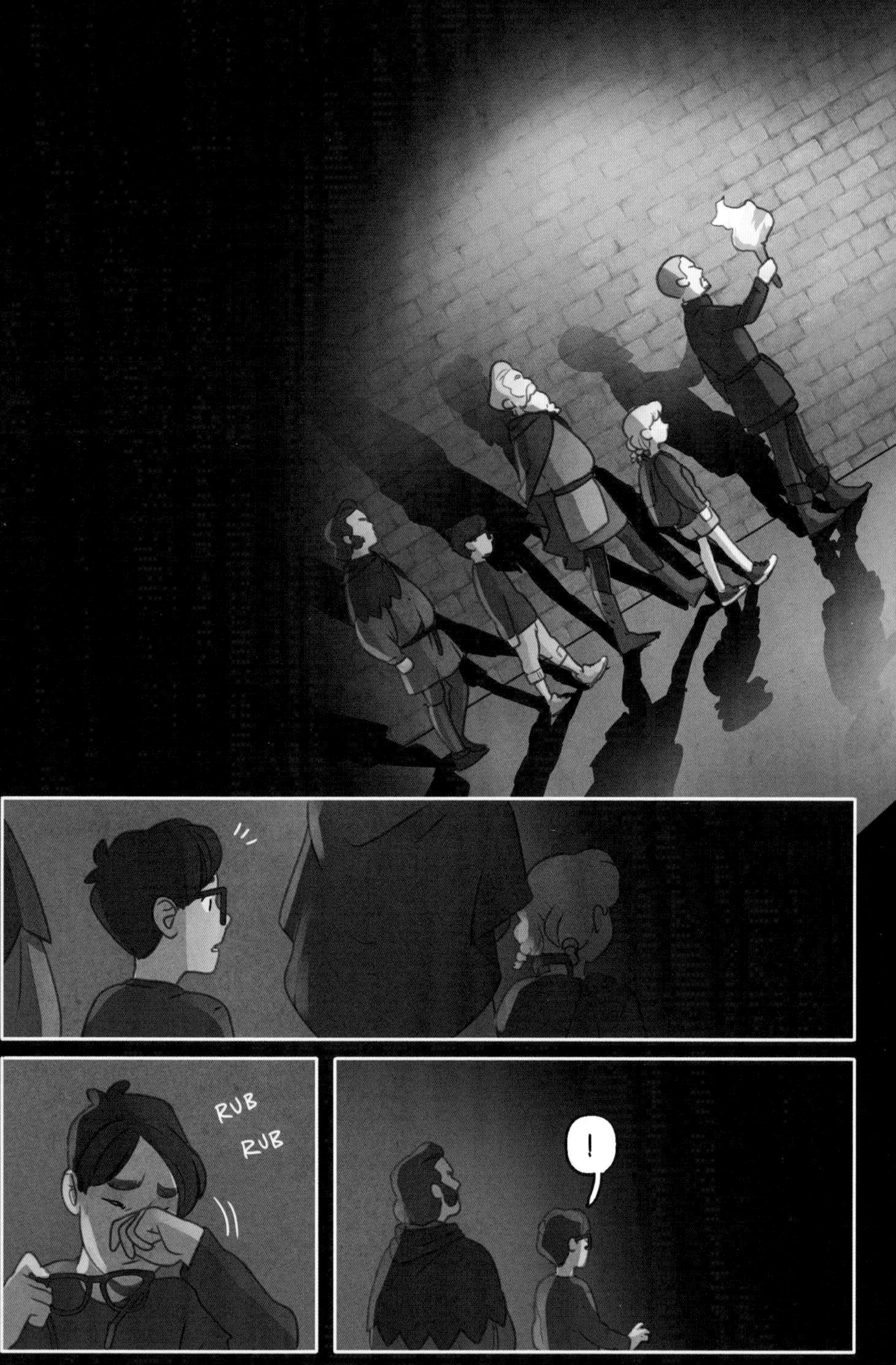
RUB
RUB
!

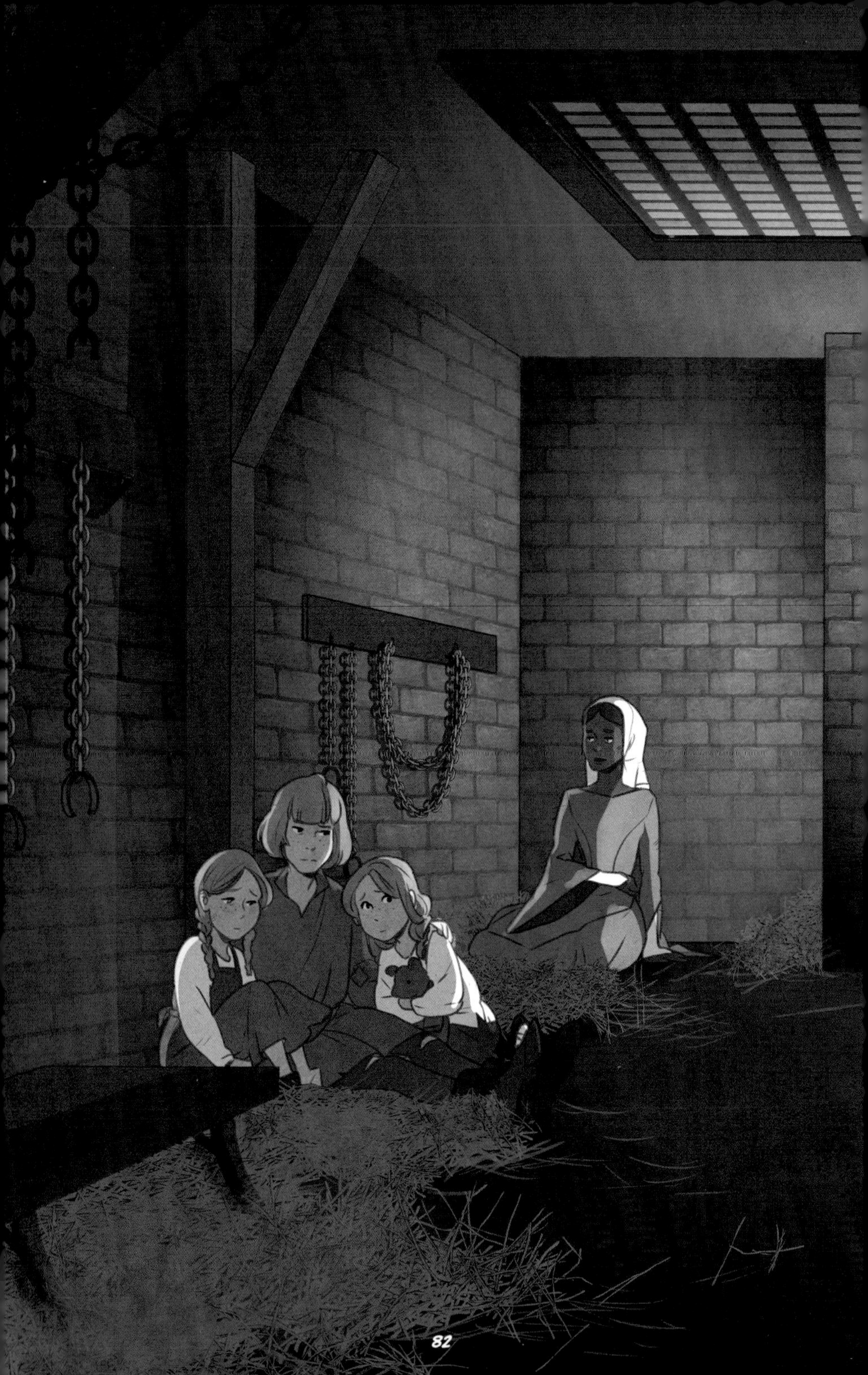

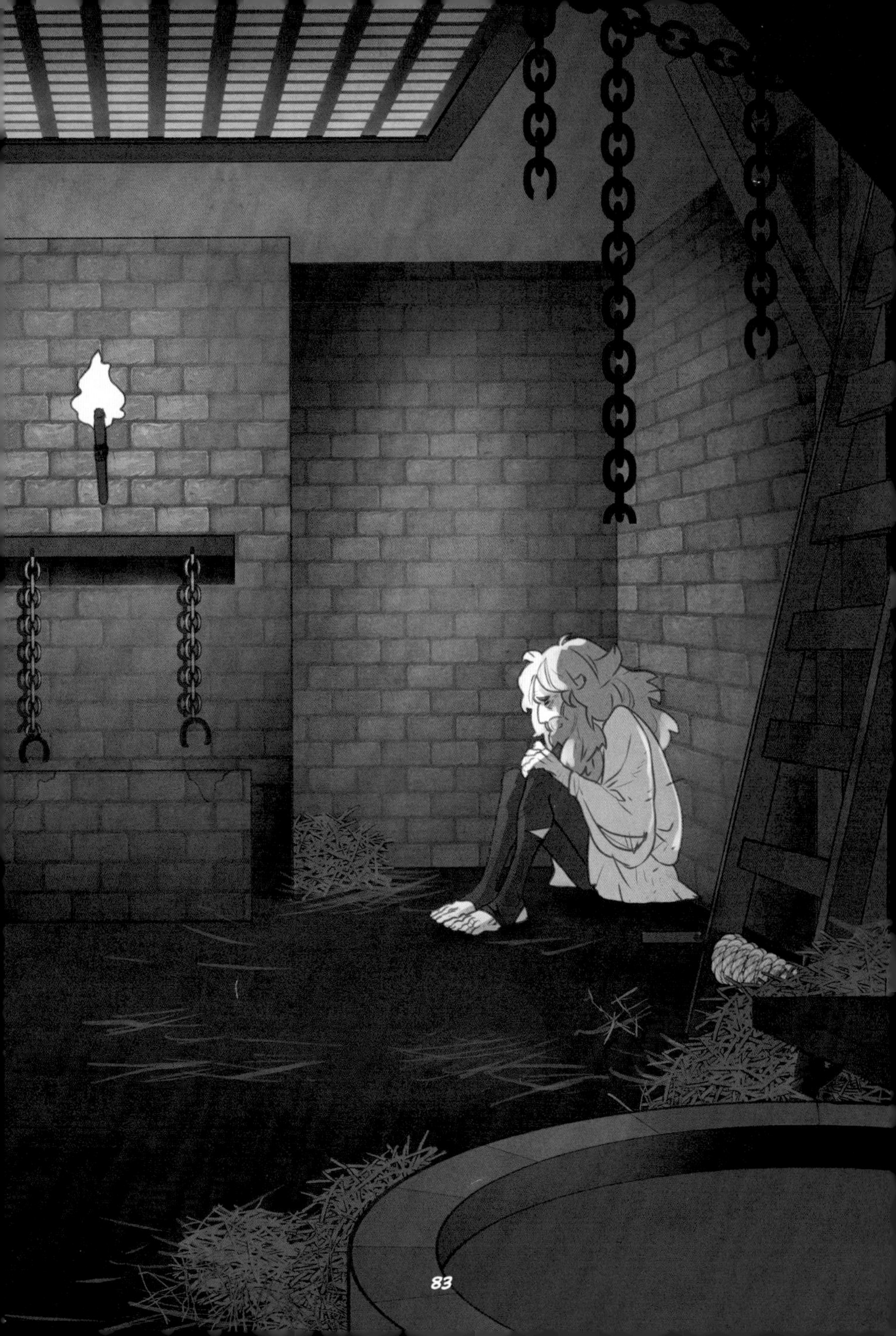

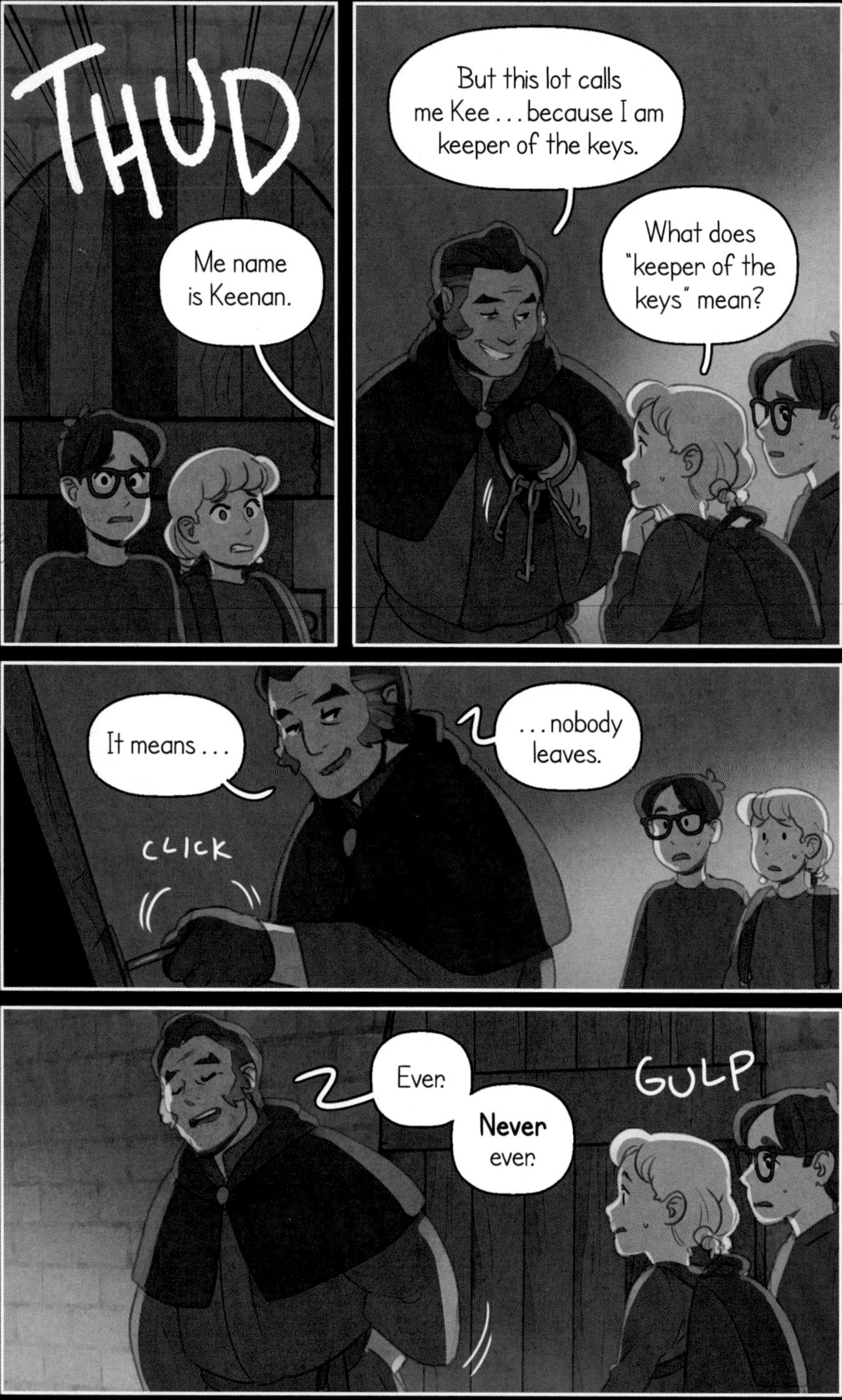
THUD
Me name is Keenan.
But this lot calls me Kee . . . because I am keeper of the keys.
What does "keeper of the keys" mean?
It means . . .
. . . nobody leaves.
CLICK
Ever.
Never ever.
GULP

87

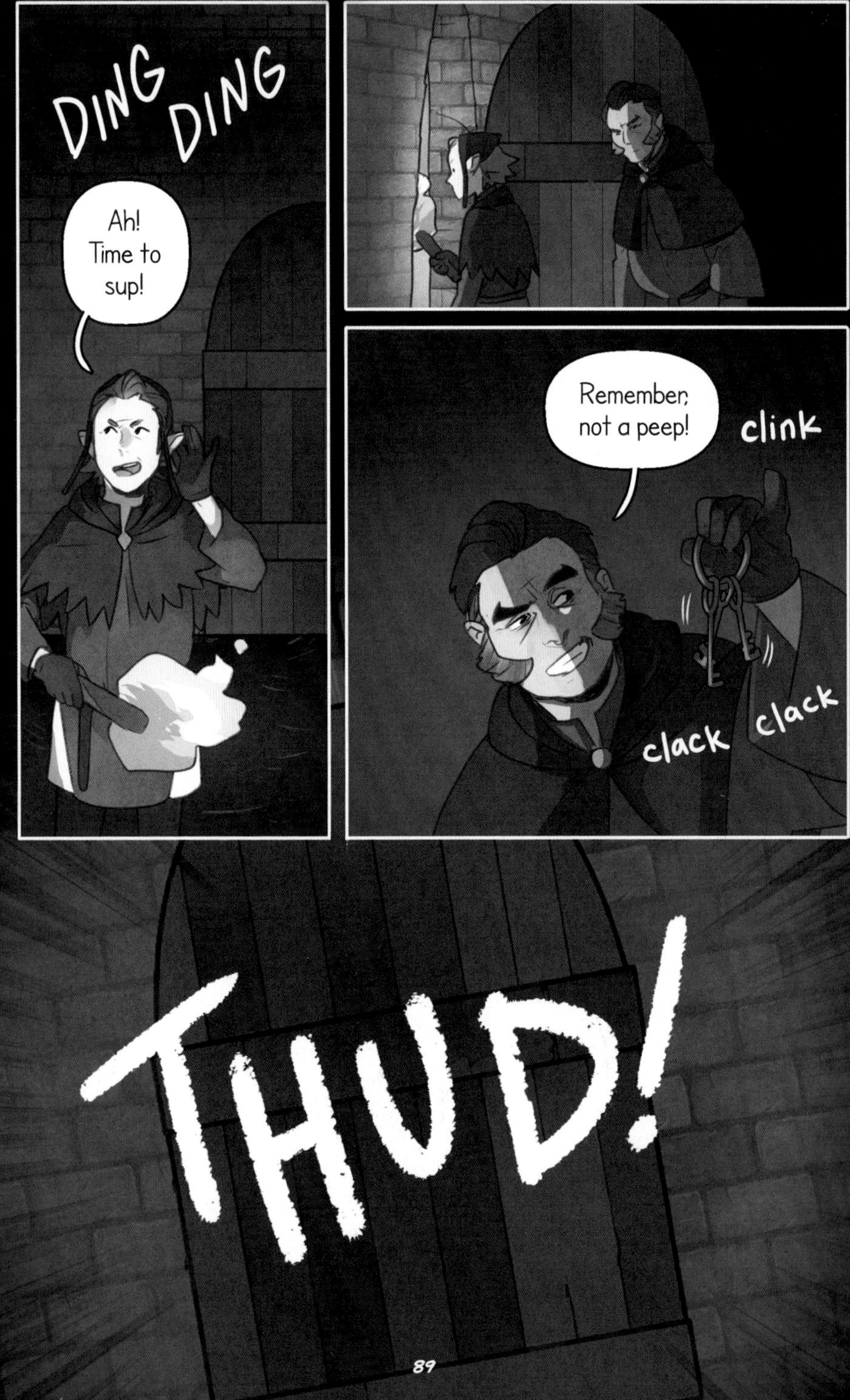
DING DING
Ah! Time to sup!
Remember, not a peep!
clink
clack clack
THUD!

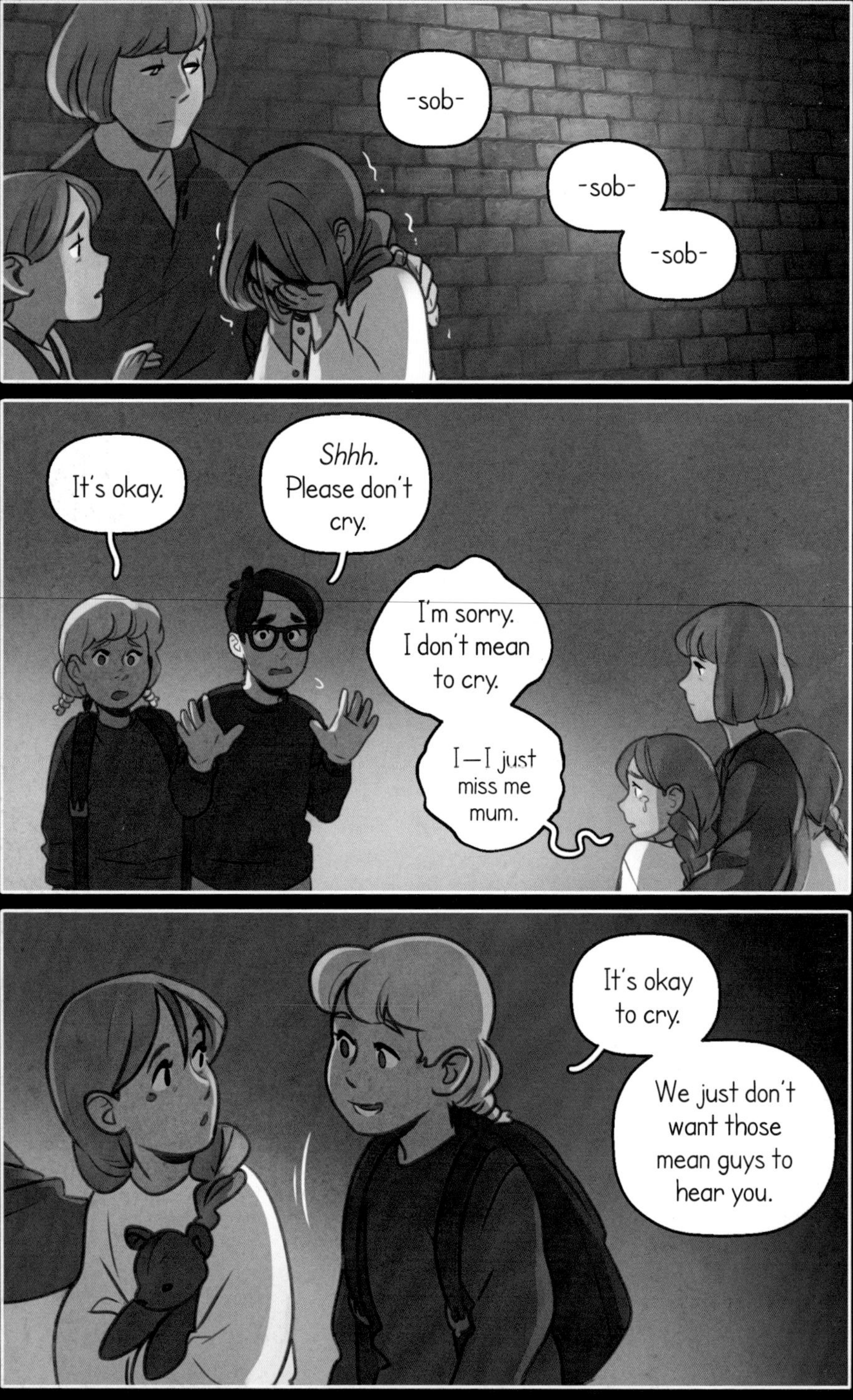
-sob-
-sob-
-sob-
It's okay.
Shhh. Please don't cry.
I'm sorry. I don't mean to cry.
I—I just miss me mum.
It's okay to cry.
We just don't want those mean guys to hear you.

If only we could find a way to get those keys from Keenan. . . .

Or maybe there's another way.
?

CHAPTER SEVEN

A Secret Passage

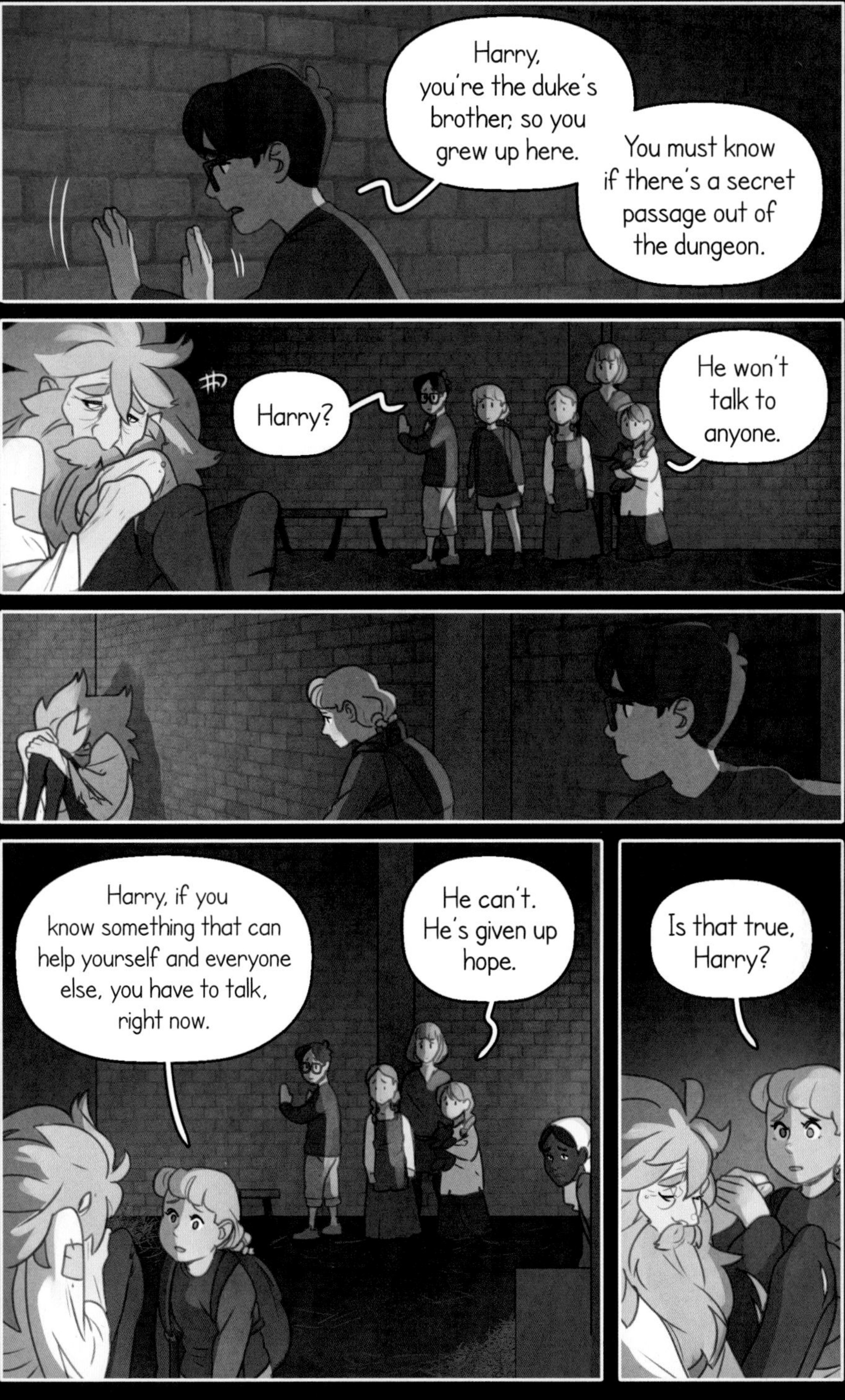
Harry, you're the duke's brother, so you grew up here.
You must know if there's a secret passage out of the dungeon.
Harry?
He won't talk to anyone.
Harry, if you know something that can help yourself and everyone else, you have to talk, right now.
He can't. He's given up hope.
Is that true, Harry?

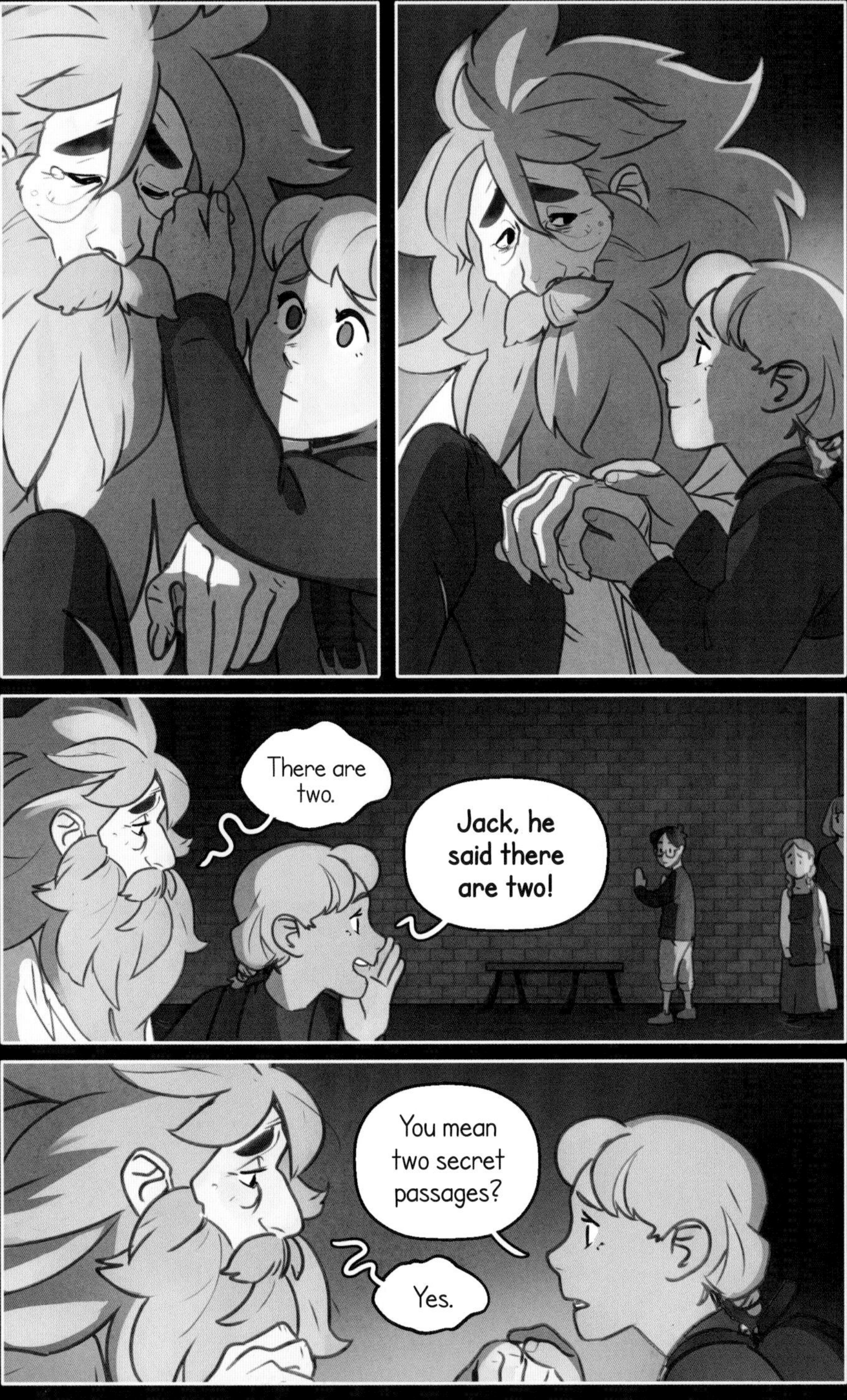
There are two.
Jack, he said there are two!
You mean two secret passages?
Yes.

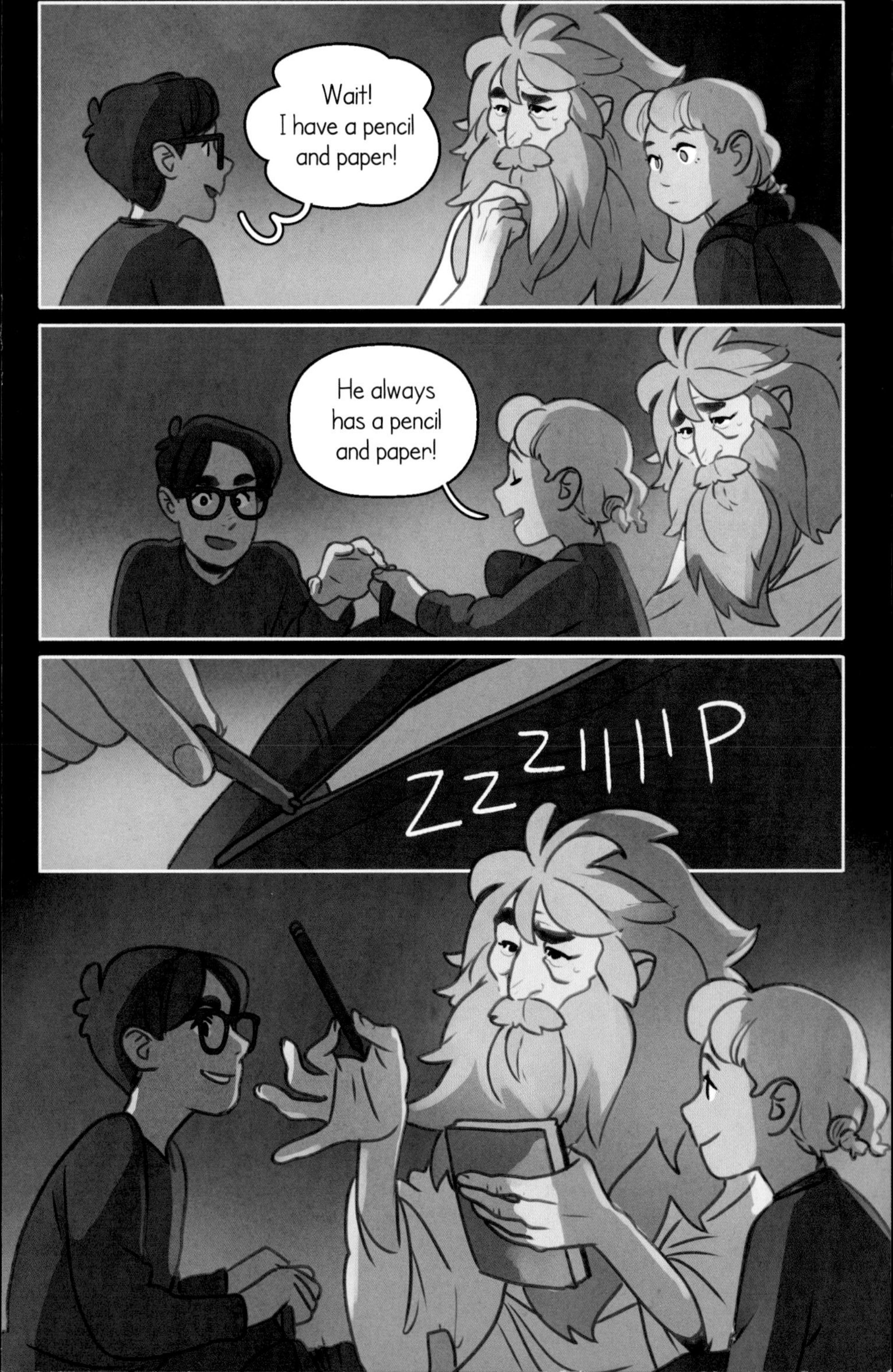

Wait! I have a pencil and paper!
He always has a pencil and paper!
ZZZIIIIP

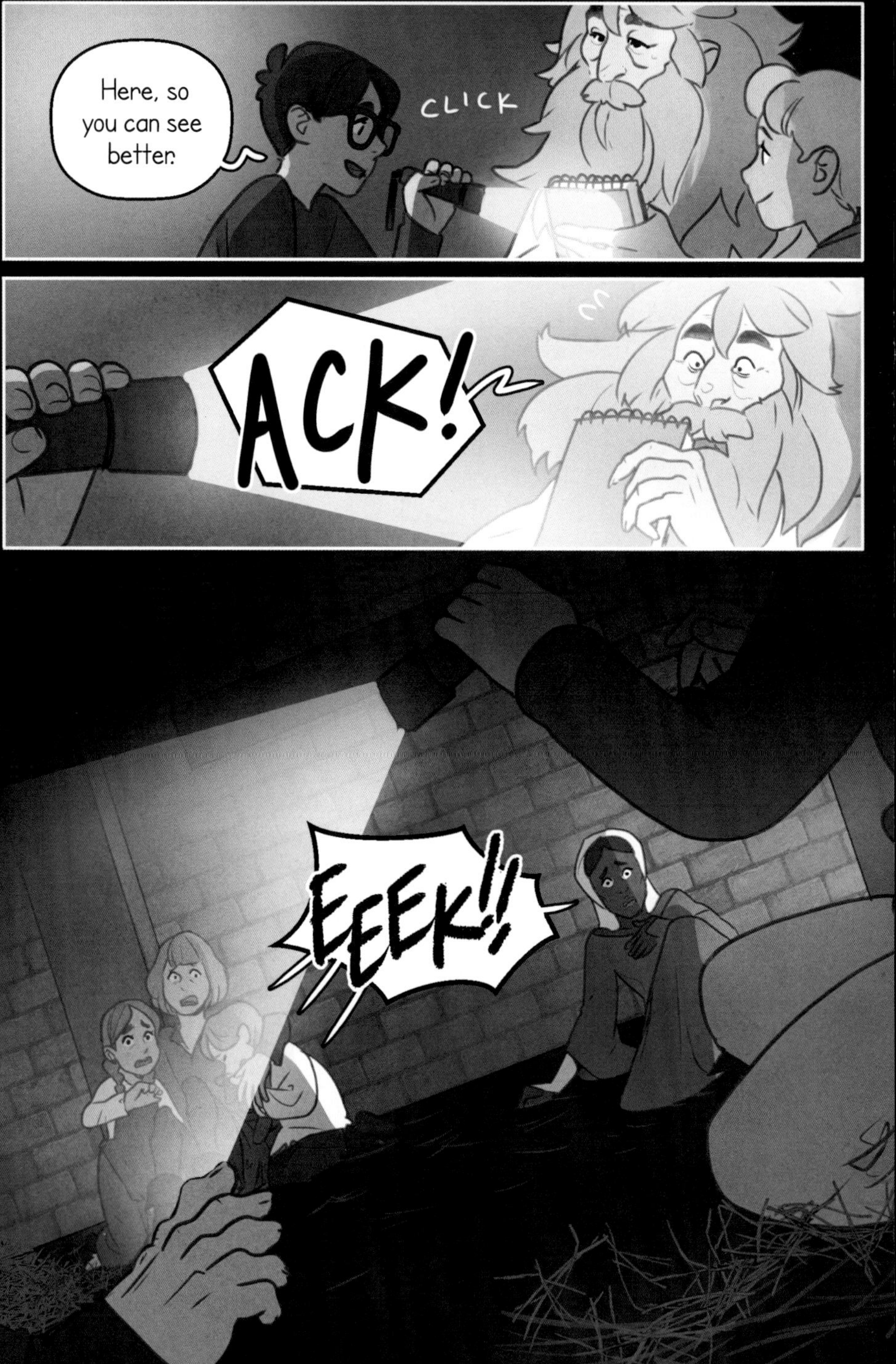
Here, so you can see better.
CLICK
ACK!
EEEK!!

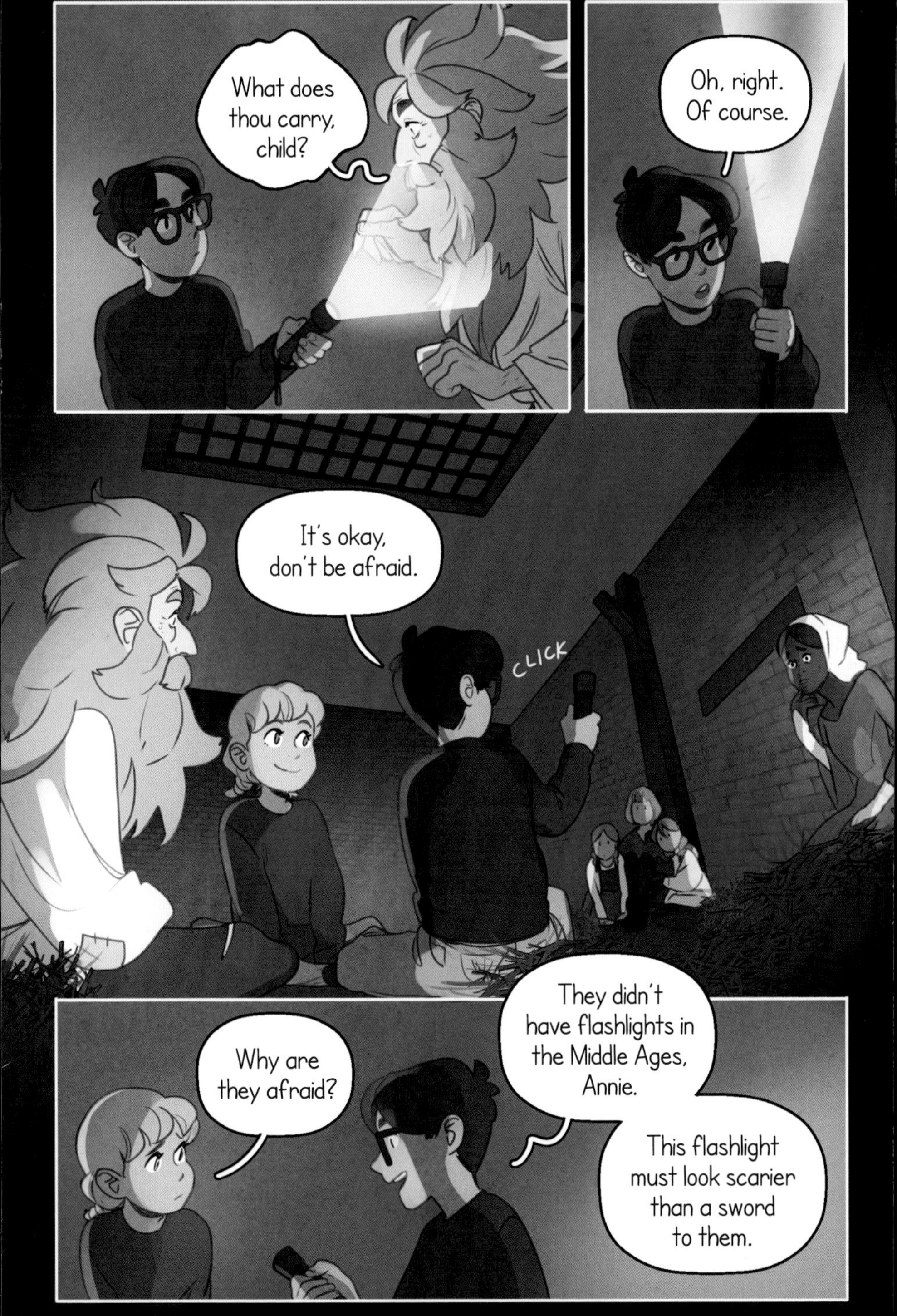
What does thou carry, child?
Oh, right. Of course.
It's okay, don't be afraid.
CLICK
Why are they afraid?
They didn't have flashlights in the Middle Ages, Annie.
This flashlight must look scarier than a sword to them.

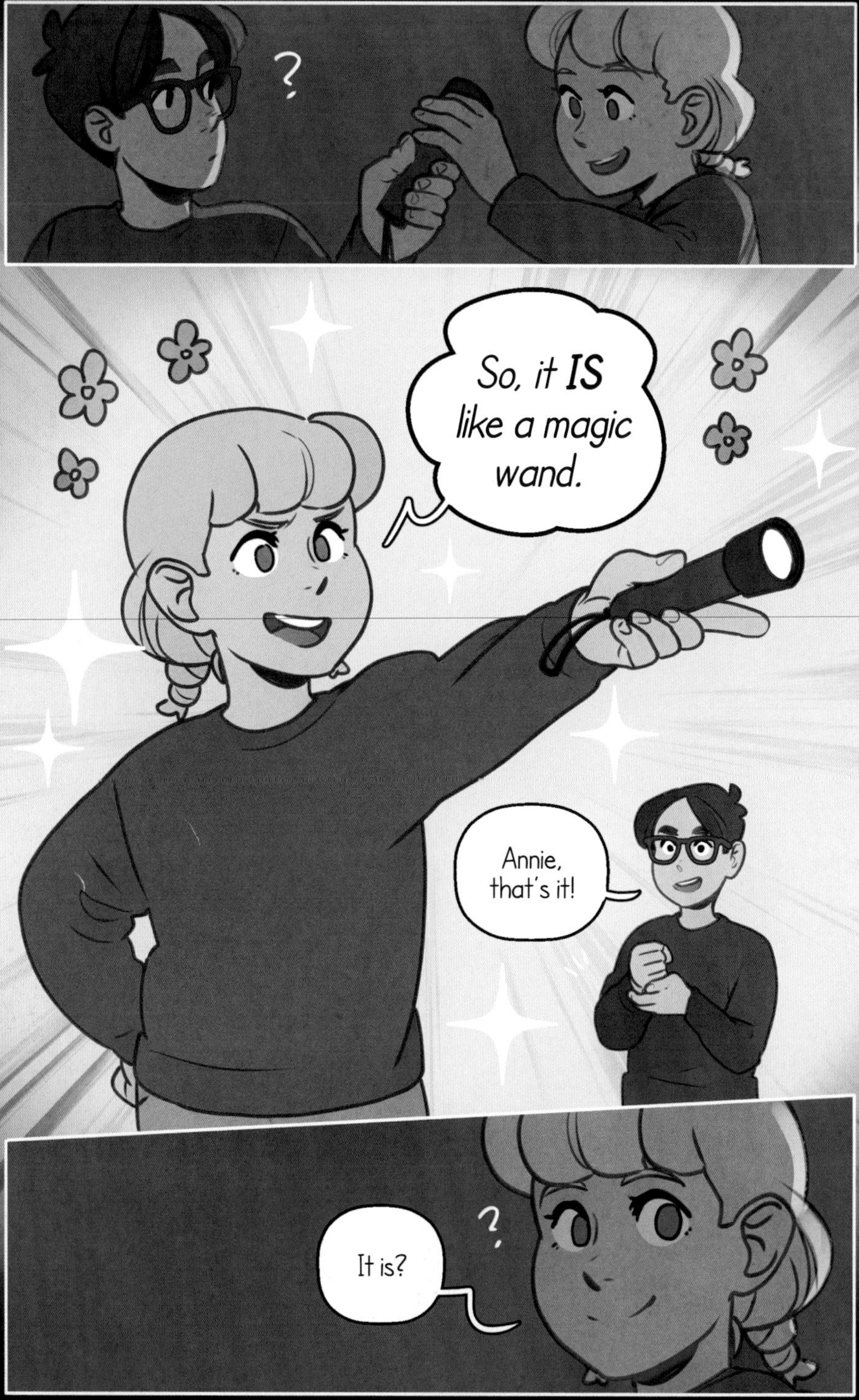
?
So, it IS like a magic wand.
Annie, that's it!
?
It is?

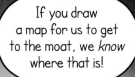

If you draw a map for us to get to the moat, we *know* where that is!

We can make our way back home from there!

And when I say go, you take everyone to the secret passage leading to the orchard.

Can you do that, Harry?

I can. And I shall.

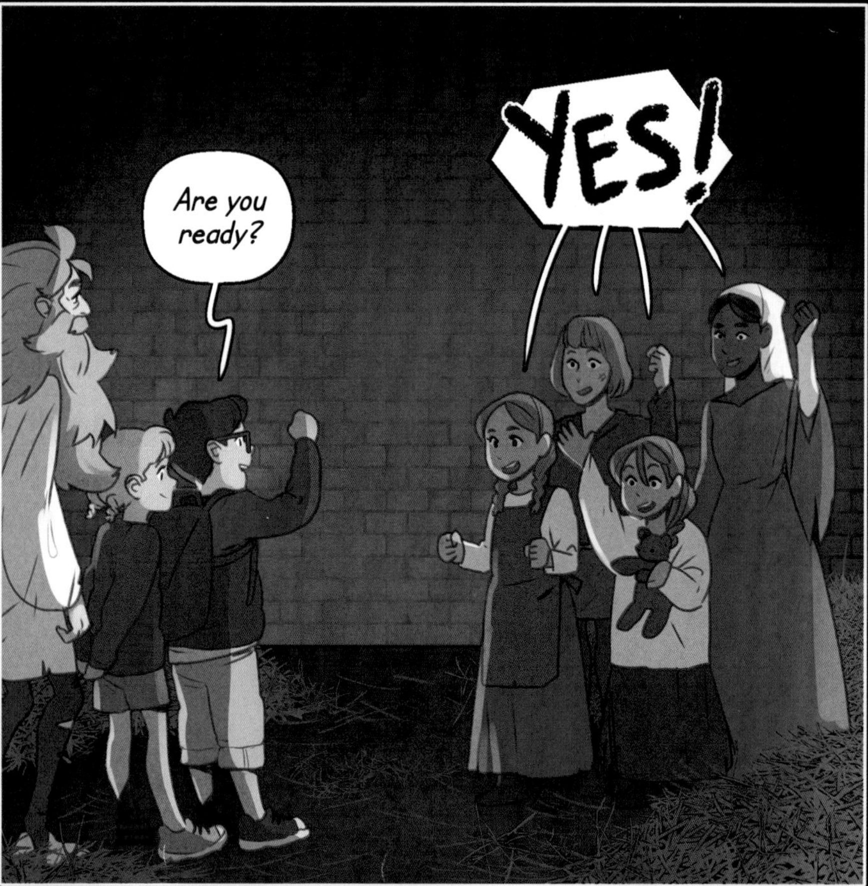
Are you ready?
YES!

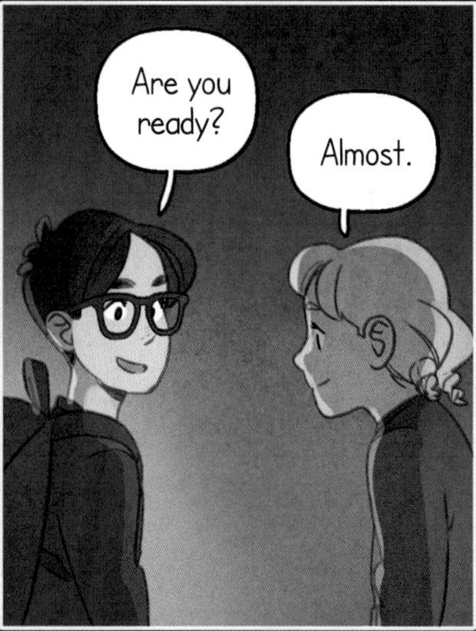
Are you ready?
Almost.

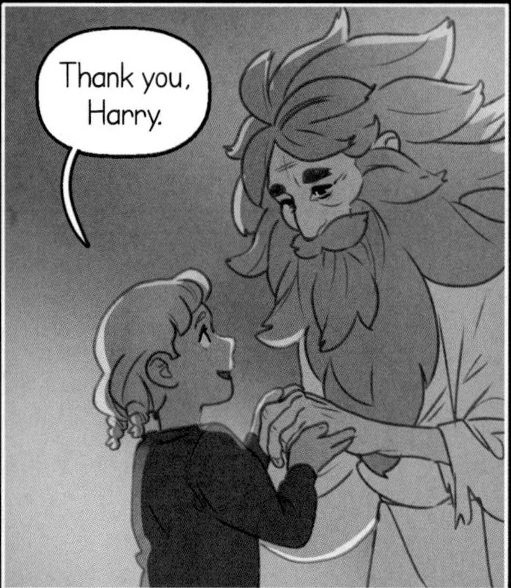
Thank you, Harry.

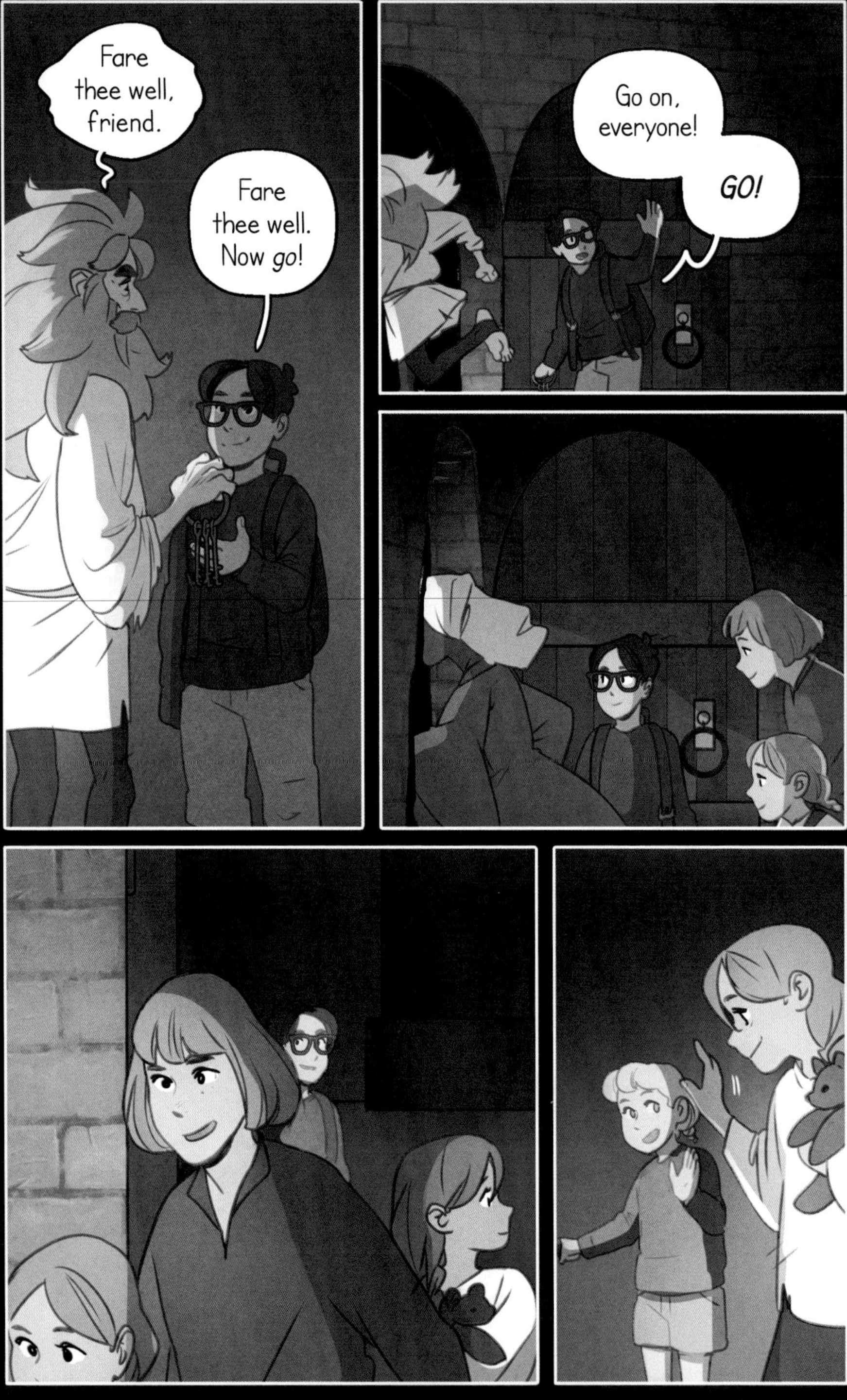
Fare thee well, friend.
Fare thee well. Now *go*!
Go on, everyone!
GO!

CHAPTER EIGHT
The Knight

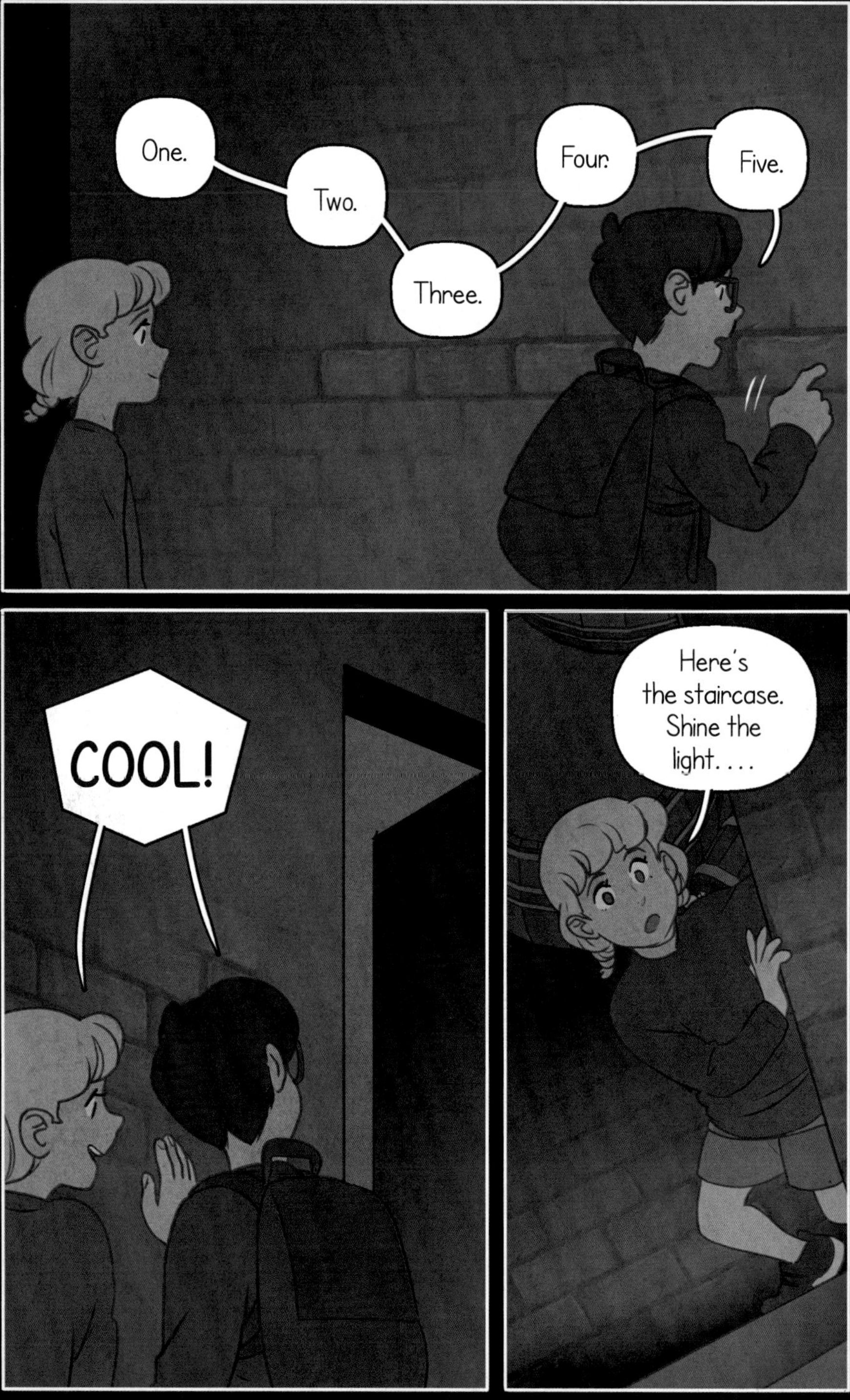
One.
Two.
Three.
Four.
Five.
COOL!
Here's the staircase. Shine the light. . . .

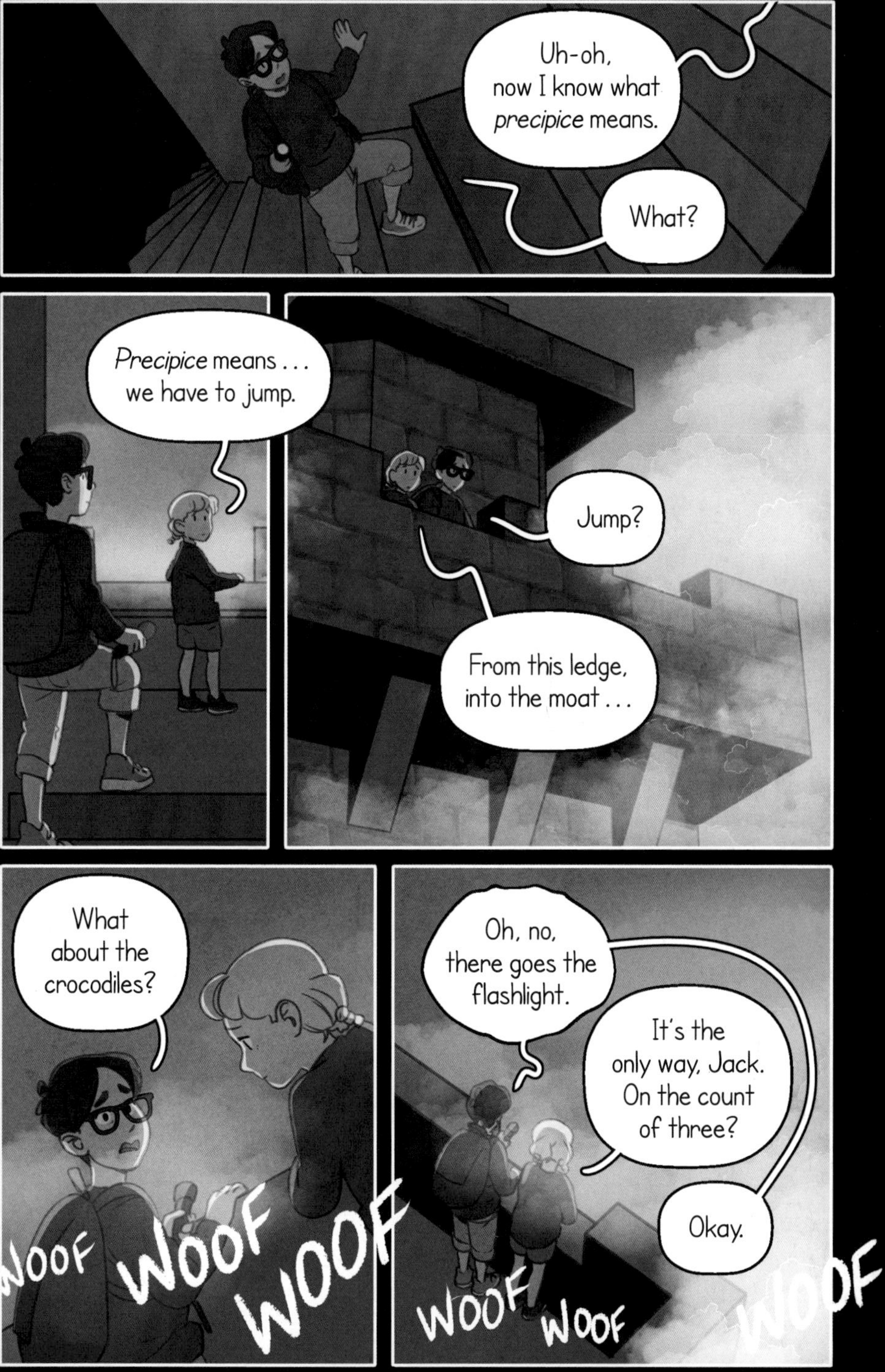
Uh-oh, now I know what *precipice* means.
What?
Precipice means . . . we have to jump.
Jump?
From this ledge, into the moat . . .
What about the crocodiles?
WOOF WOOF WOOF
Oh, no, there goes the flashlight.
It's the only way, Jack. On the count of three?
Okay.
WOOF WOOF WOOF

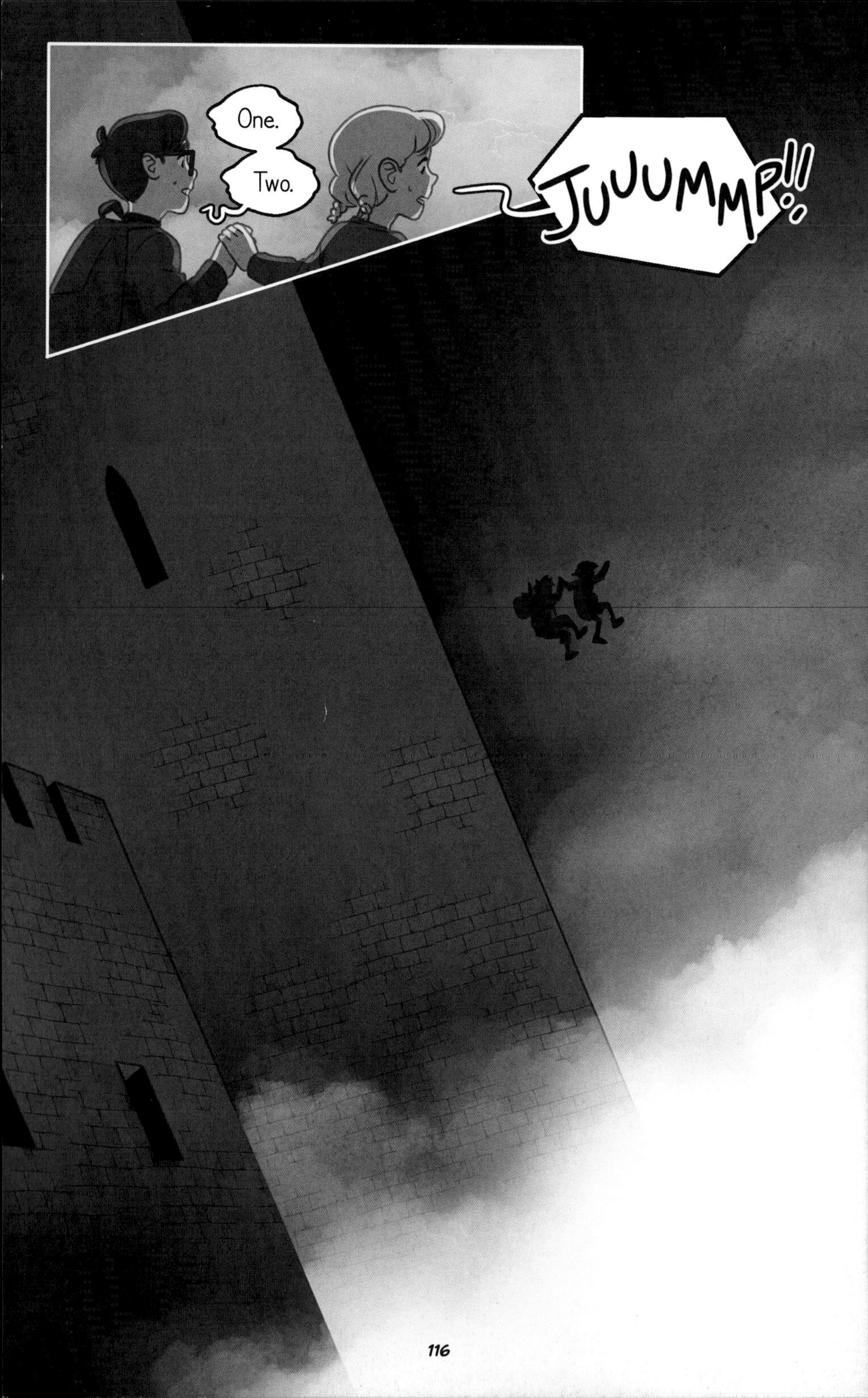
One.
Two.
JUUUMMP!!

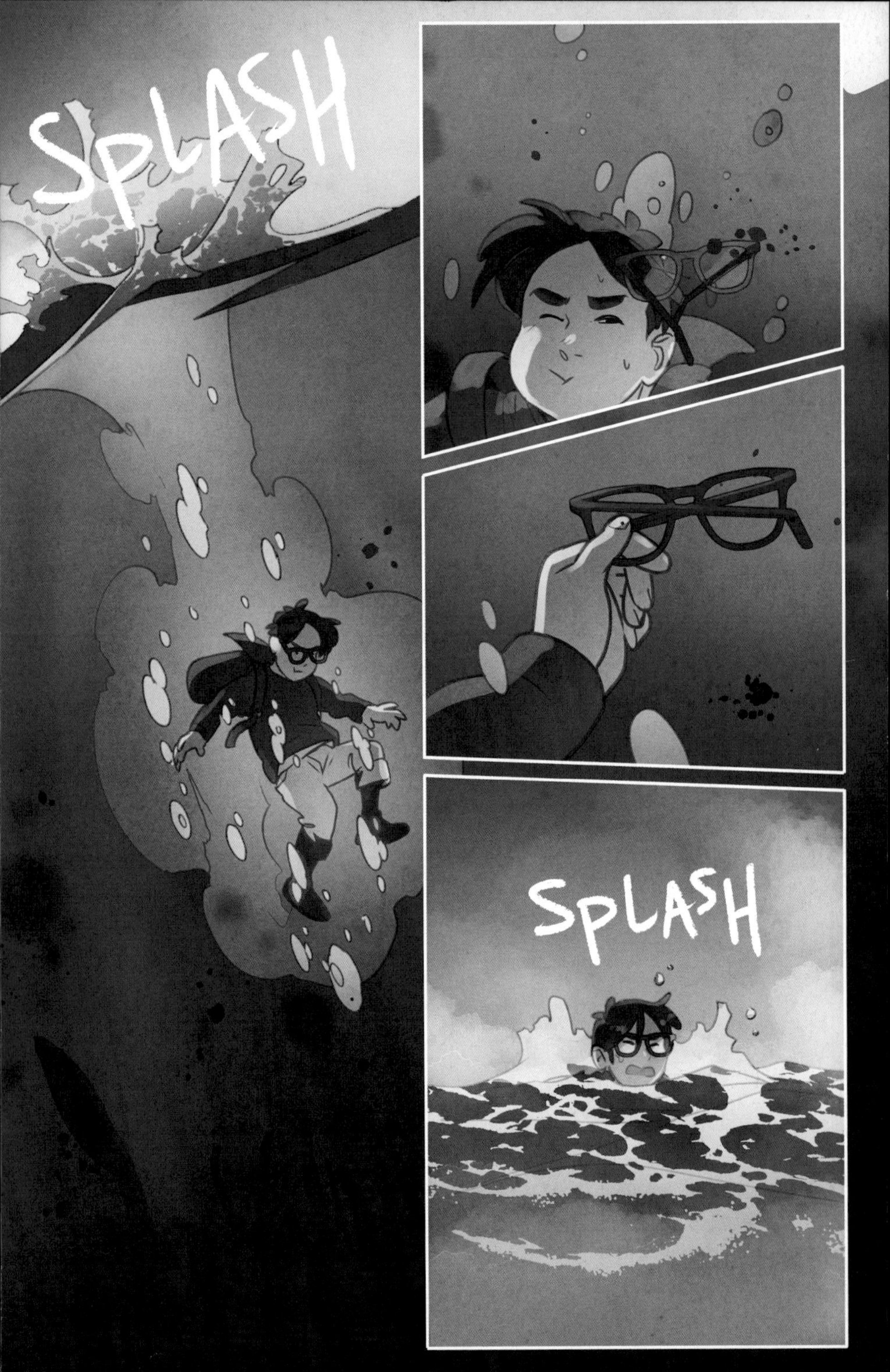
SPLASH
SPLASH

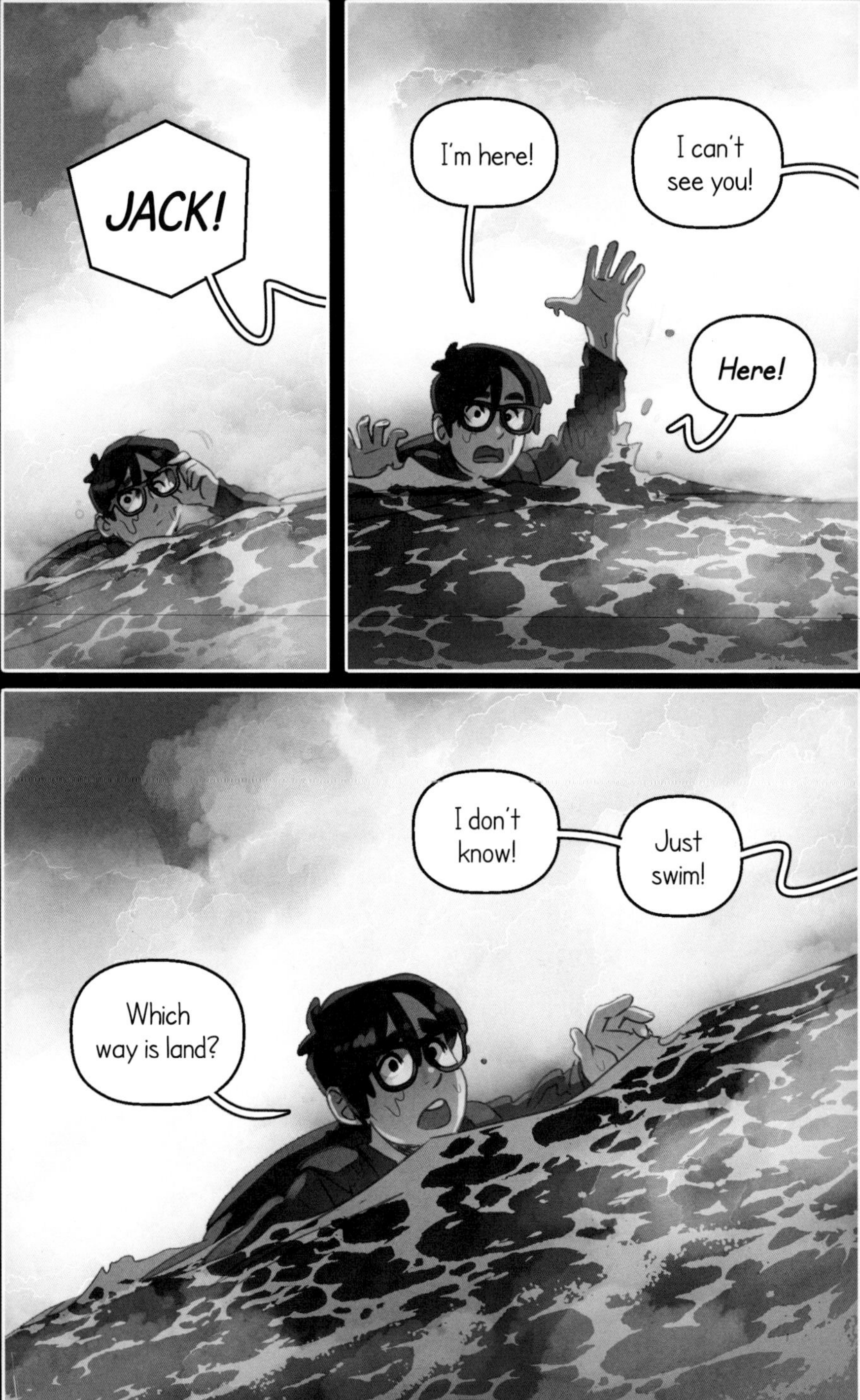
JACK!
I'm here!
I can't see you!
Here!
Which way is land?
I don't know!
Just swim!

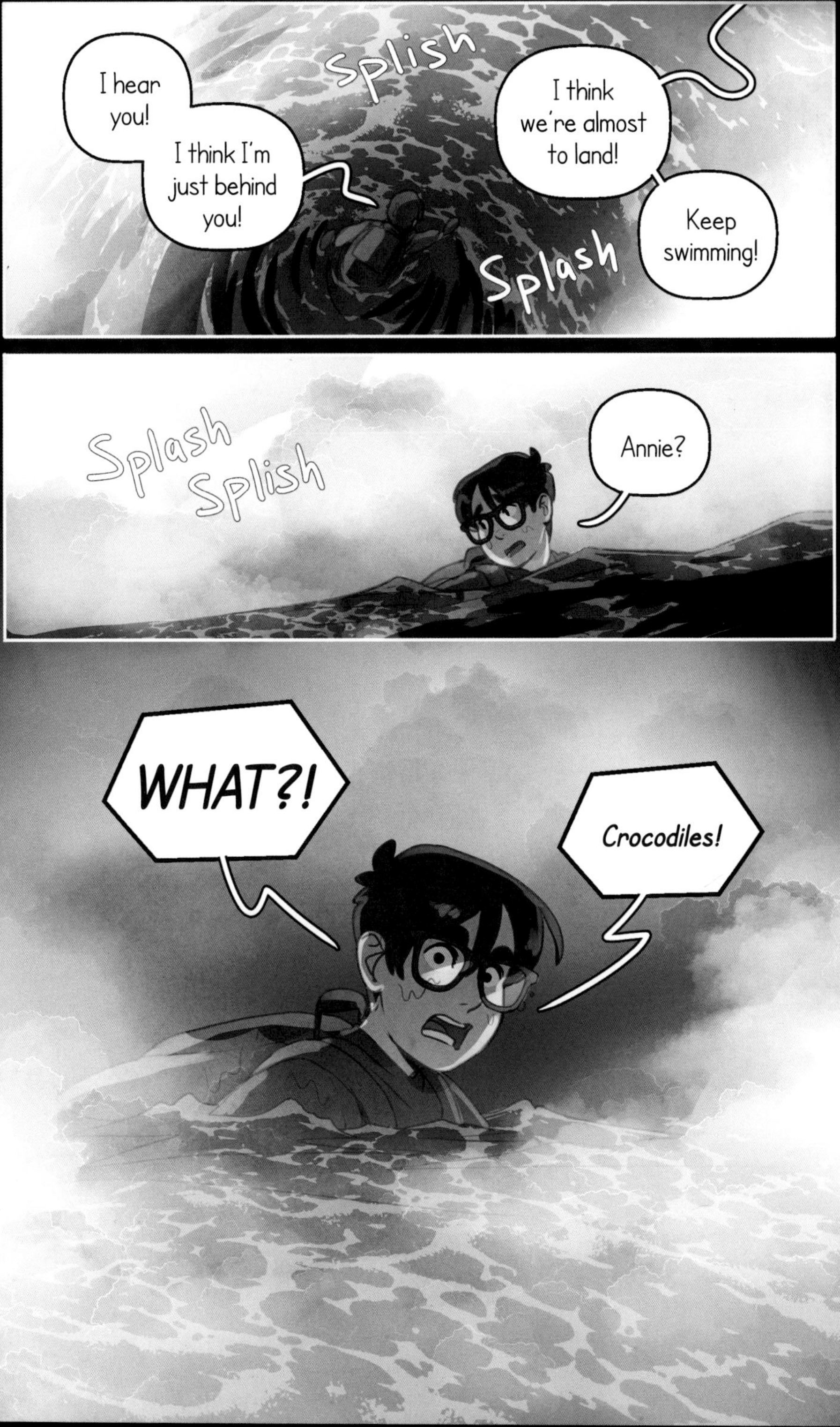
Splish
I hear you!
I think I'm just behind you!
I think we're almost to land!
Keep swimming!
Splash
Splash
Splish
Annie?
WHAT?!
Crocodiles!

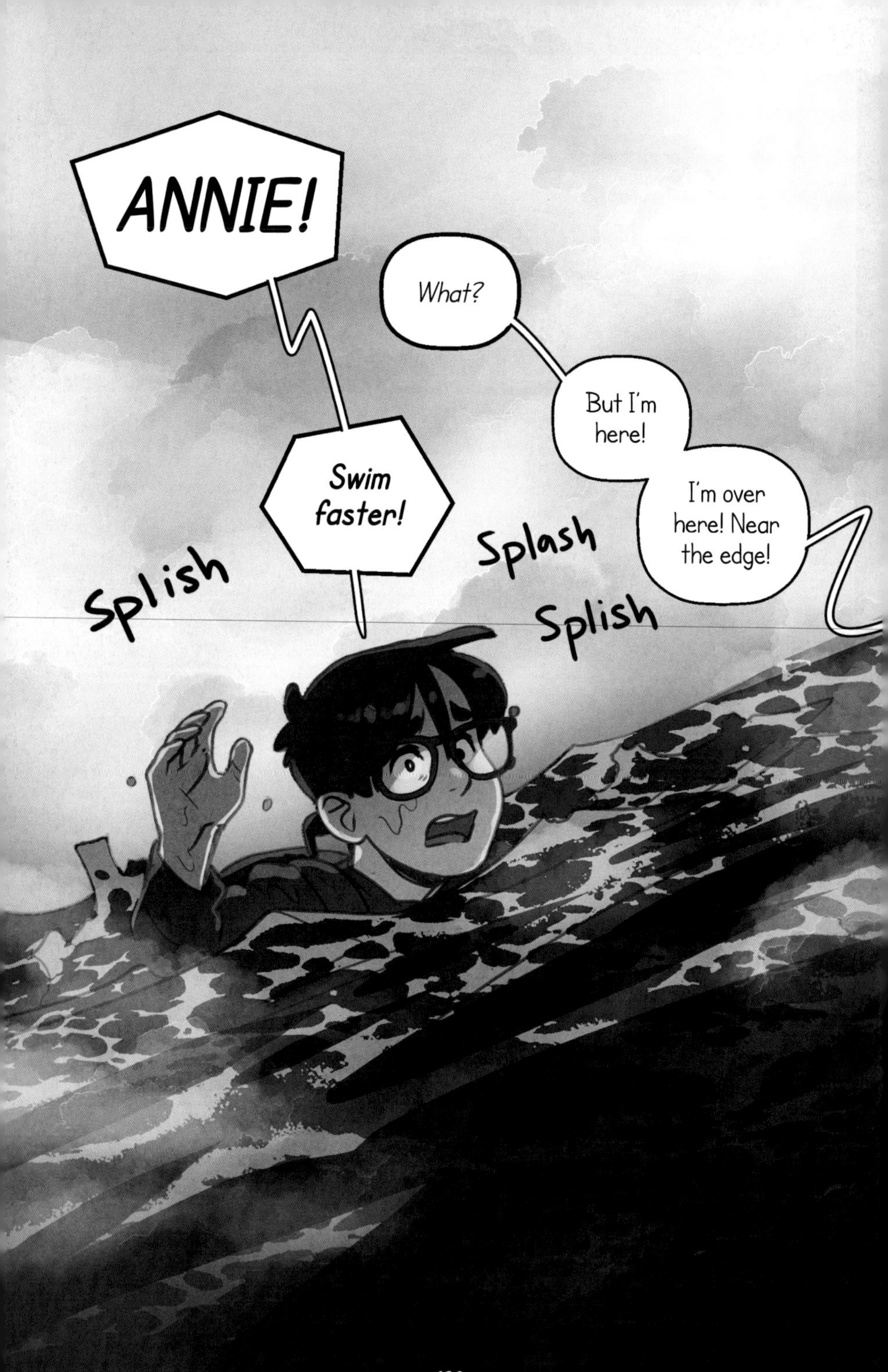
ANNIE!
Swim faster!
What?
But I'm here!
I'm over here! Near the edge!
Splish
Splash
Splish

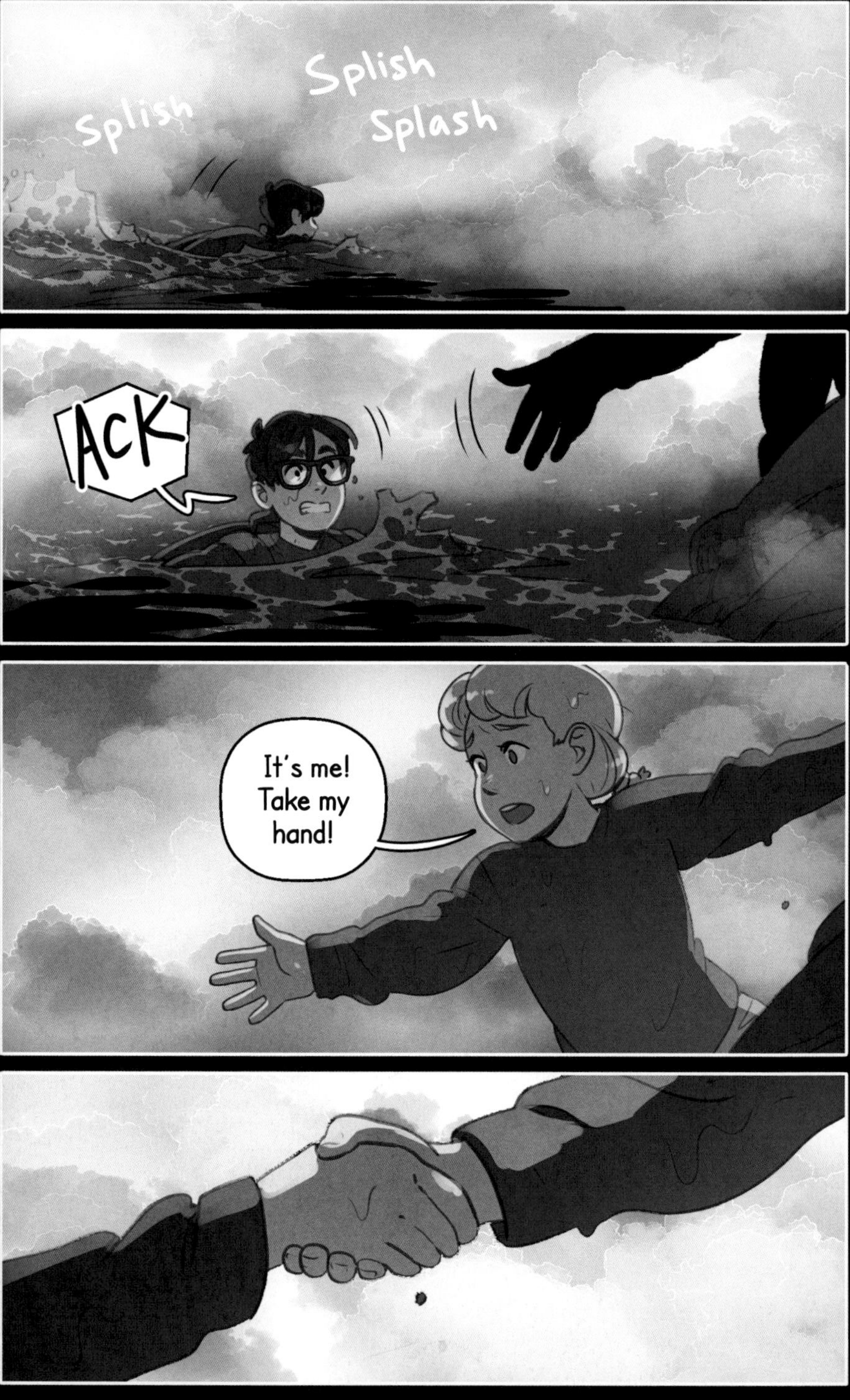
Splish
Splish
Splash
ACK
It's me! Take my hand!

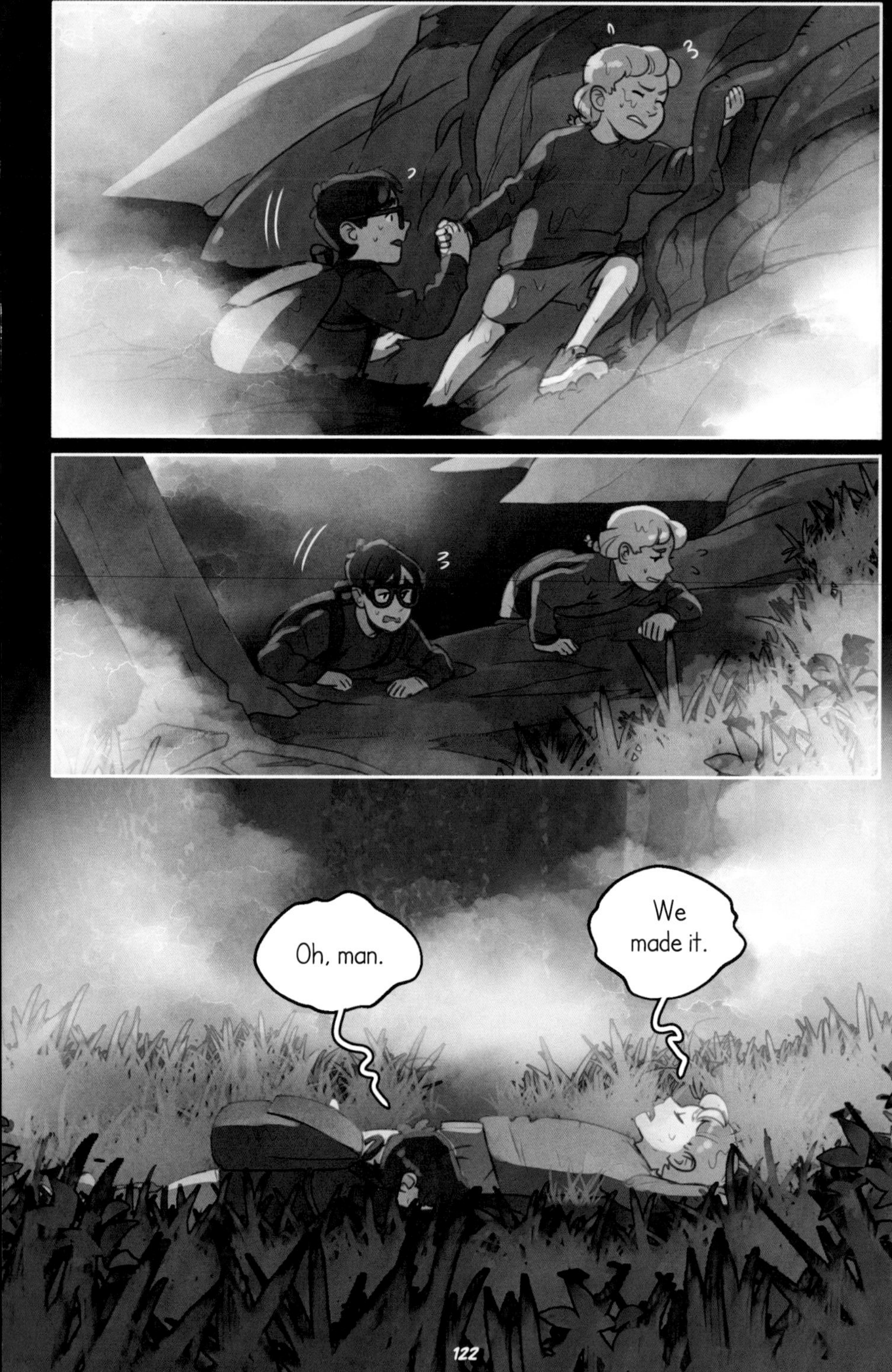
Oh, man.
We made it.

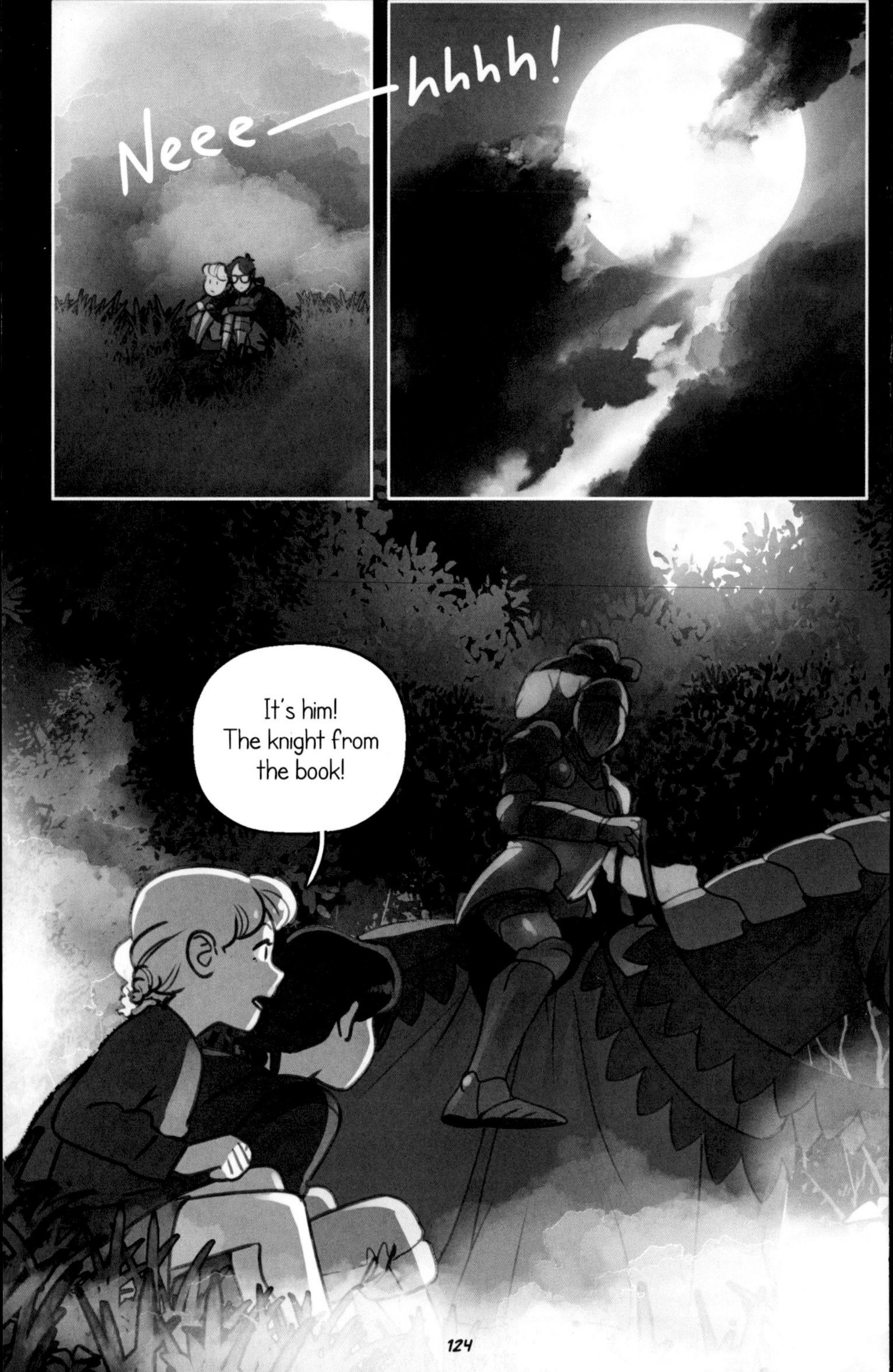
Neee—hhhh!
It's him! The knight from the book!

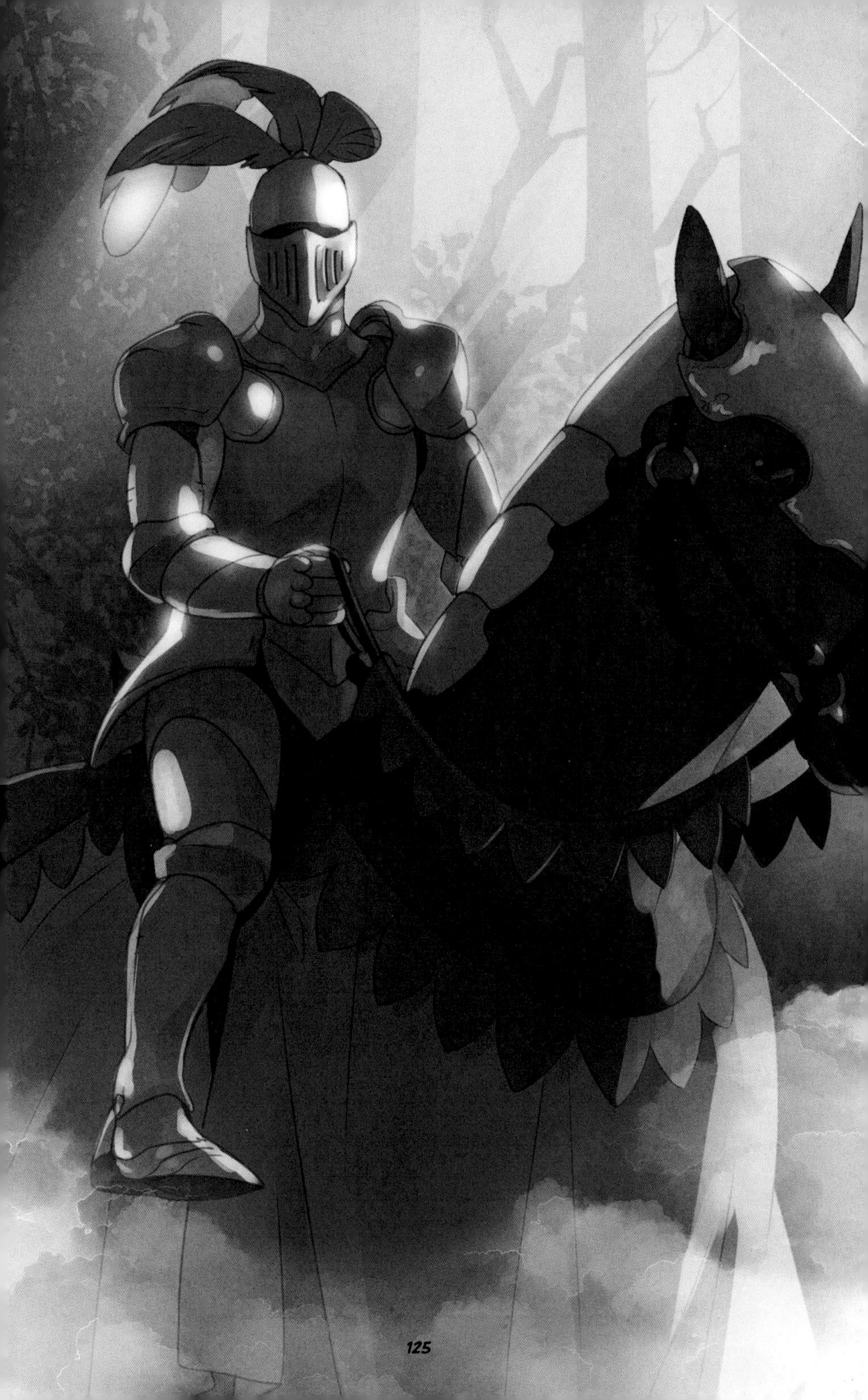

CHAPTER NINE

Under the Moon

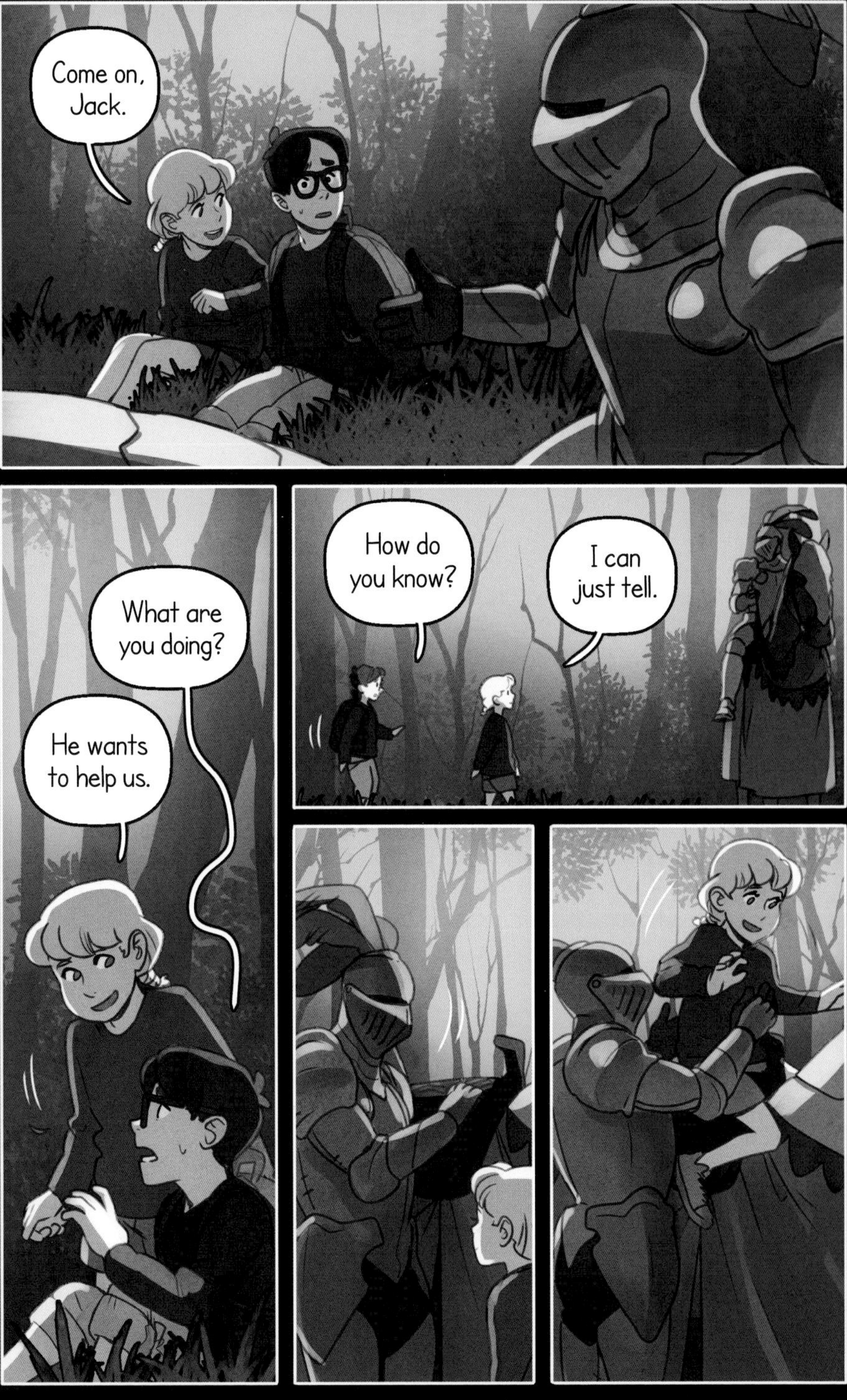
Come on, Jack.
What are you doing?
He wants to help us.
How do you know?
I can just tell.

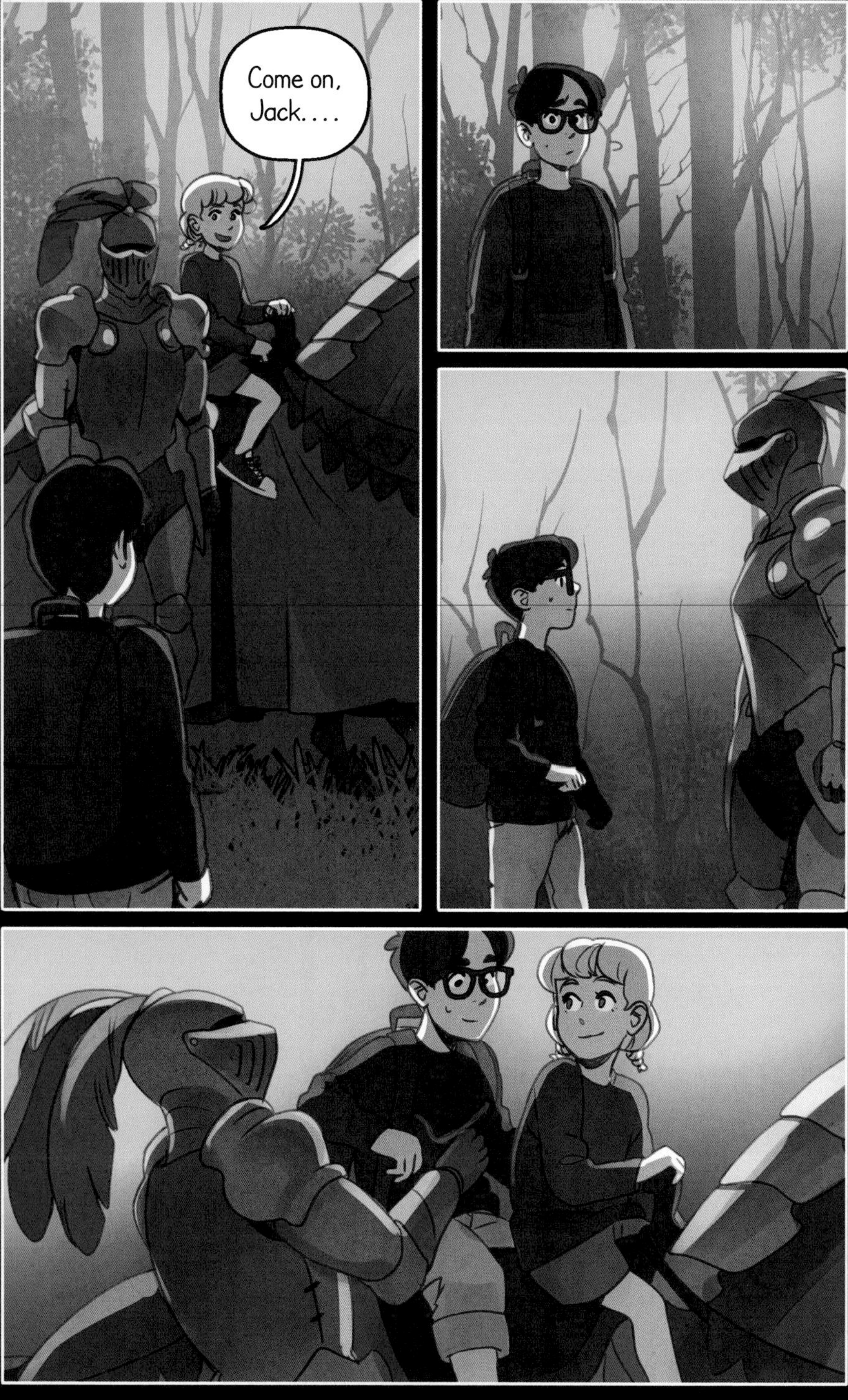
Come on, Jack....

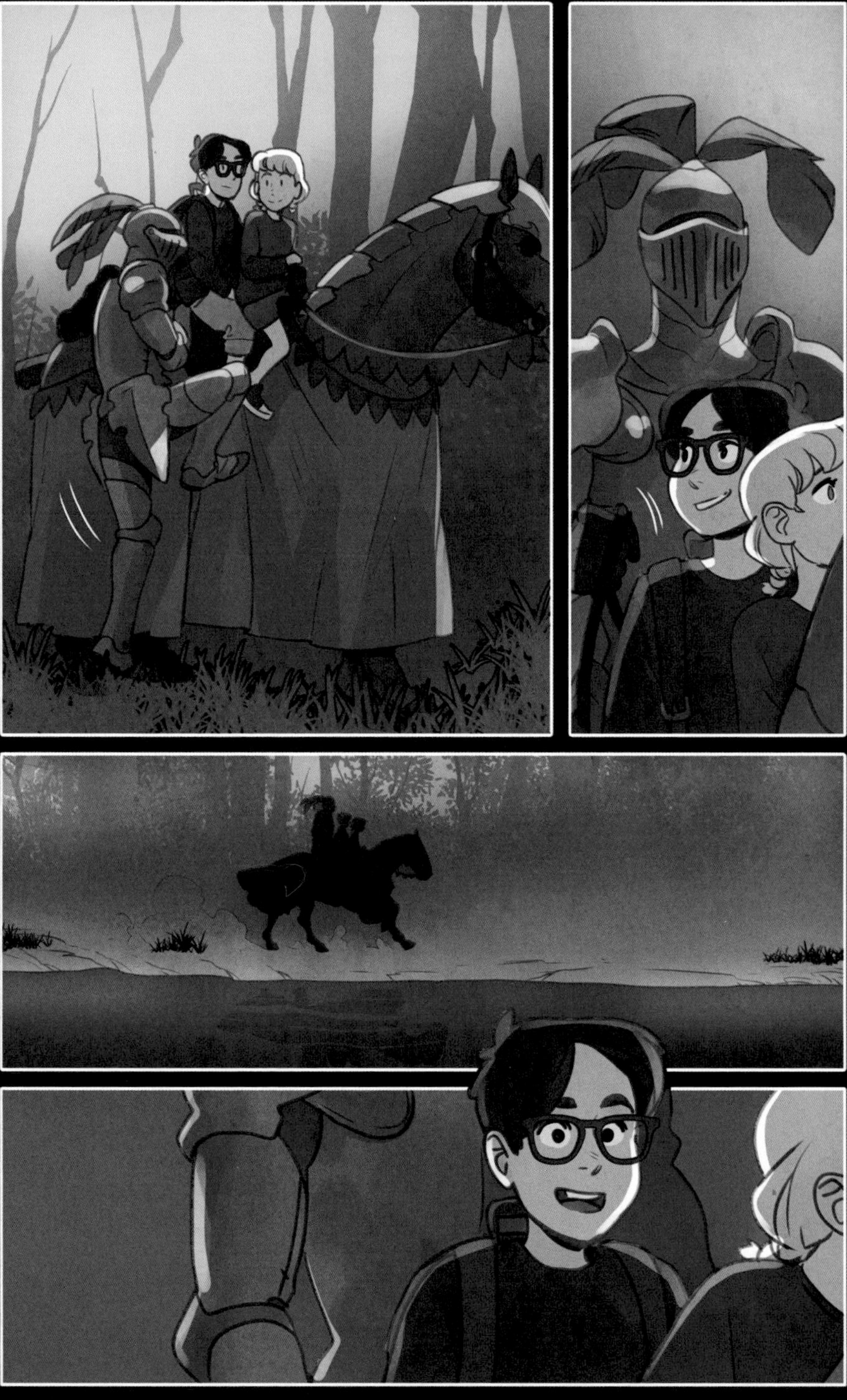

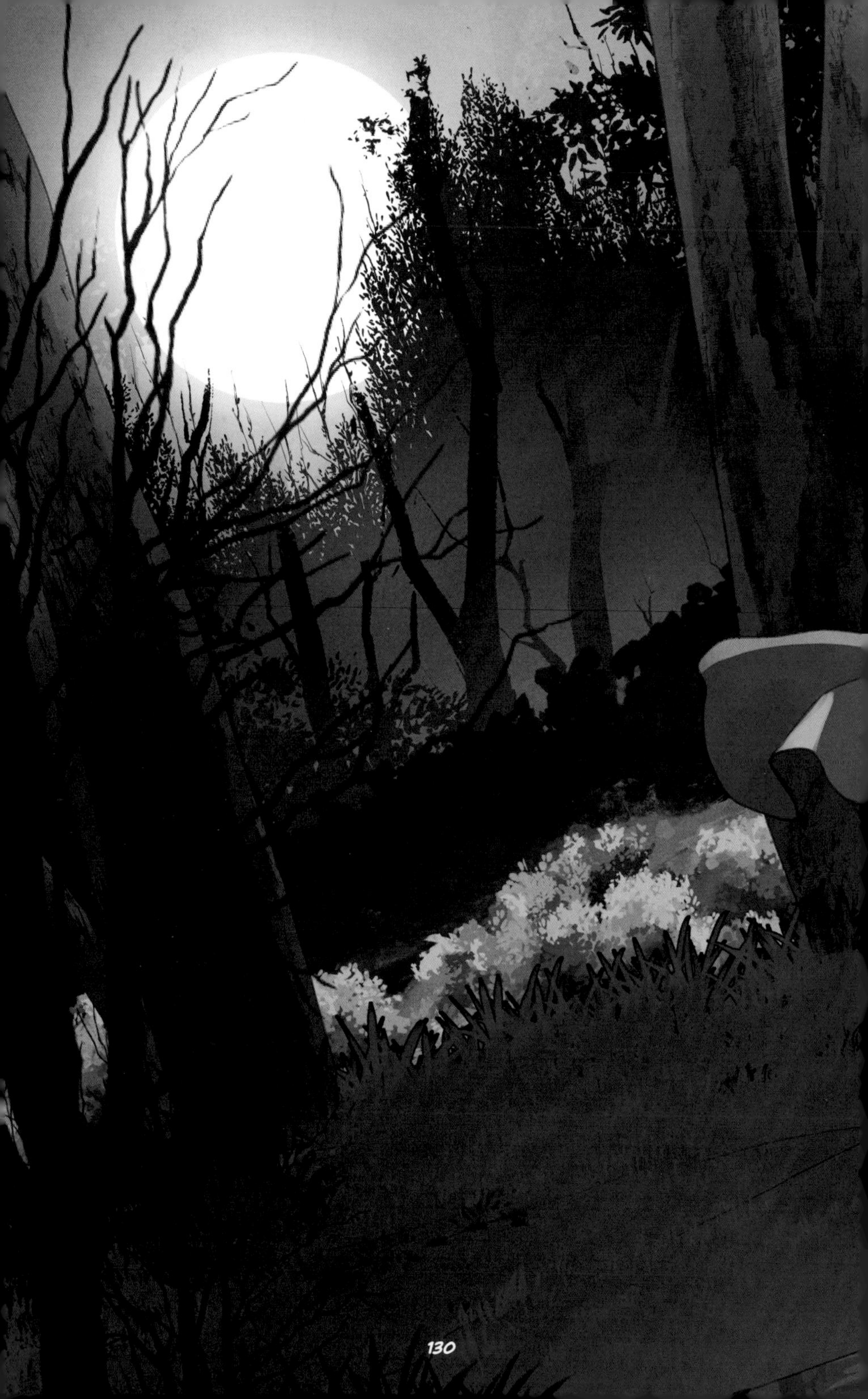

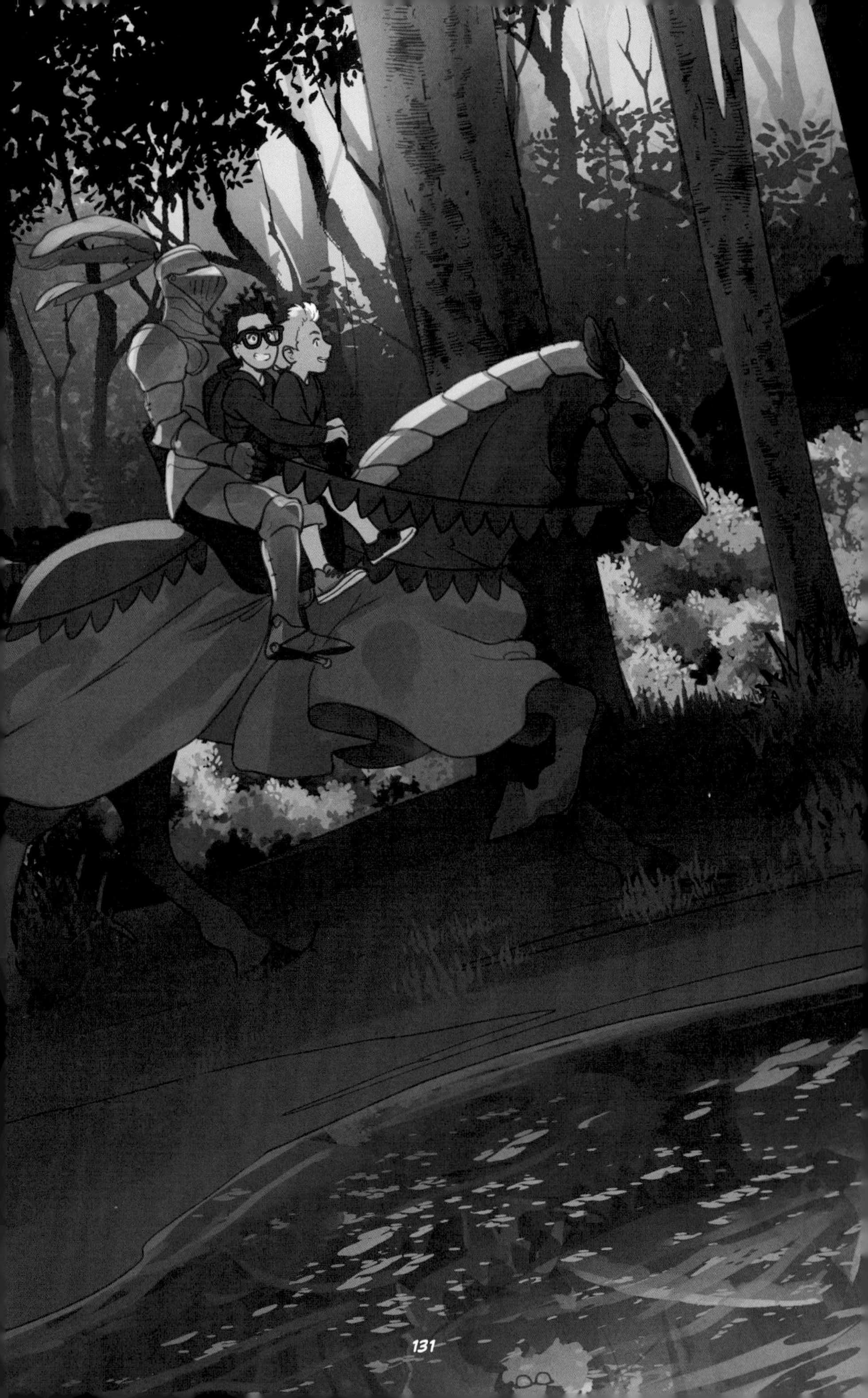

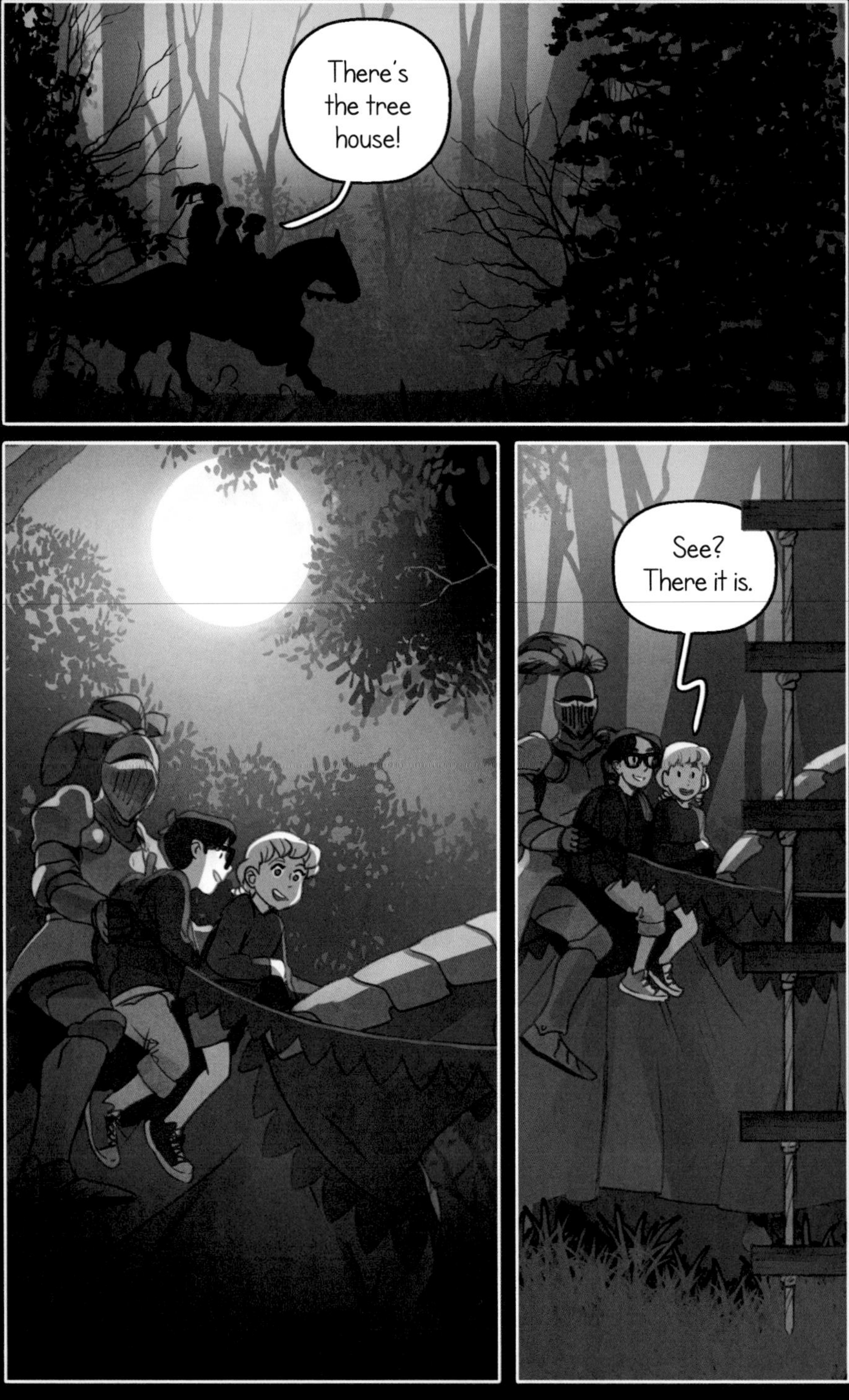
There's the tree house!
See? There it is.

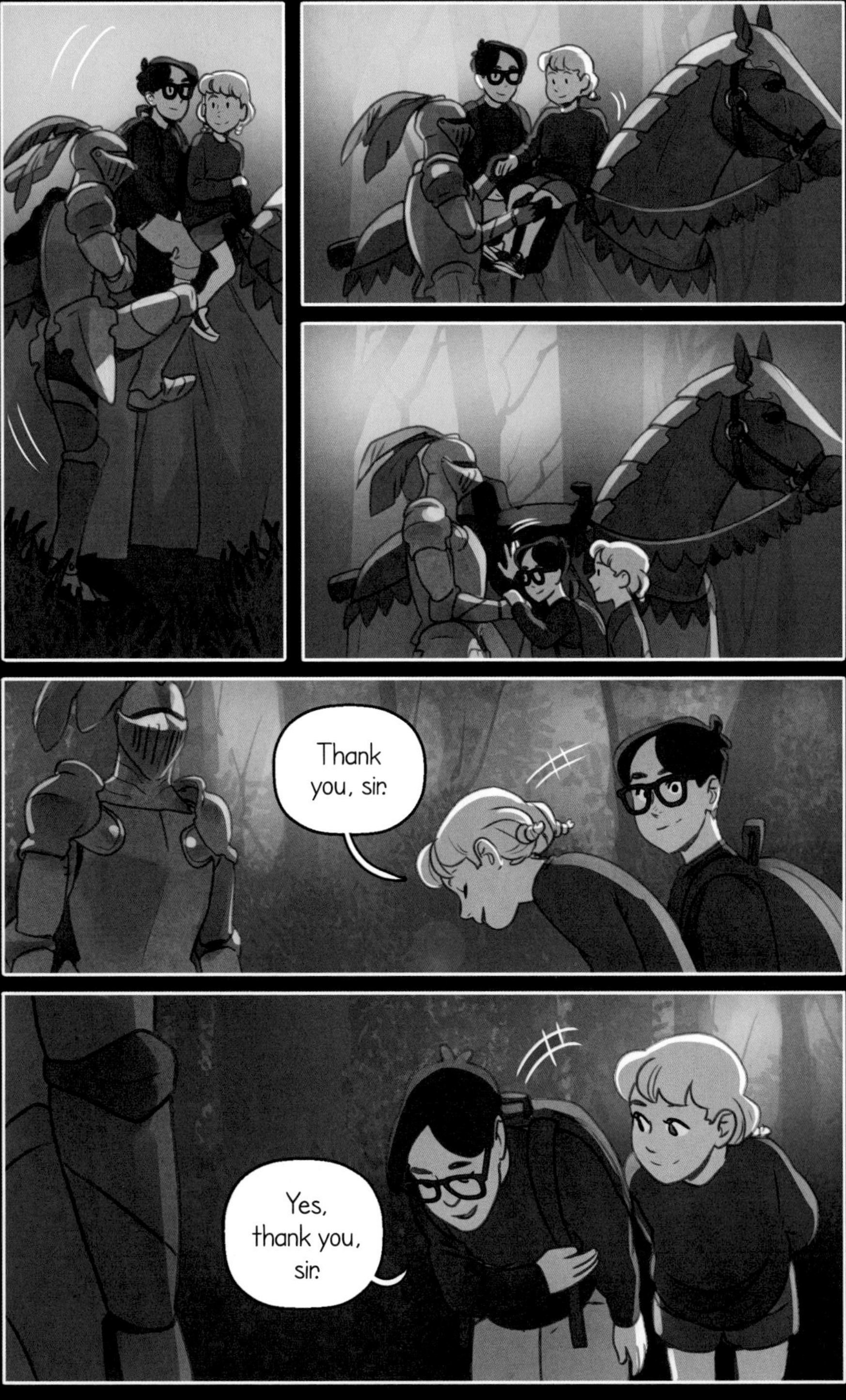
Thank you, sir.
Yes, thank you, sir.

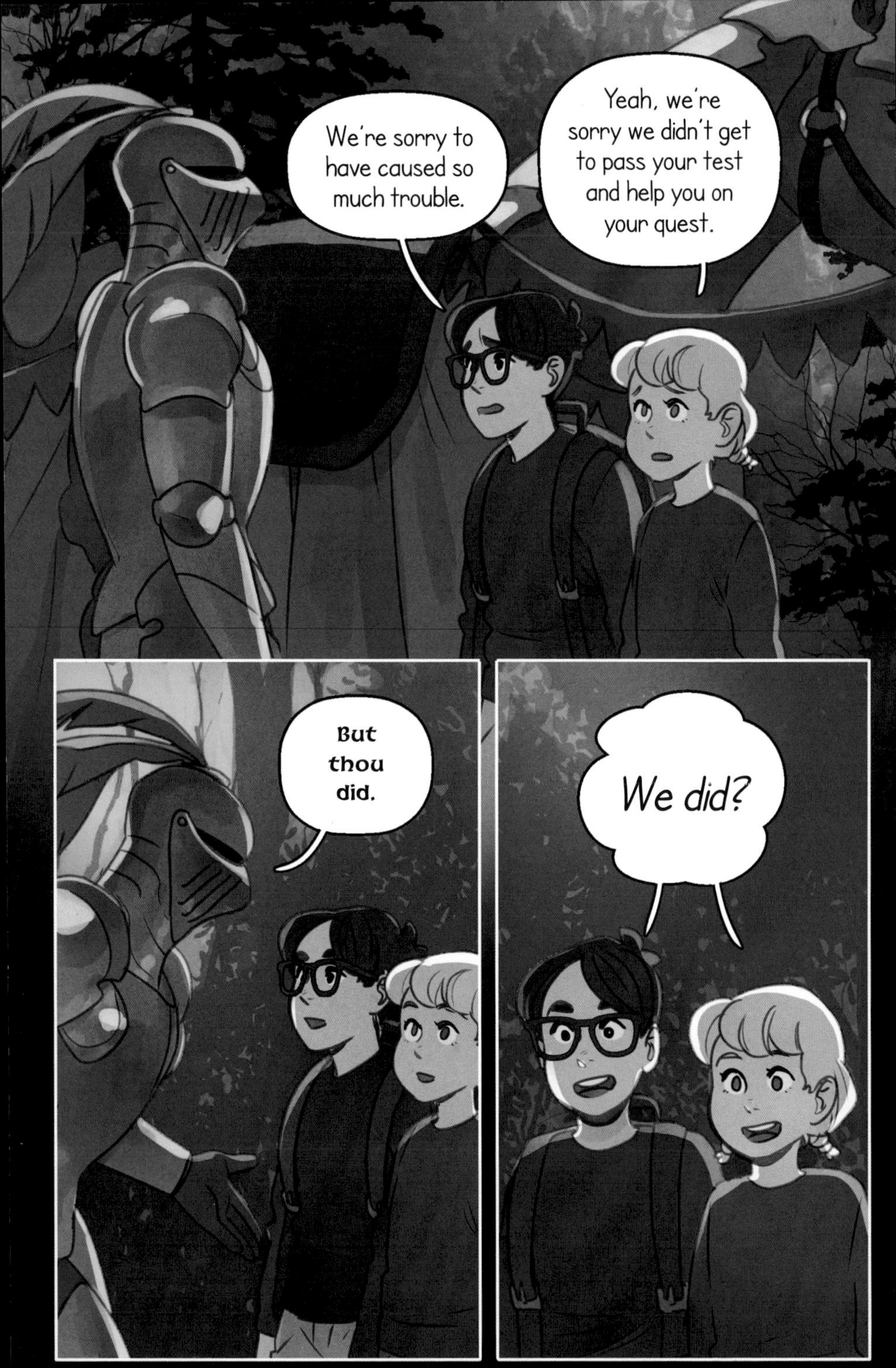
We're sorry to have caused so much trouble.
Yeah, we're sorry we didn't get to pass your test and help you on your quest.
But thou did.
We did?

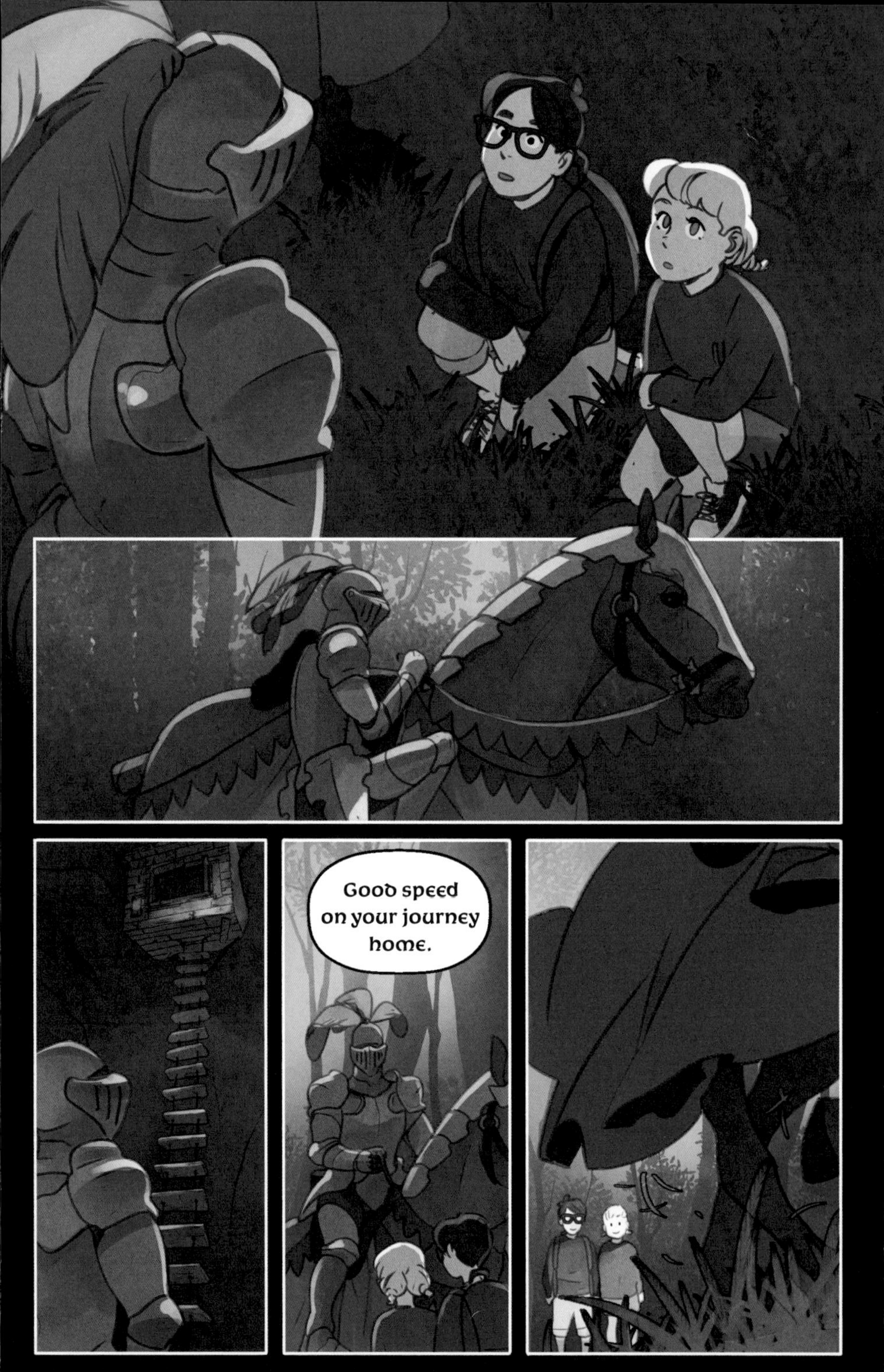
Good speed on your journey home.

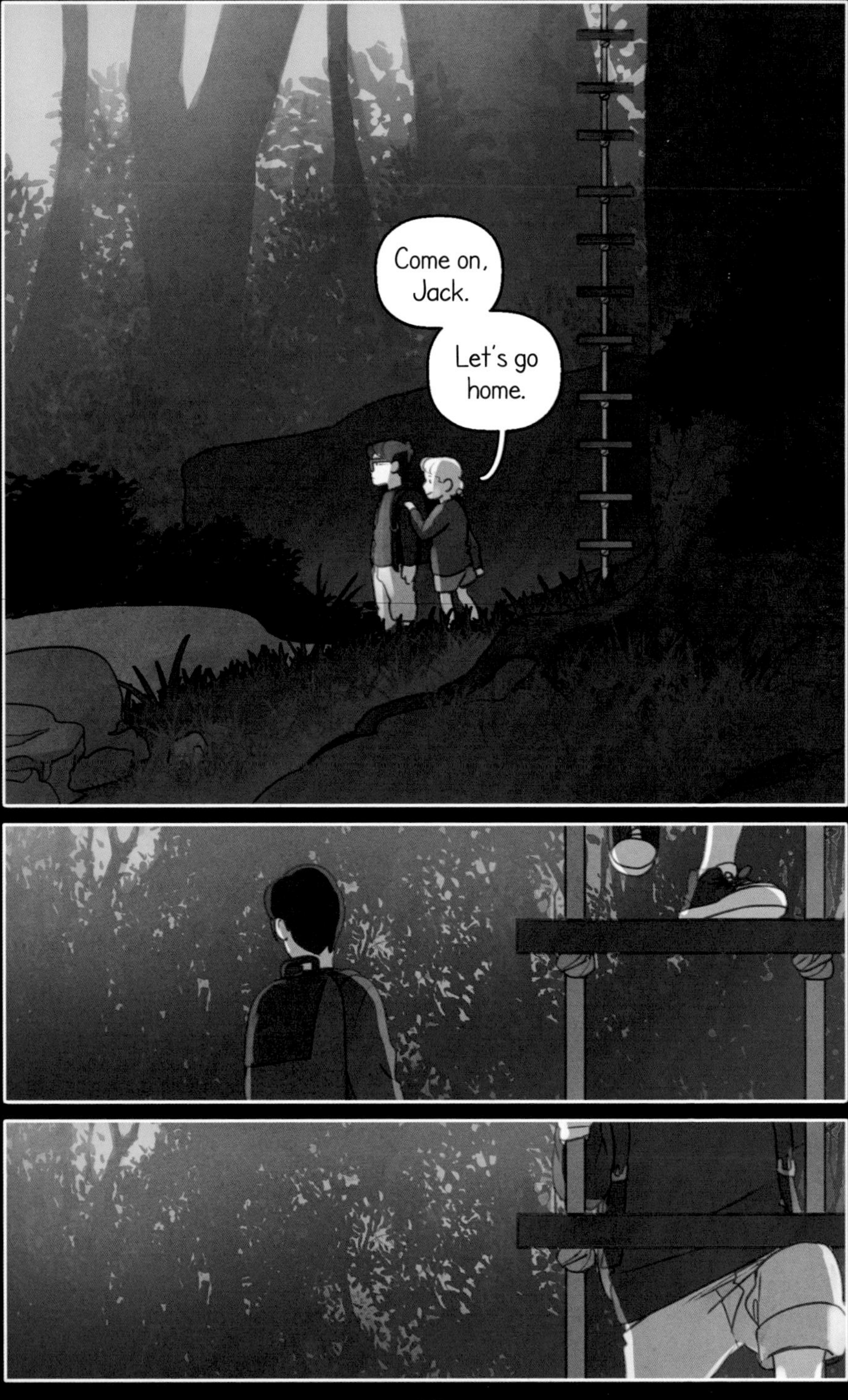
Come on, Jack.
Let's go home.

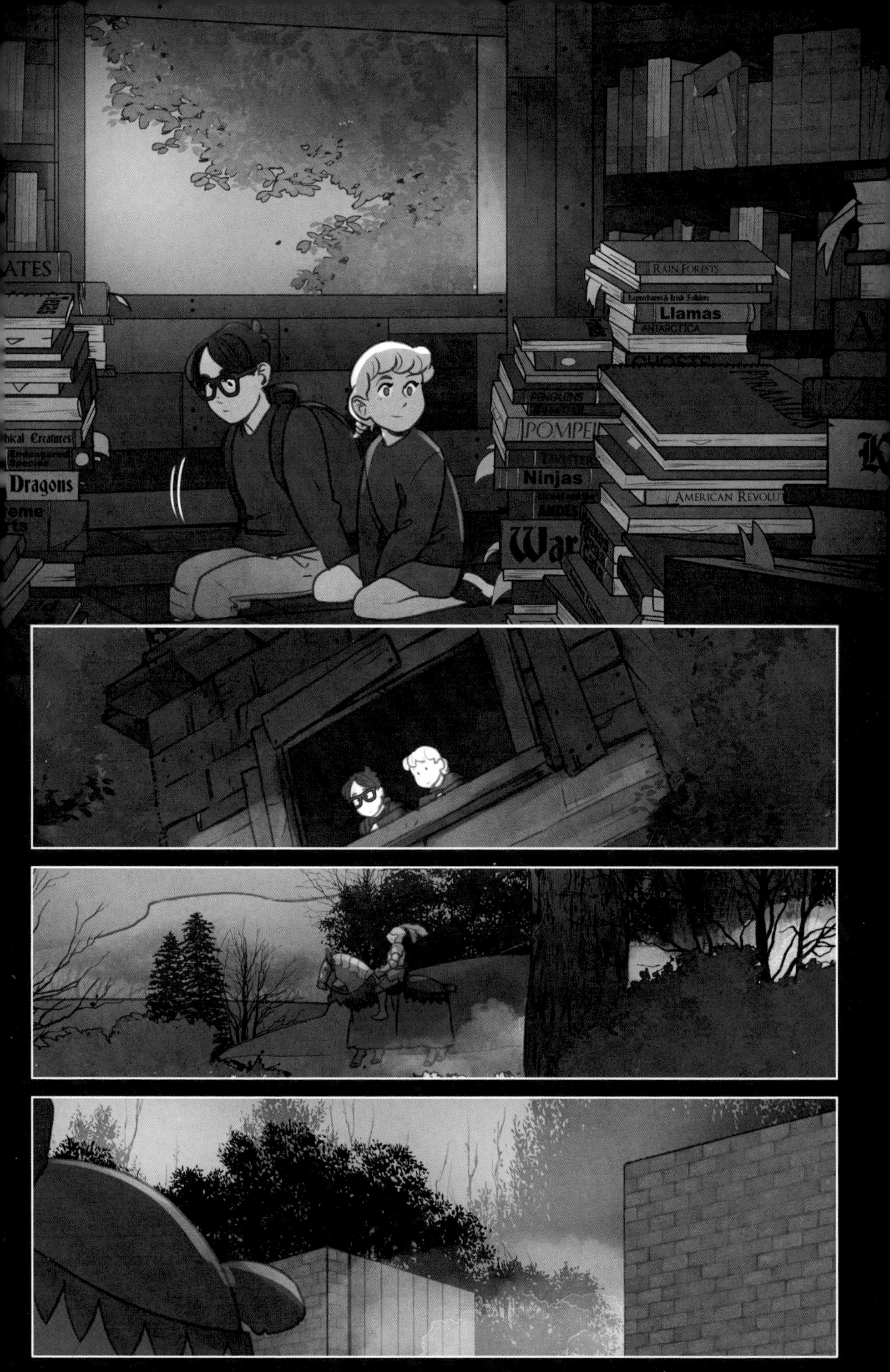
RAIN FORESTS
Llamas
ANTARCTICA
PENGUINS
Ninjas
War
Endangered Species
Dragons

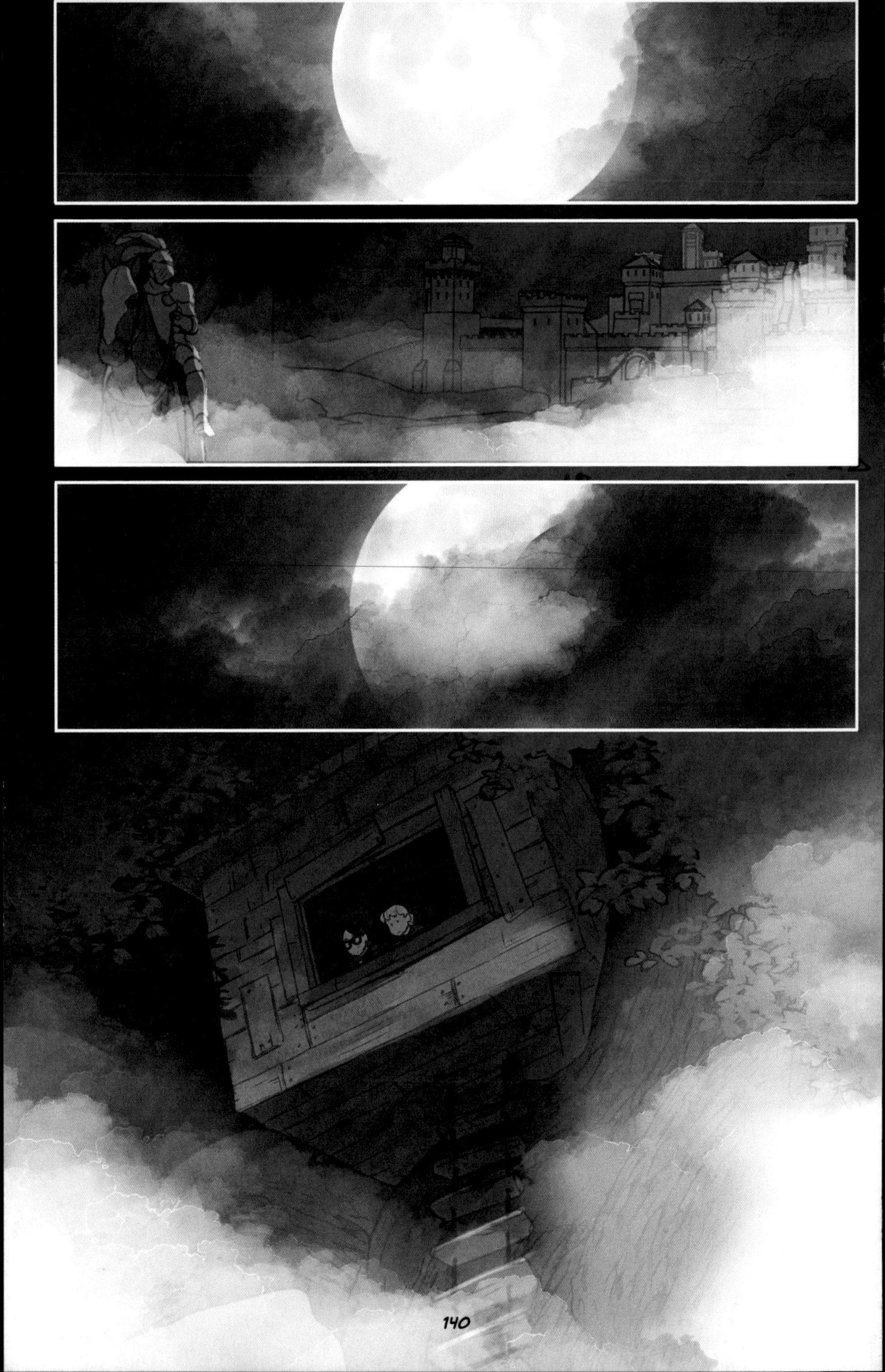

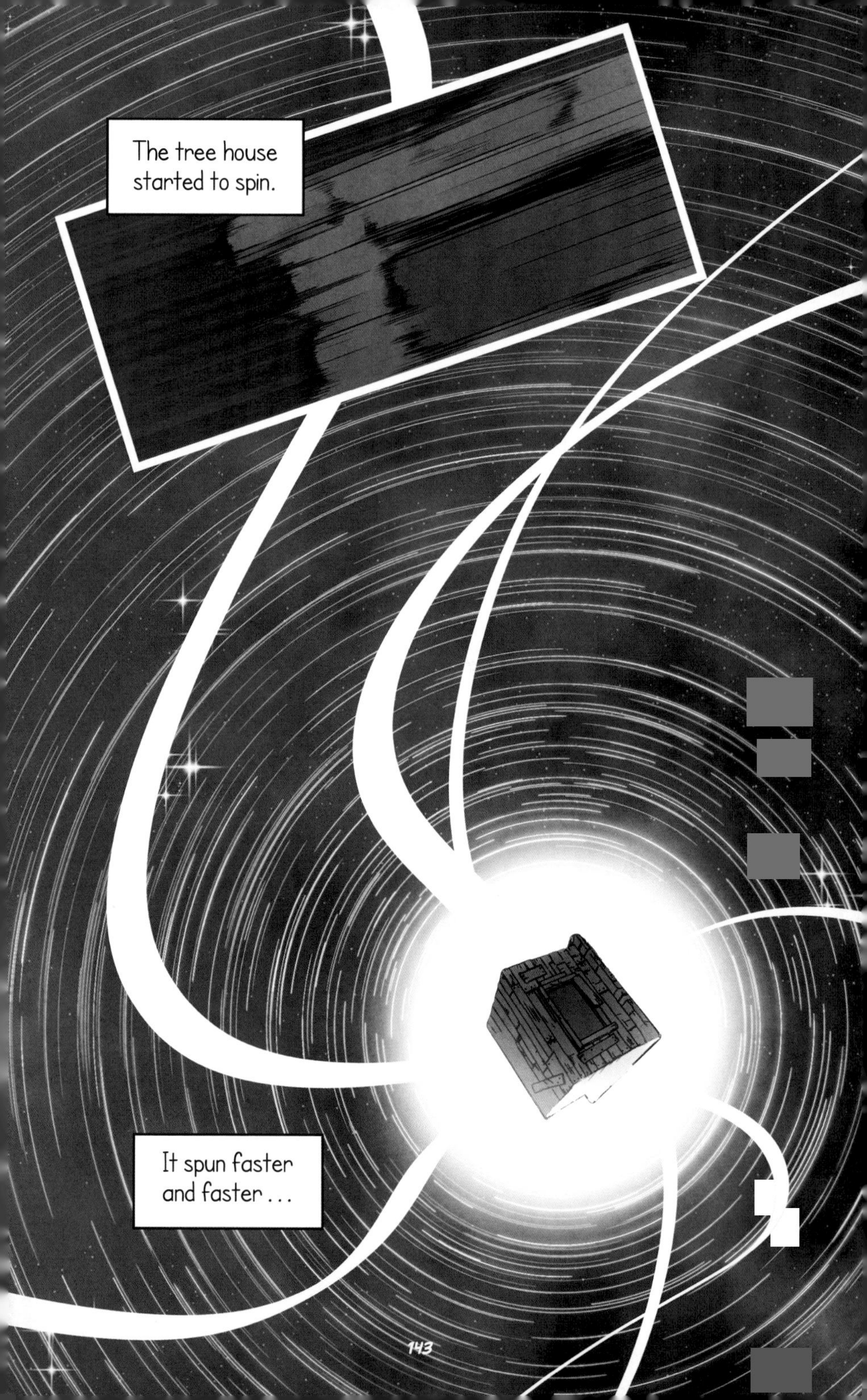
The tree house started to spin.
It spun faster and faster . . .

CHAPTER TEN

One Mystery Solved

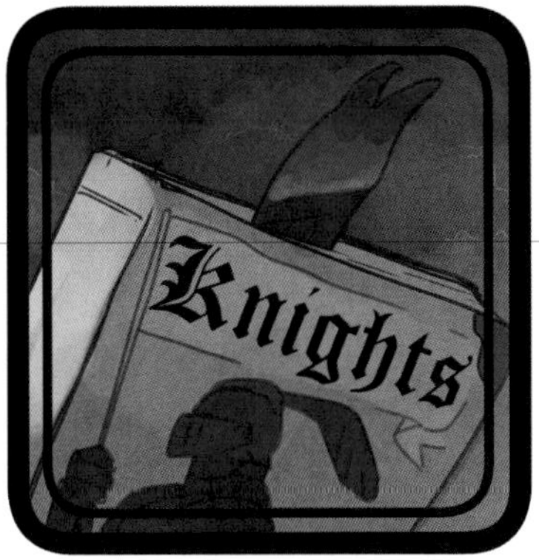
Knights

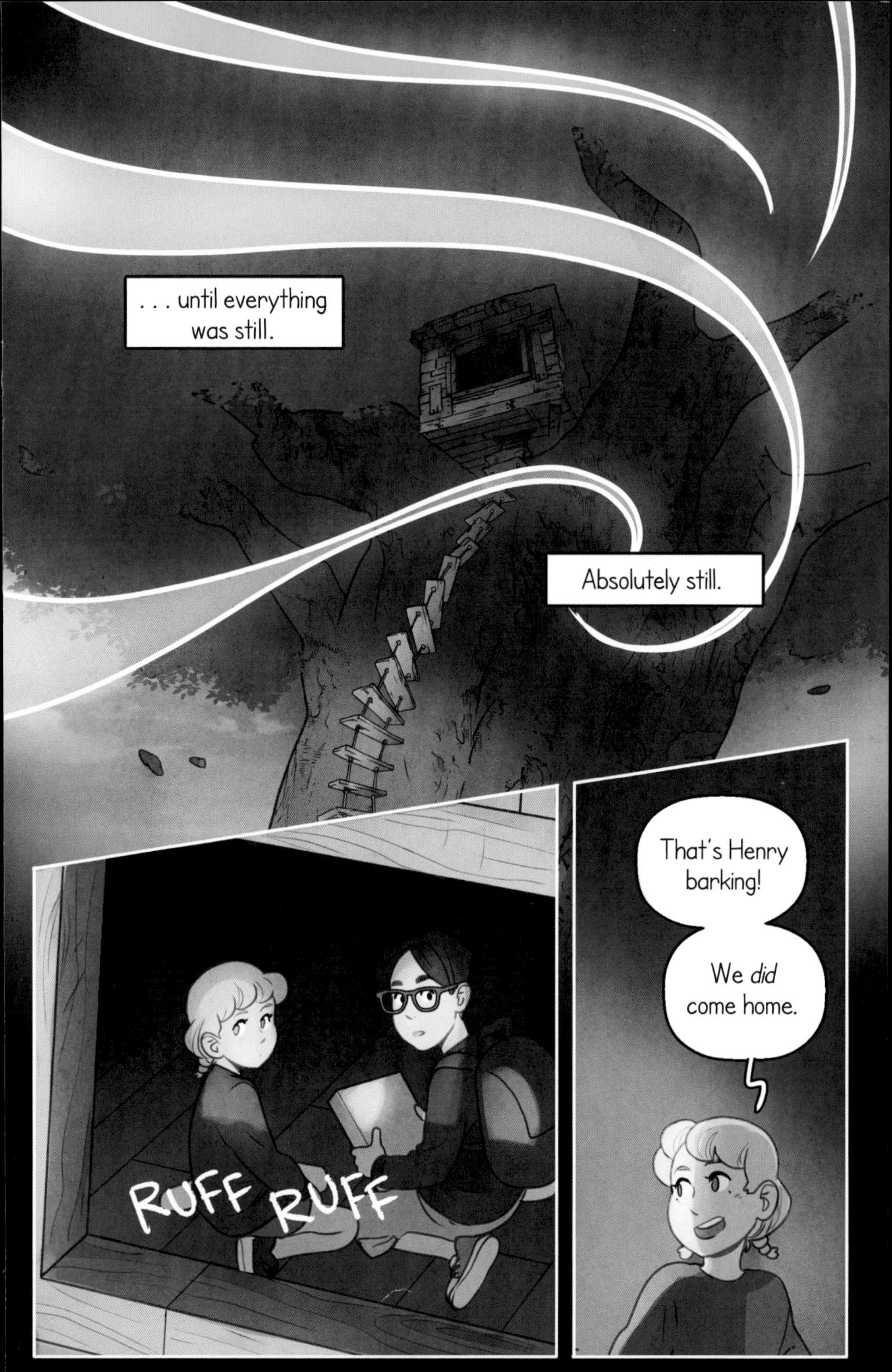
. . . until everything was still.
Absolutely still.
RUFF RUFF
That's Henry barking!
We *did* come home.

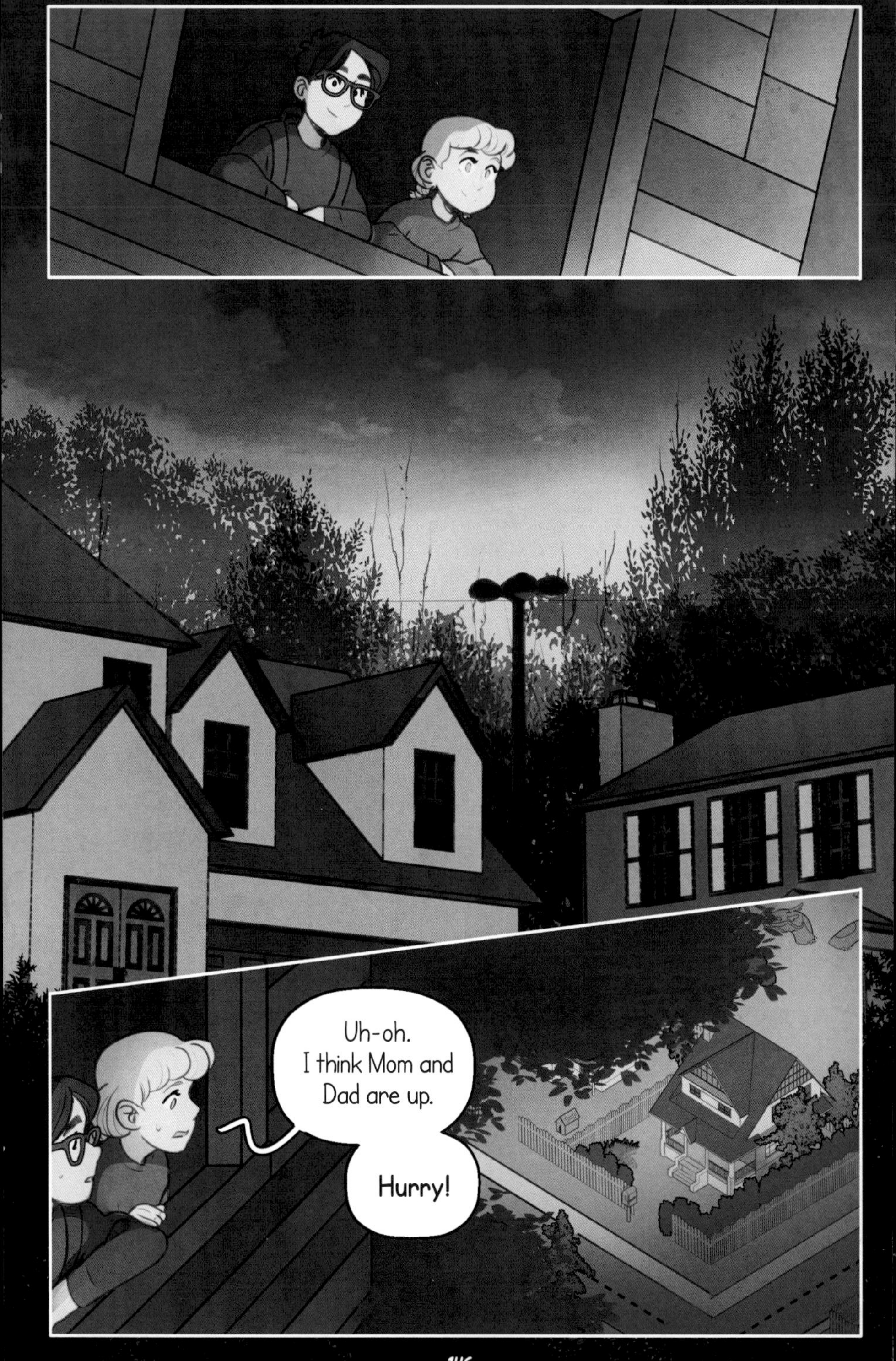
Uh-oh. I think Mom and Dad are up.
Hurry!

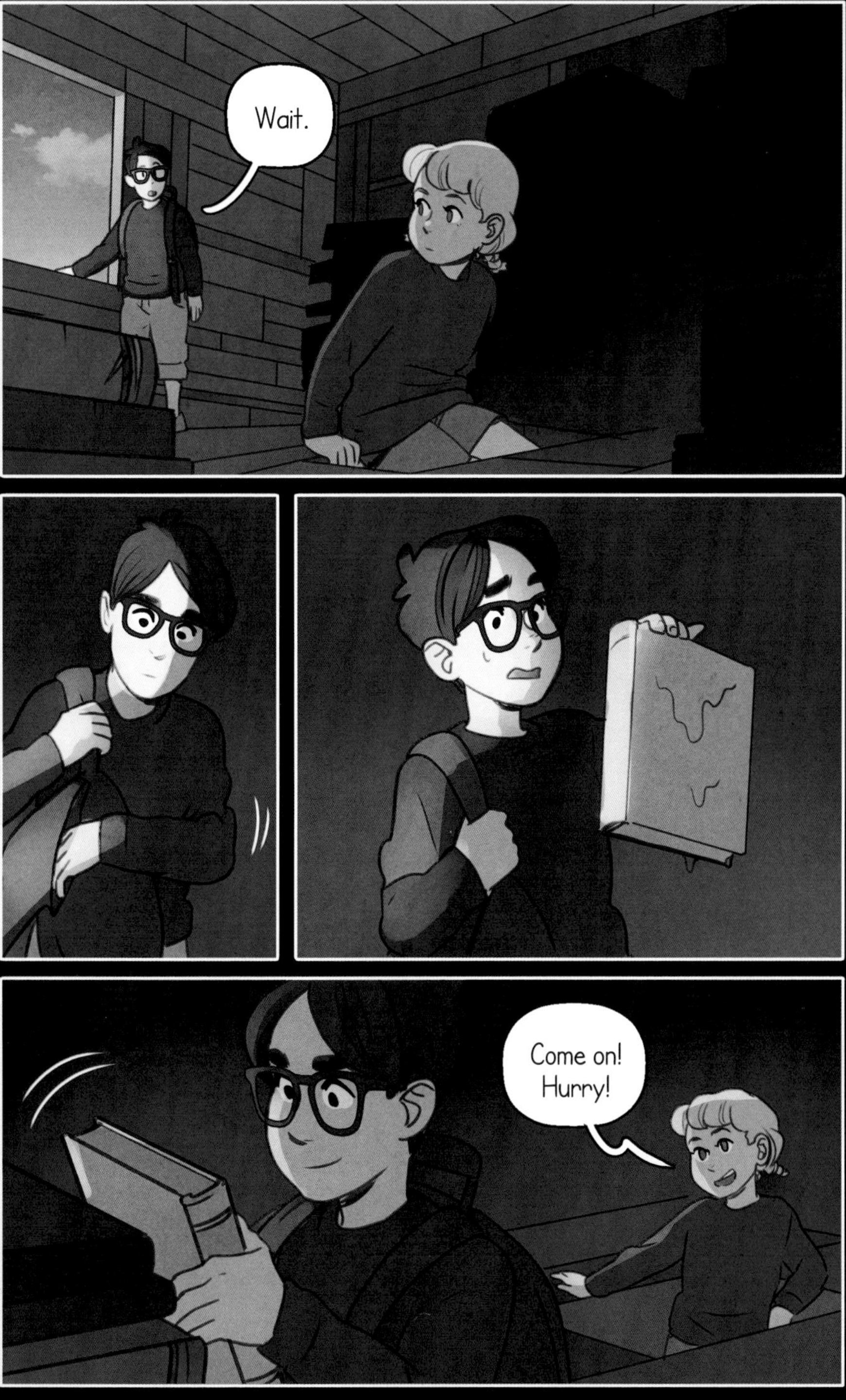

Wait.
Come on! Hurry!

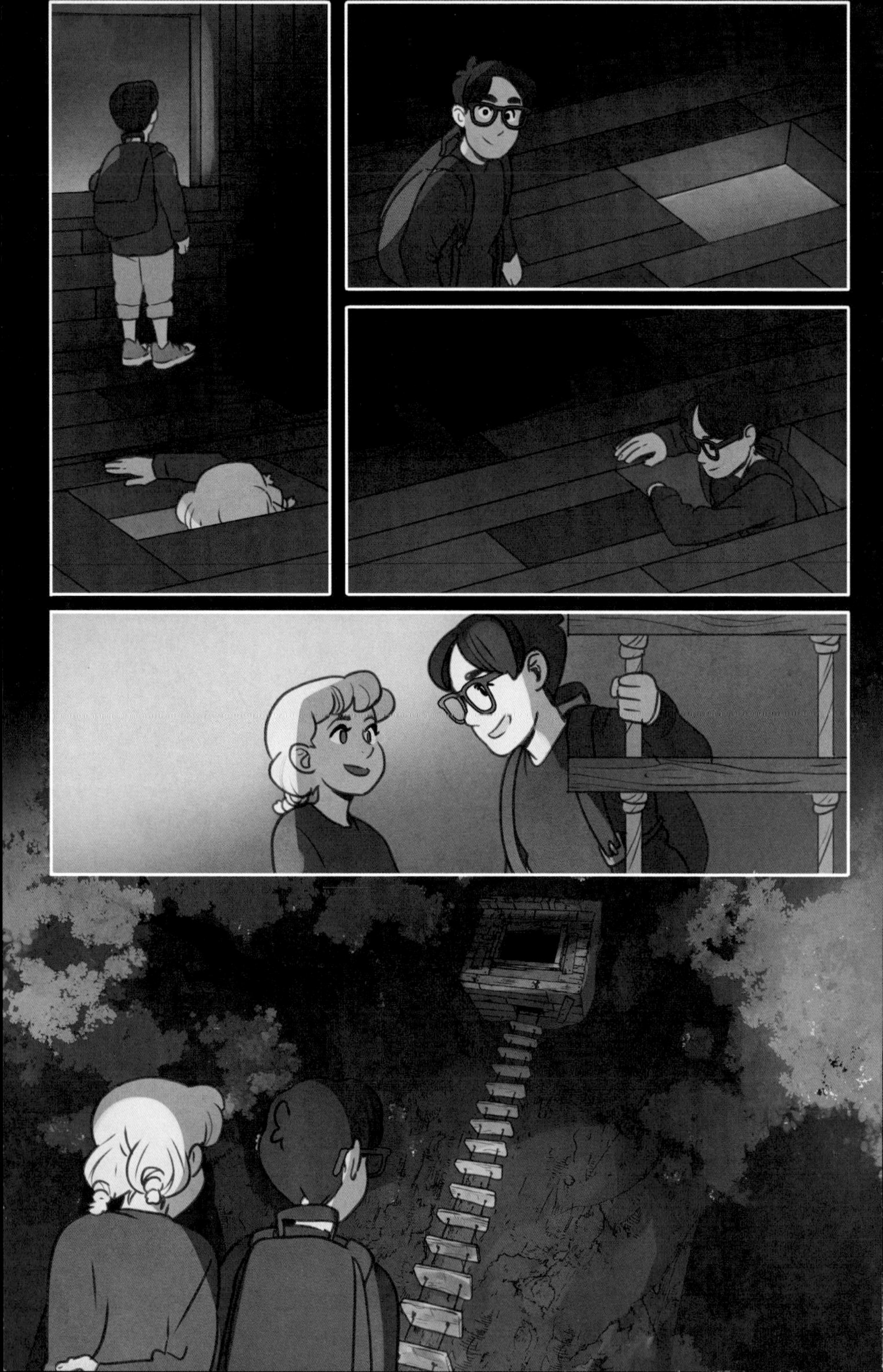

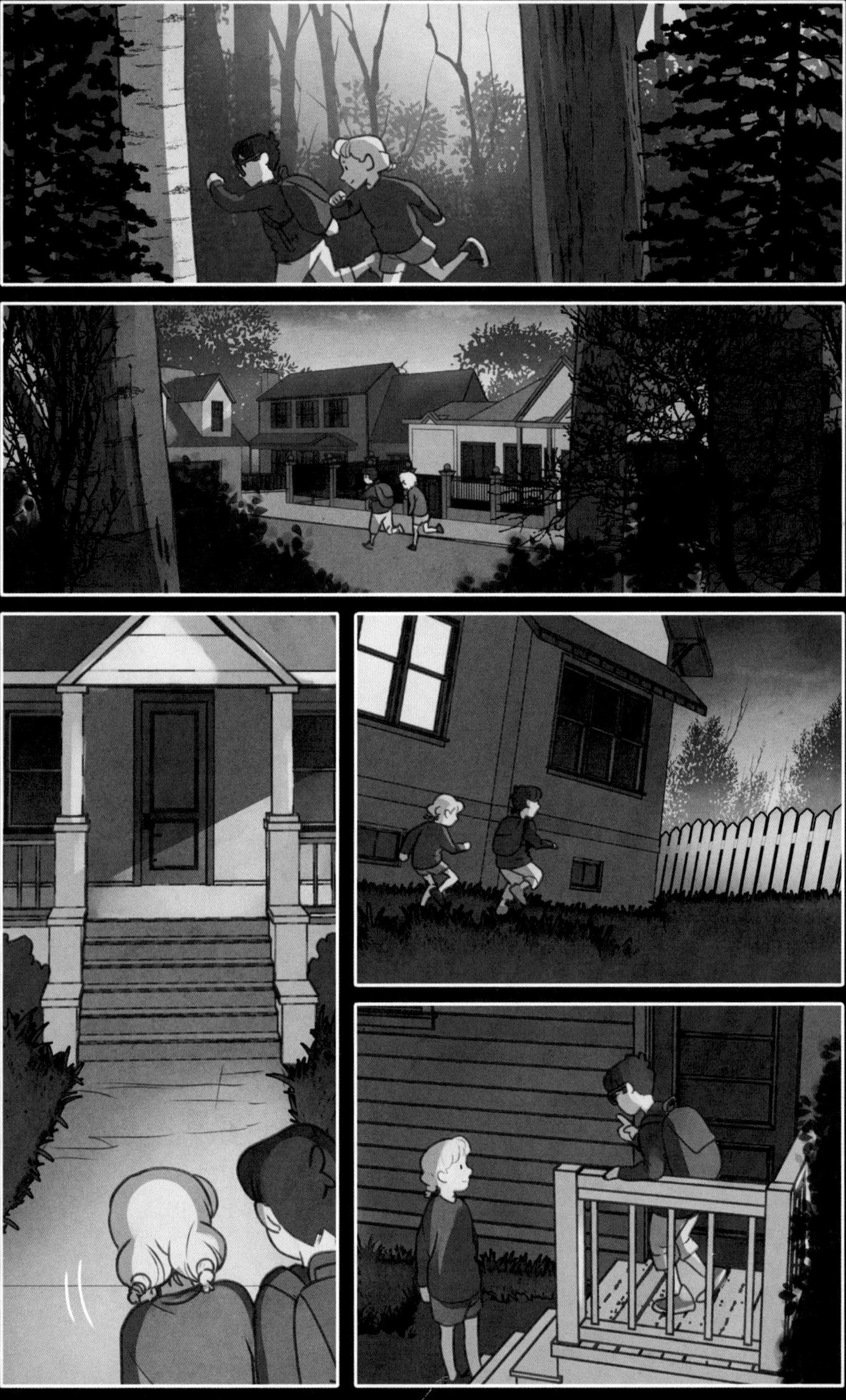

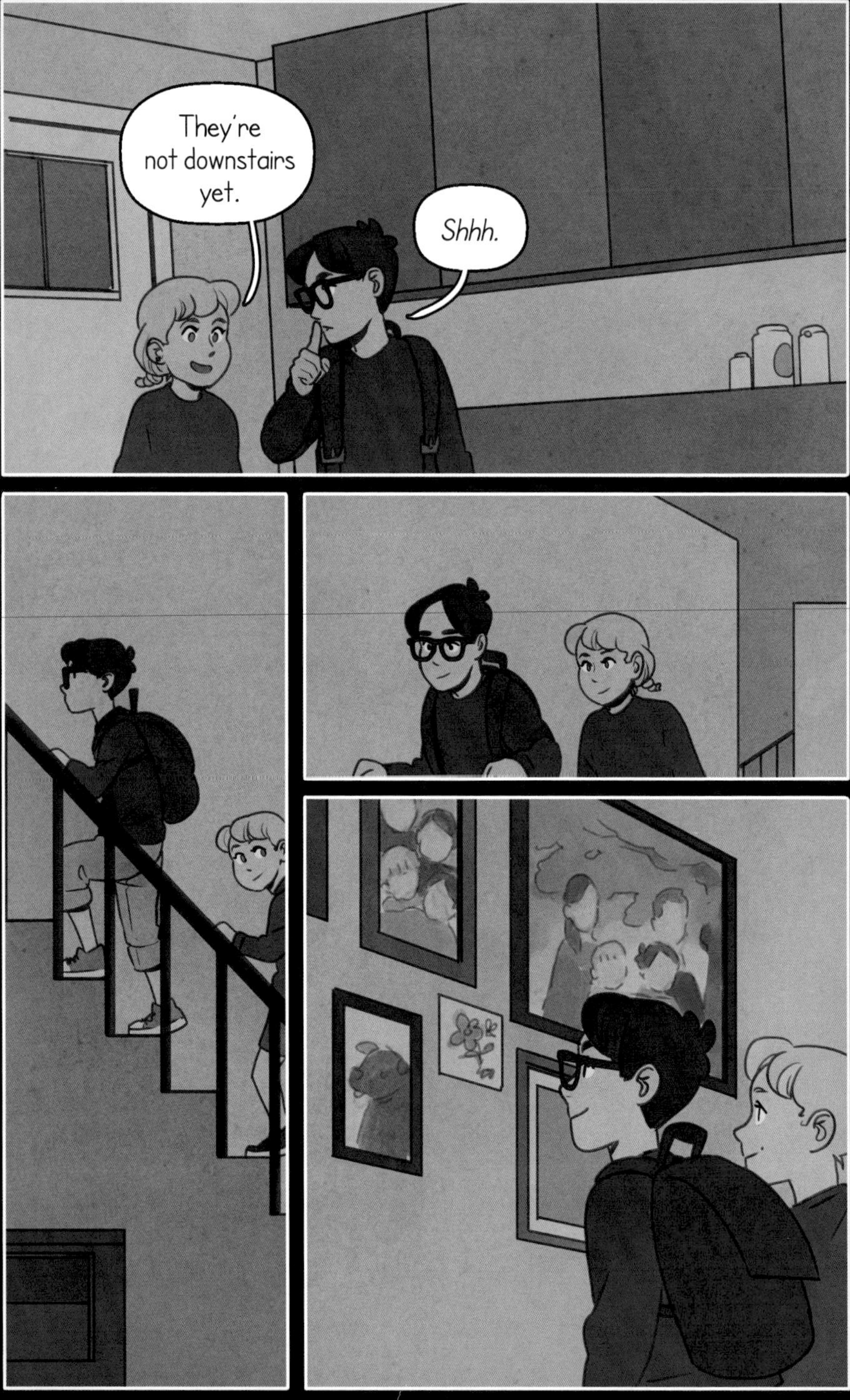
They're not downstairs yet.
Shhh.

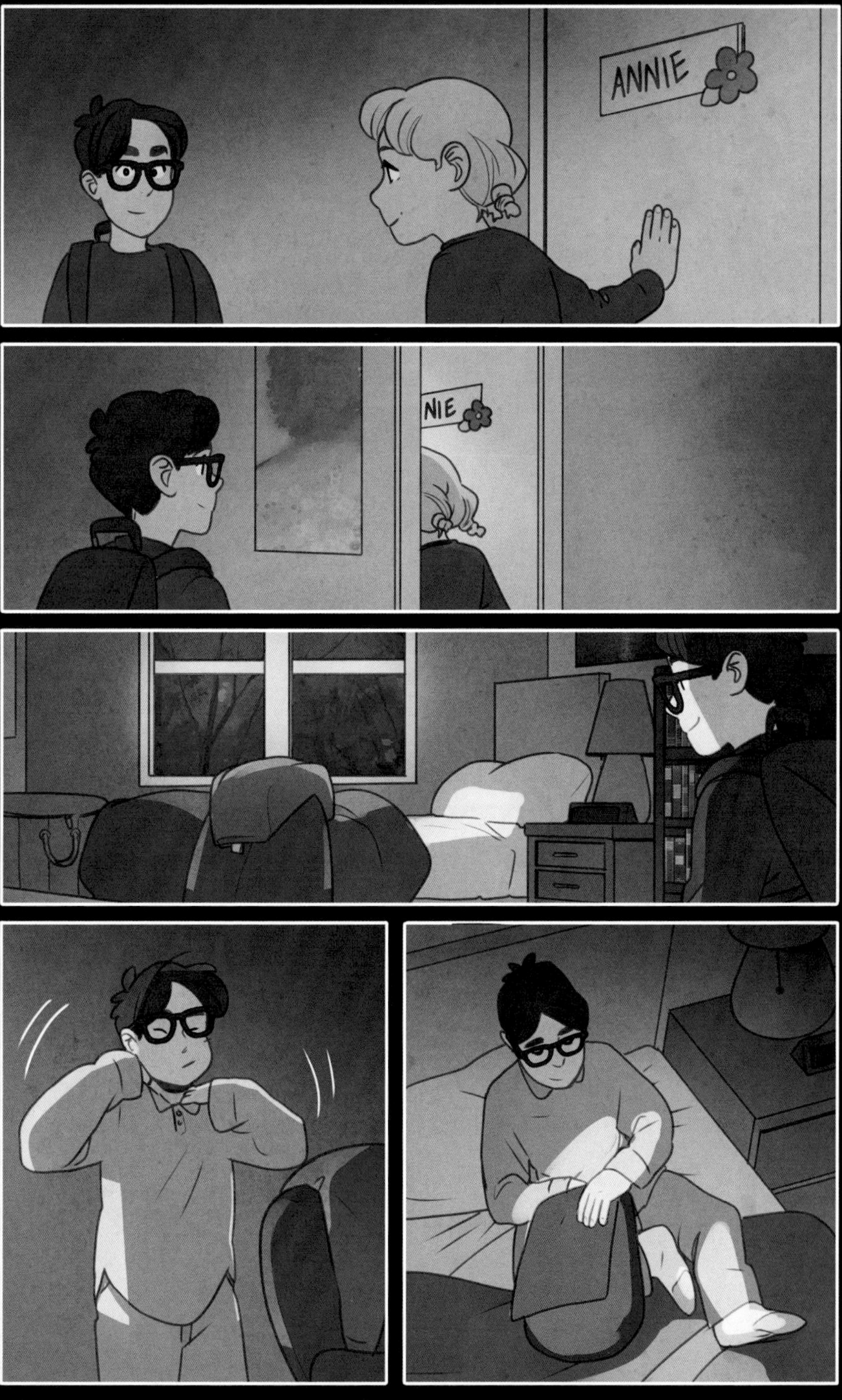
ANNIE
NIE

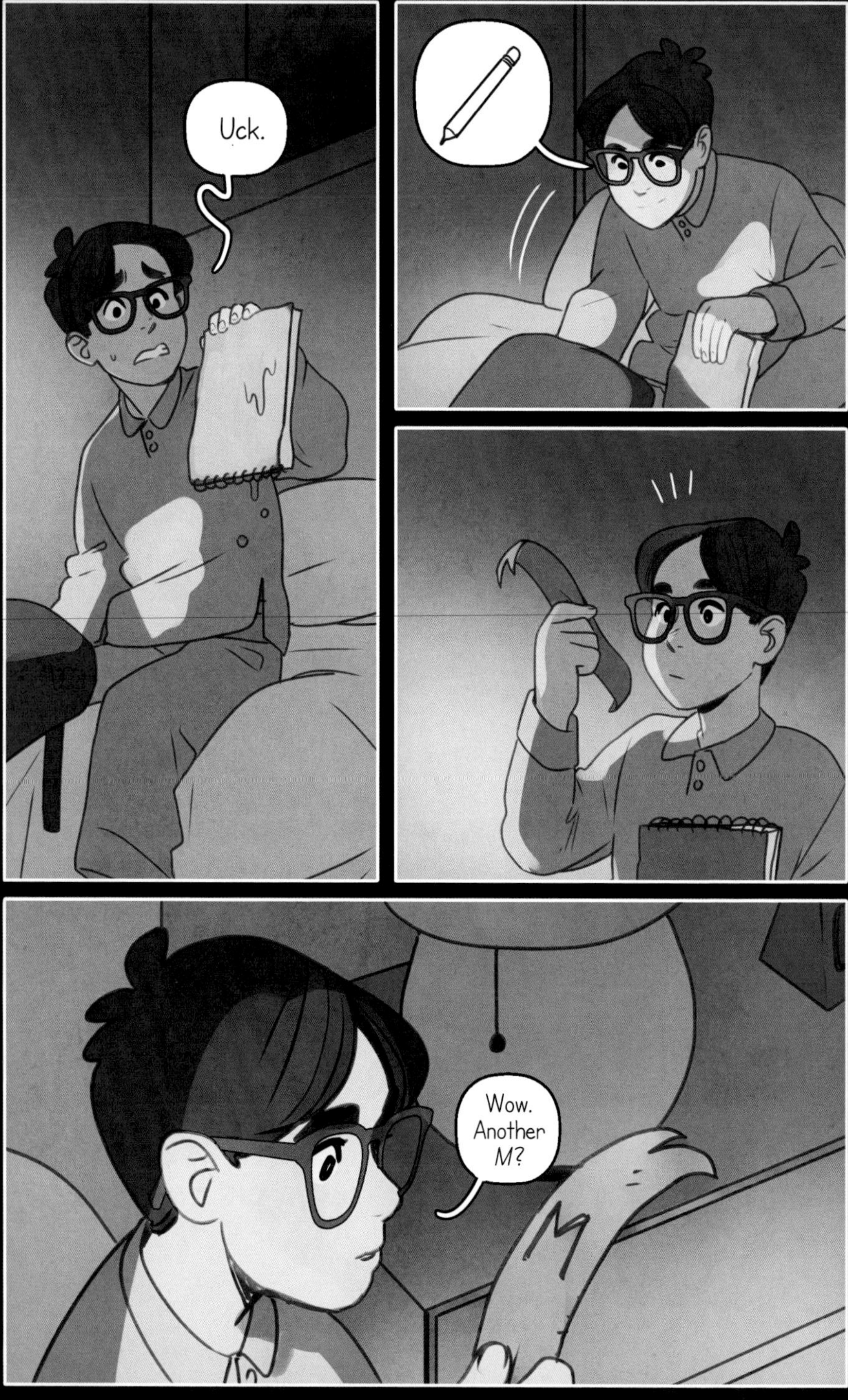
Uck.
Wow. Another M?

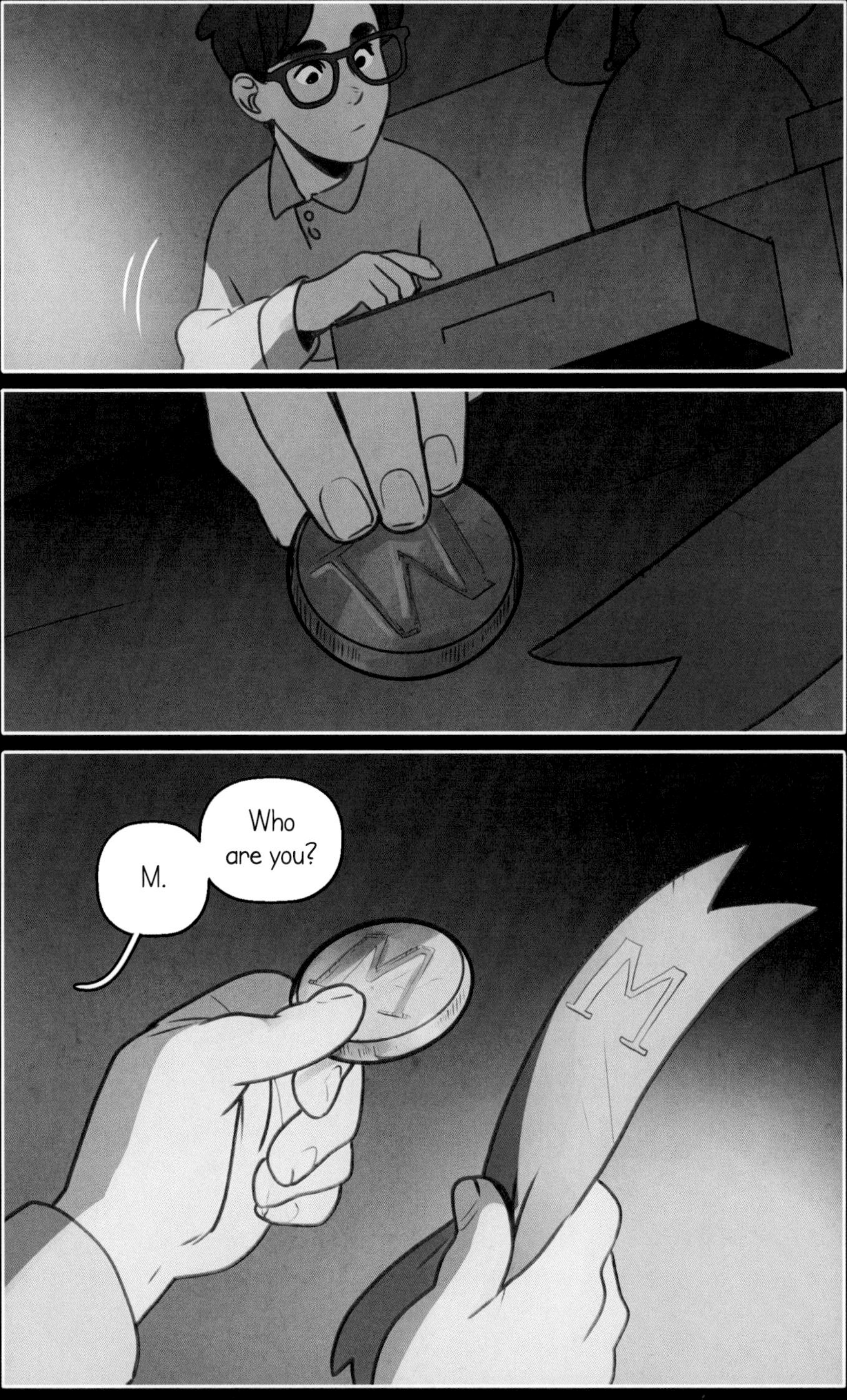
M.
Who are you?

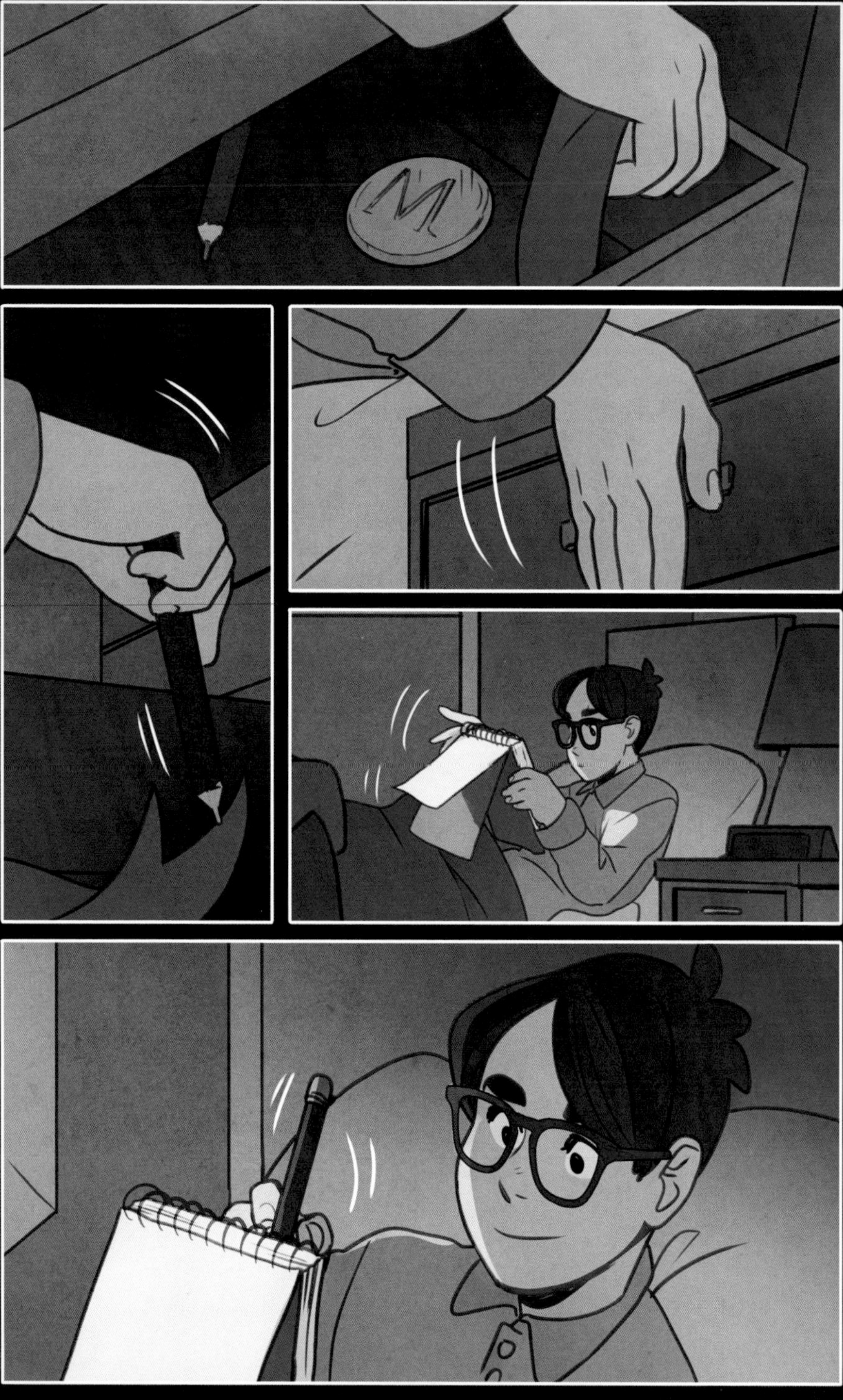
M

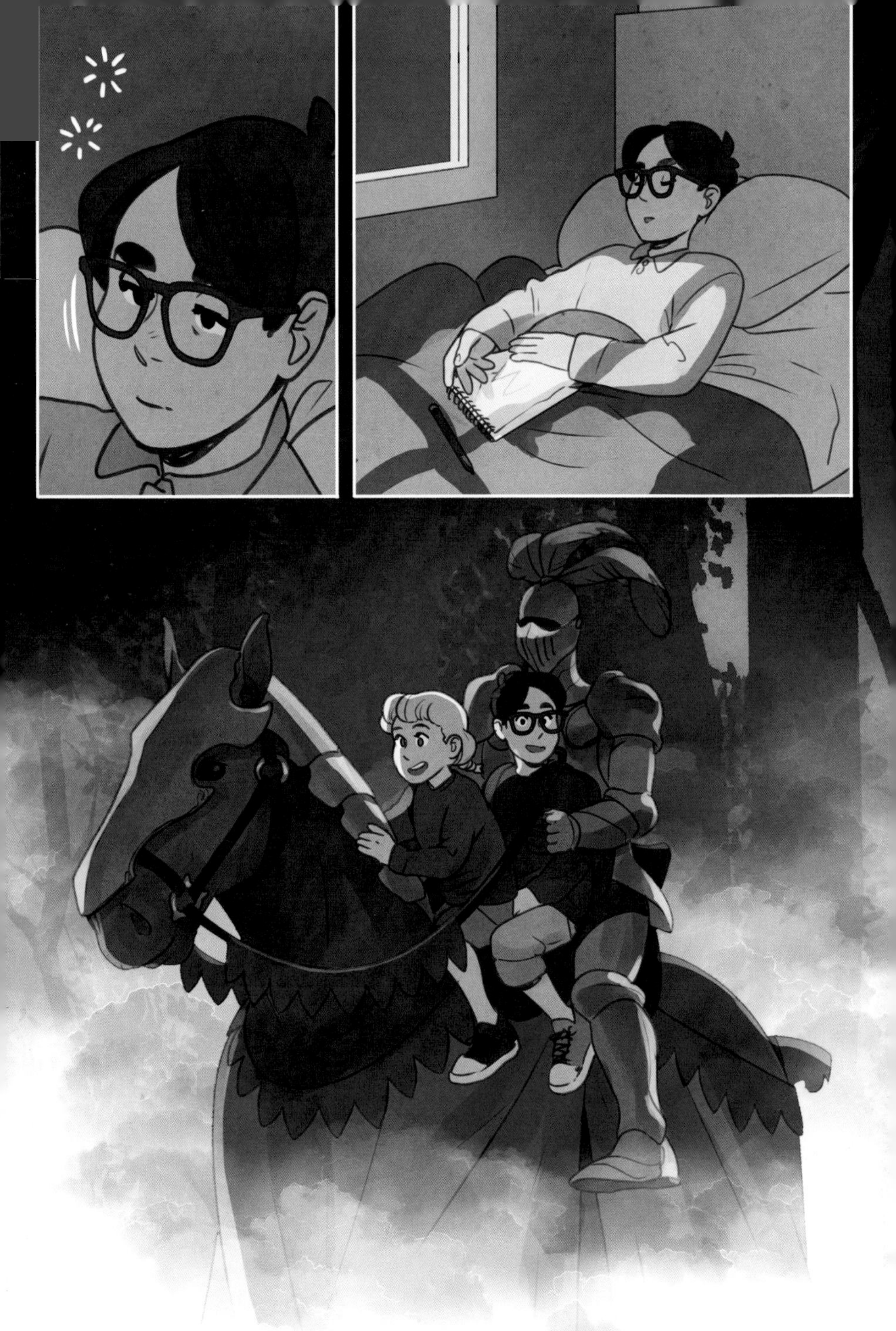

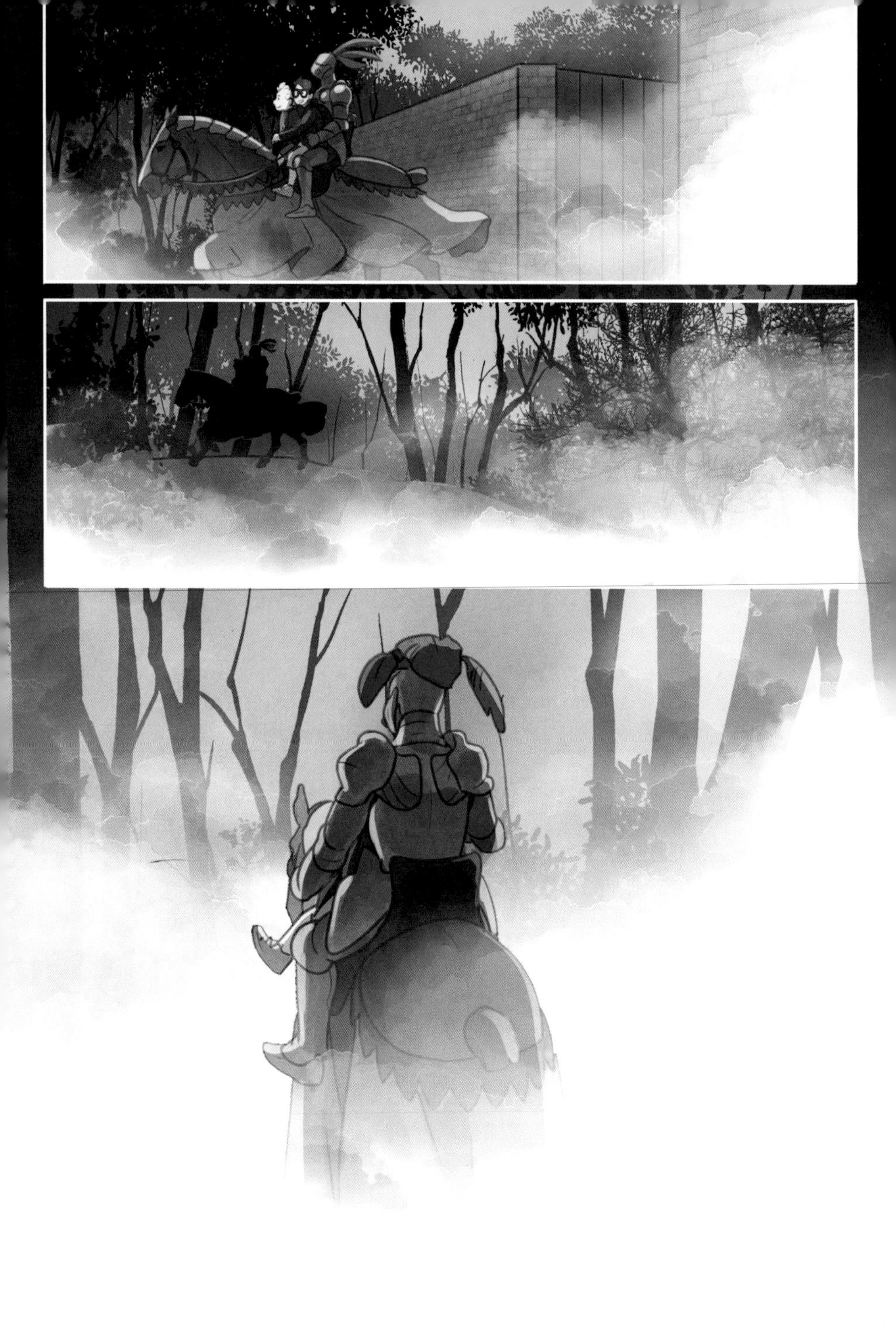

Missed the first adventure? Get whisked back
to the time of dinosaurs with Jack and Annie in . . .

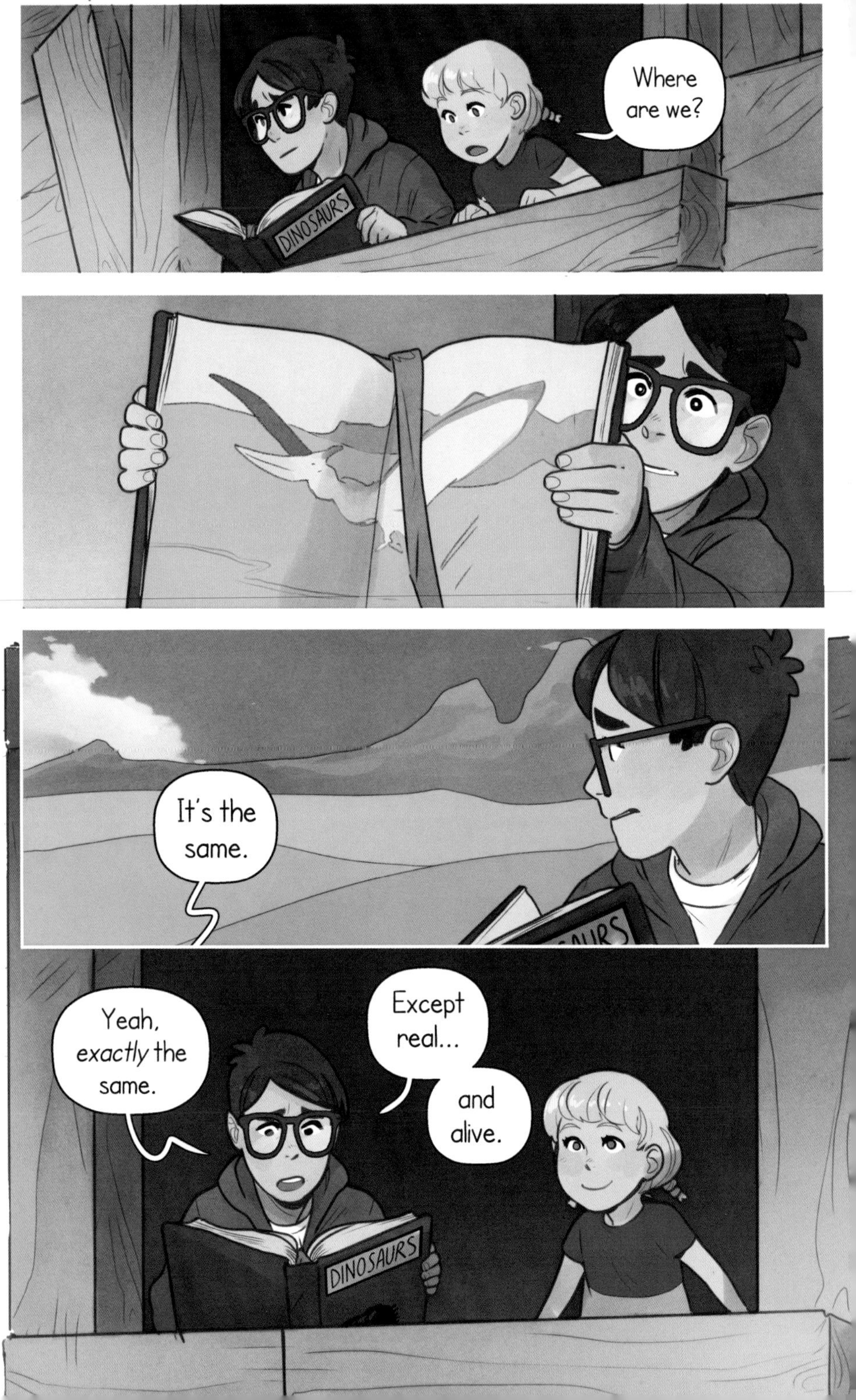
Where are we?
DINOSAURS
It's the same.
Yeah, *exactly* the same.
Except real...
and alive.
DINOSAURS

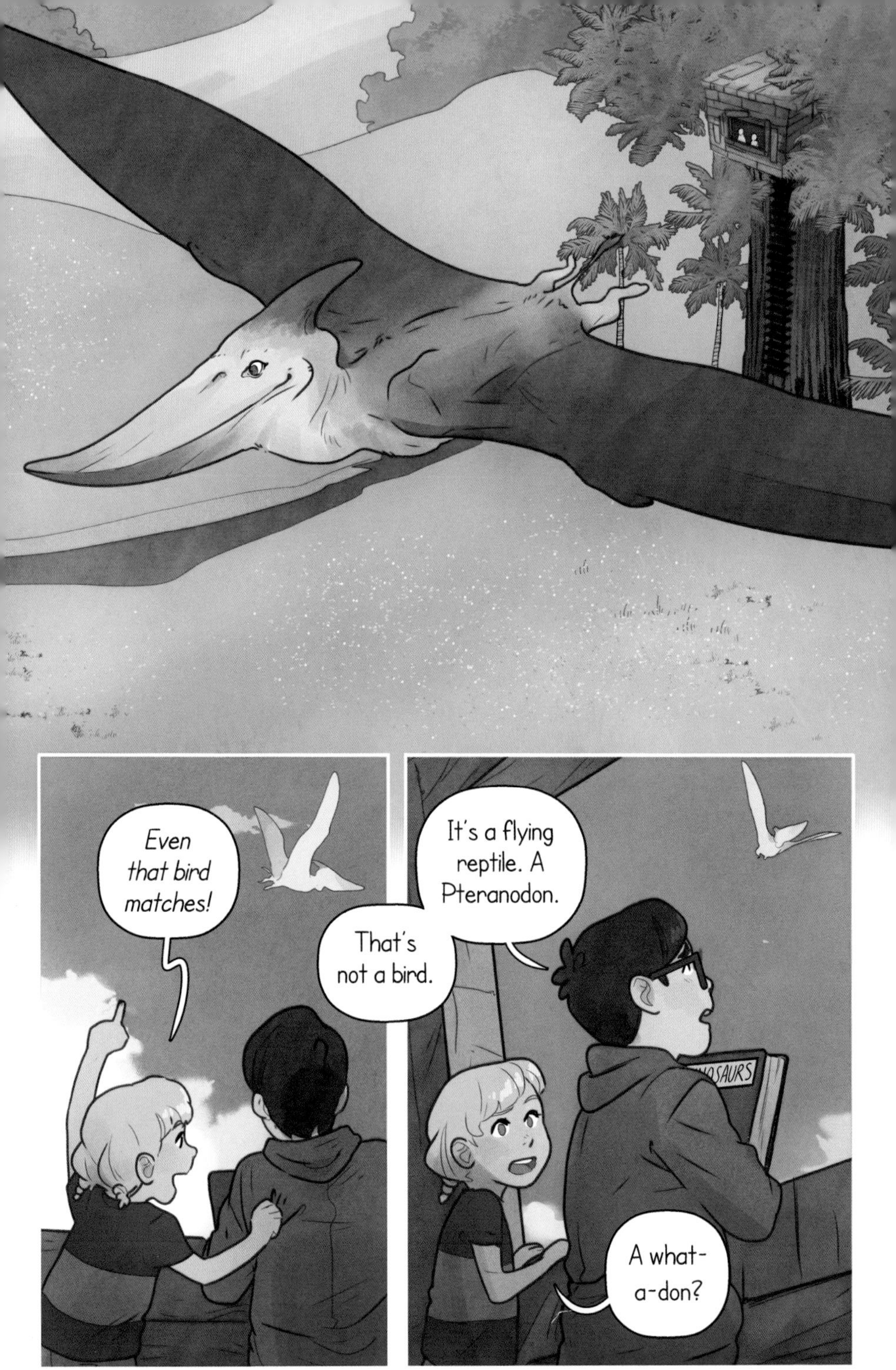
Even that bird matches!
That's not a bird.
It's a flying reptile. A Pteranodon.
A what-a-don?

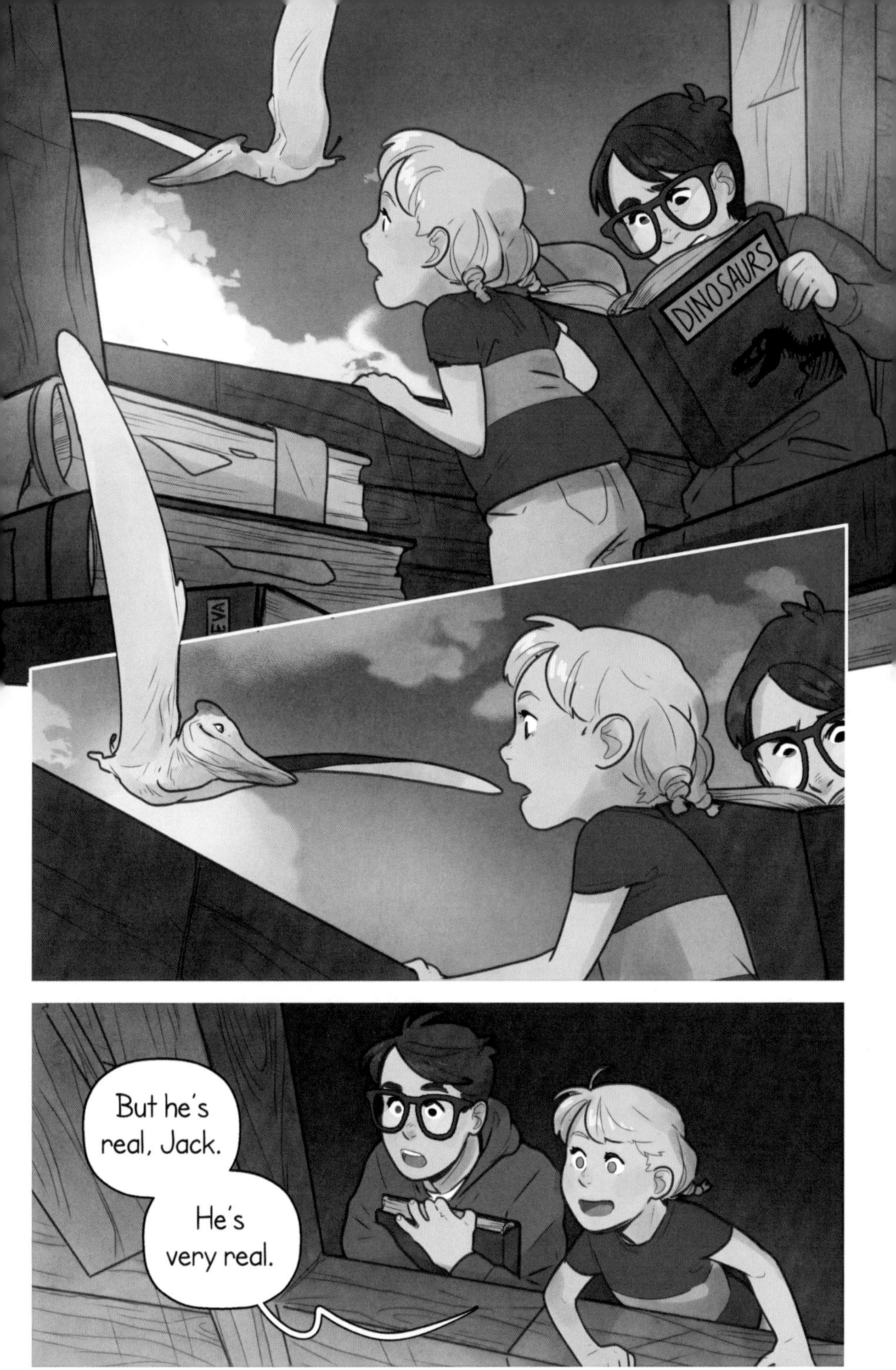
DINOSAURS
EVA
But he's real, Jack.
He's very real.

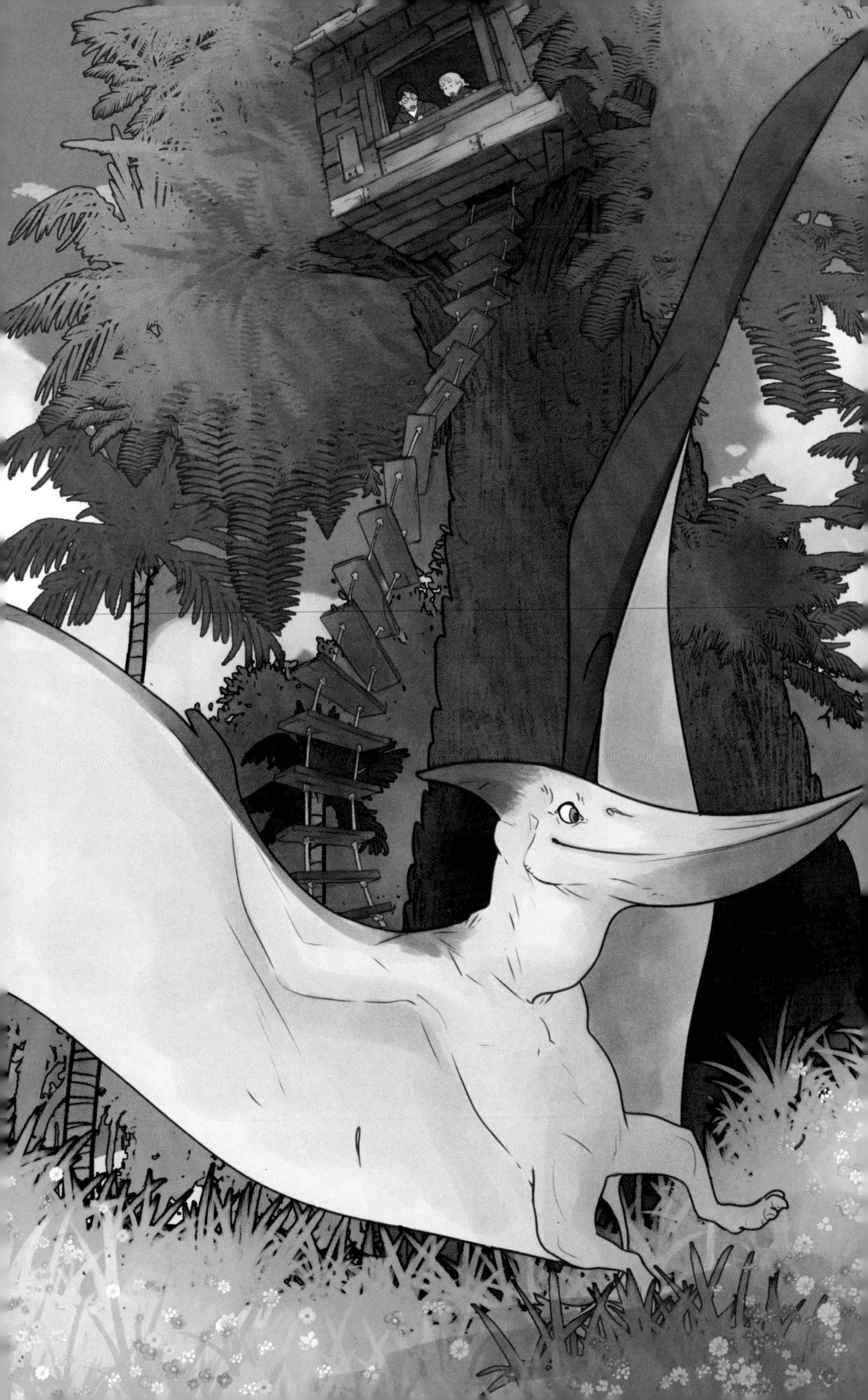

LET THE MAGIC TREE HOUSE® WHISK YOU AWAY!

MARY POPE OSBORNE
MAGIC TREE HOUSE®
#1 Dinosaurs Before Dark
#1 NEW YORK TIMES BESTSELLING SERIES

MARY POPE OSBORNE
MAGIC TREE HOUSE®
#2 The Knight at Dawn
#1 NEW YORK TIMES BESTSELLING SERIES

MARY POPE OSBORNE
MAGIC TREE HOUSE®
#3 Mummies in the Morning
#1 NEW YORK TIMES BESTSELLING SERIES

MARY POPE OSBORNE
MAGIC TREE HOUSE®
#4 Pirates Past Noon
#1 NEW YORK TIMES BESTSELLING SERIES

MARY POPE OSBORNE
MAGIC TREE HOUSE®
#5 Night of the Ninjas
#1 NEW YORK TIMES BESTSELLING SERIES

MARY POPE OSBORNE
MAGIC TREE HOUSE®
#6 Afternoon on the Amazon
#1 NEW YORK TIMES BESTSELLING SERIES

MARY POPE OSBORNE
MAGIC TREE HOUSE®
#7 Sunset of the Sabertooth
#1 NEW YORK TIMES BESTSELLING SERIES

MARY POPE OSBORNE
MAGIC TREE HOUSE®
#8 Midnight on the Moon
#1 NEW YORK TIMES BESTSELLING SERIES

MARY POPE OSBORNE
MAGIC TREE HOUSE®
#9 Dolphins at Daybreak
#1 NEW YORK TIMES BESTSELLING SERIES

MARY POPE OSBORNE
MAGIC TREE HOUSE®
#10 Ghost Town at Sundown
#1 NEW YORK TIMES BESTSELLING SERIES

MARY POPE OSBORNE
MAGIC TREE HOUSE®
#11 Lions at Lunchtime
#1 NEW YORK TIMES BESTSELLING SERIES

MARY POPE OSBORNE
MAGIC TREE HOUSE®
#12 Polar Bears Past Bedtime
#1 NEW YORK TIMES BESTSELLING SERIES

MARY POPE OSBORNE
MAGIC TREE HOUSE®
#13 Vacation Under the Volcano
#1 NEW YORK TIMES BESTSELLING SERIES

MARY POPE OSBORNE
MAGIC TREE HOUSE®
#14 Day of the Dragon King
#1 NEW YORK TIMES BESTSELLING SERIES

MARY POPE OSBORNE
MAGIC TREE HOUSE®
#15 Viking Ships at Sunrise
#1 NEW YORK TIMES BESTSELLING SERIES

MARY POPE OSBORNE
MAGIC TREE HOUSE®
#16 Hour of the Olympics
#1 NEW YORK TIMES BESTSELLING SERIES

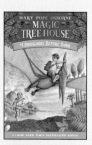

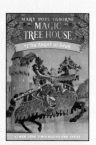

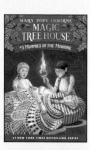

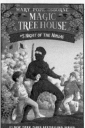

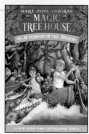

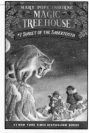

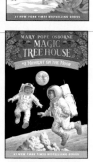

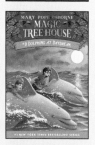

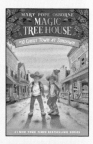

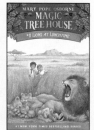

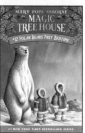

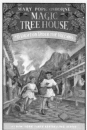

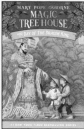

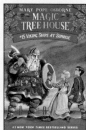

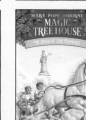

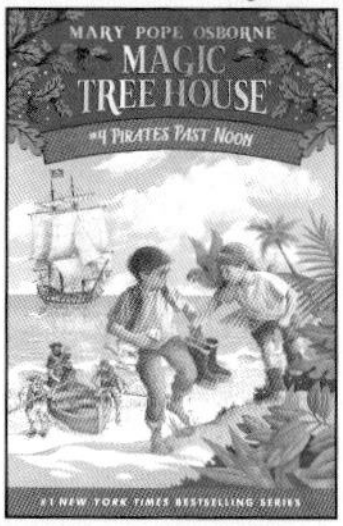

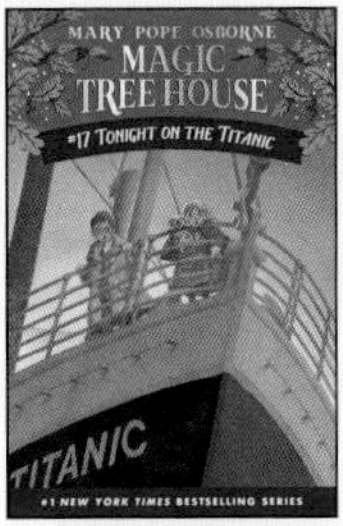
MARY POPE OSBORNE
MAGIC TREE HOUSE
#17 TONIGHT ON THE TITANIC
TITANIC
#1 NEW YORK TIMES BESTSELLING SERIES
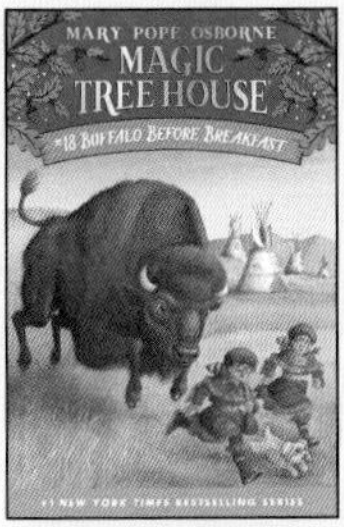
MARY POPE OSBORNE
MAGIC TREE HOUSE
#18 BUFFALO BEFORE BREAKFAST
#1 NEW YORK TIMES BESTSELLING SERIES
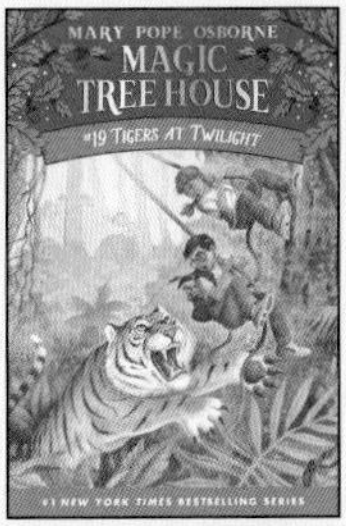
MARY POPE OSBORNE
MAGIC TREE HOUSE
#19 TIGERS AT TWILIGHT
#1 NEW YORK TIMES BESTSELLING SERIES
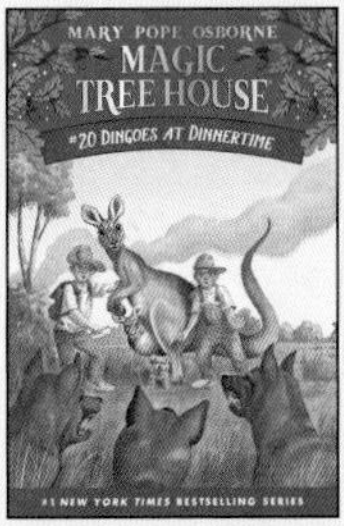
MARY POPE OSBORNE
MAGIC TREE HOUSE
#20 DINGOES AT DINNERTIME
#1 NEW YORK TIMES BESTSELLING SERIES
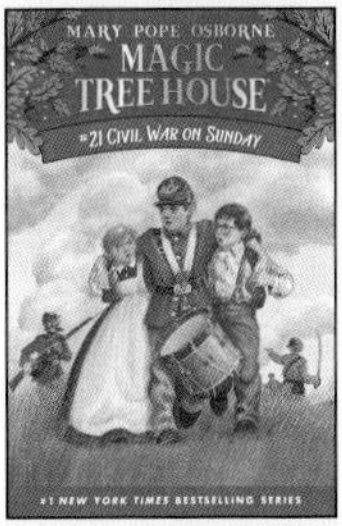
MARY POPE OSBORNE
MAGIC TREE HOUSE
#21 CIVIL WAR ON SUNDAY
#1 NEW YORK TIMES BESTSELLING SERIES
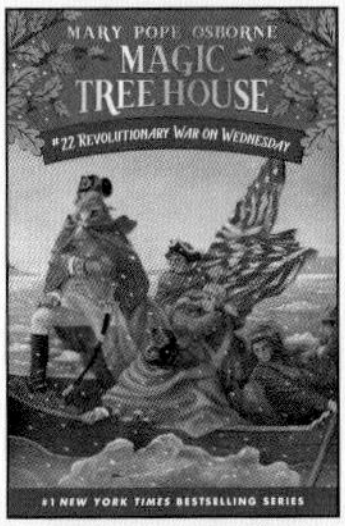
MARY POPE OSBORNE
MAGIC TREE HOUSE
#22 REVOLUTIONARY WAR ON WEDNESDAY
#1 NEW YORK TIMES BESTSELLING SERIES
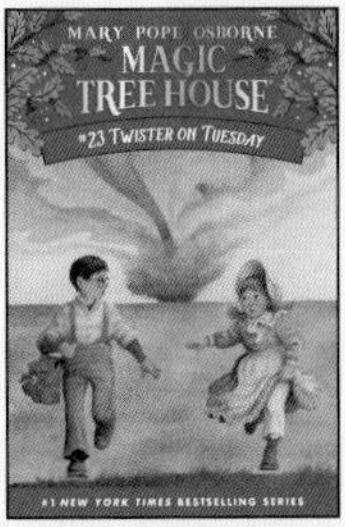
MARY POPE OSBORNE
MAGIC TREE HOUSE
#23 TWISTER ON TUESDAY
#1 NEW YORK TIMES BESTSELLING SERIES
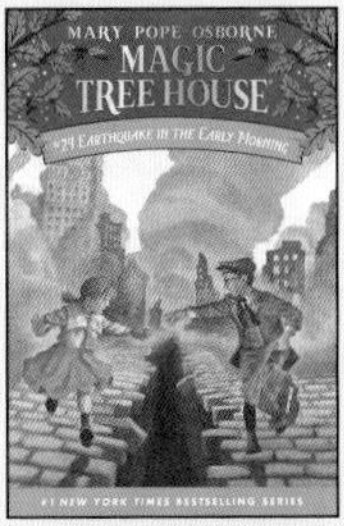
MARY POPE OSBORNE
MAGIC TREE HOUSE
#24 EARTHQUAKE IN THE EARLY MORNING
#1 NEW YORK TIMES BESTSELLING SERIES
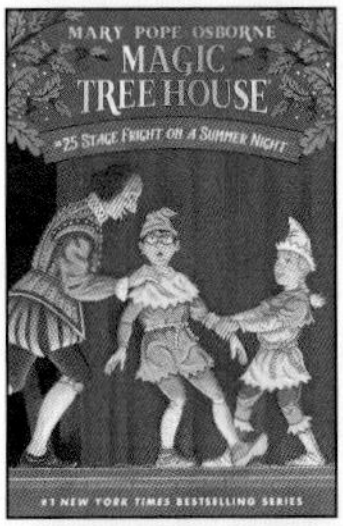
MARY POPE OSBORNE
MAGIC TREE HOUSE
#25 STAGE FRIGHT ON A SUMMER NIGHT
#1 NEW YORK TIMES BESTSELLING SERIES
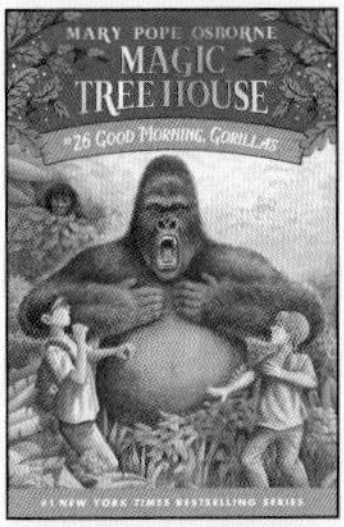
MARY POPE OSBORNE
MAGIC TREE HOUSE
#26 GOOD MORNING, GORILLAS
#1 NEW YORK TIMES BESTSELLING SERIES
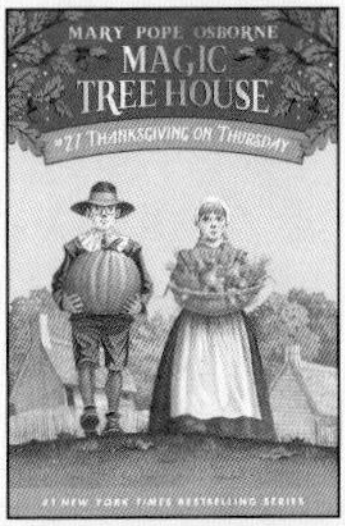
MARY POPE OSBORNE
MAGIC TREE HOUSE
#27 THANKSGIVING ON THURSDAY
#1 NEW YORK TIMES BESTSELLING SERIES
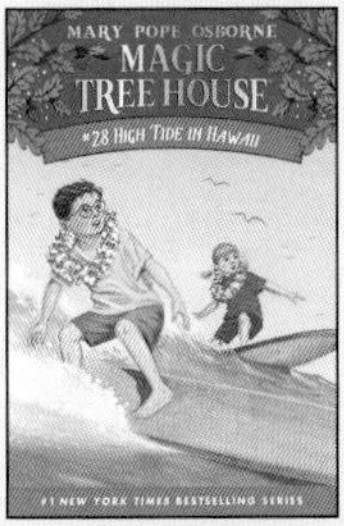
MARY POPE OSBORNE
MAGIC TREE HOUSE
#28 HIGH TIDE IN HAWAII
#1 NEW YORK TIMES BESTSELLING SERIES
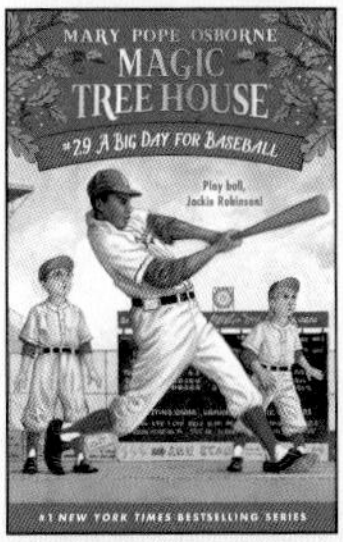
MARY POPE OSBORNE
MAGIC TREE HOUSE
#29 A BIG DAY FOR BASEBALL
Play ball, Jackie Robinson!
#1 NEW YORK TIMES BESTSELLING SERIES
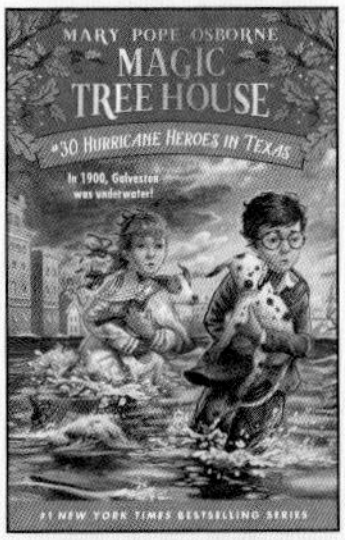
MARY POPE OSBORNE
MAGIC TREE HOUSE
#30 HURRICANE HEROES IN TEXAS
In 1900, Galveston was underwater!
#1 NEW YORK TIMES BESTSELLING SERIES
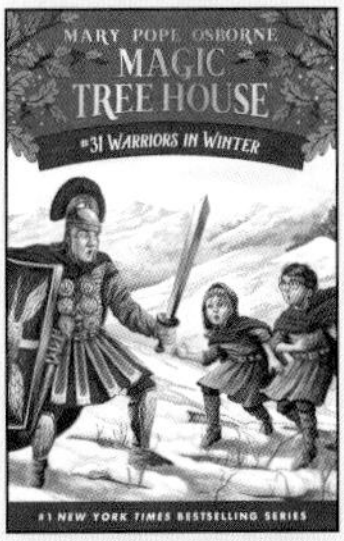
MARY POPE OSBORNE
MAGIC TREE HOUSE
#31 WARRIORS IN WINTER
#1 NEW YORK TIMES BESTSELLING SERIES
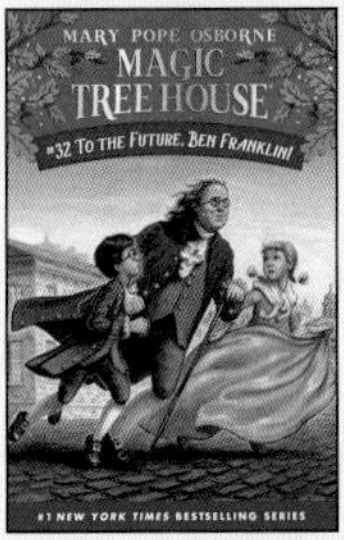
MARY POPE OSBORNE
MAGIC TREE HOUSE
#32 TO THE FUTURE, BEN FRANKLIN!
#1 NEW YORK TIMES BESTSELLING SERIES
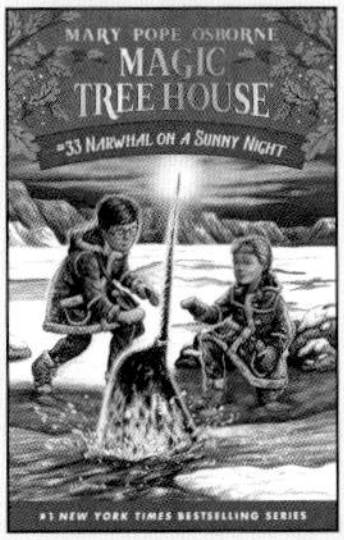
MARY POPE OSBORNE
MAGIC TREE HOUSE
#33 NARWHAL ON A SUNNY NIGHT
#1 NEW YORK TIMES BESTSELLING SERIES
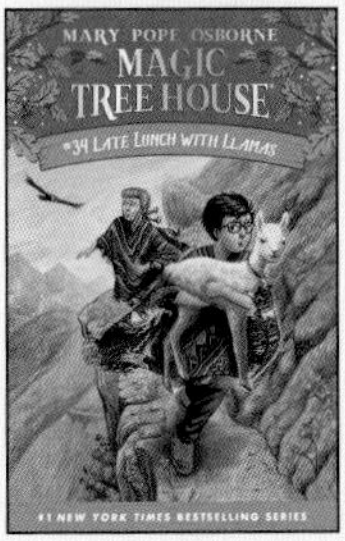
MARY POPE OSBORNE
MAGIC TREE HOUSE
#34 LATE LUNCH WITH LLAMAS
#1 NEW YORK TIMES BESTSELLING SERIES
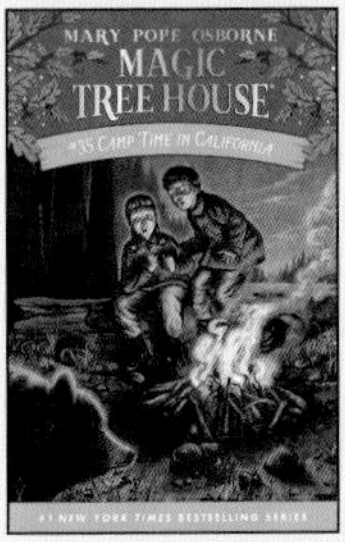
MARY POPE OSBORNE
MAGIC TREE HOUSE
#35 CAMP TIME IN CALIFORNIA
#1 NEW YORK TIMES BESTSELLING SERIES

TRACK THE FACTS WITH JACK & ANNIE!

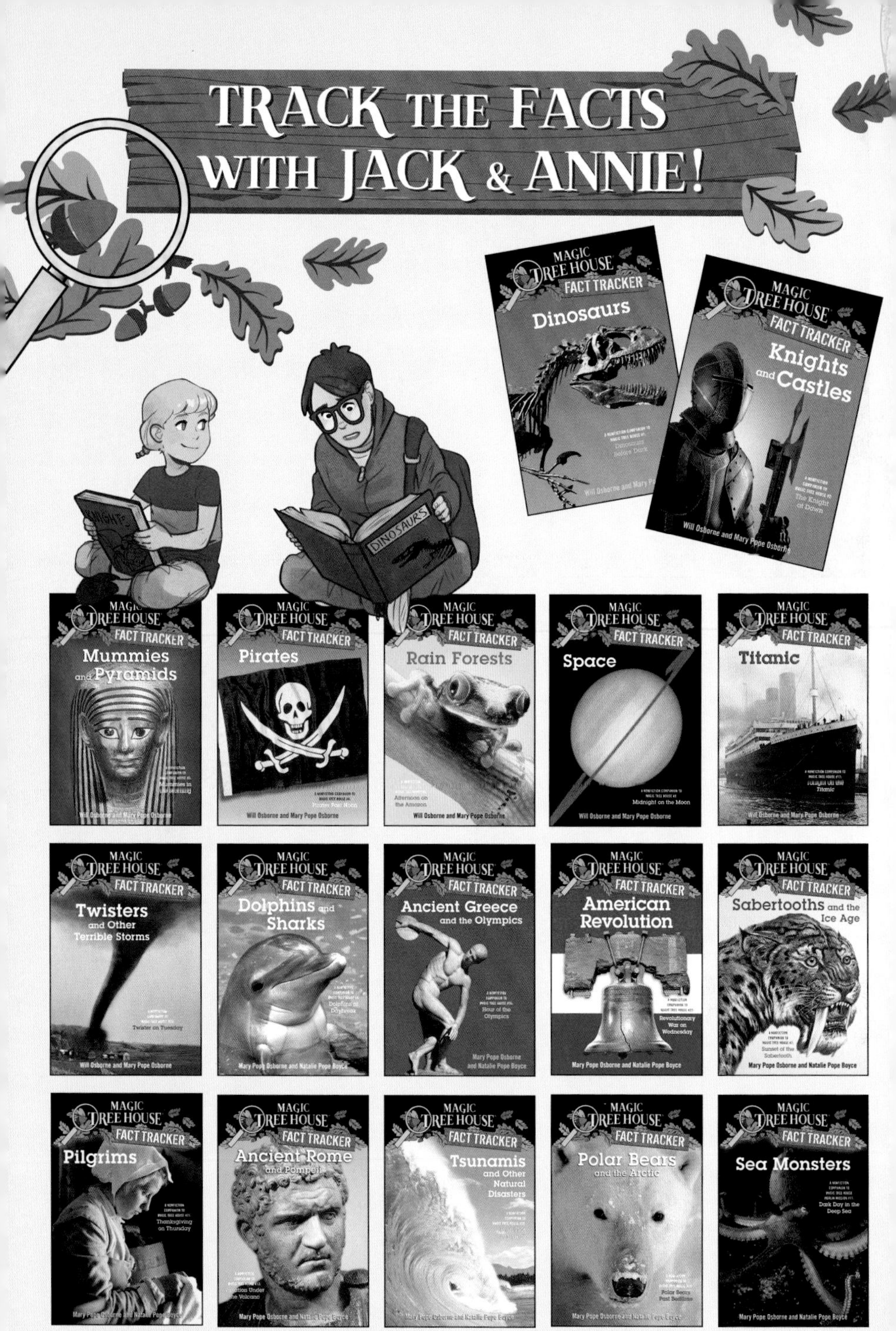
MAGIC TREE HOUSE FACT TRACKER
Dinosaurs
Knights and Castles
Mummies and Pyramids
Pirates
Rain Forests
Space
Titanic
Twisters and Other Terrible Storms
Dolphins and Sharks
Ancient Greece and the Olympics
American Revolution
Sabertooths and the Ice Age
Pilgrims
Ancient Rome and Pompeii
Tsunamis and Other Natural Disasters
Polar Bears and the Arctic
Sea Monsters
Will Osborne and Mary Pope Osborne
Mary Pope Osborne and Natalie Pope Boyce
DINOSAURS

MARY POPE OSBORNE is the author of many novels, picture books, story collections, and nonfiction books. Her #1 *New York Times* bestselling Magic Tree House® series has been translated into numerous languages around the world. Highly recommended by parents and educators everywhere, the series introduces young readers to different cultures and times, as well as to the world's legacy of ancient myth and storytelling.

JENNY LAIRD is an award-winning playwright. She collaborates with Will Osborne and Randy Courts on creating musical theater adaptations of the Magic Tree House® series for both national and international audiences. Their work also includes shows for young performers, available through Music Theatre International's Broadway Junior® Collection. Currently the team is working on a Magic Tree House® animated television series.

KELLY & NICHOLE MATTHEWS are twin sisters and a comic-art team. They get to do their dream job every day, drawing comics for a living. They've worked with Boom Studios!, Archaia, the Jim Henson Company, Hiveworks, and now Random House!

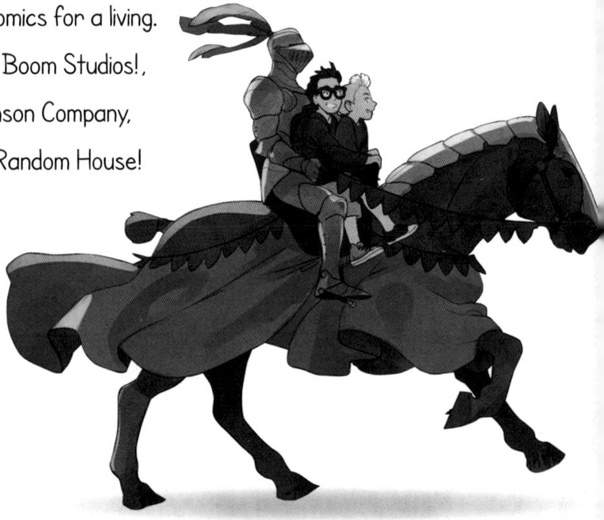